Finn's Quest

ANDY MUNRO

Copyright

Copyright © 2020 - A Munro

All rights reserved. This book or any portion thereof may not be reproduced or used in any manner whatsoever without the express written permission of the copyright owner except for the use of brief quotations in a book review.

Any references to historical events, real people, or real places are used fictitiously. Names, characters, and places are products of the author's imagination.

Cover design by A Munro.

First Edition   @ Dec-2020
Second Edition @ Feb-2021
Third Edition   @ Mar-2021

ISBN-13 : 979-8588054720
ASIN : Paperback : B08RH5N1RL
ASIN : eBook : B08R6GGGWC

For contact via Twitter use @KirklandFinn

Table of Contents

Prologue	1
Chapter 1 - Santa Fe, New Mexico	2
Chapter 2 - Camp Griffin, Helmand, Afghanistan	16
Chapter 3 - Taluca Campsite, Carson NP, NM.	23
Chapter 4 - Camp Griffin	39
Chapter 5 - Prickly Pear Roadhouse, NM.	54
Chapter 6 - Kirtland AFB, Albuquerque, NM.	61
Chapter 7 - Prickly Pear Motel, NM.	68
Chapter 8 - El Paso, Texas.	81
Chapter 9 - Iron Fist Base, Lubbock, TX	91
Chapter 10 - Foresight Ent. Office, El Paso, TX.	104
Chapter 11 - Car Crash, El Paso	118
Chapter 12 - Iron Fist Base	126
Chapter 13 - Motel, El Paso	132
Chapter 14 - Iron Fist Base	153
Chapter 15 - Motel, Lubbock	156
Chapter 16 - Akron Airport, Ohio	186
Chapter 17 - DEA	204
Chapter 18 - Iron Fist Base	216
Chapter 19 - Akron Police Station	222
Chapter 20 - Gulfstream Jet	230
Chapter 21 - Kandahar Airport	243
Chapter 22 - C-5 Galaxy	254
Chapter 23 - SOG Safe House, Kandahar	265
Chapter 24 - Marshall	276
Chapter 25 - Zafar's Compound	285
Chapter 26 - SOG Safe House	295
Chapter 27 - Amir Zafar	308
Chapter 28 - Intel	319
Chapter 29 - Briefing	336
Chapter 30 - Assault	342
Chapter 31 - Kathy	360
Epilogue	374

Acknowledgement

Thanks to my partner Christine McLoughlin for all your help in the writing and editing of this book. XX

About the Author

I am a retired design engineer from the UK. Finn's Quest is my first published book. I took the opportunity to start writing when I retired. Finn's Quest took nine months to complete. With over 95,000 words the book was a steep learning curve and involved lots of research.

Finn's Quest features two main characters I created, Kirkland Finn, a Captain in the SAS, and Nico Torres, an FBI special agent. Both characters will feature in separate books in the future.

Follow Kirkland Finn's career in the second instalment END OF EXISTENCE.

I hope you like my book.

Contact me via Twitter @KirklandFinn

Andy

Prologue

The young shepherd boy stood on the bank of the Arghandab river and stared at the black speed boat stuck on a mud bank. Occasionally a wave would lift the rear of the boat up and he urged it to move.

The bells of the goats grew quieter as they continued away from him, running between the peach trees. Catching up he flicked the slowest with a long stick convincing it to speed up and overtake the rest. He laughed and ran behind until the goats gathered in a circle. Pushing through the goats he discovered a figure dressed all in black. A battered and broken body lay on its back on the dusty ground.

The boy moved closer and looked down at the man's face seeing dead eyes staring upwards at the sky. He followed the dead man's gaze until he reached a peach hanging on a branch above his head.

He kneeled and checked the pockets on the black uniform. He screamed with excitement as he pulled out a bundle of dollar bills. He stopped and looked around nervously. Seeing no danger, he continued the search, finding a picture of a woman with a child. Seeing no value in the prize he threw it to the floor. A goat began eating the picture while he checked the last of the pockets, finding nothing of interest. He stuffed the money into his pocket then smacked the nearest goat forcing it to run away, the rest followed. His eyes returned to the peach, a grin appeared on his face as he pulled it from the branch and ran away to join them.

Chapter 1
Santa Fe, New Mexico

FBI special agent Nico Torres woke on the sofa and looked around his Santa Fe apartment. *What time is it?*

He fumbled on the coffee table for his mobile phone, knocked the empty beer bottle and watched as it smashed on the tiled floor. The small screen yielded the answer. *09:48.*

Pulling himself up off the sofa, he walked to the bathroom, avoiding the glass scattered on the floor. He relieved himself before washing his hands and throwing cold water on his face. Reaching for the towel, he dried the water from his eyes. He stared at himself in the mirror and used the water on his hands to sweep his near-black hair from his eyes. The reflection confirmed how he felt, at thirty-nine and in his twelfth year at the FBI, work, and time, had taken its toll on the detective.

He continued to look at his face analysing his reflection while in his mind, he saw their faces again. The noise of his mobile phone ringing, vibrating its way across the coffee table, snapped him back to reality.

Returning to the living room, to collect the phone, he stepped on a piece of glass, making him shout out aloud. He grabbed the mobile phone and dropped backwards onto the sofa, holding his foot. He looked at the name on the screen, pressed the green icon and placed the phone between his shoulder and cheek, "Dawson!"

"Good morning Nico, how are things?"

"I'll let you know when I've got this glass out of my foot."

Gripping the splinter of glass with his fingernails he slowly removed the shard and placed it on the table.

"How bad is it?" Dawson asked.

"I'll live! Anyway, why are you calling me? I assume you didn't call me for a chat."

"We've just taken a call from a Sheriff up your way, a case involving multiple murders in the Carson National Park." Dawson said, adding, "I know you're familiar with the area."

"That's one way to put it, the Carson covers a large area, mainly forest and mountains, with lots of ways in and out. Did you say multiple murders?"

"Three women!" Dawson declared, "It also appears another has been kidnapped. Wait while I get the details up on my screen..." The line went quiet for a moment, "Okay I've got the report here in front of me. I'll read it out for you. Carson National Park. Four English women on a camping holiday. The park ranger checked the campsite this morning and found three murdered, the fourth is still missing. The Sheriff, Cranshaw, passed the case on to the FBI because of the missing woman. She was either kidnapped or is involved in some way, maybe even the killer. You're the nearest FBI field agent Nico. Do you want me to hand over the case to you or should I give it to the Albuquerque office?"

"No! Assign it to me." Torres demanded, "Send me an email with all the details. I'll go up there later today and take a look at the crime scene."

"Okay, call me when you receive my email. If you need anything additional just ask and I'll run support for you from here at HQ." Dawson hung up.

Torres heard the click and threw the mobile on the sofa.

He lifted himself up and walked on his heel to avoid getting blood on the floor, slowly edging his way into the kitchen. He grabbed a paper towel, wrapped it around his foot and collected a dustpan and brush out of the cupboard. He stumbled awkwardly into the lounge, cleared the broken glass and dumped it into a bin.

Torres opened his laptop and read Dawson's email. He sent the most relevant details to a printer, quickly packed an overnight bag and called Dawson back.

"I've got all the information thanks. You're right, it requires closer investigation. I'm just about to set off." Torres looked at his watch, "Depending on the traffic it'll take me an hour or two to get there. I'll call you with an update once I've visited the crime scene and collected more information."

Torres arrived at the Carson National Park access road after a seventy-mile drive. Taking the road past the park office, gift shop and up towards the main gate.

During daylight hours the gate would normally be open. Local police officers, posted as guards since the incident, now prevented anyone entering or leaving the park without permission. Seeing the car approaching, one of the police officers stepped out into the road, raised his hand and Torres stopped. The officer walked around to the driver's side window and tapped on the glass. Torres pressed the button and the window slowly descended revealing the FBI badge in his other hand.

The officer turned away and shouted to his colleague, "Smith, open the gate it's the FBI." He leaned towards Torres, "Follow the signs to the Taluca campground. Be careful, the road has a few forks so look out for the signs."

"Don't worry I've been here before."

A hundred and seventy-five miles north of Albuquerque, New Mexico, the Carson National Park is popular with campers, tourists, cyclists, mountain bikers, hunters, and hikers. To most people it was just a great place to hang out and relax, however on occasions bad situations developed there. Due to the proximity to his home in Santa Fe, the FBI agent had already been involved in several incidents, most involving a mixture of excessive alcohol, or drug use, and idiots having access to guns. He had given up counting the number of cases where a simple argument over nothing important had led to a dead body and life term in prison.

Occasionally, the national park threw up a case which required real detective work. Torres had kept the file of an unsolved murder case on his desk for nearly two years. An unidentified woman, her battered body dumped in a shallow grave by her killer. Animals, scavenging for food, dug up the bones leaving them on display for hunters to find. Torres was at a dead-end, without any leads to go on, and no way to identify her. But he refused to give up on trying to solve the mystery. The case file lived on his desk as a daily reminder to never forget her. He made a point of opening the file every day to look at the images of a headless pile of bones. He lived in hope one day someone might find her skull or even a jaw bone. Something to check against dental records, or maybe to do a facial reconstruction, and a route to find her identity.

Like the unsolved murder the current case intrigued him. There had never been an incident before resulting in three dead women, one missing and no reported witnesses.

The police officer stepped to the side and waved Torres on. He took the main road and turned onto a branch road with a gradual elevation, bordered on both sides with mixtures of Douglas Fir, Limber Pine and Gamble Oak trees. At the next junction, he turned onto a steeper road which began winding with hairpin bends taking him up the side of the mountain. The trees gradually changed to Ponderosa Pine, Subalpine Fir and Engelmann Spruce, signalling a height of over seven thousand feet.

Torres had never driven as far, or as high, into the national park as the Taluca campsite, a remote location far away from the more popular campsites near the park entrance. According to Dawson's report the Taluca had no facilities making it suitable only as a stopover for hunters. *Why did the young women come so far up here?*

After driving into the park for sixteen miles Torres noticed a sign indicating the elevation was now eleven thousand feet. He continued for another mile until he found a wooden arch with the words 'Taluca Campground' burnt into it.

He drove through the archway into the main campground car park, parked his black FBI sedan, grabbed his FBI windbreaker jacket off the back seat and climbed out.

The air was warm and scented with a mixture of tones, the smell of pine infused with burnt rubber and plastic. Parked around the car park he noticed several law enforcement vehicles, the Sheriff's SUV, two local police cars and a white New Mexico medical investigators van. In the middle he spotted a burnt-out saloon car. *According to Dawson's report, it was the smoke from the victim's car fire which raised the alarm.*

Torres knew the number of people walking around the car park would make any relevant evidence gathering near impossible. He continued to survey the car park and noticed a small sign guiding hikers to the trail pathway and the nearby campgrounds. *They parked over there and walked with their camping gear.*

Torres walked up to the local police officer guarding the entrance to the trail, "Torres, FBI, is the crime scene up there?"

"Yes, the Sheriff is up there waiting for you, he said you were on your way."

"Who's in charge of the forensics and CSI stuff," Torres asked.

"Rivera, the Chief Medical Examiner for the state, she's over there." The police officer pointed towards the burnt-out shell, "At the rear of the vehicle, in the hazmat suit"

"Okay, make sure no one leaves the car park until I come back and have a chance to speak to them."

The police officer raised the tape across the entrance to the trail, Torres stooped under it and started walking up a wide dirt path between the trees. The sunlight darkened in the shade of the trees and the path became muddy. He followed the sign towards the main campsite area and began to wonder what he would find when arrived. *Can it be as bad as Dawson's report said?*

Torres would know soon enough.

The sunlight stung his eyes as he walked out from the trees into a large round clearing. A lush green landscape with a small river running through the centre and surrounded by Engelmann spruce trees. From where he was standing, he followed the route of the hiking trail with his eyes, across the clearing to where it disappeared into the trees on the far side.

Torres noticed the women's camp site in the middle and

walked over. Two small tents, arranged so they faced each other with a campfire. Scattered around the location he discovered various items of clothing, food wrappers and tins. The campfire and scattered food told him when it happened. *They'd just woken up, preparing breakfast.*

Torres pulled out latex gloves from his windbreaker and began slowly walking around the crime scene, taking time to fully survey the area, reviewing every object and footprint, using his mobile phone to take pictures as he went. He investigated the tents seeing sleeping bags and women's clothes scattered around inside.

"Torres?" a man in his fifties appeared from behind a tent wearing a large Stetson hat and a gun belt with a holster containing a wild west style revolver. The man extended his hand. "I'm the Sheriff, Cranshaw's the name."

"Sheriff, Nico Torres, FBI, Santa Fe Office." Accepting and shaking his hand Torres quickly got down to business, "Can you tell your men to make a perimeter in the car park so we can protect the evidence around the burnt-out car. They are trampling everything down there."

"Shit!" Cranshaw cursed in a strong Texan accent, "Do I have to do ev'thang round here," then turned towards a nearby police officer. "Mason, get your arse down to the car park and set up a twenty-foot perimeter around that damn burnt-out car."

Cranshaw stood, watched the police officer running down the dirt path and turned to Torres, "I'm not sure sometimes how these guys get a badge".

Torres continued, "Thanks! What have you got for me Sheriff?"

Cranshaw rested his hand on the handle of the revolver,

"Overall it's a mess, as you can see for yourself. Down here the local wildlife had fun with the food and clothes. That happened before we arrived. Apart from that it's exactly how the women left it."

Cranshaw paused, took out a small notebook and read his notes aloud to Torres, "The park ranger said four young women, around twenty-five to thirty years old, with English accents, checked into the park two days ago. They registered and paid at the main office then he escorted them up here."

Torres interrupted, "Does he normally do that?"

"He said it was to make sure they found the campsite and to help them get the tents set up in the best location. To be honest I suspect the guy was probably trying it on. I've heard rumours that he's the type."

"Do you trust him?"

"Sure 'nuf, he's worked here for a few years now, never had any issues or complaints about him."

"He may not be a suspect but he's one of the last people to see them alive so I'll need to talk to him. Go on."

Cranshaw referred to his notes, "He said that he spoke to them a few times during his regular patrols. Doing normal camping stuff, going out hiking during the day, enjoying the area and sightseeing. 'Just a group of young women having fun on holiday is what he said."

The Sheriff stopped talking, flipped his notebook over to the next page and continued. "He got a call from early morning hunters further down on the mountain side. They called to report a forest fire higher up from their location. He drove up here to check it out and discovered the women's burnt-out car still smoking in the carpark. I dread to think what a mess we would've had if they'd parked the car closer to the trees. If the fire spread, we would've lost everything. After finding the car he decided to check on the women, walked up here and found this mess. Plus..."

Cranshaw stopped talking. He felt exasperated, he noticed during his recital the FBI agent was not listening, busying himself investigating the crime scene instead.

"Torres, darn man, I'm fixin' to blow a fuse, are you listening to me?" Cranshaw said angrily.

Torres just held up a hand, continued looking at the floor and spoke, "Yes I'm listening. Did he say if he noticed any other campers up here either before or after he found the crime scene? What about hunters? Did he see any vehicles on the road up here?"

Cranshaw looked at his notes, "No, he said only the women were here, he didn't see anyone else. That's not a surprise Torres, this site is remote, most visitors like to use the campsites further down the mountainside with toilets and showers."

Torres looked at the Sheriff and said sarcastically, "I know, but it's obvious someone was up here and they must have used a vehicle. Unfortunately, it'll be a waste of time looking for any fresh tyre tracks in the car park."

The comment angered the Sheriff who was about to protest when Torres held up his hand to stop him. "Look, forget I said that."

"No, if it needs to be said son just come out and say it, that's the way I like it and you're definitely a straight shooter."

"That's how I like things Sheriff. Let's move on, I'll go over what I've seen so far. It looks to me like four people wearing military-style boots. There's no evidence of the women wearing them, that's why I asked about hunters. I suspect the culprits are ex-military or have at least had some basic military training. That's judging by how they've tried to cover up the evidence, they thought the fire from the burning car would spread to the trees and destroy the campsite."

"You sure about that?" Cranshaw probed, "One woman is missing you know, what if she arranged it and then ran off with these other people? It's been known to happen."

"Possible, but very unlikely. There's absolutely no evidence around here to support that theory." Torres said dismissively before adding, "Come with me. I'll show you."

Torres walked towards the campfire and pointed at the ground, "Look, four different tread patterns from military issue boots, the sort hunters wear. The only other footprints are from sneakers and sandals with a woman's shoe size. There are Coyote paw prints all around, they probably ate the food. Oh, and as for the missing woman, I doubt she was involved because they dragged her out of here towards the car park"

Cranshaw looked around and asked, "How do you know that?"

Torres pointed along a trail of marks in the soil leading down to the car park then turned to the Sheriff, "Your report said four women checked in. We now know one got dragged off...correct?"

Cranshaw nodded with a new and greater respect for the FBI agent. *Damn this guy is good, seems to know his stuff, where did he learn to analyse a crime scene in such detail and so quickly?*

Before he could ask, Torres looked around the campsite and said forcefully, "So where the hell are the other three?".

"They're up there." Cranshaw gestured towards the tree line on the ridge above, "But I warn you it's not a pretty sight."

Torres did not expect it to be, he had seen plenty of dead bodies and Dawson had already warned him with his report. Cranshaw walked towards the tree line, found a gap and disappeared inside. Torres followed into the trees and out of sight of the campsite area. After a walk of twenty-five feet the Sheriff stopped and pointed towards a line of trees. Torres looked and found the bodies of three women, each tied to a separate tree, slumped on the ground in a kneeling position.

Cranshaw spoke, "Only the ranger and myself have been up here so the site is pretty much as it was."

Torres walked forward leaving Cranshaw standing. He paced around the bodies, analysing the scene, he noticed the women had their hands tied behind their backs using thick black tie-wraps. *Like they're used in the military to capture prisoners.*

Each woman shot, execution-style, with a single bullet to the side of the head. Blood from the wounds had run down the sides of their faces onto their torn clothes and the floor. Along with the blood he found evidence of torture with random bruises on their faces and bodies. Despite the torn clothes exposing their underwear, he found no evidence of sexual abuse. *Evidence of intimidation and torture, what information did the women have?*

Torres began the task of examining the surrounding area, taking care not to disturb the carpet of pine needles. In the muddier areas near the trees, he discovered more evidence of the military-style boot treads. Disappointed at not finding any shell casings he moved to the fourth tree. Behind he found several cut black tie-wraps.

Torres summed up mentally what he had discovered from the crime scene. *This isn't some random act of stupidity. The fourth woman watched as the culprits tortured and murdered her friends, then they took her. They must have wanted some information from her, executing the others so they could not identify them. A professional job overall, little to no evidence left behind, no witnesses, in and out, some torture, intimidation. Military training? What was so important to these guys they felt happy to kidnap one woman and kill three others?*

To avoid jeopardising the evidence gathering process he kept his thoughts to himself and walked over to Cranshaw, "Did the park ranger take copies of women's ID's? Please tell me he followed the rules and recorded everything."

"Well actually…I was trying to tell you earlier." Cranshaw took out a small pocketbook, flipped the pages, found the one he needed and started reading the text aloud. "Four women from the UK. From their passport photos I can confirm the identity of these three." He pointed to the bodies as he read, "Linda Stafford, Mandy Smith and Lydia Williams."

"And the missing one?" Torres demanded.

"Katherine Finn, twenty-eight years old, lives in London."

"Has anyone tried to contact the families?" Torres said.

"Not yet. I was waiting for you to turn up as I thought you may know the best way to handle it. I'm not sure who to speak to."

"Their British so start by contacting the British Embassy and inform them about the death's, their families need to know."

"What should we do about the missing woman? I called the number in her passport. A man answered and said he was not her next of kin but a friend of her brother. Once I explained what'd happened here the person told me the brother was in the British Army, currently stationed in Afghanistan. I tried calling the Army offices in London but they were no help, with the time difference and military security, I'm not sure we'll get hold of him anyway. Maybe someone at the FBI can help? You guys have connections with the CIA, NSA or whatever agency does military stuff abroad, don't you? Maybe they can get through to the British Army?"

Cranshaw sounded desperate, making it obvious he was uncomfortable with telephone work. Torres guessed the Texan was a face-to-face type of man and patted him on the shoulder, "No problem let me have all the details and I'll get Dawson at HQ to start the ball rolling. I need to speak to this brother, what was the name again..." Torres looked at his notebook "Finn."

Torres put his notebook away and the two men returned to the campsite area.

Torres spoke, "Sheriff, stay here and gather all the evidence you can, I want the full area searched, we need to find something we can use to trace culprits. We also need autopsies completed quickly on the bodies to see if they can tell us anything, maybe a bullet fragment or stray DNA. Make sure the forensics team checks the area around the bodies carefully, we may get lucky, one of the bullets may have lodged in a tree. I'm going back to the car park to speak to the head of the forensics team and the park ranger, and I need a full copy of your notes and the details of the women."

Cranshaw looked at Torres and motioned to respond but before he could Torres turned, and walked away, heading down the trail towards the car park.

Torres stopped briefly and looked back, seeing Cranshaw shouting at a police officer then carried on down the dirt path and disappeared between the trees.

Chapter 2
Camp Griffin, Helmand, Afghanistan

Kirkland Finn was taking some well-deserved rest in his barracks room. At thirty-six years old Finn had been in Military service since his teens, working his way up through the ranks arriving at his current rank of Captain in the 22nd Special Air Service, part of the British Army. Finn's sixteen-man unit specialised in covert operations including surveillance, eliminating terrorist groups, recovering hostages, and supporting other military units.

The type of work that Finn did never ended up in the newspapers. He provided an invisible protection service, eliminating troublemakers or anyone who presented a threat to life in the UK. The nature of his work required that he be ready for deployment, at short notice, to anywhere in the World.

Sometimes Finn wore a uniform, sometimes he was undercover in civilian clothes, but regardless, he always focused on the job, like a machine tuned to perform at its best. To the UK government Finn was a highly trained asset, skilled in combat, intelligent with tactics, dependable to the last, and when the day came, expendable.

Finn had seen his fair share of combat and, when required, had killed, using a wide range of weapons including his bare hands. He was not proud of everything he had done while in the military but it was his job. They gave him orders and he carried them out. No questions asked.

Over the years Finn had built up a small network of people within British and US military units, soldiers that he'd trust with his life, and theirs with him. Having lost good men, and friends, along the way, outside of his unit, Finn preferred to work alone.

Finn, now stationed in Afghanistan with his elite sixteen-man squad, had become settled into life at Camp Griffin. Six months into a tour of duty at a secret British Army base positioned between Sangin and the Kajaki Dam on the Helmand river. A perfect location, and staging area, for covert military operations within the Helmand and Kandahar provinces of Afghanistan. Constructed on a flat plain close to the western banks of the Helmand river, giving easy access to the northern areas of the country which borders Iran and Pakistan. With many terrorist groups, insurgent factions, drug trafficking rings, religious fanatics, and tribal leaders in great supply across the region, the unit was never short of work.

Operations carried out from the base involved a range of transport methods, trucks, jeeps, boats, and helicopters. Whichever method ensured the men got to where they had to be, as quick as possible, without detection.

Due to the nature of the clandestine work performed by the men stationed there, Camp Griffin did not appear on any maps. The men often joked that at least they did not have to endure feelgood visits from journalists, celebrities, or members of the Royal family.

Finn sat on his bunk, unlocked his iBOW communication device. *No messages.*

It came as no surprise. It was the life he chose for himself. Apart from his sister Kathy, Finn did not have any other family members to care about him. Their parents died in a speedboat accident while on holiday in Cyprus. Finn never forgave his parents for leaving them alone, especially when he discovered later that they consumed alcohol before they died. He was twelve, forced to grow up fast, taking responsibility for his younger, four-year-old sister.

After the funeral Social Services put them into foster care with a family in Salisbury. The foster parents loved and did their best for them. Once old enough Finn joined the British Army and Kathy continued her education at university. Of course, there had been girlfriends and he came close to marriage a few times. Eventually the subject of his life in the military, getting a proper job and starting a family would come up forcing him to quickly move on.

Finn decided many years ago Kathy was the only family he wanted, or needed. He never discussed his work in the Army. She did not know what he had done and what he was capable of. When he was abroad, to her, he was just another British soldier sent on a 'waste of time' deployment.

His lifeline to stay in touch with her was the iBOW, a handheld, military grade, communication device which he received during an undercover mission and neglected to return it. To everyone else it looked like a fancy mobile phone. The iBOW included encrypted software applications for route planning, secure messaging, data storage, photography and other tasks. The iBOW also included a tracker. Finn told his friends the device was perfect for covert operations…and for listening to music.

Finn continued to fiddle with the iBOW, and logged into the browser interface. He opened the BBC News application and read about current events back home. *The usual tripe, lying politicians, overpaid footballers and misbehaving celebrities. I wonder how Kathy is doing on her holiday?*

Bored with the news he opened Facebook and searched for Kathy's profile. *No new posts or updates. Strange. Maybe she's just too busy having fun to remember to update me. Good for her.*

Looking at the small bright screen made him drowsy, tiredness crept over him, he scrolled through the music library and found his favourite Jimi Hendrix album. Fitting his headphones, he laid back on to the bed, pressed play, closed his eyes and drifted off.

∴ ∴ ∴ ∴

Finn woke to the usual sound of helicopters ferrying soldiers in and out of the camp. Sunlight streamed in from the crack in the makeshift curtains one of the guys had created from an old blanket. In the beams of light, Finn watched the minute specks of dust floating in the air and his mind drifted away, only for it to kick him back to life. Something did not feel right. *Kathy?*

Sitting up, he swung his legs over the edge of the bunk. *Why have I not heard from her? She spends half of her life on her mobile phone either texting, tweeting, or Facebooking.*

He quickly checked the iBOW again, finding no new messages. He looked for her last Facebook update, two days ago, which said she was in New Mexico getting ready to move on to a new campsite in the mountains. Something told him she was in danger, he did not understand why and the thought caused a cold shiver.

"Finn" He turned to see Dave Dunn, the latest and youngest member to join the unit, standing in the doorway, "You'd best get yourself to the command centre, Adams wants you."

Finn picked up a bottle of water from the table and drank it in one before turning to Dunn, "It's Captain Finn to you."

"Yes sir, sorry, but it sounded urgent."

Finn threw the empty plastic bottle across the room, it hit the wall and landed in the waste bin. *Urgent? Adams likes a good drama.*

Dunn knew bad blood existed between Adams, the Commanding Officer, and Finn the 2nd in Command. The men in the squad told Dunn it had something to do with a past failed mission where several of Finn's men returned home in body bags. Only Finn and Adams knew the truth. Dunn had asked, they warned him off, told him to forget it, to leave it alone. Finn had not left it, to him there was a score to settle with Adams, and he knew one day he would make it happen.

"All I know Captain is what Baker has told me. He said someone in the UK top brass phoned Adams, an urgent call. When he finished speaking Adams shouted out of his office door demanding that Baker got hold of you straight away. He called the barracks here and I got the short straw to come and wake you, sorry." Dunn shrugged his shoulders and left the room.

An officer calling from the UK? Why would they be calling here, what does it have to do with me? Is it Kathy?

He sensed something was wrong and quickly put his boots on, grabbed a clean T-shirt from his locker and ran from the barrack block, making his way across the hot, dusty, compound to the door of the command centre.

As he entered the main command centre room, he noticed the sounds of the normally active room slowly descend into a strange quiet. Only the sound of electronic equipment filled the room. Finn glanced towards Adams' open office door. As usual, sitting behind his desk with a worried look on his face. He walked between the desks, avoiding eye contact with the soldiers in the room and opened the office door.

"Sir, what's this about? I've got a strange feeling this might have something to do with my sister Kathy, does it?"

Adams stood up and walked towards the door "Captain Finn, come in and sit down."

Finn entered the small office and sat at the chair in front of the desk. Adams closed the door behind him and returned to his chair behind the desk.

"Finn, I've just had the top brass in London on the phone. They've been contacted by the authorities in the US. They need you to speak to an FBI in New Mexico."

Finn reacted angrily, "What? New Mexico that's where Kathy is on holiday. Cut the crap, Adams is this about my sister or not?"

Adams moved uncomfortably in his chair, "I don't have the details," Finn noticed Adams nervous look. "All I know is an FBI special agent called Nico Torres has been trying to track you down and the enquiry ended up with the top brass in London. As you know this place technically doesn't exist which is why he could not find you. The authorities in the US called to say he needs to speak to you urgently. They've given me his number. Stay here and I'll get Baxter to call him for you. He'll route the call to the phone here in my office...just wait a moment."

Adams stood up and left the room, closing the door behind him. Finn watched through the glass partition as Adams walked across the command centre and spoke to Baker, the communications officer for the unit. After a few minutes, the phone in Adams' office began ringing and Adams gestured for Finn to pick up the phone up. Finn raised the receiver and waited for the caller to speak…

Chapter 3
Taluca Campsite, Carson NP, NM.

Torres arrived at the trailhead and addressed the police officer guarding the entrance, "You said Rivera is the Medical Examiner, can you point her out again?"

"No problem, she's kneeling at the rear of the burnt-out car...over there."

Torres followed the direction and spotted a figure wearing a full-body blue protective suit, latex gloves, and a clear face mask. He noticed a small section of blonde hair sticking out from the side of the elasticated hood.

Walking over to the rear of the burnt-out car Torres tried to get a detailed look at the woman's figure, taking a moment to follow the lines of her tightly fitting hazmat suit before speaking.

"Mrs Rivera, I'm Nico Torres, FBI, can you give me a minute?"

Rivera looked up through the full-face clear mask to see Torres standing over her. He could now see her young-looking face and beautiful blue eyes. *Stunning.*

She noticed his stare, analysing her face and features, then returned to her work saying, "Sure, give me a moment to finish up here...oh and its Miss not Mrs."

Torres used the time to continue studying the woman's figure and features. *She looks around thirty-five, stunningly beautiful looks, nice firm body, my type of woman...and a Miss!*

Rivera finished her work, put her tools away in the white van and approached him, "Torres, I'm the Chief Medical Examiner for the state of New Mexico, how can I help you?"

Torres gestured as if to push his own hair back and pointed to Rivera's hairline. She raised her hand and pushed her hair under the hood.

"Thanks. It's as hot as hell in this thing, I can't wait to get it off."

Their eyes met, stimulating them both to break into a smile. Torres liked the suggestion and found himself staring at her before quickly glancing away.

He composed himself and asked, "You said you're the Chief, do you normally do field investigations?"

Rivera smiled, "I'm based in Albuquerque. I like to investigate the major crimes like this in person, plus the victims were foreigners so it's only right I handle any official contact with the families and embassy staff."

"That's good. Can you confirm it with Cranshaw? I get the impression he doesn't like doing that type of work." Rivera nodded acceptance and he continued, "So what have you learned so far from the crime scenes down here and up there?"

"Down here all we have is the women's car. Burned using a plastic container full of petrol, you can see the remains of it melted on the back seat. I took the chassis number and a police officer ran it through the police computer system for me. He said it's a hire car out of Texas, hired by a Katherine Finn."

Torres spoke, "Cranshaw has just confirmed that's the name of the missing woman."

So, if you wanted to find this woman all you'd need was details of the hire car and someone with access to NPR. Monitor the system, follow her for miles then snatch her when it was convenient. This is not just another random crime. This could involve people who are capable of hacking into the road traffic camera grid. They've got to be either Agency or Military?

Rivera, noticing the thoughtful look on the FBI agent's face and asked, "Are you still with me?"

Torres nodded saying, "Sorry, please continue."

"Why you'd feel the need to kill three women who are on holiday, kidnap another, burn their car, is beyond me...it just seems totally crazy. Well anyway, that's your job, right?"

"True," Torres agreed. "But I could do with some help finding the culprits."

Their eyes connected again, a smile appeared on Rivera's face before she continued, "But why burn the car, it just seems pointless?"

"Evidence. They searched the car before going up to the campsite. They burned it to destroy any DNA they may have left behind. I also suspect they wanted to start a bigger fire with the trees which would've destroyed all the evidence up there as well. Luckily for us the fire didn't take hold."

"It may have worked, at first glance it looks like there's nothing left here to go on but we may get lucky and find something. We'll keep looking."

"What about the crime scene up there? I've just asked Cranshaw to arrange a full search of the area in case they left anything behind we can use to trace them. Have you looked at the bodies? Can you tell me what happened?"

"All shot at close range, roughed up a bit to start with but nothing sexual."

"That's what I thought. It looks like there were four culprits, we need to analyse the boot prints up there. Is that something you can help with?"

"No problem I'll liaise with Cranshaw, collect up what evidence I can over the next few hours and get a preliminary report over to you before doing in-depth analysis over the next couple of days. Which FBI office are you working out of?"

"Santa Fe, here's my card, email the report, my mobile is on there as well, just in case you want to speak to me."

"Are you returning to Santa Fe tonight?"

"No. I think I'll stay in the area until I'm sure I've seen everything I need to. I'm just going to find a motel later. Hopefully there's one nearby with decent air-con, clean sheets and a bar which serves steak and cold beer. Do you know the area?"

Rivera smiled, "Not very well but I've been here quite a few times in the past. It's a popular place for hunters and there've been several shootings that have required investigation. When I stay over, I always use the Prickly Pear Motel on Highway 64. It has clean rooms and air-con. Next door there is a roadhouse which serves great steaks and plenty of cold beers to choose from."

"Thanks for the tip. Drop by if you fancy sharing a cold one with me later"

Rivera smiled again, "You never know, I might just take you up on the offer."

Torres quickly changed the subject. *It's too easy to talk to this woman.*

"Do you know where the park ranger who reported the crime is?"

"Yes, he's over there," she pointed to a man in a green and beige uniform, "the good-looking guy near the police car. He's not the sharpest person you'll ever meet, but he makes up for it in his looks I suppose. His name is Scott. A local police officer told me he's a loner with a reputation as a player when he's around women. Not my type and he didn't like me asking him questions."

"Don't worry he definitely won't like me doing it."

Torres thanked Rivera for her time and walked over to Scott. He approached the man on the blindside making sure he could not see him until it was too late. He got up close, invading his personal space. An intimidation trick Torres had used many times in the past to get someone on the back-foot. It worked again.

"Scott! The park ranger, tell me what you know."

Scott twitched with the shock of seeing Torres standing next to him. "Eh, what, well, there's not a lot to say really, the four foreign women checked in at the park office a couple of days ago and asked about camping. They wanted a quiet place to camp so I suggested this place. I took all their details and then drove up here with them to make sure they found the campsite and helped them with their tents."

"Do you normally do that? You seem to have taken a lot of interest in these young foreign women."

"No I don't normally do it but because they were foreign I guessed it'd be best to show them. This site is remote and I didn't want them getting lost."

"How did they seem? Happy? Sad? Drunk? Drug takers?"

"No nothing like that. Just a group of normal young women on holiday. They said they were on a road trip, driving from state to state seeing the sights."

"What about other park visitors, any strange reports or stuff which might give me an indication of what happened here? What about the people who did this? Other campers? Anyone check out in a rush? What about people entering the park during the night?"

Torres noticed Scott starting to fidget with the constant questions and sweat appeared on his forehead.

"The lock on the main gate was broken sometime during the night but I never heard or saw anything, I was at my cottage. Apart from that, I don't remember seeing any suspicious vehicles or visitors in the park, but it's a large area with multiple roads. Look, I think I've told you all I know."

Scott edging away nervously. Torres anticipated his action and moved, keeping an equal distance between the two men.

"Do you live in the park Scott? Married? Girlfriend?"

"I live here at the ranger cottage near the park office, it's included with the job. I'm not married anymore I left that miserable life behind years ago"

"And a girlfriend?"

"Err...well no...just me"

Torres sensed the deception in Scott's response, as if holding information back, maybe something to do with the crime or details which could cost him his job. He continued probing, "So, you spend nearly all your time here on the site, live in a cottage near the entrance gate and never saw or heard a thing? Do you expect me to believe that? You're either out driving in the park, in the office or at your cottage and you're telling me you never saw, or heard, anything last night?"

"That's right, I saw and heard nothing." Scott mumbled.

Seeing an opportunity to get to the truth Torres continued to probe, "How many staff work here Scott? Apart from you."

"There's just myself..." he paused, "and Mary. She works in the gift shop during the opening hours."

Torres concluded why Scott was twitchy, "Tell me about Mary, is she married? Where does she live?"

"Yes, she's married. She lives in a town outside the national park. Why do you ask? She won't know anything about what's happened on the mountain."

Torres got closer to Scott and barked, "I'll be the person who decides that." He stepped back and deliberately changed the subject, "What about security cameras in the park?"

Scott mumbled a nervous response, "Well there are cameras in the entrance, at the site office, the gift shop and in the main car park. We've got several cameras around the park which we use to monitor animal migration.

They're on a live stream which members of the public can log into so they can watch the animals."

"What about this car park and the campsite? Are there any around here?"

"No, this area is not included in the camera loop. It's too far from the main office."

Torres moved away from Scott, "Take me to where the camera hard-drives are stored. You drive your pickup truck and I'll follow in my car."

Scott turned away from Torres and walked to his truck, climbed in, started the engine and turned the vehicle around in the car park. He drove through the archway and waited on the side of the access road. Torres pulled up behind and flashed his lights to indicate to Scott to move on.

Torres returned down the snaking road following Scott's truck until they arrived at the entrance gate which was in the open position. The police officer noticed the ranger truck and Torres's car approaching and waved them on. On the left of the gate Torres spotted the main car park, with the park office and gift shop. Scott drove into the car park, Torres followed. Several spectators and a couple of TV camera vans had gathered in the car park. *It doesn't take those guys long to get involved. I need to speak to Mary before Scott does.*

They parked side by side outside the main office door and climbed out. Torres showed his badge to a police officer standing at the door stopping people entering the office and gift shop. The officer quickly looked then swung the door open for him.

On the way in Torres turned to Scott "You wait outside, if I need you, I'll call."

The gift shop was empty apart from a middle-aged woman behind the counter. Torres took out his badge and showed it, "Hello, I'm from the FBI, are you Mary?"

"Yes, do you know what's going on? They won't tell me anything. 'Just stay here' that's all they'll say to me. I've got to go home soon to look after my children."

"Scott has told me he was with you last night."

Mary was surprised by Torres's tone, "With me?"

"That's why he didn't hear someone breaking the lock on the main gate and a vehicle driving into the park. Is that right?"

"Err..." she mumbled nervously.

"He said you're married so Mary it's up to you. We can either do this the easy way by you telling me the truth now while you can, or, if you prefer, we'll do it the hard way. I can interview both you and your husband at the local police station."

Mary cursed under her breath, "That guy is an idiot."

Torres knew she meant Scott and said calmly, "Look Mary, I'm not interested in what you do. All I need to know is what happened here in the park last night?"

Mary swore again and moved from behind the counter to face Torres. "Look, mister, it was just a bit of fun, no need to involve my husband, or my kids. You've met Scott. You can see the type of person he is. He's got good looks and a fit body but he's got a brain like a bag of beans. To be fair to him it was me who led him on but frankly, it wasn't worth the trouble."

"And what about last night, the lock on the main gate was broken, did you see or hear anything?"

"All I remember is hearing something while I was getting ready to leave his cottage around midnight. I heard a sound like someone banging on metal followed by a truck engine. He was just lying on the bed."

"What did you do then? Did you go outside to look?"

"No, I didn't! I'm not stupid. I told Scott what I'd heard and he said 'forget it'. He started pleading with me to come back to bed but I'd already lost interest by then. Once was enough…if you know what I mean. It was late and I needed to get home. By the time I'd put my shoes on, ready to leave, he was fast asleep so I just left him to it."

While she spoke, Torres looked into the woman's eyes, analysing what she was saying. After a few thoughtful moments he went to the door and called Scott to come inside.

As he entered the office Torres got up into his face and barked, "Stop messing me about. Last night while you were having fun with Mary someone broke the lock on the main gate, a truck came in and you did nothing. Because of you, three young women are dead and another kidnapped. I'll be putting your conduct in my report. Now show me the security camera tapes, starting with the main gate, around midnight."

Scott went into the main office, logged on the PC and opened the camera system selecting the camera on the main gate.

"Start the tape at eleven pm" Torres ordered.

Scott played the tape on a medium-fast forward speed until what appeared to be a large black SUV appeared.

"What was that?" Torres asked.

"Wait I'll rewind the tape and play it in slow motion."

On the slow replay the two men watched as the SUV drove slowly up to the main gate. A large man dressed all in black got out of the passenger seat. Another, also in black, got out of the rear door with an assault rifle in his hands. The armed man walked slowly towards the buildings before stopping, crouching down on one knee, and pointing his gun.

Torres slapped Scott across the back of the head, "Damn fool! If Mary had opened the door a few moments earlier she'd probably be dead now."

"Leave it, man, you can't do that." Scott protested.

"Shut it! You're looking at losing your job, if you want, I can make it a lot worse for you. Play the tape!"

The video tape continued and the first man to get out of the SUV hit the padlock several times with a hammer, easily breaking the lock, he lifted the barrier and held it while the SUV drove into the park. The man with the gun walked backwards, still covering the buildings with his rifle and climbed into the SUV. The first man lowered the barrier, returned to the SUV and it headed into the park, out of the camera view. Due to the camera angle, and darkness, Torres struggled to see the license plate.

Torres thought to himself. *With the driver, that shows at least three of them, the other was probably still sitting in the back.*

He asked Scott, "At what time did the hunters report the fire to you? Was the sun up?"

"The fire was reported just after I started at eight twenty. Sun up is around six, I normally start my rounds at seven, that's when I normally unlock the gate but this morning I found it broken."

"And seeing it broken didn't warn you that something was wrong?" Torres shook his head in disbelief. "Start the tape at six am."

Scott fast-forwarded the tape from six. No cars entered or left the park until Torres shouted, "Stop! There..."

Torres spotted the barrier rising and moments later a black Escalade SUV driven out of the park at high speed.

Torres wrote down the time, six twenty-seven, "Go backwards, slow it down, freeze it, I need to see the license plate. Stop, there, I can't see it, damn the quality is poor, can you zoom in, stop it there, show me the rear of the SUV."

Scott fumbled with the controls and zoomed in as best as the software allowed but the unclear image made reading the license plate impossible. Torres noticed three figures on the backseat, one in the middle wearing lighter clothes than the others dressed in black. *Four on the way in and five on the way out...that confirms it, they took the woman, we need to trace that vehicle.*

Torres hissed, "Give me the hard drives, I'll get them analysed at the FBI labs in Washington."

Scott gathered the security hard drives, as he handed them over, he tried to speak but Torres stopped him, "Shut it! I don't want to know." He snatched the drives and walked from the office into the gift shop and growled to Mary "Get yourself another job, the idiot in there's not worth ruining your marriage over, think of your kids."

It sounded to Mary like Torres was talking from experience, had he been in the same shoes as Scott, responsible for ruining someone's marriage? Or was it the marriage and the kids he was trying to protect? All she could say was "Too right."

Torres walked outside into the sun and put on his Police sunglasses.

A large group of journalists and TV reporters approached him shouting questions, "Are you the officer in charge? What's your name? What happened? Is there a statement? How many are dead"

Torres ignored the questions and pushed past the vultures. He unlocked his car, placed the hard drives in a sealed evidence bag and secured them in the boot before getting into the driver's seat.

Starting the engine his mind wandered to the beautiful woman he had just met, *Rivera! She even has a beautiful name.*

A warm feeling passed through his body and he quickly changed his line of thought. *I need to find the motel she mentioned, I've got a bunch of calls to make, starting with the brother in Afghanistan? How do I track him down?*

∴ ∴ ∴ ∴

As Torres drove along highway 64, he saw a sign advertising the Prickly Pear Motel and Roadhouse on the roadside. He smiled to himself. *What a name for a Motel, well at least it is rememberable.*

After a further five miles of driving, he pulled into the motel carpark. After waking the half-asleep receptionist, he completed the check in process, which involved handing over twenty-five dollars. He parked directly outside the room door and grabbed his gear from the boot.

The motel room looked just like so many more he had stayed in during his FBI career. A TV on the wall, king size bed, table with two chairs, a fridge and a small bathroom with toilet and shower.

He hung his spare clothes up and unpacked his laptop, setting it up on the small table. He unplugged the room telephone. Took out a black box from his bag and plugged it into the telephone wall socket and plugged the room telephone into the black box. With his secure telephone line set up he started the task of trying to track down the brother of the kidnapped woman, *Kirkland Finn.*

Torres called FBI headquarters, "Dawson, how do I get in touch with a guy who is in the British Army. I think he is in Afghanistan?"

"Afghanistan? That'll be very difficult. You'll need to speak to someone at the NSA. They should be able to set you on the right track of who to speak to in the UK."

Following several calls to different agencies within the US, Torres managed to get the number of a US Army General based at Bagram air base.

"General, thank you for taking my call. I'm Nico Torres of the FBI. Can you please help? I'm trying to get hold of a British soldier stationed at a base in Afghanistan. I've tried everything. You're my last hope."

The General growled, "Listen son do I look like I'm running a missing persons unit to you? And another point, how the hell did you get my number?"

Torres decided to calm the situation and give the irate man some background details, "I'm sorry General but I can't say how I got your number but it's very important that I speak to a British soldier whose sister has been kidnapped in the USA."

"Kidnapped? What's this soldier's name and unit?"

"I don't have a unit General, only a name, Kirkland Finn."

"Finn! British Army!" The General barked, "You mean Captain Finn son."

"You sound like you know him."

"Hell son, the Captain is held in high regards in these parts. Give me the details and I'll see what I can do for you."

Torres told the General about the crime scene, the murdered women and the military style abduction of Finn's sister, Kathy.

"So, you're telling me someone in the USA has kidnapped Finn's sister? Damn son, he's not going to take that news well. Finn and his unit are an important part of what we are trying to achieve out here. Now, I assume you're intelligent enough to know we operate very strict security policies out here son. There's no way I can give you direct access to a secure UK military base so I'll tell you what I can do for you. I'll speak to the top brass in

London. If they agree to let you talk to him, the CO over there will arrange for Finn to ring you back. Goodbye!"

The line suddenly fell silent and Torres smiled to himself. *Strange character.*

He put his mobile phone on the table and got the laptop out of his rucksack. He checked his emails, replied to some, deleted the rest, and began typing his case report. A courier driver interrupted when he knocked on the motel door to collect the hard drives.

Torres handed over the package, "This is very urgent, it must arrive at FBI HQ by tomorrow morning."

"No problem, they'll be flown out from Albuquerque tonight for delivery before eight am. Sign here..."

Torres signed the paperwork and shut the door. He finished his report and decided on a long shower and a shave. After the shower Torres changed into jeans and looked through his bag. He pulled out a black 'Metallica' T-shirt and pulled it over his head. He massaged gel into his hair, reached for a comb then changed his mind and decided to style it with his fingers instead. He took a last glance in the mirror to confirm that his new six-foot rocker look would allow him to blend in with the locals. *Ready.*

Feeling happy he thought of the steak and cold beer he had promised himself earlier in the day. He reached for the door handle and the telephone began to ring.

Chapter 4
Camp Griffin

Baker typed in the telephone number and after a delay, the phone rang, "Torres."

Baker responded, "Hello Mr Torres, my name is Baker, I've got Captain Finn on the line for you. Hold while I transfer the call, the next voice you'll hear will be the Captain's."

Torres waited for Finn to pick up the telephone.

"This is Captain Finn speaking, can you confirm your full name and the agency you work for?"

"Hello Captain. I'm Nico Torres, FBI special agent working out of Santa Fe, New Mexico."

"Why are you calling me?"

"Captain Finn it's taken me a long time to track you down. I've been on the phone for hours to the different security agencies, NSA, CIA, NSC. Eventually, I managed to speak to someone who said they would help, called the British Army in London and arranged for this call for me."

"That's great to hear but does not answer my question, why are you calling me?"

"It's regarding your sister Katherine. When did you last speak to her?"

"I've not spoken to her for weeks, We keep in touch via email and Facebook but there've been no updates for a couple of days. What's going on Torres?", Finn responded in an agitated tone. "Is she hurt or in trouble?"

Torres noted the tone and decided on a direct approach, "I'll give it to you straight, she's missing. At this stage we're not one hundred percent sure what has happened but evidence suggests she has been kidnapped."

Finn was speechless, frozen by the news as it slowly sank in.

Torres waited for a response. After a few moments of silence he continued, "She was staying at a campsite in New Mexico with three other women. They arrived a couple of days ago. I can't go into all the details over the phone as it's an ongoing investigation. What I will tell you is that we've identified three women at the campsite, but there's no trace of your sister. The last confirmed sighting of all four women together was by the park ranger around five yesterday evening."

Finn mumbled, gathering his words carefully, "Torres, you've already identified three women, are you saying they're..."

"Dead?" Torres interrupted, "Yes. Can you give me some background on the women, who they are and why they're travelling with your sister?"

"Kathy's friends from university, they get together for an annual holiday. How did they die?"

"At this stage it's best not to go into the specific details of the crime."

"Torres!" Finn growled. "You're not telling me anything. First you tell me someone has kidnapped my sister, then you tell me her friends are dead, but you can't tell me anything else. Cut the crap, get to the point and tell me about my sister."

Finn stood up, with the receiver in his hand and turned to look out of the office window. He noticed that some members of his troop had appeared in the command centre. Seeing the guys staring at him with concerned looks on their faces unnerved him and Finn turned to look at the notice board behind Adams' desk.

Torres continued, "Mr. Finn, I'm sorry but I can't go into the specific details of an active investigation. What I know is that whoever has taken her has done it for a reason. I don't know why. I can't find a motive that's why I asked. A motive would give me a lead and I can get on with searching for her. My priority is finding your sister. Are there any other family members she could have contacted or somewhere she'd go if she was in trouble? Is there anyone in the US that she'd get in touch with?"

A red mist descended on Finn as he gripped the receiver tightly, "No Torres, I'm the only family she has. We've an agreement. If she's in trouble when I'm away on active duty, she calls the numbers I've given her. Then they'll contact me. If she was in trouble, and able to call, believe me I'd know."

Finn struggled to stay calm, his training kicked in and he composed himself before continuing, "So what exactly happened to her friends?"

"At the moment it looks like a group of four men came into the park during the night. They took your sister and killed the other three. They set fire to their hire car hoping to destroy the evidence. That's all I can you at the moment."

"Thanks for letting me know, and yes I appreciate it's difficult for you. Can you tell me what you're doing to find her?" Finn asked.

"We are still processing the crime scene and the CCTV footage from the area needs to be analysed. I am looking into a couple items of evidence but my biggest lead is the vehicle the killers used, a black SUV. The video footage was poor quality making it impossible to read the license plate. I've sent the video to the FBI image processing lab. If they can get a license plate it'll allow me to put out an APB. I've also circulated her picture to all the local agencies and added a flag on the national database. If we get the license plate, or she turns up in public we'll know. I'm sorry to give you bad news Captain Finn, but that's all I can tell you at this stage. I appreciate you need information and being so far away from home makes you feel powerless however I can assure you we're putting lots of resources into solving this. We're at the very early stages of the investigation and we're just starting to put the evidence together. The man I spoke to before, Baker, has my number. If you need to speak to me, or hear anything from, or about, Kathy, then call me straight away. In the meantime, I'll contact you in a few days with an update."

Finn growled, "No chance Torres, I'm not just leaving my sister to the system. I'm sure you're a diligent investigator but I don't know you or your methods. She's my sister and I'll do everything I can to find her, starting with coming to New Mexico to speak to you. I'll find her and deal with the people who've taken her. If they've harmed her in any way, they'll pay the price for it."

Torres hesitated, "Captain, that's not a good idea, you're best staying there and I'll get in touch if I receive new information which I can share with you."

"You're not listening to me Torres. I'm not letting Kathy's file end up in a pile of unsolved crimes on your desk. Another missing person case among thousands of other ones that happen every year. To the FBI she'll just end up becoming a statistic, to me…she's family. I'm coming to the States to find you. When I get there, make sure you have more information for me." Finn slammed the receiver down.

Finn paused, collected his thoughts, glanced at the floor, and calmed down. He felt like a trapped animal, miles from home, miles from the US and miles from Kathy. The dilemma played out in Finn's mind, *Fuck, how do I get out of this place and to New Mexico? What has happened to Kathy? Who are the four men? Why did they kill her friends and take Kathy? What do they need her for?*

Finn ran through his options and realised he had to call the only person in the US who could help him, *Colby*.

After working with Colby and his covert ops team on several joint task force missions in the past, Finn knew Colby owed him a big favour.

Finn picked up the receiver, "Baker, get hold of Robert Colby for me. He's the Head of the National Clandestine Service, Special Activities Division (SAC*). Call your contacts at the US base at Bagram, they should be able to direct you to the CIA office where he's currently stationed, he'll be in the field somewhere."

Finn replaced the receiver, sat down, and waited.

Adams opened the door and walked in "What's happening Finn?"

"What's happening? I'm getting out of here, that's 'what's happening'. I need to get to the US. My sister is missing, they think she's been kidnapped."

"Kidnapped? By who? And what are you saying about going to the USA? There's no chance of you getting out of here at such short notice. I'm sorry to hear about your sister but it's probably best to leave it to the authorities in the US. The FBI are dealing with it and I'll see what I can do to get access to the investigation."

Finn ignored Adams and continued to stare at the phone, urging it to ring.

"What are you doing now? You can't just sit in here all day. You're best keeping active, we've got a mission briefing to organise."

Finn looked up and stared into Adams' eyes. It was a look Adams had seen before, he hesitated, then decided to leave Finn alone. He left the office, shutting the door behind him and returned to the command centre.

Corporal Gray, one of the men in Finn's troop, approached Adams, "Sir, what's the problem with Finn?"

"Family problems, just leave him to calm down"

After twenty minutes of waiting the phone rang and Finn impatiently grabbed the receiver. Adams noticed him pick up the phone through the glass partition of his office. He looked around at Baker who put his head down.

Adams walked over, "Baker who is Finn talking to now? You're not supposed to use the comms system without authorisation. I can get you into a lot of trouble if you don't tell me."

"Sir, it's someone from the CIA. Finn requested the call, I was just following his orders"

"The CIA? Who was the caller?"

Gray overheard the conversation and pulled Adams to the side, "Leave it, Adams...if you know what's good for you."

Adams looked around and noticed all of Finn's squad in the command centre looking at him. He knew their loyalty was with Finn, deciding not to risk conflict he removed Gray's hand from his arm. Everyone in the command centre stared through the glass partition into Adams' office watching Finn talking on the phone.

After a few minutes, Finn placed the receiver on the desk, opened the door, and shouted, "Adams, you've got a call, it's from the US...and I'm leaving."

Finn walked across the command centre and past his men. O'Neill grabbed his arm "Finn, what's happening?"

Finn stopped, "My sister has been kidnapped in the US. I'm going over there to get her back. I'll be gone for a while so listen to what Gray tells you...don't let Adams get anyone killed."

He continued out the door and ran across the compound to the barracks. He returned to his room and hastily packed some basic gear into a rucksack. Leaving the barracks, he walked out into the blistering desert sun. The dryness of the desert air mixed with the intense heat caught his breath. He looked around the compound, spotted a helicopter and headed towards it. He found the pilot Greenwood, sitting in a chair under a makeshift tent created from a poncho and ropes tied to the helicopter fuselage and some crates.

Finn noticed the pilot was asleep so kicked the chair, "Greenwood, wake up, you're flying me to Bagram."

"What?" Startled, Greenwood opened his eyes, "Shit Finn, I was asleep. You know how hard it is to get forty winks around here. What are you saying, Bagram? You know I can't just get into a helicopter and start flying without authorisation. Plus, more importantly to me...it's my break time."

Finn grabbed Greenwood by the collar and lifted him off the chair, "The only thing that's going to break is your neck if you don't get off your lazy arse and get into that chopper...Now!"

Having been at Camp Griffin for some months Greenwood knew it was best not to get on the wrong side of Finn.

He adopted a calming tone, "Finn, mate, I don't know what this crap is about but you know I can't just fly you out of here. We'll get shot down by either our guys on the towers, the insurgents out there and definitely by the US if we go anywhere near Bagram."

Finn slowly lowered Greenwood to the floor, once again he felt trapped.

In the command centre office Adams put the telephone down and reflected on the call he had just taken from Colby. *Top brass in the US and UK bending over backwards for Finn. Why? Two weeks leave...a Helicopter...*

Adams left the command centre, walked out into the central compound, and searched for Finn. His quest stopped when a helicopter flew over the base and made a wide arc around the perimeter, ensuring the British soldiers in the guard towers noticed the US Air Force markings on the fuselage.

The British soldiers stared at the hybrid design, a plane with a helicopter body. Wings on the fuselage and a tail section with a propeller inside a circular cowl. The mystical appearance included a special type of paint, a strange blue and grey colour which appeared to change as the helicopter moved along the skyline, a kind of stealth technology.

The pilot moved the helicopter into the centre of the base, hovered over a patch of clear ground and landed. He climbed out and took a moment to look around the base. Some soldiers walked over and following a short discussion he ran in the direction where the soldiers had pointed. He ran past Adams who shouted after him, "Hey, I'm the CO here, can I help?"

The pilot stopped running and returned to Adams, "Captain Finn?"

Adams pointed to where Finn was standing with Greenwood. The two of them walked over to Finn and Adams noted, "I'm not sure how you've managed to pull this off Finn. The top brass in London have given you two weeks leave to go to the US and find your sister. The US Air Force has sent this guy to take you to Bagram."

"Finn?" The pilot stretched out a hand, "Sorry for the dramatic entrance. I was in the area and my orders were to get here ASAP and pick you up. I hear you're on your way to the USA."

Finn accepted the hand, "Thank you, that's a fancy looking helicopter. I've never seen one like that before."

"It's a prototype, they call it the X-49 Speedhawk**. We can talk about all the technical stuff later but don't expect any on-board service. Enough of the chit chat, let's get out of here."

"Definitely!" Finn reacted, grabbed his pack, and turned to his commander with a look in his eye that would freeze vodka, "I'll catch up with you later Adams, when this is over, we are finishing it."

A feeling of panic swept over Adams. He knew what Finn was capable of.

Finn and the pilot ran over to the X-49 and within minutes the helicopter was in the air, rising to a safe height and disappearing over the horizon. Once airborne the pilot turned to Finn and said, "Cooney."

"What?" Finn was miles away, staring out of the window, all he could think about was Kathy. *Who could've taken her...Why did they take her...What are they doing to her...Bloody Hell!*

"My name's Cooney, you look beat man. Try to get some sleep, this baby is fast but it'll still take at least three hours to get you up to Bagram. They're arranging for you to board on a transport plane that's due to leave there later today. When the transport lands in Germany they're flying you onwards on another bird to the States."

"Sorry mate, I'm beat like you say. It's nice to meet you, thanks for your help". Finn tapped Cooney on the arm to acknowledge the greeting. "I'll take your advice and get my head down" Finn rested his head on the window and within seconds he was asleep.

※ ※ ※ ※

Finn woke with a jolt as the X-49 touched down at Bagram Air Force Base. He quickly gathered his thoughts and looked around the US airbase. He noticed lots of US military aircraft parked in locations around him, in the open on the tarmac and inside the hangers.

"Grab your gear, time to get you on the way to the States, but first I need to get your clearance documents."

Cooney jumped out and ran over to a waiting Black SUV. Two men dressed in the typical CIA uniform of black suit and sunglasses got out and talked to Cooney for a moment then handed him an envelope.

Finn did not like the CIA guys who wore suits, experience told him that you could not trust them, always looking to stab someone in the back to get a promotion. Finn had worked with the suits in the past. He preferred the guys in the US military or the undercover staff that Colby had, he knew he could trust those guys. He climbed out of the cockpit and jumped down onto the tarmac. He grabbed his bag from behind the seat and started walking towards the SUV.

Cooney returned to the helicopter and spoke to Finn, "I hate those guys, they give me the sweats, like a couple of vampires."

The two men laughed together. Finn, despite only meeting him briefly, liked Cooney, he knew he was one of the good guys you could trust, and count on when it mattered.

Cooney passed an envelope, "Here are your papers, you'll need them to get into the US, don't lose them. Your plane leaves in less than an hour so that's just enough time for a quick freshen up and a cold beer, come on, I'm buying."

The two men ran over to the main airport building with Cooney leading the way.

❖ ❖ ❖ ❖

The US Marine transport touched down at Ramstein AFB Germany at 7.23 am. Finn grabbed his pack and cleared the gate security check. On the other side a US Air Force sergeant escorted him to the command centre. After passing more security checks the sergeant showed him to an interrogation room with a single table and two chairs.

"Wait here Captain Finn, there's someone keen to meet you."

Finn dropped his pack to the floor and sat at the desk. He looked to his left and noticed a large mirror that covered the wall. *I wonder if someone is in there watching?*

Suddenly the door swung open and a booming voice shouted, "To attention Finn!"

Finn spun around to see a large six-foot, US Marine officer standing in the doorway, "Crowe, never in the world."

Finn stood up and the two men shook hands. Finn knew Crowe from when they worked together behind enemy lines in Afghanistan. Each had the other to thank for saving their lives on more than one occasion. That kind of bond and friendship never fades.

"Finn, there's no way I was going to let you pass through here without saying hello."

"You're a sight for sore eyes Crowe, I thought they shipped you back to the States."

"That was the idea, then they said they had an important job for me and I've ended up stuck here for the last four months. Man, I wish I was back out there dealing with the trash. Getting fat sitting behind a desk is not for me."

The two men pulled out a chair and sat at the table.

Crowe tapped on the table for a moment, thinking, then spoke, "They said you were flown up to Bagram then onwards to here on express transport orders which came from the top. The pilot told me he watched you at Bagram getting out of some fancy helicopter. Come on, spill the beans, what was it like?"

"There's nothing to say really. All I remember is that it was fast and had wings on the side, anyway, I slept most of the way to Bagram. One thing I'll tell you is the pilot was a good guy...he looked after me."

"What's his name?"

"Cooney."

"Yep, he has flown me in and out of a few scrapes over the years, you were in good hands, they've given the new gear to the right guy." Crowe paused and looked intently at Finn, "One thing is for certain Finn. Uncle Sam still loves you that's for sure. You have some powerful friends in the States ready to help. What's this business about?"

"All I know is what the FBI agent told me. Four men have snatched my sister from a campsite in New Mexico. They killed her three friends as well."

"Any clues as to who it could be? Do you think it's something from your past? We've both made enemies around the world."

"No one knows about my sister, only the top brass in the UK and your guys at the NCS, and she knows nothing about what I do, she thinks I'm just a regular soldier. I've never told her about my real work."

"So, what you're saying is that if they've found information on her it could only have come from a leak on your side…or ours. It doesn't make sense though. If she knows nothing, why take her? She can't tell them anything about what you've done."

"That's what's worrying me, if it's connected to me and they think she knows something then they may torture her, get nothing, and finally decide to just kill her."

"Don't start thinking like that, it could just be something random. You know there are quite a few people in my country that have no brains but have access to guns."

"I know!" Finn nodded, "It makes no sense, that's why I need to get over there and find out for myself. You know me, I need to be involved. I'm not just going to relax and let the situation play out...It's not how I do things."

Crowe banged the table with his fist, "Damn, I wish I was coming with you. If you need any help while you're in the States call me. I may be able to open a few doors for you. Come on let's get you on the plane and off to the States, you've got work to do."

The two men left the room and Crowe accompanied Finn to the transit area, "Wait here and I'll get your flight details."

Crowe went into a side office and reappeared with another soldier. "Finn, this is officer Barrett he'll take you straight to the plane, and he's got your clearances, good luck brother, stay safe."

The two men shook hands. MP's escorted Finn to the security gate and he immediately boarded his next flight to the US.

The Special Activities Centre (SAC) is a department within the CIA's National Clandestine Service. The SAC and the extended Special Operations Group (SOG) form the NCS's Special Activities Division that's responsible for clandestine or covert operations which the U.S. government does not want to be overtly associated with. Typical operations include terrorist tracking and elimination, raids, ambushes, unconventional warfare, and sabotage. SAC members are employed as Paramilitary Operations Officers and Specialized Skills Officers and as such, they don't typically wear a uniform. The CIA's paramilitary operations officers typically come from respected military groups including Navy SEAL Teams, Army Special Forces, U.S. Army Rangers, and the US Marine Corps.

** *The X-49 Speedhawk is an experimental four-bladed, twin-engine, high-speed helicopter with wings on the fuselage. Developed by Piasecki.*

Chapter 5
Prickly Pear Roadhouse, NM.

Torres left his motel room and headed across the car park to the roadhouse next door. The telephone call with Finn played on his mind. *Will he really try to come here? Surely not!*

Torres stood and reviewed the outside of the building finding only a handful of cars and two motorbikes in the car park. To the side of the entrance door in the window there was an illuminated 'Coors Light' sign. As he approached the door, he noticed the 'No Firearms' sign and laughed to himself. Pulling the badly fitting door open he stood in the entrance, looked around and found just what he expected, a rural bar.

On his left along the wall, he found a long wooden bar, empty, apart from the bartender and two guys at one end sitting at stools. From their look Torres identified them as the owners of the motorbikes. To his right, on a small stage, a guy performed a country and western song on acoustic guitar. Positioned between the bar and stage several round tables and booths along the walls occupied by people eating food. Torres counted thirteen people in all, not including the bar staff and the waiter. He proceeded to the bar, pulled out a stool and sat down.

The bartender, a young woman, walked over to him, threw a beer mat on the bar in front of him and asked, "Evening, what's your poison?"

Torres smiled, "I'll have a draft beer please, an IPA if you've got one, oh...and the menu."

The bartender took a glass from under the counter and started pulling a draft beer, "Here you go, Alligator IPA, folks like it round here." She placed the beer in front of him and walked away.

"And what about the menu?" Torres protested.

"No need for a menu. It's either steak or burger, and you can have chips or salad with it, or both if you like. If the burger does not do it for you then the chef also does a mean chilli con carne, hot and spicy." She smiled and added, "The chef is Mexican, he just cooks what he likes, but it's all damn good stuff."

"Steak, rare, chips and salad then," Torres confirmed.

"The food will be about fifteen minutes or so, enjoy the beer." The bartender walked away and disappeared through a doorway at the rear of the bar.

Torres watched her walk away admiring her body as she went. He took a mouthful of his beer and moved his attention to the sports channel on the TV above the bar. Not actually taking any notice of what was happening on the screen his mind drifted onto the events of the day. *What a mess, why kill those young women? I've got to save the other one.*

The bartender broke his concentration as she placed a plate of food in front of him, "Here you go, I'll bring you some cutlery and I guess you'll need another draft beer?"

He looked at the empty glass in his hand not realising he had already drunk all the contents, "Er...yes please, thanks."

The bartender walked away and returned with some utensils and various sauces, placing them next to his plate. She noted the thoughtful look on his face.

"Can I ask, did you work here yesterday?"

The bartender started pulling the draft beer, "I thought for a moment you were going to ask for my number," She smiled and put down the beer next to his plate, "Why do you ask?"

"I planned to meet some friends here but I got delayed and I was just wondering if you'd seen them in here. It was four guys."

"There was one group of four men, ignorant macho types...rude, loud, sexist."

Torres nodded, "I guess that sounds like them."

"They came in here around ten last night, sat at the booth over there near the stage. Ate lots of food and drank lots of beer, left around midnight, total assholes...they didn't even leave a tip."

"I don't suppose you heard them talking?" Torres enquired, fished for any information that might give him a lead on the killers.

She looked at him with an angry look on her face, "Are you a cop or something? Look mister I serve beer and food. I don't snoop on the customers." She looked towards the bikers at the end of the bar and raised her voice, "I like how I look and want to stay that way."

Torres said calmly, "Sorry, I don't want to get you into trouble with anyone." He pointed to the CCTV camera behind the bar, "Do these cameras work?"

"No chance, they've not worked for years, they're just for show. A bar like this wouldn't survive if customers knew we had cameras recording their activities."

"No worries," Torres said dismissively, "Anyway it sounds to me like it was them. I'm sure I'll catch up to them later."

"Are you sure you want to? Do you need friends like that?"

"Actually, they're not really friends, it's more of a work thing."

"Find a new job." The bartender shouted as she walked down the bar to serve another customer.

Torres returned to his food, eating it all. He drank his cold beer, then ordered another.

∴ ∴ ∴ ∴

The loud banging on the motel door woke Torres. *What time is it?*

He grabbed his mobile from the bedside table, flipped it over and looked at the screen. *07:13. Never!*

He rubbed his eyes, "One moment."

Sitting up, he dragged himself off the bed, grabbed his jeans from the floor and pulled the T-shirt over his head. He quickly looked around the room making sure no evidence remained of his time spent with the bartender. Another loud knock followed and he yelled at the door, "I said just a moment."

He fumbled on the floor for his socks. A third knock caused him to curse aloud, "Damn!"

Angrily he threw his socks on the bed, walked over to the door, and yanked it open. The morning sun hit Torres's eyes. He looked away briefly as his eyes adjusted to the light, then turned back, finding a beautiful blonde-haired woman standing outside holding two cups and a paper bag. *Rivera.*

"Good Morning Torres! I've brought us both some Breakfast." She took a good look at him before continuing, "My you look a welcome sight. One too many beers at the roadhouse by any chance?"

"What do you mean?"

Rivera pointed at him, "The T-shirt!"

Torres looked down to see that he had put his t-shirt on inside out. *Damn.*

"Can I come in?" she looked past Torres into the room seeing the bedsheets in a mess. "Not interrupting anything, am I?"

Torres opened the door. Rivera walked in placing the cups on the small table in the corner of the room before pulling out a chair and sitting down. "I brought you coffee and cream doughnuts. I hear that's what cops eat, am I right?"

"I'm not a cop."

The smell of sex still hung in the air, "Did you meet Jenny at the bar? She's a beauty, right?"

"Jenny?" Torres stared at her, acting innocent. "Can you give me five minutes to get a quick shower, tidy myself up and I'll join you for breakfast."

Torres picked up his suit trousers from the chair and collected a clean white shirt from the wardrobe before moving into the bathroom. After a few minutes he returned wearing his work clothes.

"That's a much-improved look." Rivera complimented.

Torres smiled at her and took a seat at the table. He took a mouthful of the lukewarm coffee and said, "They stopped off here, at the bar, on the way to the campsite, the bartender confirmed they left around midnight. That fits in with our timescales."

"You mean the four guys from the SUV? Did she give you a description or any other information which you can use to trace them?"

"No. Just typical meatheads and the CCTV in the bar doesn't work so it looks like a dead end. Did you get anywhere with the evidence you collected at the crime scene? Anything new for me to work with?"

"The autopsies told us what we already knew, they were executed. No evidence of drug or alcohol use. No bullets left at the scene. Not a lot to go on. You did however leave your mark on Cranshaw, he seems to have found a new enthusiasm for police work. He told his men to make plaster casts of the boot prints you discovered. I photographed them and circulated the images to military surplus stores in the area just to see if anyone could identify the tread pattern."

Rivera paused for a moment to take a drink of the coffee and a bite of a doughnut.

"And…did you get anywhere?"

"I was coming to that. One store owner in Farmington identified them as MN95GTX combat boots. He said they're the top of the line, costly, he only sells them to serious hikers and hunters. He did say they're used by military forces around the world. Your hunch that the killers might have links to the military could be right. Or maybe it was hikers?"

Torres reacted angrily, "Hikers don't execute women."

He picked up a doughnut, took a single bite, twisted his face, and threw the remaining piece in the bin.

Rivera smiled at him, "Who's a big bad grump in the morning. I'll bring bagels next time."

Torres smiled, "Can we trace the boots via sales receipts? Surely they don't sell lots of them?"

"You'd be surprised. They're widely available across the US in surplus stores and via online sales."

"So, it's another dead end." Torres said disappointedly.

"Not necessarily. If you catch a guy wearing a pair then we may be able to match the tread pattern and wear. The tread pattern on a piece of footwear can act in the same way a fingerprint does. The chances of two boots becoming worn down the same is near impossible. It won't stand up in court but it'll confirm if a person should be a suspect or not. Did you manage to trace the SUV from the camera footage?"

"Still working on it. The FBI lab has the best software available for analysing images, maybe we'll get lucky and they'll pick out the license plate. I need to call Dawson at the Washington office but he doesn't start work for another hour."

Torres took a drink of cold coffee and turned to Rivera with a glint in his eye, "So what do you think we should do with an hour to spare?"

Chapter 6
Kirtland AFB, Albuquerque, NM.

The US Air Force plane landed at Kirtland Air Force Base, on the outskirts of Albuquerque, at 10:47. Finn slept lightly on the plane and was in no mood to hang around. Once the seat belt sign extinguished, he jumped up, grabbed his pack from the overhead bin and made his way towards the front. He stood in a queue with other military personnel and waited for the cabin door to open, seconds seemed like minutes and he thought of Kathy.

The soldier behind him tapped him on the shoulder, "Your turn to go buddy."

Finn apologised and the queue edged towards the door, eventually he walked out into the warm New Mexico air. The sky a perfect blue without a cloud, for a moment Finn thought he was back in Afghanistan.

He followed the instructions of the ground staff directing everyone towards a doorway. As he approached the door two US Military Policemen appeared and blocked his way, a sergeant and a private. Finn noticed one holding a picture of him. The police officers gestured for him to move out of the queue of passengers.

The senior MP spoke, "Captain Finn can you come with me sir. We've got a jeep ready to take you directly to the command post."

Finn was too tired to protest, all he wanted was to get outside, to find a means of transport and to track down the FBI agent. He knew the only way to get a clearer picture of what had happened to Kathy was to speak face to face with the investigator. Once he had all the information, he could start the job of tracking down Kathy and the kidnappers...with or without Torres' help.

The two MPs led Finn outside to the jeep, one opened the back passenger door and he climbed in. After a short journey to the command centre the MP's took Finn to a room and a waiting security officer.

"Can I have all of your papers including your ID and warrant card."

Finn handed over documents and the officer checked them against his copy. The officer noticed Finn becoming impatient, "This shouldn't take too long Captain, it's just a formality." He continued reading the documents then handed them back. "All is in order, Captain Finn. There's an officer here to meet you from SAC. He told me to tell you Robert Colby sent him."

The officer turned to the MP's, "Gentleman take Captain Finn to the ops building and present him to SAC officer Miller."

Finn shook his head while replacing the documents into his pockets. *Here we go again, what now, I just need to get out of here. Colby has pulled off a miracle to get me here but I need to start looking for Kath.*

The MPs took him to the Operations Building. The driver stayed in the jeep while the other escorted him to a meeting room.

"Captain Finn, please wait here, would you like some water or coffee? Any food? I heard the officer say you've had a long flight."

Finn put his pack on the floor and sat at a desk, "No thanks, I'm fine."

After a short wait the door opened.

"Hello Finn, I'm Miller. Colby asked me to meet you once you got stateside."

Finn stood up to greet the man as he walked across the room towards him. Miller was a few inches over six foot, slim, with swept-back long blonde hair, dressed in a Hawaiian shirt, shorts, and trainers. To Finn it looked like the guy had come direct from a beach holiday. The two men shook hands before sitting.

"Did I mess up your holiday?" Finn said, pointing to the shirt.

"You know how it is, I wouldn't get far in the SOG wearing fatigues", both men laughed before Miller continued, "Colby sent me, I'm your personal travel guide. He's told me to give you one hundred percent support while you're here, just ask and I'll do what I can."

He passed a mobile phone to Finn, "Take this. It's a burner phone, not traceable, plus there's unlimited credit. I've stored my number in there, so just select the contact, hit that green button and call anytime, day or night. If I don't pick up, just leave a message and I'll call you back as soon as I can. I've also got a car for you, nothing fancy, and a room at the Holiday Inn in Albuquerque. Here's the key card, room 208, I've already checked you in. Stay as long as you like the CIA is paying the bill so don't forget to use the mini bar."

"Is there any more news on why Kathy was taken? Is Torres on the case like he promised? Has he found any evidence to trace on the culprits? I've been in the dark since leaving the base in Afghanistan."

"I don't know anything more than you regarding the kidnapping. I only know what Colby told me. He's started an internal investigation using a select number of covert officers, of which I'm one. At this stage he wants you to meet up with the FBI agent, Nico Torres, he's staying at the Prickly Pear Motel on 64 near the crime scene here in New Mexico. He doesn't know that you're here in the states. Colby thought it was best you hook up and make your own bond."

Miller took out a cigarette and offered the packet to Finn who dismissed the offer, "No thanks, I never did see the point in those."

Miller took out a lighter and lit his cigarette before continuing. "Colby has spoken to his opposite number at the FBI and they've agreed to give Torres a free reign on this one. All the internal reports I've seen say Torres has a very good reputation as an investigator. He's focussed, knows his stuff and more importantly you can trust him. If you want anyone out in the field looking for your sister with you it's him. Also, you've got this..."

Miller took out a letter from his pocket and threw it on the table in front of Finn. "That's your get out of jail free card, don't lose it. It's a letter signed by both his boss at the FBI and Colby. It explains to Torres that he's now part of a joint SAC, FBI, task force. I hope this guy is a team player because he's just become part of the covert group Colby has set up. The letter makes it very clear he's to work with you to recover your sister. His job is to find

Kathy, arrest the men responsible and find out why they took her."

Miller paused for a moment taking some time to study the man in front of him, "Finn, we both know something doesn't add up here and the boss feels it could be part of something much bigger which he's been investigating. He's keeping his cards close to his chest and only wants a small number of people involved. Information is given out on a need-to-know basis. He's not even told me what it's related to but I know him well enough to know when something is bugging him. He's said we must work covertly and outside the normal channels. He trusts you and that's why he's bust a gut to get you over here. Whatever it is he's obviously worried about leaks so keep things simple and only trust the people in the team. Just keep your head down and don't involve any civilians. We don't want the local police, the military or other agencies involved."

"And what about the four guys who've kidnapped my sister and killed her friends? I can't guarantee to you, or Colby, what I'll do if I find out they've harmed her."

Miller smiled, "He said you'd say something like that. Let's focus on finding your sister, I'm sure the other pieces will fall into place along the way. As for the kidnappers, well I don't care much for soldiers who kill innocents, it's not what soldiers do, so what you decide to do with them is fine by me."

Finn stood up, "Thanks Miller, tell Colby I owe him a big one for doing all of this, and I appreciate you coming to meet me but I just want to get started looking for my sister."

"He obviously has a lot of respect for you," he paused to stub out his cigarette, "One day you'll have to tell me why, and yes you're right, let's get going."

The two men walked out into the hot afternoon sun. Miller headed towards a silver-coloured Dodge SUV parked nearby, Finn followed. He pressed the key fob on the way to open the doors.

"Here you are, it's all yours, look after her. I even gave you a full tank of gas, well actually the CIA paid. Just remember Torres doesn't know you're here and until you give him the letter, he won't know about Colby. He's highly trained so don't underestimate him. The Prickly Pear is on 64 about a hundred miles north of here. A colleague rang the reception. He's still there but I'm not sure for how long though. Grab yourself a map and some food at a local gas station and get going."

Finn looked around, noticing several dents and scratches on the bodywork before turning to Miller and taking the keys. "It's perfect, thanks again."

The two men shook hands and Finn opened the vehicle door, "How will I know which person is Torres? Do you have a picture or car registration?"

Miller grinned, "Getting access to that information would lead to questions, but don't worry it'll be easy, up there he'll stand out as law enforcement. A guy with your skills will pick him out soon enough."

Finn threw his pack on the back seat, climbed into the SUV, slammed the door, and started the engine. He gave a final gesture to Miller through the window before heading out of the car park towards the security gate. Once clear of the Air Force security he was finally on his own with a clear plan in his head. *Find Torres, then Kathy.*

Chapter 7
Prickly Pear Motel, NM.

Torres rolled over on the bed and picked up his mobile phone from the bedside cabinet. He glanced at the time on the screen, *10:47*.

He unlocked the screen and speed dialled a number, "Dawson? Have you got any news for me on the license plate?"

"Morning Torres. We've managed to pull a few images off the camera footage and analysed them with the software. It's given us a licence plate which I've traced. The problem is it's not clear cut who actually owns the vehicle."

"Just tell me what you know, I've not got all day."

"Am I keeping you from chasing women and beer?"

"Very funny. I wish I had the time."

"The SUV is owned by a shell company registered in the Bahamas. A company called Foresight Enterprises. When I searched the database all I discovered was a head office address located in El Paso, Texas. The office is right on the border, you can practically walk into Mexico from there. What is strange is I can't find any evidence of any business activity, no tax records, no employment records, it's just a ghost. The only connection to Foresight I can find is the lawyer who set up the shell company. A guy called Smithson based in Austin, Texas. Our records show he's well known for setting up shell companies. We suspect some of the companies are involved in illegal activities like money laundering. We've never had enough evidence to arrest him, he seems to have a guardian angel. I've tried to call Smithson at the law office where he works but all I get is an answering machine."

"It's not much to go on Dawson but at least I've finally got a lead. This Foresight business sounds like it could be worth checking up on. If it's a shell company then why have an office near the border? I need to go and investigate the place. Apart from the border is there anything of interest nearby? Did you check Google Earth to see what the place looks like?"

"On Google Earth there's nothing unusual, just a two-story building in a row of shops and offices. The shops are on the ground floor and the business offices are based upstairs. The area is a bit run down. Do you want me to send a local Texas based agent out to check the address?"

"No. If there's anyone there who's involved in this mess then they'll get spooked. We'll lose any chance of finding out what's going on. You should know me well enough by now to know I prefer to see things for myself."

"Very true."

"Send all the information you've collected by email and I'll go there."

"El Paso must be a good five-hour drive from where you are."

"More like six, but at least I can call in at home on the way and pick up some clean clothes. Keep looking into this shell company for me, we need to find out who's behind it and using it as a shield. It doesn't make sense that they'd want to attract unnecessary attention by killing and kidnapping people. Try and find out who the investors or benefactors are."

"No problem. If anything turns up, I'll send you an email so it's there when you next log on. Also, give me a call when you're at the Foresight office and I'll coordinate with you. If it's required, I'll be able to get a couple of local FBI agents to support you."

"Great stuff...thanks Dawson." Torres hung up the call, and took a cigarette from a packet on the bedside table.

Rivera, now fully dressed and putting her shoes on, said "I guess that means you'll be leaving?"

"I've got to go to El Paso to follow up a lead...I'll call you when I get a chance."

Rivera grabbed her bag off the floor, opened the door, and turned to Torres with a smile, "No you won't. Stay safe special agent Torres."

Torres motioned to respond as she shut the door behind her. He dressed, switched on his laptop and checked his email messages. In among the many unread emails, he spotted the one he was waiting for. *Well done Dawson.*

He ran the events of the case back through his mind, trying to match up the scraps of evidence, formulating an action plan, and searching for a motive. *Who's behind Foresight? Where do they fit in with the crime? Something doesn't add up, unknown persons, possibly military trained, taking a woman who they've obviously tracked. They're using an SUV that's registered to a business that doesn't appear to exist. The SUV and office are all I've got to work on.*

He packed up his gear, loaded the car and checked out of the motel. Upon leaving the motel lobby he noticed the roadhouse next door open for business. He climbed into his car and moved to the front of the bar. *Lunch first.*

Torres walked in and sat on the same stool at the bar. He noticed a different bartender working behind the bar, an older woman who, upon seeing him sit down, approached him.

"Good afternoon, what can I get you."

"I'll have a pint of the Alligator IPA."

"Do you want to order any food with the beer?"

"Yes please, steak, rare, with chips and salad?"

The woman walked away before returning with the beer, a table mat and cutlery. "Food will be with you soon. Do you want anything extra on the side?"

"Mushrooms, if you've got them."

The bartender smiled, "That's not what I meant…never mind."

Torres shrugged his shoulders, picked up his beer and watched the woman walk away. He turned his gaze to the TV and thought of the six-hour journey to El Paso he had in front of him. The steak arrived and Torres stared at his meal, something told him the next few days would be interesting.

⋅ ⋅ ⋅ ⋅

Finn took the road out of the airbase and pulled into the first petrol station he spotted, making sure to park the SUV away from any security cameras. He went into his pack and pulled out a baseball cap, pulling it down low above his eyes before getting out. He walked across the forecourt and into the station shop, keeping his head down to avoid any inside cameras. He picked up some sandwiches, an apple and a couple of Gatorade drinks. He looked around for the map stand, finding it near the pay counter. He placed the items on the counter and returned to the stand to flick through the maps.

"Can I help you Hun?" The middle-aged lady behind the counter asked.

Finn smiled "New Mexico? I need to get on to the 64."

Noticing Finn's accent, she said, "You're not from round here are you, 64 is easy to find, you just...." At that moment a man dressed in jeans and a black hoodie burst into the store and ran up to the counter. Finn stood by the map stand and noticed the barrel of a gun sticking out from the sleeve of the hoodie. The missing teeth, haggard face and dirty clothes told Finn the man was most likely a drug addict.

The man noticed Finn looking and turned to point the gun at him, "Stay out of this man or I'll kill you...then her." The robber turned to the counter and yelled, "Okay bitch, give me all the money in the till and clear out the safe as well."

The woman reached down behind the counter. Finn and the robber instinctively knew she was going for a gun. The robber raised his handgun towards her. Finn reacted quicker by pushing the map stand over, knocking the gun out of the robber's hand, onto the floor and under a food rack. The man watched the gun disappear and hesitated. In the blink of an eye Finn struck him across the neck with his right forearm while placing a leg behind him. The addict landed on his back and reached for the gun. Finn spun around and dropped down with a knee into the addict's groin making him scream out in pain.

A voice announced, "Stand back Hun…I've got this now."

Finn looked behind to see the woman pointing a pump action shotgun at the robber…and him.

Finn stood up. "I don't want any trouble and I can't stick around to talk to the police, I just need to get to the 64."

"No worries, you take the drinks and other stuff, grab the New Mexico map over there…the red one, and I'll sort out this mess."

As Finn moved away from her, she advanced towards the robber, "Sonny, do you really think you can come in here threatening me? I'm sick to death of addicts like you taking liberties..."

Finn left her to it, grabbed the drinks, map and turned to the woman, "Thanks."

"No, thanks to you, stay safe out there, come back anytime."

Finn ran out the door and proceeded across the forecourt to the SUV, getting delayed answering police questions was the last thing he wanted. He climbed into the driver's seat, threw the food and drinks into the passenger footwell, and opened the map. *64, 64, come on, there, ok, right, 125 east, then 285, about 150 to 200 miles, I'll work out the rest later.*

Finn put the map on the passenger seat and pulled out of the petrol station as two police cars drove in at high speed from the other direction. Within minutes he was on the freeway heading north. He figured once he found the start of the 64, he would keep driving until he discovered the Motel along the way.

Finn completed the journey to the Prickly Pear in just over three hours, only stopping on the way to eat the sandwiches, use a truck stop toilet and to read the map. He slowly pulled into the Prickly Pear car park and drove along the parked cars outside the rooms. The Motel at this time of the day was mostly empty and none of the cars looked like what he imagined an FBI agent would drive. At the end of the Motel, he noticed a saloon car parked at the front of the roadhouse next door. He parked his Dodge a few spaces further down, put his baseball cap on and climbed out. *I bet he's inside drinking beer instead of getting out there and looking for Kathy...this doesn't sound like the guy Miller spoke about.*

Finn took a few moments to cool down before walking into the bar. Like a creature of habit Finn quickly looked around him, surveying the room. Within seconds he had built up a complete view of the bar, entry points, exit points, toilets, and customers. He moved over to an empty booth which gave him a wide field of view.

A server came over, "Drinks or food? Or both." she asked.

"Just a bottle of Bud."

"Coming up."

Finn looked around the bar until the server returned with the beer, twisted off the cap and placed it in front of Finn, "Enjoy, let me know if you change your mind about the food."

At that time of the early afternoon, with few customers, the job of identifying Torres was easy, just like Miller said. Finn spotted a guy in suit trousers and white shirt sitting on a bar stool. *That must be him. Not doing much police work, chatting to a bartender, drinking, and eating.*

Finn picked up his beer, walked over and stood behind Torres. He composed himself before pulling out the stool next to the FBI man and sat down. Facing forward, not making any eye contact with the FBI agent, Finn sipped his beer and watched the sport on TV.

Torres sensed a presence and turned to see a man sitting next to him. He looked up and down the bar. *Twelve empty bar stools and this guy decides to sit next to me.*

"You okay there buddy? Have trouble finding a seat? It's surprising how fast this place fills up on an afternoon, isn't it?" Torres sarcastically announced.

Finn placed his bottle on the bar and turned to look at Torres, "I'm not your buddy. No one likes a wise guy Torres and while you're sitting in here drinking, eating, and making jokes my sister and the killers are getting further away."

Torres recognised the determined look in Finn's eyes. A look he had only seen a few times before and it was not a look he liked, "Sorry buddy you've got me mixed up with someone else. What are you saying about your sister? Have we met before?"

"Cut the crap Torres. My name is Finn, we spoke on the phone yesterday."

Torres paused for a second, put his beer down and took some time to look over the guy next to him. *The brother? How the hell did he get here so quickly from the depths of Afghanistan? It's not possible is it?*

He looked all-round the bar to make sure no one else was watching before turning to Finn, "I'm still not getting it friend, who's this Torres you're asking about? It looks like you've got me confused with someone else."

Finn felt his anger rising and motioned to climb down from the bar stool. Torres grabbed his forearm to stop him before gesturing for him to return to the empty booth. He shouted down to the bartender, "Two beers for me and my buddy, we'll take them in the booth. Can you pack this up for me? I'll take it to go and we'll have the cheque at the same time, stick it all on my tab."

Finn picked up his beer and moved over to the booth. Torres took another bite from his steak and picked up his beer before joining him.

The two men stared at each other, neither spoke. Torres studied the slim dark-haired man in front him. Finn did the same.

After a few moments the server returned with the beers, and a dish with the cheque. Torres spoke to her, "Thanks, now give us some private time and there'll be a nice tip in it for you."

"No problem," the server walked away.

"Look buddy, I don't like people getting in my face. You said you're called Finn? Have you got any ID with you to prove that?"

"And how do I know you're Torres?"

"True. We seem to have a dilemma, we can stay here, stare at each other and get drunk, or we can start to trust each other. You look like a trustworthy guy. How about showing me some ID?"

Finn stared at Torres, then handed over his ID card and Miller's letter. The FBI agent checked the ID then quickly read the letter and returned it, "It appears I'm now at your disposal. To say I'm not happy about it would be an understatement but that's the world we operate in." He offered his hand. "Pleased to meet you, Nico Torres, FBI."

Finn stuffed the letter in his pocket, shook the agent's hand and said "Kirkland Finn, just call me Finn."

"I must say Finn, I'm surprised to see you. When you said you'd be coming here, I thought you were just blowing off steam, something I could understand in the circumstances. I'm not sure how you did it but I guess you know some big shots at the CIA, you must be well thought of for them to get you out here so quick"

"I told you I'd come and I do what I say. How I arrived is not important. We can either work together as a team and find out who these bastards are, what they want and get my sister back. Or, we do it separately, and I take matters into my own hands." Finn picked up his beer, took a long drag on the bottle and placed it back on the table, "I'd prefer the first option but, either way, I'm getting my sister back."

Torres stared at Finn. *This guy looks like he can handle himself and the letter came from the very top…best keep him close.*

"I'll go with the first option, but..." Torres paused, picked up his beer and took a swig as if mimicking Finn, "...not until you fill me in with your story. If we're going to work together it'd be good to know more about the person I'm working with."

Finn stared at the table, considering his response then raised his head to look at Torres, "There's not a lot to say, as you already know I'm in the British army, the SAS. I can't discuss anything about what I do, or where I do it, but what I will tell you is I'll not give up until I get Kathy back. She's the only family I have."

Finn continued to tell Torres about what happened to his parents and how as young children both he and Kathy had developed a strong bond together.

Torres drank while he listened to Finn's story then spoke up, "SAS, that's special forces isn't it? And I'm sorry to hear about your parents. Growing up can't have been easy for you both but you seem to have done ok…you said she's a lawyer now? That's the other end of the law-and-order business to where I'm."

"Have you got family Torres?" Finn asked.

Torres put his head down, the question stirred a vision that flashed through his mind.

Torres raised his head, looked sadly at Finn and mumbled, "No…not anymore."

Finn realised his question had unsettled the big man. He saw the distress in Torres's teary eyes and cursed himself for asking. He avoided eye contact and drank his beer.

Torres composed himself and continued, "It happened four years ago while investigating a drug lord operating out of Florida. He was importing cocaine products from Colombia and distributing them around the US using the Cuban underworld. I got very close to putting him away, due to a leak somewhere in the agency he discovered where I lived and put a contract out on me. The killers he hired visited my home during the night and put a bomb on the garage door. They connected the trigger to the door remote control system. I assume they expected me to be at home, but I was away, on a stakeout. The next morning my wife got in her car, taking our daughter to school, and pressed the remote...they both died instantly."

"Shit!" Finn swore, then considered his next response carefully, "I don't know what to say Nico, I'm really sorry." He touched Torres's arm, "You made them pay...right?"

"Damn right...I made sure the bastards never saw the inside of a courtroom. Afterwards, I requested a transfer and moved from Florida to New Mexico for a fresh start. Now I live with guilt everyday..." Torres stopped, wiped his eyes and took a swig of beer, "It seems life has dealt us both bad cards in the past Finn but there's no joy in looking backwards, let's just focus on what we need to do today...get your sister back!"

Finn finished his bottle and said angrily, "And don't forget we need to also get the bastards who killed her friends!" He paused for a moment and calmed down, "Where do we start? What evidence have you discovered so far that we can follow up on?"

Torres finished his bottle, put a twenty-dollar bill and the cheque under the empty bottles and announced, "I'm on my way to El Paso and you're coming with me. How did you get here? Did you get dropped off or did you drive?"

"I've got a car outside. Why are we going to El Paso?"

"What we know is four guys came into the campsite during the night, waited till the sun came up, grabbed the women, tied them to trees, executed three of them and took your sister. They set fire to the hire car and we have no witnesses. I managed to get a license plate from the park CCTV system. The vehicle is registered to an office in El Paso, it's our only lead." Torres stood up. "Look let's get moving, you follow me in your car to my house in Santa Fe. I need to collect some gear first. We'll leave your car there and we'll go together in mine. I'll fill you in with the evidence we've discovered so far on the drive."

Chapter 8
El Paso, Texas.

Thud. Marcus grabbed Kathy around the neck and punched her in the stomach hard enough to wind her. "Shut up bitch, can't you just sit still."

Thud. He hit her again.

Troy looked around from the front passenger seat and shouted, "Marcus, leave the merchandise alone, you damage her and I'll damage you."

Sanders, sitting on the other side of Kathy pulled her up straight on the seat and placed a water bottle on her dry lips, "Drink, it's just water."

She opened her lips and quickly gulped the water down.

Sanders turned to Marcus, "You're an asshole, why'd you do that?"

Marcus shrugged and looked out of the window, "She wouldn't sit still, I'm sick of her fighting all the time."

"Shit man! She's got her hands tied behind her back, a blindfold on, just been dragged out of a campsite, seen her friends shot and you think she'd be happy?"

Troy spoke, "Don't get too friendly with her, if they don't pay or try to rip us off, she's next for a bullet."

Kathy gasped as she heard the comment.

Sanders continued to badger Marcus, "Why exactly did you shoot those women? Did it make you feel brave? They came here on holiday for Christ's sake. Is killing innocent women what we joined the military for?"

Troy cut in, "Shut it Sanders, once we get her to the drop off point and get our money we're out of here. We can all go our separate ways. This is the last pay day for me, I've done too much dirty work for these guys. And now we know they're working for both sides, I'm out. We all lost good friends in Afghanistan and to know these guys are in bed with the scumbags turns my stomach."

The SUV swerved to miss a Coyote which had ventured out from a corn field into the middle of the road. Suddenly noticing the speeding SUV coming towards it, the Coyote darted back under cover.

Thrown about in the rear Marcus shouted, "Baxter you need to get control of this thing. And just so you know Troy, I'll not hand this baby over till I see the cash, you don't trust them and I don't trust you."

Troy laughed aloud, "Good to see we all got into this in the spirit of trust and teamwork. That's fine by me Marcus. We cover each other's backs at the drop-off, we hand her over, then we all split, four points of the compass. Agreed?"

The four men all nodded in agreement.

Kathy's breathing returned to normal. She rubbed her head against Marcus's shoulder and managed to move the blindfold enough to allow her to see out of the corner with one eye. She looked at the driver, Baxter, a large black man with a beard and bald head. She looked ahead, ensuring the others did not discover her looking.

The SUV continued to race through the backroads of New Mexico, past farmers' fields and areas of barren wasteland. Locusts bounced off the windscreen as swarms flew across the road from the fields on either side of the road.

Baxter spoke, "It's sixteen thirty-four, what time is the drop off? And where's it taking place? All you've told us so far is that we need to get to El Paso. Is that where we're doing the swap?"

Troy replied, "All I know is we'll get our instructions the way we've always done, at the office. Given that this place is on the border my guess is they want to make the drop in Mexico."

Marcus cut in, "No way! I'm not leaving US soil. If we manage to get over the border with her, we'll not see the money. Plus, they can easily make us disappear over there. Over here they'll be careful about involving others which helps us. Over there anything can happen."

Sanders spoke "I agree, you need to tell them we want to see the cash before we do the exchange and it takes place here in the US, in Texas. Those guys in Mexico are brutal. When I worked with the DEA, we saw all kinds of shit. You cross those guys and they'll torture you for days, cutting bits off you just for fun, keeping you alive so they can carry on cutting bits off you till your body just gives up. I'd prefer to keep my head on my neck and not leave it on a gate post in Mexico."

Baxter turned to Troy "Sort this shit out man. I'm with the others, we hand her over here in the US."

"For god's sake you guys are unbelievable, we don't even know where they want us to do the exchange so calm down. If they say Mexico, I'll tell them it's a no go, okay?"

Troy noticed the sign for the Texas state line, "Baxter, slow this thing down and take it easy, there are loads of border patrols and police around here. We don't want to draw attention to ourselves with her in the car."

The SUV approached the city limits of El Paso, taking the backroads until they arrived at Pera Avenue. They drove slowly down the empty road, the shops and offices appeared closed for business as they passed. Each soldier checked for potential threats as they drove past the office door on their right and continued down the road.

"Looks all clear. Baxter, let's park up over there in the alleyway." Troy pointed to a small access road on the opposite side of the street to the Foresight office building.

Baxter did as Troy instructed, drove a little further down the road, turned left into the alleyway and parked.

"Great, turn off the engine. What's the time?"

Baxter replied, "Nineteen thirty-six. What's the plan?"

Troy turned to the men in the back, "Marcus, use the passageway on the other side and get to the rear of the building. Recon the area, if they've got any spotters out one is bound to be around the back. If it's clear find a hiding place and watch the back entrance…and stay in contact, report anything suspicious."

The four men used a secure military short range communication system with earphones and a mic button on a strap around the neck. Pressing the button allowed the user to talk to the other people in the loop.

As Marcus got ready to climbed out Troy added, "Check the main street is quiet and leave the assault rifle, we don't want some 'do-gooder' phoning the law after seeing your dumb ass with a gun."

Marcus grinned at the comment and climbed out of the SUV, pushing his pistol into the belt of his pants, and pulling his jacket down to cover it. He walked to the corner of the alley and spotted the office door, opposite on his right. Walking across the empty road, he instinctively checked for pedestrians and observers at the windows, finding it clear he walked down the passageway. He reached the rear corner of the building, turned, and walked along the back alley of the office block building. Constantly checking the surrounding area and any blind spots for danger. At the rear fire escape of the Foresight office, he stopped and looked up and down the alley.

The area was empty, apart from the rubbish bins and an old abandoned truck. He progressed to his right and spotted the rear entrance for the Foresight office. He stood back and looked at the skyline of the building for activity on the roof. Happy the area was safe he pressed the comms button on his neck to report, "The street is clear, no pedestrians, observers or moving vehicles. The area at the rear of the office is also clear, I think you're safe to progress."

Troy replied "Good man. Now stay there and keep your eyes peeled, if anything moves report it straight away."

"Understood," Marcus confirmed.

Troy turned to the remaining men, "Stay here, I'll go into the office and get the delivery instructions. Don't do anything that attracts attention, just keep a lookout for Winter's men and any trouble. It all looks safe but things can quickly change…and make sure you look after her."

Baxter turned to Troy, "Good luck buddy, if anything happens give three clicks on the coms button and we'll come and back you up."

Troy grabbed his pistol from the glovebox and opened the door, "Just make sure you look after her…she's worth a million dollars."

He jumped out of the SUV and took a quick look up and down the alley before moving out into the main road. He spotted an old dodge car driving towards him, returned to the alleyway and hid while the vehicle drove past. The driver, an old Mexican, turned to face him then returned his attention to the road. He waited until the car disappeared then ran across the road. He stood on the path, checked the area for activity, then casually walked up to Foresight office door. He looked through the glass panel door, found no light or activity then keyed the access code into the keypad on his right. The keypad made a beep sound and the door lock sprung open.

Troy grabbed the handle and cautiously opened the door onto a staircase which led upwards to the first-floor offices. He pulled out his pistol and slowly climbed the stairs. At the top he edged the office door open with the barrel of the gun, and peeked inside. Finding it empty he pushed the door wide open and ventured inside.

The state of the interior told him that no working business had occupied the open plan office for years. The only remnants of past activity included a couple of tattered chairs and a table. The dusty room had plaster crumbling from the walls. Electrical cables, papers, cardboard boxes and other bits of rubbish scattered around the floor, discarded items with no value to the last tenants.

Troy spotted the telephone on the wall at the far end of the room near two doors. The room had a window along the rear wall with a door allowing access to the fire escape and a window all along the front looking down onto the road. He checked the rear door and found it locked, then progressed through the room scanning for bugs and security cameras, finding nothing. He cautiously opened the two doors near the phone, finding a store cupboard with more rubbish, and a toilet with thick brown water in the bowl. The rancid smell briefly caught his nostrils and he quickly shut the door. Taking one last look around the office to confirm to himself it was safe, he lifted the phone receiver and dialled '0' as instructed by the label.

After a short pause an automated voice answered, "Foresight Enterprises, enter your access code after the tone."

Troy waited for the tone then keyed in his ID code and waited for a response.

The automated voice played a message, "Pick up, current location, twenty-three hundred hours."

The line suddenly disconnected, Troy replaced the handset and looked at his watch to confirm the time. *Great we're doing it here, that should make the guys happy. Less than four hours. Baxter and Marcus are already wired, unless I keep them under control they'll be at each other's throats. We just need to avoid detection, do the handover, and get the money. Then I can get away from here and start a new life.*

Troy walked over to the rear window and spotted Marcus. The two men exchanged a thumbs up before he walked over to the front window to check the road outside was still empty of traffic and pedestrians. Seeing the coast was clear he ran to the door and down the stairs. At the front door he checked again before proceeding outside to the path. He jammed the door stop down, to make sure it could not lock itself, then ran over the road and climbed into the SUV.

Sanders leaned forward "How did it go?"

Troy looked at him, ignored the question and pressed his comms button to allow all the men to hear his report, "Marcus, the drop off is going to happen here at twenty-three hundred. Stay there on guard, and make sure you stay alert, these guys will be just as happy to kill us than hand over any money. Baxter is going to guard the roof, Sanders and myself are going inside to do the handover. Remember, as long as we've got her, we're safe."

He released the button and continued "Baxter, first you take us over to the office and we'll take her inside. Then return to this side of the road and park up around the back of the building. Get up on the roof somehow and set yourself up with the sniper rifle. Stay alert, I always need you to have eyes on me. You should be able to see clearly into the room as the windows are big enough. If anything happens, I'll signal you in the usual way."

"No problem."

"Sanders, you take her, she's your responsibility. She doesn't go anywhere until we've got the cash. The door is already open. When we pull up outside, take her inside, straight up the stairs and get her comfortable. I'll bring the weapons. Once we are inside you get moving Baxter."

Baxter reversed the SUV out of the alley into the main road, drove along on the correct side of the road for a hundred yards or so and swung it around to the opposite side stopping with the passenger door opposite the office door.

Sanders grabbed Kathy under the arm and opened the door with his spare hand. He climbed out and dragged Kathy with him until she stood on the path. Looking from under the blindfold she noticed that she was in a public place. *In the open. This is my chance.*

Sanders eased his grip on her arm as he closed the door and Kathy struggled to pull away from him.

He cursed, "Take it easy bitch, we're going for a walk, that's all"

She protested, "Let me go you pig." Then started screaming at the top of her voice, hoping someone would hear her protests. In a split-second Troy punched her in the face knocking her unconscious. Sanders struggled to hold on to her limp body.

"Do you think you can handle her now?" Troy barked.

Sanders lifted Kathy, dragged her towards the door and opened it wide. Once inside he put her over his shoulder and carried her up the stairs into the office. Troy unloaded the gear, banged on the roof to signal to Baxter to get moving, then carried the gear upstairs joining Sanders, and Kathy, in the office.

In the office, Sanders looked around, spotted an area in the corner with a wooden floor and laid Kathy's limp body down. He checked the tie-wraps on her hands and the blindfold. He positioned her on her side, ensuring she could breathe easily, with her face pointing into the room and her back running parallel to the wall. He collected his assault rifle and some extra magazines from the bags and took up a position guarding the rear window and door. He spotted Marcus kneeling between a bin and an old truck and gave him a thumbs up.

Troy took up position at the front window guarding the entrance and the main road outside.

"Baxter, can you see me?" A red laser dot appeared on Troy's chest and his eyes followed the beam towards the opposite roof, "Good man, stay alert...now we wait."

Troy checked his HK416 assault rifle, tucked some extra magazines into his hip pockets and stepped back into the shadows. He watched the road observing random vehicles transiting the area. His mind drifted as he began to dream about the new life he had planned.

Chapter 9
Iron Fist Base, Lubbock, TX

The Iron Fist camp, situated on a converted ranch on the outskirts of the city of Lubbock, Texas, was busy as usual. Service personnel went about their duties, trucks moved gear and men around the facility and military planes arrived and departed at regular intervals.

Little remained of the original farm complex apart from the old farmhouse. The modified large wooden building retained most of the original architectural features. Painted red, with white railings and window frames which made the building stand out among the drab military buildings and hardware. The ranch house, set back, away from the runway, barracks, and hangers now used as a home and office for the base commander, the leader of Iron Fist Security.

General Cofax Winter, stood looking out of the window of his study as the security guards patrolled outside. In the distance he noticed a group of soldiers training on the parade ground, the latest recruits for his private army. He cursed the situation he found himself in. From decorated US Army General to living every day at the disposal of drug traffickers and corrupt government officials.

A knock at the door distracted him, "Come in."

The door opened and the head of his security team walked in, "You wanted to see me sir?"

Winter turned, "Ward, we need to be in El Paso at twenty-three hundred hours to collect the woman. I want to be there earlier so we can make sure the area is safe. We'll need a team of eight men and make sure they know how important this woman is. She has to be taken alive, I don't want any fuckups, ok?"

"And what about the money boss? Who is going to do the handover?"

Winter laughed aloud, "What money?"

The comment puzzled Ward, "You told Troy he'd get a million dollars to kidnap the British woman and bring her to you."

"You're correct, I did, but that was before they started shooting up half of New Mexico and killing people. Storming into a campsite and executing people is not exactly discrete is it? That's not how we operate. A bit of common sense was all they needed to use. Police would've forgotten a simple missing person's case after a few days. They've started a shit storm for me. This mess has the potential to affect my bottom line and my clients here in the US have already been on the phone to kick my arse. Do you understand Ward?"

Ward nervously agreed, "Yes sir."

"Marcus and Baxter are a liability. I've warned Troy about taking them on jobs but he's loyal because of their time together in the Marines. That boys club stuff has finally caught up with him."

Winter paused, took a cigar from a box on the desk, lit it, took a big drag, leaned backwards and blew the smoke towards the ceiling, "Ward, I sometimes get the impression you think I sit on my arse all day smoking cigars. What you don't realise is that I've a greater responsibility than you can possibly fathom. We've got two sets of clients that we must pacify. Firstly, the government who fund our legitimate business here, supplying soldiers for their dirty deeds in the East. And secondly, our drug dealing friends who pay us handsomely for acting as a conduit, enabling the chain of supply and demand. Any attention drawn to my business makes those clients uncomfortable. Kidnapping is not my business. I went along with it to smooth the waters with our partner in the East. Waters that have become, should we say, rippled recently. Do you understand?"

Ward thought about his response, knowing the wrong answer could result in an explosive reaction from Winter. He decided on the easy option, "Yes, of course sir."

Winter smiled, "You see Ward that's why I like you, you're never frightened to blow smoke up my arse."

Winter laughed to himself and continued his rant, "By killing those women the British are going to get involved and I don't want them poking their noses into my business. The last time that happened resulted in a cut in our supply lines. It's taken years to build the supply chain back up, and that's the only reason I agreed to take this woman. I don't like involving civilians in my business, but I'm a soldier like you and must follow orders. An FBI special agent has been assigned to the case as part of some joint task force. There is no information coming out of the NCS about it, they've closed all the doors. That covert government stuff just gives me a headache. What I understand is he's the type of officer who'll make it his lifework to find this woman and solve the murders. If he manages to trace those idiots to this place it'll draw undue attention to my business."

The thought provoked Winter to angrily stub out his cigar, "You see Ward, I'm the man whose job is to make everyone happy, and this mess is making people unhappy. That's why I've no intention of paying those idiots. My main priority is to cover up the mess they've created."

"Do you want me to get one of my guys to investigate the FBI agent? I could arrange for him to have an accident?"

"At this stage just try and find out what you can about him, the usual sources are still on the payroll, make them work for it for once. I want to know everything about him, even down to the colour of his socks."

Ward nodded in agreement, "I'll get onto it straight away sir."

"So, what the hell are you still doing in my office busting my chops? I thought I said I needed to get to El Paso urgently."

"Sir?"

"Well move dumb ass!"

"Sir." Ward stood to attention and left the office.

∴ ∴ ∴ ∴

After spending over an hour gathering the security team members and the transportation required for the trip to El Paso, Ward returned to Winter's office.

"Sir, the men are ready to go."

"Okay, well let's get going then." Winter put on his flight jacket and grabbed a handful of cigars from the box on his desk, stuffing them into his inside jacket pocket.

The two men left the ranch house and approached two black SUVs waiting outside along with the team Ward had assembled. The squad of ex-military stood patiently. Highly trained soldiers with many hours combat experience between them. All wearing identical black uniforms with assault rifles across their chests.

Ward fitted out the security squad with the same type of comms system as Troy's men. He passed a set to Winter, "Here sir you'll need this so you can communicate with the team."

Winter snatched the equipment from Ward and climbed into the passenger seat of the lead vehicle. Ward sat in the front passenger seat of the vehicle behind. Once all the men and gear were onboard, they began the five-hour drive to El Paso.

Winter slept through most of the uneventful journey until the driver woke him, "Sir, we're on the outskirts of El Paso, nearly at the office."

Winter opened his eyes and the headlights of the oncoming cars blinded him. The sun had set while he slept and he cursed. After giving his eyes time to adjust he looked around the area, "Drive slowly, stay on the back streets. What time is it?"

"Twelve minutes past ten."

The SUV left the main road and proceeded to Pera Avenue stopping at the end of the road. Winter looked all the way up to the far end noticing no other traffic or people.

Winter pressed the comms mic button on his neck, "Ward, we've got twenty-eight minutes until we pick up the package. The office is half way down on the right. These guys are heavily armed and dangerous. Take your vehicle to the other end of the road and drop off two men to guard the street, one at the front one at the rear. I'm sending two of my guys to do the same at this end."

Two men climbed out of the back door of Winter's SUV. One began standing in the shadows of a shop front while the other ran down to the corner of the alleyway. Ward's SUV pulled out from behind Winter's, drove down to the far end of the road and pulled into an empty shop parking lot. The back doors opened, two more security guards jumped out and followed their orders.

※ ※ ※ ※

"Troy, they're here. I've just seen a vehicle drive down to the end of the road and it looks like there's another parked up at the other end." Baxter reported.

Troy shouted over the comms system, "Right men! They're getting ready to do the exchange, everyone stay alert, no shooting unless I give the order,"

※ ※ ※ ※

After a few moments the two sets of security guards called in to Winter.

"T1 to leader, ready."
"T2 to leader, ready."

"Leader to T1 and T2, stay alert, if you see anything suspicious call in. Ward, it's time to get moving. We'll park outside the office front door. Park your vehicle behind mine. We'll both go in together to do the exchange with one guard each."

With both SUVs parked outside the Foresight office door Winter picked up his mobile and dialled the number of the telephone inside. Inside the office the telephone began to ring. Troy picked it up and waited for the caller to speak first.

"It's time for us to do business Troy. I've got the money and you've got the woman. Let's get the deal done." Winter growled.

"That's fine with me, come in. Just remember, if you try anything Winter, I'll make sure I kill you first. All we want is our money and no trouble."

"Calm down, we are all friends here Troy, once we get this deal done you can be on your way."

Winter hung up the call and stuffed his mobile into his pocket and climbed out of the SUV, the others followed. Standing at the door, Winter keyed in the access code and the door unlocked.

Winter pointed to the security guards, "You two go in first."

He turned to Ward, "You next, I'll follow."

The first guard opened the door and with the others following moved slowly up the stairs. At the top the two security guards entered the room with weapons drawn. They looked around the room and discovered Sanders standing on the left at the rear window, a woman on the floor near him and Troy on the right near the front window. The men took up covering positions on either side of the doorway with their guns aimed at Troy and Sanders. Ward entered and stood in the doorway to confirm it was safe then signalled for Winter to enter.

The General entered the room with his usual swagger carrying a black hold-all bag and announced, "Troy, my good fellow, how are you?" He looked towards the rear window, "And Sanders, nice to see you again. Where are Marcus and Baxter? Are they joining us?"

Troy ignored the question, "The mighty Cofax Winter has come to see me in person, I feel privileged. I've been doing your dirty work for years and this is the first time I've seen you get your hands dirty. Must've taken something very special to get your fat arse off a chair. I guess you couldn't trust anyone else with your money."

In the corner Kathy pushed the side of her head against the floorboards rolling up the blindfold just enough to allow her to observe the room. She twisted her hands to see if she could break the tie-wraps but found the plastic too strong. She fumbled around on the floor, found some plaster stone pieces which had broken from the wall, and tried those. Each time she forced the fragile stone against the plastic it broke into smaller pieces. While she worked at the plastic tie-wraps she investigated the room, trying to note as much information as she could.

She observed a group of men dressed as soldiers and an older grey-haired man, sixty plus, five foot ten, grey hair, pot belly. *Cofax? That's an unusual name.*

She continued her observations and looked at the man Winter was speaking to. *So, he's Troy, right?*

She struggled to focus her eyes, still drowsy from the punch which knocked her out. She continued to study Troy. *Six foot plus, long blonde hair tied in a ponytail and a goatee beard. He's a handsome man.*

She continued to look around the room noting the appearances of the other soldiers until her gaze returned to Winter talking to Troy.

"That's not a nice way to greet your friends Troy." He dumped the bag on the floor in front of him and pointed towards Kathy. "I'm here to collect this special person and make sure she gets out of here safely. And as for doing my dirty work, that's the way of the world. I do someone's dirty work and you end up doing mine, call it capitalism."

He put his hand into his inside jacket pocket impelling Troy and Sanders to raise their weapons towards him. Winter's security guards followed, each taking a man, one on Sanders, the other on Troy. An uneasy atmosphere descended over the room as they stood in silence and stared at each other.

Winter calmly removed his hand, "Easy boys we're all friends here…Cigar anyone?"

Winter gestured for everyone to lower their weapons before lighting his cigar and taking a drag, "You didn't answer me about Marcus and Baxter."

"Don't worry Winter they're here, just like you I like to have security."

"What happened to friends trusting each other?"

Winter turned his attention to the woman on the floor. He walked over and knelt in front of her, pulling her blindfold all the way up onto her forehead.

He looked into her eyes and asked, "Tell me young lady have these men been nice to you?"

Kathy struggled on the floor, all she could do was shout at him, "Fuck off! Whoever you are, let me go scumbag."

"That's nice!" Winter looked up to Sanders, "You're polite to people and that's how they respond...that's why I lose my temper so much."

He turned to Kathy and stroked her face, "I like your spirit young lady. Keep it up, you'll need all your will and strength over the next few days, you're going on a journey. In the meantime, I suggest you start showing some respect to the people who are, should I say, caring for you."

Winter stood up and turned to Troy. "Okay, good work but your methods have created a lot of problems for me. I'm not sure I can use your services anymore."

He looked down and pointed to the black bag at his feet, "That's half of what I promised, five hundred thousand. That's all I can spare right now. I've picked up a lot of expenses trying to clean up your mess in New Mexico. These murders have created a lot of trouble for me. Mistakes come at a heavy price in our game, you know that. Tell me, who killed the women? Baxter, right?" After a pause for thought he added, "Or Marcus? Or possibly both. My dear Troy I told you to not take them with you. I warned you that they'd be a liability and it's ended up costing you a nice payday."

Sanders aimed his assault rifle at Winter's head and shouted, "Fuck you Winter, where's all the money you promised? The deal was to get the woman, there she is, now give us what we agreed. Troy you're not going to put up with this bullshit...are you?"

Troy held up his hand, "Easy Sanders I'll sort this," gesturing for him to lower his weapon, which he did.

Troy looked directly at Winter, "So you're going to rip me off after all the years I've worked for you?" Then held up his right hand making a fist gesture. Instantly a red laser dot appeared in the centre of Winters' chest.

Winter looked down and responded with his usual bravado, "Ah, now we know where Baxter is." He shook his head disapprovingly then continued, "Look Troy, get your men under control, if you kill me...you're all dead. There are four of us in here and four more outside. You'll never get out of this office alive."

Troy lowered his arm and the laser dot disappeared.

Winter grinned, "Good man. Look, I'm sorry you feel short changed but it's a circumstance of the business we operate in. I'm sure you are aware that in business there are always winners and losers. In this case you feel like a loser but once you're out on the road, a free man with all that money, you'll soon realise you're a winner. It's still a very good payday and think of the new life you can have."

Winter moved to the bag and slowly unzipped it taking out a bundle of dollar bills. He showed Troy the rest of the bundles in the bag. "There you see, lots of lovely cash for you and your men." Winter replaced the money and slowly zipped the bag closed.

Troy realised he had little alternative other than to concede the situation. He walked over, picked up the bag and returned to his position next to the window then growled, "Believe me Cofax if I ever see you again…I'll kill you."

Winter blew smoke from his cigar towards Troy, "No problem, I can live with that. People have been saying things like that to me for years but I'm still here my dear boy."

Troy reacted angrily, "Arrogant asshole. One day someone will wipe that smile off your face."

Winter nodded, "Yes, but not you Troy. I'm glad you got that off your chest but if you're ready I'd like to conclude our business?"

"Go on."

"This is how we'll do it. My guards will take the woman, you keep the cash. Then I'll leave and Ward will follow. You stay here while I collect my other men and depart the area. You leave with your team in thirty minutes. Agreed?"

Troy nodded to Winter who in turn gestured to his men to get moving. They picked up Kathy and disappeared out of the office. Winter headed towards the door, announcing as he left, "Enjoy the rest of your life Troy."

Ward guarded the doorway until the General had descended the stairs then quickly followed.

At the bottom of the stairs Winter pressed his comms button and ordered, "All teams regroup".

The two guards checked outside for traffic before exiting the office. One opened the boot of the SUV while the other carried Kathy, with his hand over her mouth, threw inside and slammed the door.

All the men returned to their vehicles and they drove away at high speed.

Watching the vehicles speed away down the road Troy turned to Sanders, "I'll get that bastard, this is the last time he's going to get away with ripping me off."

"Not if I get to him first." Sanders cursed, "You're going to get a lot of shit from the other two when you tell them he's only given you half the money."

"I'll sort it...."

Chapter 10
Foresight Ent. Office, El Paso, TX.

Torres finished the story and turned to Finn, "...so that's why we are going to El Paso. Unfortunately, this Foresight company is the only lead we've got at the moment, we'll follow it and see where it takes us. The start is the office, it could just be a dead end, an address the lawyer uses to register the shell companies, but it still needs checking. The location, close to the border, seems very convenient to me. We may only ever find the connection between the killers, your sister and Foresight by going there."

"Sounds okay to me, lead the way," Finn grinned. "Sorry, no pun intended. How far is it from here?"

Torres shook his head then glanced at the Sat Nav, "About ten miles."

"Good, we both know the longer these guys have got hold of Kathy the smaller her chances of her survival become."

"We don't know why they took her yet so don't start thinking like that."

"You're right," Finn said. "Hopefully the office will give us some answers, something to indicate where they've taken her. What do we know about the place? Security? Is it guarded? Layout?"

Torres nodded while concentrating on driving, "Dawson said it's a first-floor office in a typical downtown area. A mixture of shops and offices. I'm not expecting any security other than locks on the doors and maybe some cameras. I'll be surprised if anyone is there at this time of day. Let's just have a good look around and find out what's there. We don't want any trouble, you're unarmed, remember!"

"True! But I still have my bare hands and not having a gun or knife won't stop me if they've got Kathy in there."

Torres smiled and said, "I suspect you're right but at this stage can we do things my way? Step by step. Slowly, slowly...catchy monkey."

Finn looked at him with a puzzled look on his face, "Eh... What's that mean?"

"Look, just follow my lead. This is how we'll play it. We'll park up out of sight. You can take the rear entrance and I'll check the front door. If there's someone inside the office then I'll talk to them, make a general enquiry. If not, we'll see if we can break in via the rear entrance and then search the place. Okay?"

Finn nodded, "Agreed, but...do FBI agents 'break in" to properties?"

"A slip of the tongue, I meant 'gain access'." Torres turned the FBI cruiser into Pera Avenue just as a Black SUV came around the corner at high speed, nearly colliding, "What the...Idiot! He nearly wiped us out."

As he entered the street, he noticed an empty car park in front of a shop and pulled up. The two men got out and looked around them, surveying the area. They found a road occupied by run down shops and businesses, empty of any traffic or pedestrians.

"Looks a bit of a dive around here. Makes you wonder where that car came from in such a hurry," Finn said.

"I was just thinking that," Torres confirmed.

Finn grabbed his leather jacket from the back seat, "So where's the office then?"

"Judging by the images Dawson sent me it's on this side of the street about half way down, there's also an alley running behind the buildings. Use the passageway over there to access it, then walk until you find the fire escape and rear entrance to the office. If you see anything suspicious don't get involved, just stay out of sight and observe. If I manage to get inside, I'll signal you somehow from the back window."

Finn cautiously asked, "And how will I know which fire escape leads to this particular office? I've never been here before."

"Good point!" Torres said, "you'll just have to hope there's a dustbin or a sign with the Foresight name written on it. Also check the escape ladders."

Finn looked at him in disbelief, then ran down the passageway towards the rear alley. Torres continued along the footpath towards the office, checking the shops as he passed, finding them empty and closed for business. He noticed the shop below the Foresight office, realising he was close, checked the street was still empty of pedestrians and moving vehicles, then drew his pistol.

He cautiously approached the glass office door and spotted a Foresight sign above a keypad on the right side of the frame. He peered inside, glanced up the staircase and noticed a dim light shining out onto the landing from a doorway on the right. He tried the door, which was locked, then studied the keypad.

Baxter noticed movement in the street and used the comms system, "Troy there's someone outside the front door of the office."

Troy, heard the words in his earphones and quickly moved to the front window. He looked down and found his view blocked by the canopy over the footpath.

"Damn!" he cursed and pressed the comms button. "Who the hell is it Baxter? I can't see anything. Is it one of Winter's men?"

Baxter used the scope on the sniper rifle to get an improved view, "No, Winter and his men have just driven off, I'd say he's an undercover police officer. He's also got a pistol in his hand. I've got a clear shot Troy, do you want me to take him out?"

"No! That'll bring too much heat down on us. We need to get away safely. If it's a police officer, he'll see the office is closed for business and may just walk away."

Baxter released the pressure on the trigger and removed his finger, "What happened with Winter, did you get the money?"

Troy turned to Sanders who shook his head, advising him not to reply. Troy shrugged his shoulders, "We got the money, but not all of it. Winter has ripped us off."

"Not all of it? The thieving snake…I'll kill him," Baxter growled.

Marcus interrupted and barked, "You're shitting me! I told you we couldn't trust that maggot. This is the last time he rips me off…" A moments silence followed before he added, "Fuck you Troy. I'm coming to get my money."

Troy calmingly said, "Guys, one thing at a time. I'm not going to prison for the rest of my life, so stay focused. If this person is a police officer like Baxter said, then he may have called for backup, which means we've got about three minutes to get the hell out of here. We need to get the gear and money into the SUV before they arrive otherwise there's going to be a bloodbath."

Troy quickly formulated a plan in his head and ordered, "Marcus, make your way round to the front and see if you can cut the man off. Baxter, go back to the SUV and get ready to move on my order. As soon as Marcus gets rid of the police officer, drive to the front door to pick us up. Once we're mobile we need to get as far away from here as possible." He paused, then spoke sternly, "Then, we'll regroup and make a plan on how to get our money from Winter."

Marcus proceeded towards the front door of the office. He moved out from behind the bins, into the alley and headed towards the small passageway leading to the main street. Finn, still moving along the alley in the shadows, froze as the two men almost bumped into each other.

Marcus noticed Finn at the last second and reached for his pistol. Finn anticipated the move, rolled forward over his head, onto his back and kicked Marcus in the stomach. Losing his balance, Marcus let out a groan then stumbled backwards onto the ground. Instantly the two men jumped to their feet.

The pistol fell from the back of Marcus's belt making a loud clatter as the metal hit the concrete alleyway. Marcus realised he would need to turn his back on his attacker to collect it and chose his knife, pulling it out in one rapid movement from the sheath on his hip. The big man, much bigger than Finn in weight, height and width grinned and held it threateningly.

Finn looked at the seven-inch hunting knife waving around in front of his face. He focused on the serrated edge and the highly polished steel. *This guy is serious.*

Marcus beamed, "Come on...let's play!"

Finn responded sarcastically, showing no concern for the knife, "I'm not here to play mate, I'm just looking for my sister."

Marcus noted the English accent and realised he meant the kidnapped woman, "You're out of luck limey! The bitch is long gone, they're taking her overseas. You've got no chance of finding her."

Marcus continued to wave the knife from side to side taking up a defensive stance in front of Finn, who copied with his hands as defence. The men maintained a distance of a few feet as they moved from side to side. Finn desperately looked around the area for a weapon, finding nothing suitable.

Marcus shouted, "Come on...let's see what you're made of limey." He lunged forward, leading with the knife, swiping it from side to side.

Finn followed his movements, dodging from side to side, using his arms and feet to fend off the repeated attacks, and the hunting knife blade.

Marcus broke through the defences and slashed across the front of Finn's leather jacket, cutting the material, but not deep enough to draw blood.

Marcus continued to grin as he made another assault. Finn fended off the blade with his left arm and an opportunity for a counter-attack opened. In an instance he landed a hard blow on Marcus's chin with his right fist. The blow startled the big man and he stumbled backwards, dazed and lightheaded.

Finn advanced as Marcus spread his legs to steady himself, he landed another blow into the big man's groin with his right boot. The force of the kick prompted Marcus to bend forward and pull his arms inwards towards his body to protect his genitals…a natural reflex.

Finn moved forward, linked his hands together to form a club and hammered a blow down on Marcus's neck. The weight of the blow forced the big man to fall forward on to his face, letting out a loud groan.

Finn stood back and looked at the motionless body in front of him. He waited, unsure if it was a trick, kicked the lifeless body and received no reaction. He turned the body over with his foot and discovered the hunting knife sticking out of the chest.

Finn, removed the knife, wiped the blood on the front of Marcus's jacket and stashed it in his belt. He considered the pistol then kicked it away into a pile of rubbish. Instinct took over, he returned to the shadows and surveyed the area around him, looking for possible accomplices, finding none. He decided to conceal the body and returned to where the big man lay. He struggled with the weight of the corpse, staggered to a dumpster and threw it inside.

Sanders, watching from the rear window observed the fight and shouted to Troy, "Fuck! Some guy has just iced Marcus in the back alley."

In anger Sanders smashed the window with the butt of his assault rifle and aimed downwards to Finn. Hearing the glass smashing above him, Finn glanced upwards, noticed the barrel of the rifle at the window and dived behind the dumpster for cover. Sanders began firing off rounds in short bursts towards the bin. Bullets ricocheted off the concrete alley and tore into the refuse, throwing bits into the air. Finn kept his head down as scraps of food from the nearby takeaway rained down on him. This was not the first time he had been shot at or covered in shit.

Torres, hearing shooting coming from the rear of the building, stood back and shot the lock from the office door. Troy heard the noise, moved over to the doorway and shot wildly down the stairs. The glass in the door shattered as the armour piercing rounds sprayed around the entrance. Torres spun around and pressed his back against the outside wall. He looked briefly at his Glock 17M handgun and considered the imbalance in firepower between the shooter and himself.

Baxter, also hearing the shooting, drove the SUV to the corner of the alley opposite and noticed Torres taking cover against the wall. He leaned out of the driver's side window and began shooting towards the FBI man.

The magnitude of the situation dawned on Torres, trapped between the shooter upstairs and the SUV driver opposite, unless he moved…he was dead. He made a split-second decision to run for the passageway alongside the office door. He dived into the gap between the buildings whilst Baxter's bullets ricocheted off the walls around him.

Troy shouted to Sanders, who stopped shooting at Finn and turned, "I've got the money! Let's get the fuck out of here. When we get downstairs, I'll cover, once you reach the SUV, you cover me."

Sanders grabbed the gear and ran to the doorway to join Troy. With bullets no longer spraying rubbish around him Finn's attention turned towards the shooting at the front of the building. He quickly ran down the passageway towards the front. He grabbed the stumbling Torres and pulled him to the ground, away from Baxter's bullets.

The two soldiers in the upstairs office grabbed the bags and proceeded down the stairs. They held their assault rifles on the shoulder strap and at the hip, ready to shoot anything which came into view at the doorway. The front door just a frame with glass scattered all around the floor, both inside and out.

Baxter, noticed Sanders appear at the front door, stopped shooting and pulled the SUV into the road. He spun the vehicle around in the road with smoke burning from the tyres. With a quick jerk of the steering wheel, he slammed the passenger side wheels against the curb stone alongside the office door.

By moving the SUV Baxter lost sight of the passageway which allowed Finn to move to the front corner, he watched as the SUV pulled to an abrupt stop.

From the office door Troy shouted to Sanders, "Go!"

Sanders sprinted out through the door frame onto the footpath. Troy watched as his friend reached the side of the

SUV and grabbed for the door handle. In a split-second Finn threw the hunting knife. Troy watched as it spun, rotating in the air, and landed in the centre of Sanders' chest. Sanders dropped to his knees and slumped at the rear wheel of the SUV. Taking tight hold of the money, Troy jumped out onto the footpath and immediately started shooting his assault rifle in the direction of the knife thrower. Bullets shot along the street and into the passageway, ricocheting off the walls and smashing windows.

Finn retreated into the passageway, finding Torres getting to his feet and recognised the danger. If Troy chose to move to a position where he could shoot down the passage, both men would die. Finn instinctively grabbed Torres's Glock from the ground and shot random bullets down the passage, into the main street.

Troy heard the shots, stopped shooting and seized the opportunity to escape. He pulled the passenger side front door open and jumped inside with the money bag. He shouted, "Go! Go! Go!"

Baxter floored the accelerator leaving a trail of smoke and rubber behind them. The Heavy SUV swerved and weaved along the road.

Baxter shouted at Troy, "Who were those guys?"

Troy turned to see if anyone was following, "Sanders and Marcus didn't make it." He slapped the bag in front of him, "but at least we've got the cash. Get your foot down, we need to get as far away from El Paso as possible. Police and border guards will be all over this place in the next few minutes."

Finn realised the shooting had stopped and heard the screeching tyres. He moved to the corner of the passage, arriving in time to see the black SUV speeding away. He turned to Torres and shouted, "Quick, get to the car, we're going after them."

The two men ran out into the main street. Finn handed Torres his Glock and snatched the hunting knife from Sanders' chest as they ran along the footpath. They returned to the FBI cruiser and quickly climbed inside. Torres turned the ignition key and the engine sprung to life.

Finn shouted, "Floor it! We can't let them get away. They know where Kathy is."

Without hesitation Torres sped out of the car park and onto the main road, tyres smoking, in pursuit of the SUV. Torres switched on the blue lights and siren. He looked at Finn with a grin on his face, "Just so people know we're the good guys."

The superior handling of the FBI cruiser allowed them to accelerate and corner at higher speeds than the heavier SUV. Within moments they increased speed, gaining ground as the SUV appeared on the road in front.

Finn pointed out of the windscreen, "There it is!"

"Got it," Torres acknowledged.

Baxter looked at Troy, "Where to?"

Troy looked behind and noticed the blue lights flashing, "Head back the way we came. We need to get out of the city…and lose those fools."

Baxter came up to a slow-moving car in the lane ahead, forcing him to pull out into the oncoming traffic. Cars in the lane began to swerve and brake ahead of him. Once past the slow car he quickly pulled the SUV back into the correct lane. The constant abuse of the brakes and engine strained the SUV to its design limits. Baxter swerved the SUV around a ninety-degree bend and felt the vehicle getting away from him, losing control. To stop the SUV turning over he braked hard and pulled the steering wheel sharply to one side, correcting the spin. He floored the accelerator, looked in the rear-view mirror and watched the cruiser rapidly approaching behind.

"Shit! They're almost on top of us," Baxter yelled with a hint of panic in his voice.

Troy turned to look through the rear screen only to see Torres and Finn staring at him with the FBI cruiser almost touching the back bumper.

Baxter shouted to Troy, "Get in the back! Shoot them."

Troy climbed over the front seat, knelt on the back seat and aimed the assault rifle out of the rear window. He pressed the trigger on the HK416 assault rifle in short bursts, shooting at the heads of Torres and Finn. The armour piercing rounds generating flames as they exited the barrel of the gun. In an instance a row of bullets appeared across the windscreen of Torres's car.

Seeing the man, and the gun, Torres and Finn instinctively ducked down below the dashboard before the bullets arrived. Troy stopped firing when he noticed the men had disappeared. Cursing to himself he resumed the assault, this time aiming at the car engine and tyres.

The FBI cruiser lurched as the front tyres burst and the engine gave out a loud growl like a dying animal. Torres pulled the wheel hard to the right to direct the car away from the bullets. The engine died, the car slid sideways and came to a rest as it crashed into the rear of a parked car. Instantly the safety airbags activated, into the faces of Torres and Finn.

Troy watched as the cruiser crashed and shouted aloud, "See ya later chumps! Maybe next time."

He climbed into the passenger seat and patted Baxter on the shoulder saying, "Well done buddy, they're out of the game."

Baxter sighed a breath of relief and smiled. He noticed the roadside sign for 'Columbus NM-9' and turned onto a side road that ran parallel with the Mexico border.

He looked at Troy and announced, "We're in the clear."

"Great!" Troy declared, "Slow down, there are border patrols around here. We've had enough drama for one day. Let's just get as far away from El Paso as possible."

Baxter slowed to a modest fifty miles per hour on the New Mexico backroad.

Baxter enquired, "Do you think Winter sent them to finish us off? It was an unmarked police car but they didn't behave like police officers. Did you see how quick that guy dispatched Sanders with the knife? It must've been some of Winter's agency men."

"They weren't cops, that's for sure," Troy confirmed.

"You said Winter short changed us."

Troy picked up the bag and patted it with his hand before saying, "Winter has ripped us off true, but this gives us a start. We need to wait until the heat is off then we'll go back and get him...even if just for Marcus and Sanders sake."

"So how much did you get? I assume we're splitting it two ways?" Baxter urged.

"He said it was five hundred thousand."

"You counted it…didn't you?"

Troy unzipped the bag and looked inside at the money. He noticed something strange about the contents of the bag. He put his hand into the bottom and fumbled inside. The blast blew the roof off the SUV and in a ball of flame still rolling on its wheels, the vehicle progressed slowly down the road, moving gradually across the carriageway and down into a ditch

Chapter 11
Car Crash, El Paso

The rear end of the parked car crumpled with the force of the crash. Engine oil dripping onto the hot exhaust pipes resulted in smoke beginning to rise from the bonnet of the FBI cruiser and a river of green luminescent coolant fluid ran into the gutter.

After several minutes Torres and Finn woke, both dazed and confused. The air bags provided protection from serious injury but the sudden bag inflation knocked their heads backwards onto the headrests.

"Are you ok? Try not to move. I'll get some help for you both," a voice declared.

Torres slowly opened his eyes. He shook his head and felt a pain in his neck. Blood trickled down his face. Feeling the warm liquid, he touched his nose and looked to see blood on his fingers. He looked forward out of the shattered windscreen, unable to focus due to blurred vision. Finn woke to a pain in both his head and neck. He rubbed the neck to relieve the pain and blinked repeatedly, forcing his eyes to focus. The two men turned towards each other, both seeing just a blurry figure.

The voice spoke again, "Hello, can you hear me? We've phoned for help. It should be here soon."

Torres turned his head towards the direction of the voice, seeing a blurry figure leaning into the car. He rubbed his eyes, looked again and realised it was a member of the public.

Finn, with his vision quickly returning, forced the car door open and stumbled out.

The good Samaritan pulled at Torres's door. Torres barged his shoulder against it from the inside. Between them they managed to open it far enough for Torres to climb out. Torres straightened and felt pain in his back and neck.

He turned towards the helper, "Thanks. Now move away, this is a crime scene."

The helper, surprised by the tone of the instructions motioned to protest but Torres pushed him away.

Finn, rubbed his back then walked around the wrecked car to stand next to Torres. The two men studied each other noting the minor cuts and bruises which both had sustained.

Finn pointed towards Torres's face, "How's the nose?

Torres felt his nose, "It's not broken."

"Good. Now let's get back to the Foresight office," Finn declared. "We need to know who those guys were. They left in a rush and may have left something behind we can use to trace them."

"You said before, 'They know where Kathy is', what did you mean?"

"A guy was hiding in the alley around the back. When I asked him about Kathy he said, 'She's already gone' and 'I wouldn't find her as she's going on a journey overseas.' What do you think he meant by that?"

Torres shrugged his shoulders, "I don't have a clue. Let's go back and ask him."

"Not much chance of that," Finn declared. "He's dead."

"Dead!"

"He came at me with a big knife. I defended myself, and in the process, he fell on the knife," Finn explained, with a wry grin on his face.

"He fell on his own knife?" Torres said with a surprised tone, "That seems a bit convenient."

"Actually...he did."

Torres raised his eyebrows and shook his head. Before he could say anymore, the sound of a vehicle approaching distracted him and he turned to see a police car. Finn quickly took out the hunting knife and threw it into the storm drain next to the cruiser.

"Why did you do that?" Torres asked.

"We need to keep going. We don't have time to stand around explaining things to police officers. If I'm found with a knife it might lead to a few awkward questions."

"Don't worry, I didn't see anything," Torres said as he walked towards the police car. He stopped and turned, "By the way, thanks for saving my life back there. Quick thinking...we were sitting ducks in the passageway."

"Don't mention it, you'd have done the same."

A loud voice behind Torres announced, "Police! Get your hands in the air."

They both looked to see two police officers standing either side of the police car, guns drawn and pointed at them.

"Relax guys." Torres said, "I'm with the FBI."

The two police officers looked at each other and the driver shouted, "Okay, FBI man. Let's see your badge."

"It's in my jacket pocket. I need to get it out so don't shoot me ok."

"Fine, do it slowly and throw it over here."

Torres chucked the ID making it land at the officer's feet. The police officer read the details then turned his attention to Finn, "And who are you?"

"You don't need to know, he's with me." Torres declared forcefully, taking control of the situation. "We're in pursuit of suspects wanted for murder and kidnapping and need to take your car. Quickly call this incident in and arrange for a car to collect you. We'll bring your car to the station later."

He pointed to his car, "That's an FBI cruiser. It needs moving to the police station garage. I don't want it ending up in the police lock up. It has a lot of technology and weapons inside…plus my clean clothes."

"And mine," Finn added.

Torres and Finn climbed into the front seats of the police car. Torres, sitting in the driver's seat, looked in the mirror and noticed the dried blood on his face. He started the engine, turned the car around in the road and returned to the Foresight office.

Entering Pera Avenue they noticed the road shut off from public access by barriers. A police officer noticed them approaching and moved the barrier aside, allowing them to enter. Torres parked, joining the police cars, a border control pickup, an FBI cruiser, and an ambulance already outside the office.

Finn noticed Sanders's body laid in the gutter with a pool of blood around him. He wondered if they had found Marcus's body in the bin yet.

Getting out of the car together Torres turned to Finn, "Let me do the talking. Stay out of the way and don't mention anything. The El Paso FBI are here and we don't want them getting involved in our investigation. Remember what Colby said."

Torres looked towards a police officer near the office door and shouted, "You! Where are the FBI agents?"

Startled by the way Torres spoke to him, the police officer nervously pointed towards the shattered office door and mumbled, "Upstairs."

Torres walked through the shattered doorway and climbed the stairs to the office, with Finn following close behind. Inside, the room, showed little evidence of the battle which had taken place outside, apart from the broken rear window.

Torres introduced himself to the two Texas based FBI agents. He explained the culprits were suspects in a murder and kidnapping case in New Mexico. The Texas FBI agents agreed to let the local police handle the crime scene and quickly left, leaving Torres and Finn to look over the office by themselves.

"Don't touch anything." Torres put on latex gloves and handed a pair to Finn, "Just have a good look around, give me a shout if you see anything of interest."

They separated and wandered carefully around the office. Torres spotted something of interest and took out his mobile. In between taking photos he gestured to Finn,

"Come over here." He kneeled and pointed with his finger, "Look."

Finn knelt next to Torres and asked, "What is it?"

Torres said excitedly, "KF scratched into the skirting board."

Finn looked closer and noticed dusty chalk marks faintly scratched into the wood.

Torres repeated himself, "K and F? KF? KF?"

Both men looked at each other and said at the same time, "Katherine Finn!"

Finn smiled, "She was here. It's a good job we returned when we did as this would've been lost forever once moisture came in through the broken window."

Torres took photos while Finn continued to look around the surrounding area, "Look Torres! There's more over there. She must've been laid here on the floor and used the pieces of broken plaster."

Torres looked at the area on the wooden floor where Finn pointed. He took more images then crouched down to get a closer look.

"It's very faint. Two words. It doesn't seem to make sense. Can you make out what it says?" Finn asked.

Torres studied the words and replied, "I think it says 'Cofax'. Like you said it's very faint and the light in here's dim. I'll use the torch on my phone."

He took out his mobile and opened the torch app pointing it at the words scratched into the wood.

Immediately the words became much clearer and Finn announced, "Cofax Winter."

"What the hell do you think it means?" Torres enquired.

A large grin appeared on Finn's face as he replied, "Torres, I think we've just found our new lead. Well done Kathy."

The two men stood up and Torres called over the CSI team members. He told them to fully process the area and to protect the evidence. Torres looked at his watch and gestured to Finn to follow him outside.

They returned to the police car.

Torres turned to Finn, "It's nearly two in the morning and we need to find somewhere to sleep. We're both beat up and tired. We're not going to find her while we're in this state. We need food and sleep. First thing tomorrow I'll contact Dawson, give him an update on what has happened and see what he can dig up on the words 'Cofax Winter'. We don't know if it's a person's name, a place or the name of a company, it could be anything, but if anyone can trace it, Dawson will."

Finn motioned to protest with Torres then common sense took over, his body agreed with Torres. The jet lag, the constant worrying about Kathy and fighting Marcus had finally caught up on him.

He looked at Torres and said, "Sounds like a good plan. You're right, we need to regroup and start again in the morning. Also, you should get your nose checked out."

Torres smiled and said, "It's not going to spoil my good looks is it?"

"It looks like an improvement," Finn quipped.

The two men laughed.

They drove the car to the police station, entered the underground car park and stopped. They spotted the mangled FBI cruiser in a corner and walked over. Torres removed his weapons, laptop, and personal items. Finn grabbed his pack from the back seat.

After dropping off the police car keys with the desk sergeant they phoned for a taxi, checked in to the nearest hotel…and slept.

Chapter 12
Iron Fist Base

The return journey from El Paso to Lubbock was uneventful. Kathy struggled in the back of the SUV with the plastic tie-wraps cutting into the flesh on her wrists. Periodically a guard would look over the back seat and offer some water. In the front passenger seat Winter wore his designer sunglasses as the sun came up and he drifted in and out of sleep.

On entering the Iron Fist Security base, the two SUVs drove straight to an area set up as a temporary prison by the security chief. Five shipping containers arranged side by side and internally converted into a dual interrogation and prison cell layout.

The two vehicles parked in front of the containers, the guards from Winter's SUV climbed out and opened the boot. They lifted the struggling Kathy out and held her up between them with her feet barely touching the ground. Winter climbed out and walked around to the rear of the vehicle.

He walked up to Kathy and pulled her blindfold off.

"Let me go you pig," Kathy shouted.

Winter slapped her across the face and she cried out in pain.

"Shut up, you don't speak unless I ask you a question," Winter said menacingly.

A searing pain ripped through Kathy's face and her cheek glowed a deep red. Tears appeared in Kathy's eyes but she forced herself to stop. She told herself to remain strong and not reveal the fear and pain she felt. She gritted her teeth and stared into Winter's eyes.

Winter stood back and took a moment to look at the young woman in front of him. Her blonde hair tied in a ponytail and her face covered in dirty marks, but no cuts or bruises. He studied her clothing. She wore a pair of white trainers, beige coloured cargo pant shorts smeared with dirt and dust, and a red 'Oasis' t-shirt. She looked exactly as he expected…a British tourist.

Winter turned to Ward, "Let's get this young woman settled in her new home. You can take the ties off her wrists. She's not going anywhere."

Ward walked behind Kathy and cut the tie-wraps with a hunting knife. Kathy pulled her hands around to the front of her and rubbed her wrists.

Winter looked at her and said, "If you try anything they'll go back on and not come off again until you arrive at your final destination. Are we clear?"

Kathy stared at him, but did not reply.

"I said, are we clear?" Winter shouted in annoyance.

Under her breath Kathy mumbled, "Yes."

"Good."

Winter walked a few feet away from her while taking a cigar and gold lighter out of his jacket. Once lit, he turned to face her, "We can't have you travelling abroad looking like this. We need you looking your best for the journey. I don't want people thinking I've neglected you."

Keeping his eyes fixed on her he shouted out, "Ward, we need clean clothes, hot water and toiletries. Make it happen."

Addressing Kathy, he said, "Once you've cleaned yourself up these nice men will bring you some hot food and something to drink. I suggest you eat and drink as much as you can because you're going on a long journey later today."

The words induced a feeling of panic and she struggled to break free from the two guards. Winter came up close to her, she smelt his cigar breath and spat in his face.

Winter raised his hand slowly towards his face and wiped the spittle away. He hit Kathy across her face with the back of his hand and snarled, "Such ingratitude after I've taken so much trouble to look after you."

Kathy's legs buckled and she momentarily lost consciousness. The two security guards continued to hold her limp body. She opened her eyes enough to see Winter walking away from her.

Winter arrived at the SUV and turned, "Ward, get on with it. You also need to discuss her travel arrangements with Martinez, I don't want any more cockups, I'll be in my office."

She watched Winter get into the SUV and followed its progress as it headed away towards a red farmhouse.

Ward pointed to the container at the end of the row and ordered the guards, "Take her to cell five, it's empty."

The two guards lifted her high enough so her feet were moving but not taking the weight of her body. They walked along the front of the containers towards the end. She heard people groaning in pain and protesting from other containers.

At the last container, a guard opened the container door and Kathy looked inside to a space which frightened her. An old desk and two chairs, Various chains and ropes hung down from the ceiling, tied back against the side walls. On the wooden floor she noticed blood stains mixed with dirt and at the rear a dividing wall with a door and barred window.

The guards carried her through the inside of the container up to the dividing wall and opened the door into a small prison cell.

Kathy looked around the small room. She noticed a bucket in the corner and a small wooden bed without a mattress, or blankets. The size of the door frame forced one guard to let go of her. The other held her tightly, dragged her inside and threw her onto the floor. Kathy let out a groan as her body hit the dirty wooden floor. She looked at the guard as he grinned, walked out of the cell and locked the door behind him.

He moved to the small barred window and shouted inside, "Enjoy your stay."

Kathy laid on the dirty floor for a few moments gathering her senses. She pulled herself up onto the wooden bed and sat for a moment taking in her surroundings and wondering what was happening. She rubbed her cheek, still warm from Winter's slap and cursed. Unanswered questions ran through her mind and provided no comfort. The anxiety and stress induced a feeling of tiredness. She laid over onto her side and slowly fell asleep.

⁕ ⁕ ⁕ ⁕

Kathy woke at the sound of the steel door unlocking. She sat up on the bed and Ward walked in with a carrier bag in his hand.

"Kathy!" He said loudly, "Wake up."

He threw the bag onto the bed next to her and stepped away to one side as two guards brought in a trolley with a large plastic tub filled with water. They wheeled the trolley into the corner near the bucket.

Ward guarded the door as the guards left the cell. He looked at her and said, "The water is hot enough for you to clean yourself up, toiletries are in the bag. Don't let it get cold, use it while you can. I'll be on guard outside, no one will be able to watch. Shout out when you're ready and I'll bring you some food."

A guard returned and passed Ward some plastic bottles. He took them and threw them onto the bed.

"There's some water, drink it," he urged. "Do you need anything else?"

Ward's eyes told Kathy he was unhappy with the situation.

"Yes…how about setting me free." She demanded.

Ward grinned and said, "If I do that, I'll end up in the container next door."

"Why am I here? From what I can see you are soldiers and this looks like a military base. Am I under arrest or something? What have I done wrong? Who were the men who killed my friends, and who's the asshole who hit me, is he in charge?" She desperately barked out questions, searching for answers. She tried to stand up but he pushed her back onto the bed and she banged her arm on the metal wall.

Ward looked at her sympathetically and said, "I'm sorry but I can't tell you anything. You should take the opportunity to get yourself cleaned up while you can. And make sure you eat and drink. I can't guarantee when you'll get more."

Chapter 13
Motel, El Paso

The next morning Finn and Torres woke early. Torres sent an email to Dawson before they checked out of the Motel. After eating breakfast at a local diner, they took a taxi to the FBI office in El Paso. The taxi dropped Finn off at a seven-eleven before arriving at the security gate.

Torres went inside the FBI building and, after making a phone call and a short wait, an FBI agent appeared from an office and handed him a set of car keys. He collected the vehicle from the underground car park, cleared security, drove out of the gates and returned to the seven-eleven to collect Finn.

"Okay, we have a car, what next?" Finn asked.

"I need to speak to Dawson."

Torres chose the car park of a large retail store and parked up. He took out his mobile phone and speed dialled. He gave Dawson a brief report on the events which had taken place the day before at the Foresight office.

"I got your email. Sounds like you've been busy," Dawson confirmed.

"True. What's the latest from the crime scenes?" Torres asked.

"Nothing new from New Mexico so far."

"What about the guys killed at the Foresight office? Have they managed to get any ID's?"

"We didn't find anything on the bodies or in the office which we can use to identify them but we may get an answer this afternoon on the fingerprints and DNA."

"What have you found out about 'Cofax Winter'. Is it a company of some kind?" Torres enquired.

Dawson laughed and said, "Not a company. It's a person. General Cofax Winter, or ex-General, he's retired now, a big bird in the US Army with lots of medals. His personnel file has a security seal which requires clearance on a level far above anything we could hope to achieve. I called one of Colby's contacts to see if they knew him and he said Winter mixes in circles that go right to the top of the administration. After his retirement from the Army, he set up a company called Iron Fist Security. It's a PMC. Do you know what a PMC is?"

"PMC? I don't have a clue, fill me in."

"A PMC, or private military company, provides armed combat or security services to governments or private companies. They'll go wherever you want if you pay them. It's big business. They refer to the employees as 'security contractors' or 'private military contractors' but basically, they're just soldiers. In the old days people called them mercenaries.

"The services and expertise offered by the PMC are like those of any national security, military or police force. Some PMCs receive contracts to work abroad for private companies. They provide bodyguards for key staff or protection of company premises and assets, especially in hostile territories. There've been reports, but nothing proven, claiming these guys go abroad to clean up stuff that's too dirty for the military, all paid for by government budgets. They normally employ top of the line ex-military trained guys. Real medal of honour bad asses who can go abroad and shoot guns without worrying about getting into trouble. Just consider for a moment what happens when agencies like the CIA or DEA are operating covertly abroad and you get the idea. According to reports private contractors now make up thirty percent of US intelligence community forces, but are taking nearly fifty percent of the available cash from the budget. We are talking big business Torres!

"What I've managed to find out about Iron Fist Security is they're one of the biggest offering services in Afghanistan. They've got a lucrative government contract which grants them unfettered transport between there and a base in Lubbock, Texas. The contract means they don't have to worry about clearing US customs. That type of security clearance comes from the top. Whatever these people are doing over there it's fully backed by the government."

Torres interrupted, "The men who attacked us were well trained, I'd be surprised if the reports on the two dead guys don't mention military histories."

"We'll find out soon enough," Dawson confirmed.

"So how do I get in front of Cofax Winter? I need to speak to him, he's our only lead. These guys are linked to him somehow and are obviously behind the kidnapping and murders," Torres asked.

"From what I understand he spends most of his time at the Iron Fist base at Lubbock. I've looked at satellite photos of the area and the base spreads over a wide area of land. The images show several military training grounds, barracks, gun ranges and a full mock up town modelled on a typical Afghan village. There's also a full-size airstrip capable of handling the biggest cargo planes."

"General Winter lives on the base?" Torres asked.

"On the photos there's an old ranch house set back from the main military complex, probably there before the land was converted. If I was looking for him…that's where I'd look."

"Send the details of what you've discovered so far and let me know once you receive more information on the bodies from the office."

"No problem." Dawson paused, then said cautiously, "Torres, be careful. There've been several CIA types calling here asking about you and trying to get information on what you're doing out in the field. If you suspect Winter is involved in something then it could open a big hornet's nest. It could be they're worried about you exposing what he's really doing for the intelligence agency guys in Afghanistan. Take care brother."

"Thanks, Dawson."

Torres hung up the phone and stared out the window, processing the information.

"Well? What did he say?" Finn enquired.

Torres continued to look out of the window and replied, "Do you know what a PMC is?"

"Yes, they're military contractors. They work all over the place. There are a lot in Afghanistan doing security details, protecting people, looking after oil pipelines, that type of stuff."

Torres looked around at him and asked, "Have you ever heard of a company called Iron Fist Security?"

"Of course. They're the main ones you see in Afghanistan. I've seen the men and vehicles at the air bases and around the major cities. They wear a uniform of black pants and beige jackets or t-shirts. Why do you ask?"

"Cofax Winter, he's the leader of Iron Fist. Retired US Army General."

Finn remembered the times when he had encountered the contractors in the past and said, "Are you saying they're involved in this business with Kathy? The Iron Fist guys I've met are just like regular soldiers. I don't think they'd have any reason to take her."

"I'll ask Dawson to see if he can link Winter, or Iron Fist Security, to the shell company Foresight. If there's anything illegal going on, they'll need a shell company to hide both the money and who's involved."

"In the meantime, we need to get to this Winter guy. Kathy wrote his name down, he's the person we need to go after," Finn challenged.

"That may be difficult, General Winter is holed up at the Iron Fist base which is a five-hour drive from here. He's not going to let us walk in there without a warrant and no judge is going to give me one unless I've got rock solid evidence that he's done something wrong. He's a decorated veteran."

"What evidence do you need? Four military contractors, an office leading to a shell company and a message from

Kathy saying Cofax Winter. We also know they're planning to send Kathy 'on a journey' so we need to move quickly. I need to get to Winter, he's the one pulling the strings." Finn complained.

Torres noticed Finn becoming irritated by his answers but continued anyway, "Finn, what we know and what we can prove are two different things. Everything you've just said is circumstantial. It doesn't open any doors for us. Yes, I agree Winter is involved but we don't have any actual evidence. If we focus on catching those two guys who escaped last night and can question them, they might give us a reason to go after Winter."

Finn replied angrily, "Look Torres, you operate within the law, I'm a soldier. All I ask is for you to take me back to my car so I can get mobile on my own. You can go after the two guys...I'll go after Winter."

Torres said calmly, "Lubbock is six hours drive from here, Santa Fe is four. When you get there you still have another five-hour drive back to Lubbock. Nine hours driving alone or six with me? Going on your own is a waste of time. Also, if you're caught by these guys without some form of backup, you'll probably not last very long. These guys are bad asses with technology and numbers on their side. All you've got is a burner phone. Come on Finn be realistic, we need to stick together."

Finn conceded, "You're right, I guess, but ask yourself how these guys are funded and how they're able to operate outside the law both here and abroad? I trust you, but I get the feeling we'd be wise not to trust anyone else. This could go all the way to the top. We're starting to see why Colby has set up a separate investigation team."

"That's a viable point Finn. We need to start watching our backs and taking care who we talk to."

"We're wasting time. Let's get to Lubbock and find out what we can about Winter, Foresight and Iron Fist, I've got a plan."

"A plan?" Torres asked.

"I suggest we go to the Iron Fist base, do a recon of the perimeter and check out the security measures that are in place. Then we'll find a motel to use as our camp. I'll speak to my contacts at the NCS and arrange to get some gear dropped off. Tonight, I'll go into the base covertly and search for Kathy. The shootout last night has taught us we're up against well trained and heavily armed soldiers who are happy to kill. To get inside undetected I need some high specification covert ops gear."

∴ ∴ ∴ ∴

On the drive to Lubbock, they stopped at a diner and Torres took the opportunity to make some calls.

Calling HQ first, "Dawson, any news?"

"You were right, the two guys killed at the crime scene were in the military. Their personnel files have a security seal, I can't see what they did. All I can find is confirmation that they left the Army four years ago then disappeared off the grid."

"No records of them buying anything or travelling?" Torres enquired.

"Nothing, one more thing though, during the night New Mexico police discovered a burnt-out SUV in a ditch with two mutilated bodies inside. The state medical examiner and a forensics team are at the site collecting evidence. If they find anything, I'll let you know. The police officer at the scene told me that it looked like a bomb or explosion of some kind. These not much left of the occupants to use to identify them."

"Dawson, these guys are bad news, they shot up that place last night without a second thought, is there anything we can use to link these guys to Winter? What about the shell company?"

"Nothing has come up yet on the guys but I've got one of the financial experts looking into the shell company to see if we can trace the money."

"Good job, keep on it. We are driving to Lubbock to see what we can dig up on Iron Fist." Torres said.

"Don't worry Nico, I'll keep looking, once I know something new, I'll let you know. The medical examiner may find something we can work with, let's see what she comes back with. The SUV had crossed the state line into New Mexico when it exploded so it's the same examiner from the campsite killings. I suppose that makes things easier for us to coordinate."

"Dawson, be careful where you look, what you dig up and who you speak to. We don't know who's involved so keep things between us for now."

"Will do."

The line went dead. Torres looked at his mobile phone considering the next call that he had to make. He scrolled through the contacts until he found the one that he required. *Rivera*.

He sat staring at his mobile phone for a few moments with his finger hovering over the green icon. He sighed and put the phone back into his trouser pocket.

They continued the drive until they reached the outskirts of Lubbock. Torres input the address on the Sat Nav and they drove towards the main gate of the Iron Fist base. Approaching the main entrance gate, they noticed heavy security with several guards with guns. They drove past and continued driving along a two-lane road running parallel to the perimeter fence of the base, with the aircraft runway beyond.

Finn observed the base while Torres drove. He turned to Torres and said, "This base covers a wide area, lots of military hardware in there and a heavy lift runway capable of taking planes of all sizes. There's a lot of security as well, cameras, heat, and noise sensors on the fences. But with the right gear we can get around those easy enough."

Torres replied in a concerned tone, "Something tells me you've done this stuff before. I'm wasting my time arguing with you. I have to play by the rules, we need to find a way for me to get in the front door legitimately and do a face to face with Winter. I ask this guy some awkward questions…"

Torres stopped talking, the intense look on his face told Finn he was thinking, considering his options. After a few moments Torres continued, "My problem is I don't have a reason at the moment which I can use to approach him."

Torres pointed out of the windscreen, "Look there's a Motel, it's close enough to the base for us to be able to observe the comings and goings. Let's use it as our base and then we'll decide where we go from here."

Finn nodded in agreement.

Torres parked and went to the Motel reception and hired two rooms on the second floor with an adjoining door. Both rooms had windows providing a clear view of the Iron Fist Security base and the airstrip.

Once settled in their separate rooms Torres knocked and opened the joining door into Finn's room. He found Finn standing at the window and walked over to join him. The two men stood together and looked out towards the runway. They discovered two planes, a C-5 Galaxy cargo plane, and a white Lear executive jet parked at the front of the large hanger. The cargo plane had both the rear and front doors open with a team of forklift trucks loading crates. A ground crew started the process of refuelling the executive jet. On the far side of the runway, they noticed a line of parked military helicopters.

"Looks like they're preparing the planes for take-off," Finn observed. "I've had a thought. Because Iron Fist is a private company all the aircraft have a unique aircraft identification number, you can see it on the rear sides of the plane. They must tell air traffic control where they're going. Do you think your guy at HQ can find out if anyone has logged a flight plan for them? At least we'll find out where they're going."

"No problem," Torres said, "but I can't see the full number from here."

"I'll go outside and see if I can get a clearer view." Finn said.

"Okay, while you're doing that I'll go out and get us some food and a few beers. There's a Seven-Eleven just down the road, is Pizza okay for you?"

"Anything will do for me," Finn declared. "And don't forget those beers."

∴ ∴ ∴ ∴

Torres returned with the food and drinks. They ate while they talked.

Torres asked, "Did you manage to get the numbers off the planes?"

"Yep, I wrote them down here," Finn pulled out a piece of paper and pointed, "That's the number of the cargo plane and that's the small jet. The executive jet took off at eighteen twenty-seven."

Torres took the paper, "Let's give the numbers to Dawson and see what he finds."

He drank some beer, threw the crust of the pizza in the box and picked up his mobile from the desk, "Dawson, can you track a couple of planes for me? Here are the numbers…" He read them out before continuing, "Find out where the planes have been, where they're going, who's operating them, what they're carrying…anything."

"No problem," Dawson said, adding, "It's a good job I don't have a date to meet because I get the feeling it's going to be a long night."

"Did you?" Torres asked.

"No," Dawson sighed.

"What about the medical examiner, did she manage to identify the bodies in the SUV?"

"She wants you to call her urgently. She's discovered some important information but said she wants to tell you first before she submits her full report."

"I'll give her a ring now."

Torres hung up and realised he could not put it off any longer. He looked at his contact list and selected 'Rivera', pressed the green icon and the phone rang.

Rivera answered sarcastically, "Nico Torres the disappearing FBI agent finally calls. Is withholding evidence the only way I can get you to call me? Dawson said you're somewhere in Texas. It sounds intriguing."

Torres responded in an apologetic tone, "I'm sorry. I should've called you earlier but it's been quite an intense couple of days. Dawson said you know something about the men in the SUV?"

Rivera chuckled to herself and said, "Back to business, that's the Torres I know. I wonder if one day we'll talk to each other as people not officials." She paused and considered her statement before continuing, "Never mind! This is what I've found. When the SUV blew up evidence scattered across a wide area and away from the actual burning chassis. In the debris we discovered an ID card for 'Troy Ramon'. I can't confirm if the picture on the ID is one of the two guys as there's not much left of them. What I can tell you is the ID is for a company called Iron Fist Security. We're trying to trace this Ramon guy to see if I can get hold of his dental records. I may be able to match them to one of the bodies. The forensics team is still looking through the debris, we may get lucky and find something on the other guy as well."

Torres replied with urgency in his voice, "Can you do me a favour and miss that information off your report and make sure no one contacts Iron Fist Security asking about the guy. We don't know who to trust or who is involved and it could jeopardise what I'm doing."

"No one will contact Iron Fist but I can't guarantee who knows about the ID card."

Torres noted a colder tone in her voice. He waited for a few moments and thought to himself. The prospect of losing her suddenly dawned on him.

"Rivera, this mess will be over soon and we'll have plenty of time to talk together afterwards. As people not officials. I'll buy you a nice dinner in Santa Fe and we can talk about anything you want." He hesitated and asked, "How does that sound?"

Rivera sighed, "We'll see. For now, just stay safe Nico Torres." Then hung up.

Torres wondered if he had missed his chance. Lost another opportunity to get his life back on track, a chance to feel love again.

Finn distracted him, "So what did they say? Do you have any leads to work on or progress you can report?"

"Yes actually, we've just had some good news. We've finally found a connection between the guys in the SUV and Iron Fist Security. Which means I've now got a valid reason to interview Winter."

"Not yet! Let's follow my plan. I'll call Miller and find out what he knows about Winter, maybe he can suggest the best way to approach him. Also, once I've spoken to him, he'll feel obliged to report our progress to Colby. That way we'll know he's fully onside with what we're doing down here."

"Okay, we'll do it your way…for now."

Finn said impatiently, "And what about those planes?"

"Dawson is checking on the planes, it'll take a little time, he'll call me as soon as he has the information."

Finn stood up and walked towards the adjoining door, "Okay, I'll call Miller."

He returned to his room, shut the door, and picked up the burner phone from the bedside table. He sat on the bed and pressed 'one' on the keypad.

The phone rang once, "Miller!"

"Hi Miller, I'm calling to let you know where we are and what's been happening. You will have seen Torres's report and the updates from Dawson so you'll most likely be up to speed anyway."

"I've been following your progress, what happened to keeping your head down and not getting into trouble?" Miller asked.

"I've been trying my best!" Finn protested, "We were lucky to get out of the shootout in El Paso alive. The men we came up against were heavily armed and I had nothing to use as protection. I need a weapon. Can you speak to Colby and ask for authorisation so you can provide one?"

"I can't see that presenting a problem, leave it with me, in the meantime tell me what you have discovered."

"We are currently holed up in a motel in Lubbock, Texas. It's located on a road which runs alongside the perimeter fence of a military base run by Iron Fist Security. Do you know them?"

Miller laughed aloud, "Finn, everyone knows who Iron Fist are. They provide security and support staff to various locations in Afghanistan. They do a lot of government work. They perform security details at private sites like the airports and hotels. That's the legal stuff everyone gets to hear about. What I also know is they work for both the CIA and the DEA on, should we say, projects, which are outside the field of security. The guys they tend to use are heavy duty ex-military bad asses who enjoy life in a conflict zone. The type of guys who join the army so they can legally kill people. I'm sure you know the type."

"Have you ever heard of a guy called Cofax Winter?"

"You mean 'the General'. He's the main force behind Iron Fist Security. There have been rumours of the company operating outside the law but no one has ever been able to prove anything and whenever evidence comes up it quickly disappears. If a whistle-blower comes forward no matter how well protected, someone always gets to them. Why do you ask?"

Finn replied, "We think he's behind the kidnapping."

"What the General?" Miller said in surprise, "No way!"

Finn continued with his report, "We traced the SUV the kidnappers used, to an office in El Paso. It's owned by a shell company registered in the Bahamas. We suspect Iron Fist owns the office. They've used some fancy lawyer to set things up and cover their tracks. The four guys who took my sister are dead. Two died at the office and two died later when an SUV blew up during their escape."

"Blew up!" Miller repeated and asked, "How?"

"At the moment we don't know but it sounds like a bomb or maybe they set off one of their own weapons accidentally, who knows? Torres said forensics found an ID card at the scene for a 'Troy Ramon', a security consultant for Iron Fist. That's the link we've been searching for, Kathy, to Ramon, to Winter. Ramon's personnel files are classified and the FBI guys don't have the level of security clearance required to access them. I know you've got your sources. Can you look into Ramon for me?"

"No problem, I'll see what I can dig up." Miller confirmed and asked, "So, if they're all dead, where the hell is your sister?"

"One of the guys told me they passed her on to someone else and they were going to send her overseas."

"You talked to him? And now he's dead?" Miller asked.

"Miller, that's not important now," Finn snapped. "It looks like they handed her over at the office. We missed the pick-up guys but for some reason the guys who took Kathy were still at the office. We arrived about five minutes late."

"None of that confirms Winter's involvement, it could just be a coincidence. Maybe the guys don't work for Iron Fist Security anymore. You'll not get anyone to move on Winter with such flimsy evidence."

"Wait! Let me finish." Finn retorted. "The reason we came to Lubbock is because when we searched the office in El Paso, we found a note from Kathy. She wrote 'Cofax Winter' on the floor. She could've only done that if she'd met him or heard his name mentioned. Winter spends all his time here at the base. If he has taken Kathy then she's most likely still inside. Security is very tight, as you'd expect. Torres wants to interview Winter face to face but I've warned him against it as it could put Winter on the back foot. He might decide to dispose of Kathy rather than be caught with her."

Miller responded in a calming tone, "Finn, give me some time. I'll investigate this Ramon character and discuss with Colby what we should do about General Winter. I think we are beginning to understand why Colby is running his covert investigation."

"Thanks Miller, I'll wait for your call"

In the other room Torres took a call from Dawson, "Nico, I've checked the planes. The small jet is heading north to Akron, Ohio. The flight log says a private flight with four passengers. The other, a C-5 Galaxy, is carrying military personnel and freight to Kandahar, Afghanistan with a stopover in Morocco for fuel. The small jet is owned by Foresight, the other is owned by the US Air Force on loan to Iron Fist."

Torres listened, then speculated, "The Foresight jet could just be moving staff around but we need to make sure they've not smuggled the kidnapped woman on board. Can you get the FBI at Akron to search the plane when it lands?"

"I'll speak to the field office up there and ask them to do a meet and greet on the plane." Dawson confirmed.

"Our priority is searching for the woman but we also need to know who the four passengers are and what the cargo is."

"Okay, leave it with me Nico, I need to get onto it straight away before it lands."

Dawson hung up. Torres opened the adjoining door into Finn's room and asked him about the call with Miller. Finn repeated the details while Torres collected two cold beers from the fridge. He twisted off the caps and waited for Finn to finish before handing one over, "At the moment Finn we don't know if Kathy is at the Iron Fist base or has been moved on to another location. We're going to seize the small jet when it lands at Akron, the flight log said four passengers, one could be Kathy. It's a six-hour flight up to Akron so it will land sometime around midnight. Dawson is going to arrange for local FBI agents to search it, if she's onboard, we'll find her."

The burner phone rang and Finn quickly answered it, "Miller."

"Finn, I've spoken to Colby. He wants you to proceed cautiously investigating Winter. It seems the General is a person of interest to him. He didn't go into any specific details but as you know Colby has a side investigation going. As soon as I mentioned Winter his mood changed. He's told me to give Torres and yourself as much support as possible to investigate what Winter is involved in at the base. But there's no official back up. He said if he brings in other intelligence agencies it'll blow his investigation wide open. He made a point of saying not to trust anyone. Basically, the three of us are on our own."

Finn replied, "Things have moved on since we last spoke, Miller. Torres has arranged to stop the private jet that flew out of here earlier when it lands at Akron. We think Kathy could be onboard."

"You need to give me the details so I can inform Colby." Miller confirmed.

Finn agreed, "I'll text you the flight number. Now back to this support you mentioned, I need you to get me some gear so I can get into the base and have a good look around." Finn pulled out a list and read out the items he required, "A person-to-person communication system. I'll need fully suppressed weapons, a HK416 assault rifle with armour piercing bullets and a decent handgun, a SIG D320 would be nice. I also need two magazines for the pistol. One with normal bullets and the other with tranquilisers. Now the hard one, can you get me one of those new covert sneaking suits your Navy Seal and Special Forces guy's wear. I saw them using them once. Also chuck in some decent night vision goggles, a few smoke, stun and sleep grenades just to be sure."

"Finn, that's a lot of gear, you're not planning on starting a war?" Miller joked.

"The men we can see in the base are armed to the teeth. They are using the latest technology weapons, like the four guys in El Paso used. I've no intention of using lethal force, that's what the tranqs and grenades are for, but if I find evidence that they've got Kathy imprisoned on the base then I'll do whatever I can to free her."

"Give me an hour to collect up the gear, there's a Naval ordnance centre not far from you. I'll get a helicopter to fly me there. I'll take one of their pickups and then drive to meet you at the motel."

"You're coming here?" Finn asked.

"Too right! I'm not going to let you have all the fun. I'll sit in at your Motel while you're both out. Someone needs to listen in on the comms system, at least you'll have some backup, even if it's not official."

"Thanks Miller, I look forward to seeing you."

Finn hung up the call, went to look for Torres, who had returned to his room, finding him working on a laptop.

Torres looked up, "Thought I'd check for any new information while you took the call, how did it go?"

"Miller has sorted things out with Colby and he's going to help us get into the base to see if we can find Kathy."

"What's your plan?" Torres asked.

"We don't have a lot of time. The ID card gives you a valid reason for getting into the base and speaking to Winter. While you're doing that, I'll cut the perimeter fence and proceed onto the base and see what I can find."

"What about backup? What if things get out of hand?" Torres asked.

Finn replied, "Colby doesn't want anyone else involved. Miller is coming to give us some backup. If we don't do this now, we could lose the opportunity to get to Kathy before they send her somewhere else. I doubt Winter will tell you anything but it'll keep him busy while I search the facility for her."

"You don't have the right gear to go snooping around in a heavily protected military base." Torres stated.

"Don't worry Miller is bringing some, it'll be here within the hour, as soon as it arrives, we get going."

Torres nodded and said, "Agreed, I'll phone Dawson to fill him in on our plan, it's best someone knows where we are, I mean, just in case something happens to us all."

"Can you trust him?" Finn enquired. "Colby warned us to be careful with who we trust."

Torres laughed loudly, "Dawson? I'd trust him with my life. I've done it many times in the past. Don't worry, we can trust him."

Finn patted Torres on the back, "No problem, I trust you and you trust him, but tell him it stays with him."

Chapter 14
Iron Fist Base

Winter, sitting behind his desk, took out a cigar, lit it and leaned back in the chair. Ward stood silently in front of him while Winter took several puffs on the big cigar ensuring it was alight. After taking a long drag Winter held the smoke for a moment then blew it out at Ward, "Is she settled into the executive suite?"

"Yes sir. We gave her what you said. She complained at first but she was eating when I left," Ward replied.

"Good." Winter confirmed, "We just need to ship her on to the client. Then we're in the clear. What time is the transport booked for?"

"The C-5 is booked to return to Kandahar at twenty-one forty-five. It's currently getting refuelled, loaded with the next batch of contractors and some replacement gear, then it'll be ready to take off again. We'll have to send security guards with her and keep her away from the other contractors. It could end up getting nasty. Those guys won't take kidnapping a woman easily, or our other business."

Winter hissed, "Ward, you're a nice guy but sometimes I think you take me for an idiot. Do you really think I would sit her on the plane in front of everyone?"

"No. Sir." Ward confirmed.

Puffing on his big cigar Winter continued, "We run two types of business here Ward. The PMC which keeps us in with the government, cleaning up their mess and our other business involving clients here in the US and over there. Without the government allowing us to fly the planes we can't run the other business. Do you understand?"

"Yes. Sir." Ward confirmed again.

"Leave the thinking to me. Now get the fuck out!"

Ward left the room. Winter sat, thinking while toying with his cigar. The telephone ringing interrupted the silence, "Yes... who... Marshall, yes okay put him through."

"Hi...yes as far as I know they're in the air...the other business? Yes, we've got her here...she leaves at twenty-one hundred forty-five...as far as I know it went smoothly...Troy? I arranged for him to have an accident. His team had become a liability...what?...say that again…he had an ID card with him? I'm surrounded by morons...no, it's not a problem, leave it with me to deal with. First, I need to get this woman out of my hair. I don't see the point in dragging this woman halfway around the world. Your hare-brained scheme to pander to his demands are getting out of hand. This could get very messy and if I go down, you'll go down with me."

Winter slammed the phone down and cursed loudly, "Marshall you bastard. What the hell have you got me involved in."

Winter continued puffing on his cigar until he had calmed down enough to pick up the phone.

He barked into the receiver, "Martinez, I need you to put together a four-man security team, including you. You're going to travel with the woman and personally deliver her to the client. The plane leaves here at twenty-one forty-five. You're travelling with the other contractors. They mustn't find out about the woman or there'll be shit to pay. Drug her to keep her silent during the flights. Ship her inside one of the crates we use for gear and they won't suspect anything. And make sure she can breathe. I don't need to remind you of what will happen to you if she doesn't get there in perfect order. Can I trust you to do that for me?"

He waited for the response he expected, and always got, then slammed the phone down. He leaned back in his chair and smoked his cigar.

Chapter 15
Motel, Lubbock

Torres and Finn prepared themselves for the nights planned events. Torres dressed in his suit trousers, white shirt, and FBI windcheater jacket. Finn in Jeans, t-shirt, and leather jacket. They sat in silence, each thinking over what they had to do in the coming hours. Torres read his notes and formulated the questions he would ask Winter. Finn looked at the scribbled map he created of the base and considered the possible locations where Kathy could be hidden.

A light knock at the motel room door impelled Finn to look at his watch, 20:12. He put the security chain on the door and slowly opened it. *Miller*.

"Come in," Finn directed him towards his partner, "This is Nico Torres."

The two men shook hands, "Nice to meet you Torres. I've heard a lot about you."

"All good stuff I hope," Torres enquired.

Miller laughed, "I can't tell you. It's classified." He turned to Finn and asked, "What do you want to do with the gear?"

"Leave it in the pickup for now," Finn said. "You can drive me to the perimeter fence and I'll get changed there. Torres will set off from the motel at the same time as we do in a coordinated attack, he'll go in through the main gate while I break in through the fence."

"Sounds good." Miller agreed, then added, "But first we need to put these on."

Miller opened a metal case containing a military grade communications system consisting of a base station and a set of linked earpieces with a built-in microphone permanently switched on. The system did not allow the users to speak independently to each other. The microphone transmitted any picked-up sounds to the other people in the loop via the earpieces. The transmitted sound contained two signals. One just static to mask the sound waves and the other a GPS tracker signal showing the position of the wearer on the base station map screen. The miniature design size of the earpiece ensured the system was undetectable and perfect for covert missions. The system used military grade encryption making it impossible to trace the signals. He handed earpieces to both Finn and Torres and watched as they fitted them.

Miller tested the sound and GPS tracker on the base station, identified the three GPS signals and declared, "Okay the system is ready."

Finn looked at the other two men and announced, "Come on let's get moving, time is running out."

At 20:34 the three men left the Motel.

∴ ∴ ∴ ∴

Torres drove left out of the car park and headed towards the main entrance gate of the Iron Fist base. He requested a meeting with General Winter and handed over his FBI ID card. The security guard made a phone call and received the authorisation from Winter to allow Torres to enter the base.

Winter had no other option, to refuse would raise suspicion, something he needed to avoid while there was a kidnapped woman hidden at the base. The guard handed Torres the ID card and directed him to a large ranch house set back towards the side of the base.

From the security gate Torres drove his cruiser between the main buildings of the camp, along a line of hangers, some barracks, and a row of shipping containers. He found the road leading towards the ranch house on the other side of the airstrip. As he drove along, he relayed information back to Miller and Finn using the comms system. Talking aloud to himself recounting what his eyes observed…number of guards, equipment, buildings, layout of the base. He looked over the runway towards the perimeter fence and thought of Finn.

∴ ∴ ∴ ∴

Miller drove his pickup truck right out of the Motel car park and along the road running parallel with the perimeter fence and airstrip. On his initial drive by earlier in the day Finn had identified an area with minimal security. He guided Miller who turned off the main road onto a dirt track and after a short drive they arrived at the perimeter fence. Miller parked and the two men climbed out.

Miller unpacked the gear while Finn stripped down to a t-shirt and boxer shorts. Miller handed Finn an aluminium flight case. Laying it down on the damp grass Finn opened it and discovered the sneaking suit. A one-piece stealth body suit with a zip up the back. Visually it looked a lot like a diver's wetsuit however it cost considerably more to make. The suit included built in rubber shoes which allowed the user to walk on many different surfaces and leave no sound signature. The body of the suit fabricated from a heavily weaved cloth, developed to provide a high level of injury protection from bullets and shrapnel. While not providing the same protection as a Kevlar bullet proof vest, which would be too bulky, the main purpose of the suit was to allow a person to infiltrate an area undetected. An added feature of the material was masking body heat making the user invisible to heat detection security devices.

After covering his legs and arms in talcum powder, Finn placed his feet into the legs, quickly pulled the suit on and asked Miller to zip the back. He collected the weapons and filled the pockets of the suit with the grenades and magazines. He put on the gloves, balaclava and fixed the night vision goggles on his head ready to move them into position. He stored the silenced pistol in a holster on his hip. He swung the assault rifle strap over his head so it ran diagonally across his body. He adjusted the strap tension to ensure the rifle remained on his back while moving, and could still swing around quickly for use, if required.

"I'm ready, cut the fence." Finn asked.

Miller nodded and got the wire cutters out of the pickup truck. He cut the fence in a line starting at the ground, working upwards, bending the wire and making an opening. Once wide enough, he turned to Finn, "Get yourself in. I'll repair it just in case someone starts snooping about, then I'll head to the motel and monitor the comms. Good luck buddy, keep your head down."

Finn nodded in agreement then proceeded through the fence into the base. He walked in a crouched position twenty feet inside, stepping on the short grass growing alongside the runway. He kneeled and looked back to watch Miller seal the fence then waited until the pickup drove away.

Finn whispered so the others in the comms loop could hear him speak, "Torres, I'm through the fence and on the base, good luck, see you later at the motel."

Miller added, "I'm on my way back to the motel. Stay safe guys."

∴ ∴ ∴ ∴

Torres continued along the road until he arrived at what he would describe as a typical Texan Ranch house. A large wooden building painted red with white railings and window frames. Constructed with two floors, five windows along the top floor and two either side of the central entrance door on the ground floor. The front had a porch with a swing seat on one side and a set of patio furniture on the other.

Torres noticed several security personnel patrolling the perimeter of the building. He noted three teams of two men walking around the building at regular intervals. He relayed this information to the others before getting out of his car. Looking out from the house towards the base and the surrounding area Torres imagined what the area looked like in the past as a cattle ranch, now spoiled forever.

Ward greeted him at the door and asked for his ID. Torres reached in his jacket, pulled out his badge and showed the guard.

"That's fine," Ward confirmed. "Can I ask why you want to speak to General Winter?"

"And who are you?" Torres demanded.

"I'm Ward. I run General Winter's private security team here on the base."

"You're not a military contractor?" Torres asked.

"The military contractors are separate to General Winter's personal security detail."

"And the guys walking around here with the guns are security contractors."

"Yes. There are others stationed around the base."

"They're heavily armed, is that really necessary?" Torres probed.

"The General takes his security seriously," Ward shared.

"To answer your question, I need to talk to him about some employee matters so can you take me to him?"

"Of course. I'll tell him you're here." Ward guided Torres through the front door into the house and a large entrance hall.

Torres noticed rooms on all sides and in front a large staircase leading to a landing with a balcony and the upstairs rooms.

Ward directed him to the side, "Stay here!" Then walked to a door on the right, knocked, went inside and shut the door behind him. After a few moments the door opened and Ward looked out saying, "Agent Torres, please come in, General Winter will see you now."

∴ ∴ ∴ ∴

Finn flipped down the night vision goggles in front of his eyes. He blinked to allow his eyes time to adjust to the bright green light. He scanned the area in front of him, using the zoom feature on the side to get a clearer view of activity on the base. He noticed the large military cargo plane at the other end of the runway near the aircraft hangers, a C-5 Galaxy. Forklift drivers continued to load crates into the cargo bay while a large group of uniformed men stood nearby, waiting to board.

Moving slowly in a crouched position Finn headed towards the hangers making sure to avoid detection. He looked for cameras, sound detection equipment, infra-red beams and heat signature detectors, the typical security devices used on a military base. He carefully moved along the grass verge of the runway, in the shadow of the runway lights. He hid behind a transformer station for a few moments then ran the last ten feet to the area behind the hangers. He knew anyone standing on the other side in the bright lights would have little chance of spotting him. The darkness provided perfect cover as he checked along the rear of the building. He spotted a maintenance ladder which ran up to the roof and climbed to the top. On the roof he crawled to the edge and looked down onto the rear of the cargo plane.

He discovered four men wearing different uniforms to the other larger group, dressed all in black, like the ones he encountered at the Foresight office. The larger group wore black cargo pants and a beige t-shirt. He identified the men as the military contractors he had seen operating in Afghanistan.

He continued to observe the four men dressed in black, intrigued to know why they were there. He listened as one of the men shouted out orders to a forklift driver, "Not that one dumb ass, I told you that one goes in last."

Finn looked around the rest of the loading area noticing a barracks, a row of containers, a training ground and some helicopters parked on the other side. The barracks building looked empty with just a couple lit windows. He looked again at the containers and spotted a group of armed men wearing all black. *What's so important about those containers that they've had to post special guards?*

Finn looked beyond the containers and spotted a large ranch house further away. *That's where Torres is.*

❖ ❖ ❖ ❖

Ward held open the door while Torres walked past him and into the room. Torres heard the door slam and glanced back to see Ward stood at the door, blocking his exit.

Standing near a desk a grey-haired man in his sixties wearing jeans and a black t-shirt greeted him, "Come in FBI agent Torres. I'm General Winter, how can I help you this fair evening?"

"General Winter, thank you very much for your time. I'd like to ask you about one of your men, a security contractor. He was involved in a vehicle accident. I'm trying to get in touch with his next of kin but don't have the information I require. I'm hoping you can help."

Winter replied with some concern in his voice, "He's dead? I'm sorry to hear that but what makes you think I can help? What's the name of this unfortunate chap?"

Torres took out his notebook and mumbled, "One second..." He looked at the pages, wasting time, "Where's it gone?" He continued to flip the pages then said loudly, "Ah yes...there it is...Troy Ramon."

Torres's performance had the desired effect and he noted the annoyance on Winter's face.

Winter turned to Ward and hissed, "Ward, Troy Ramon. Have you ever heard of him?"

"No. Sir, not that I can remember, Sir."

"It looks like you've had a wasted journey Torres. We don't know this man."

Torres detected the deception in Winter's voice but knew he had to continue to play along with the farce to give Finn enough time to do his work. He decided to bend the truth to see where it led, "I'm surprised you haven't heard of him General, because the vehicle he was driving was registered to this base, and your company."

The comment surprised Winter. *We destroyed all the links to this base, where has this come from?* He processed the data in his head then explained, "We've got lots of vehicles. We sell them at auction when we no longer need them." Winter looked at Ward again and asked, "Have any of our vehicles gone missing or been involved in an accident?"

"No. Sir."

Winter responded to Ward's answer, "Again, I'm not sure I can help you agent, it seems like you've been given some wrong information. I can only assume the vehicle has been sold and not registered properly with the new keeper."

"General, I'm sure what you're saying is correct and this is just some mix up somewhere. To make things easier, and so we can both return to more important things, can I look at your employment records? I'm sure you've got lots of people on the base and you can't be expected to remember every employee, past and present."

"The admin office is closed at this time of day but you still won't find any extra details there. We don't store employee records here. All the ex-military staff have their records classified by the government. A little insurance policy I put in place when they asked me to set this place up. And anyway, what makes you so sure we employed this man?"

Torres noticed Winter becoming increasingly annoyed by the line of questioning and decided to push a little harder, hoping to get a reaction. He looked at his notebook again for a few seconds then stated, "An Iron Fist ID card was found among the items recovered from the vehicle. The name on the ID was Troy Ramon. That confirms his employment to me despite what you're both saying. If I could just get some details of his address or next of kin, I'll get out of your hair."

"Ward, are you sure you haven't heard of this guy? Torres just wants some information then he'll leave us alone to continue our work." Winter turned to Torres, "Correct?"

Ward, unsure of what Winter wanted him to say in reply, took the easy option and announced, "I'll ask some of the guards outside, maybe they remember him."

Ward left the room.

Torres detected his line of interrogation getting under Winter's skin and decided to continue pushing. Winter, feeling agitated by the constant questioning turned to his desk, took out a cigar, lit it and took a large drag. After holding his breath for a few seconds, he blew the smoke towards Torres.

Torres didn't react to the insult. He looked at his notebook for a few seconds then raised his head and asked, "General, how many men are employed by Iron Fist Security?"

"We've got around three hundred military contractors and another hundred support staff based here and around the world. We also have about fifty men who are security contractors. I can't be expected to remember everyone that passes through here."

"Yes, I can understand that General." Torres agreed.

Ward returned, "General, one of the men remembers Ramon. He did work here as a security contractor. We dismissed him and a few others for breaking the rules. Do you remember?"

Winter pretended to be surprised, "Ah...I see. Thank you Ward."

Winter's face changed. Torres detected Ward's comments had put the General in a position he did not want to be in. He looked at Torres, "I'm sorry for the wrong information, it appears Ramon was employed here. If I remember correctly, he was part of a group of men who broke the rules. The usual vices, drink, drugs, women. I couldn't rely on them so I had to let them go."

"When did this happen?" Torres asked.

"Ward, can you remember?"

"It must be over six months ago, Sir." Ward confirmed.

Torres asked Winter, "I'm intrigued to know how much money a military contractor can earn."

"It depends on their rank but they are paid around five hundred dollars a day when they're in the US. That's doubled to a thousand when they're working in a conflict zone."

"Good money, makes you wonder why this Ramon guy would get himself dismissed."

Winter shrugged his shoulders.

"General, I'm sorry to keep asking, all I need is some information on this man, an address or next of kin. Are you sure you don't have some personnel records somewhere on the base which you can show me?"

Torres sensed Winter becoming increasingly agitated by the constant questioning, something the old General was unaccustomed to. Ward noticed the warning signs, experience told him an uncomfortable Winter could result in an unpredictable reaction.

Winter took another drag on his cigar, "Torres, do you think I've got the time to check up on contractors I've had working for me in the past? The only records I ever get to see is their military service record and that's provided by Washington."

"General, no, I don't expect you to know everyone you've employed, past or present. But I do find it difficult to believe you've not got any information available to help me trace Troy Ramon's family. It'll help me a lot, I can contact his family and let them know he's dead."

"Torres, I'll tell you what I'll do for you. Leave all the details with Ward. I'll get in touch with the family personally. I'll also arrange for a funeral and for any money he may be due to be given to his family."

Winter stubbed out his cigar and said aloud, "See mister Torres, I'm a nice man. Isn't that right Ward?"

Ward shouted from behind Torres, "Yes. Sir"

Winter clapped his hands together and said forcefully, "Good! Now that we've sorted that out, I'll let Ward escort you to the main gate."

Winter gestured towards the door, signalling for Torres to leave. Ignoring him, Torres looked at his notebook and after a few moments silence continued with his questions, "General, I've got one more question, something else I hope you can help me with"

With his anger rising Winter replied sarcastically, "Of course. I'm here to help you however I can."

"General, can you tell me anything about a company called Foresight Enterprises?"

"Never heard of it, should I have?" Winter growled.

Torres ignored the tone of the response and continued, "Ramon and his friends were involved in a gunfight yesterday evening at an office owned by Foresight in El Paso. They are also the main suspects in a number of murders and a kidnapping in New Mexico."

"And what has this got to do with me?" Winner said angrily, "Torres I think I've helped you all I can. I'm a busy man and, even though I'd like to, I can't stand around here all day talking to you."

"Foresight is a shell company set up by a guy called Smithson. The FBI financial investigation team at J Edgar have discovered a link between Foresight, Smithson, and Iron Fist Security.

"I've never heard of Foresight or anyone called Smithson." Winter replied, his voice getting louder as his anger increased. He looked at Ward, then Torres.

Torres decided to push his luck further, "I've got a murder and kidnapping case leading to a Foresight office. The men involved in the case had an Iron Fist ID Card. You can see where this is going, General. The guys at HQ are in the process of arranging for Smithson's arrest. They're going to search his offices, account books, and computers. If they find any connection between Foresight, Iron Fist and Ramon and this place then it will have to be shut down for months while it's searched for evidence."

Winter laughed out aloud and hissed, "Really? Come on Torres, please tell me you've something more to go on than groundless allegations and threats."

Looking at his notebook before continuing Torres decided to make a final push, "There's one more important thing to consider General. We found your name written on the floor next to where we discovered DNA traces of the kidnapped woman. That can't be a coincidence can it?"

※ ※ ※ ※

Finn climbed down from the roof, and edged his way along the rear of the hanger, staying in the shadows and constantly looking for surveillance devices. He moved all the way along the building until he came to the corner. He spotted some lined-up trucks, crouched down, and progressed towards them. Once there he took shelter behind one of the large tyres and continued to scan the area for danger.

Both vehicles and men moved around at the rear of the cargo plane at the other end of the hanger. He noticed that all the crates were on board and the military contractors had begun boarding. He watched as they took up seats on either side of the plane with the crates running down the centre. Once on board the four men dressed in black, including the one shouting earlier, boarded, and sat next to the last crate. As the ramp slowly closed, Finn realised it presented an opportunity to get to the other side while the activity distracted the ground crew. While considering his options he could hear Torres speaking to Winter in his earpiece. *That Winter bloke sounds like a real asshole.*

Weaving between the trucks and several large fuel storage tanks he finally arrived at the barracks on the other side. With his back pressed to the wall he crept around to the rear of the building and looked for the shipping containers. *There they are! Is that where they have Kathy held? I need to find out what's inside.*

He noticed four security guards standing in the open area in front of the containers and one container with a slightly open door and a light on inside. Finn looked around, taking time to decide the best route to the containers. He moved into the darkness, used a row of trees as cover and came out at the rear of the last container. Finn could hear the guards talking to each other at the front. The guards blocked any chance of him getting into the containers without detection, to proceed he had to get rid of them.

He removed his pistol from the holster and took a magazine from his pocket with a blue strip paint on the side. Blue signalled the magazine contained tranquiliser darts. He jammed it into the handle and took out a suppressor, slowly winding it onto the barrel of the pistol.

He moved to the rear of the line of containers, staying in the dark and picked up a stone. He threw the stone at the back panel of the open container making a metallic clang.

The security guards looked at each other, one decided to go inside the container while another moved around the side of the container. The guard stood and stared into the darkness. After a few moments he decided to walk towards the rear. When he arrived at the corner, he looked along the back of the containers.

Finn raised the pistol and shot a tranquiliser dart into the neck of the guard. The man slumped forward, dropping his weapon onto the concrete. A loud metallic clang rang out. The two remaining guards looked at each other then ran to the rear of the container to investigate the noise.

Finn, hearing the footsteps approaching, dragged the body away from the back of the container and placed it behind a generator. Looking between a gap in the generator air vents he watched as the two guards came closer.

The guards shone torches into the darkness and spoke to each other. One guard moved away from the generator while the other walked towards it. As he came around the side Finn approached from behind, grabbed him around the neck, pulled him away into the shadows, and choked him until he passed out. Finn dumped the guard next to the first. He stood up to see the last guard scanning around the area with a torch, searching for his colleague. The guard shouted a name and walked towards the generator.

Finn took out his pistol, took aim and placed a tranquiliser dart into the guard's neck. The guard twitched for a moment then fell forward onto the ground.

Finn dragged the body and put it with the others. He glanced at the three prone bodies then scanned the surrounding area with his night vision goggles for danger. *Nothing. That should take care of them for a few hours. Now the last one.*

Finn moved slowly around to the front of the container and heard the last guard walking on the floor inside. Finn decided to deal with him inside the container, avoiding detection by staff moving around on the base.

As Finn moved to the container door, he heard the jet engines on the cargo plane burst into life. He looked around and the plane appeared from behind the barracks building and slowly moved towards the end of the runway. The plane proceeded onto the main runway. The engines gave out a loud roar as C-5 increased speed and lifted off into the night sky. Finn looked at his watch, *21:48*.

Forgetting the plane, he turned to the partially open container door and peeked inside. Finn recognised the converted container layout, a typical interrogation and prison cell configuration commonly used at special forces bases. *This is supposed to be a private facility, they shouldn't have prisoners?*

Opening the door wider Finn noticed the guard standing in the cell section at the other end, facing away from him. Finn slowly crept inside, the shoes of his sneaking suit creating no sound on the floor. He closed the distance between him and the guard to only a few feet.

The guard suddenly turned around, finding a figure in all black standing in front of him. The guard hesitated for a moment, Finn did not. Reacting the quickest, he ran forward and pushed the guard backwards into the small room. The guard fell onto the floor, Finn jumped on top of him, sitting on the man's stomach with his legs holding the man's arms down. Finn landed a series of blows on the man's face breaking his nose and cutting his lip, the final blow dislodged some teeth. Blood ran from the guard's mouth as he spat the loose teeth out onto the floor.

Finn looked around the cell seeing a bucket in the corner, a wooden bed with toiletries and dirty women's clothes. *Kathy! She was here.*

Finn got up off the guard, stood over him and took out the pistol. Pointing it at the guard's head he whispered, "Get up."

Groaning in pain the guard rolled onto his side, then on to all fours before finally standing, uneasily.

Finn shouted, "Follow me!" Then moved backwards into the interrogation room section with the guard following. With his eyes fixed on the guard Finn walked to the front door and pulled it closed, ensuring none of the light escaped outside. He grabbed some ropes hanging from the steel roof and ordered, "Put your hands together."

The guard held out his hands and Finn tied the ropes in a knot around his wrists. Finn pulled on the block and tackle chain and lifted the guard off the floor.

Groaning in pain the guard pleaded, "What are you doing? Who are you? Let me go."

Finn punched the man in the face, "Shut it! I'll ask the questions. Tell me what happened to the woman you kept in this cell."

"I don't know anything," the guard protested.

Finn punched the man in the stomach with a force which would most likely cause internal damage. The guard cried in pain, swinging on his arms from side to side.

"If you don't tell me I'll put a bullet in your head and ask one of the other guards. You decide," Finn warned, and punched him again.

Gasping for air the guard decided to talk, "All I know is a woman was brought onto the base during the night. They put her in here. A guy I spoke to said she was English. Look man, I wasn't on duty when she arrived."

"Where have they taken her?" Finn demanded.

"She's not on the base anymore. She's on the plane which has just taken off."

"Shit!" Finn cursed, "The C-5?"

"Yes."

"I didn't see a prisoner boarding the plane."

"Martinez and three other guards came to get her about an hour ago. They injected her with something and when she passed out, they put her in a crate."

"Where's the plane going?" Finn asked.

"Regular flight taking cargo and soldiers to Afghanistan, Kandahar I think."

"You're saying Winter arranged for her capture and has transported her with Martinez to Afghanistan?"

The guard nodded as blood ran down from his nose and lip onto his chin and down onto the floor. Finn lifted his pistol and aimed it at the guard's head.

In a panic the guard shouted, "Hey man, I told you everything I know. I'm just a guard here, I don't do any dirty work. Winter has a team of about twenty guards which he uses for that stuff. They've some sort of scam going on here at the base but they're the only ones involved in it."

"Who are the main players," Finn asked.

"Winter, Ward and Martinez are the ones in charge."

Finn shot a tranquiliser dart into the guard's neck and he fell silent.

Finn opened the container door, refitted his night vision goggles, and looked outside. Making sure of no nearby activity, he proceeded, shutting the door behind him, and moved around to the side of the container. He decided to report what he had discovered to the others.

Speaking in a whisper, "I've just found the cell where they held Kathy. The guard said they'd drugged her, put her in a crate, then shipped her out on the cargo plane which just took off. It looks like there are four guards with her. It seems like the main military contractors are not involved in whatever Winter is up to. He said the plane is on route to Kandahar. We need to take Winter down now while we can, I'm heading to the ranch house, Torres if you are listening…I'm coming to support you."

Finn looked to the area behind the containers and discovered the distant lights of the ranch house.

∴ ∴ ∴ ∴

Winter studied Torres's face, "Torres, you're starting to get on my nerves. I think you're clueless as to the business I'm running here. I'm trying to make our Country a safer place for everyone. By investigating these unfortunate incidents, you've upset my business, upset my clients, and now you've upset me. The current administration pays me more than nine hundred million dollars a year. They pay the money because my men will do the things that they won't. However, the budgets are under constant review and making a profit is difficult. I've got costs like every business owner and to keep things fluid I need additional income streams. A business like mine involves greasing some palms while stepping on other people's toes. Making enemies goes with the territory. You've now been promoted to my enemy list and my enemies don't stay on that list very long."

Winter moved over to a table with bottles of drink, he poured out a glass of whisky for himself.

He pointed the bottle at Torres and asked, "Would you like a drink?"

Torres shook his head, "No thank you I'm on duty."

"Really?" Winter mused while looking at the label and saying, "This is good stuff, about one hundred dollars a bottle. It's not the cheap rubbish you'd drink at home in Santa Fe."

※ ※ ※ ※

Finn stopped his progress towards the ranch, Winter's words ringing in his ears, and immediately sensed the danger of Torres's situation.

Miller, also listening in on the comms system became indecisive, unsure if he should call Colby, call in the local FBI as backup, or just let the situation play out.

※ ※ ※ ※

Torres moved uneasily and said, "So you've done your homework on me Winter. I think that confirms there's a leak somewhere in the agency."

Winter drank the whisky in one gulp and said, "I've been following your progress for a while, it seems we nearly met in El Paso. Despite what you think I'm not a bad man Torres. How about you just leave this Ramon business to me? I'll make it all go away and to say thank you I'll make a nice deposit into your bank account. What do you think?"

"Not everyone is like you Winter. Some people think personal pride and self-respect is more important than money."

Winter continued, "That's disappointing. Not your refusal to take my offer but that you believe something is more important. Nothing is more important than money. A few years ago, I may have thought like you but thank god I came to my senses. I've spent years getting shot at and cleaning up other people's mess. One day I asked myself, 'what for?' I'd nothing to show for all my troubles while other people had gotten richer. I decided to take advantage of my situation here and get in on the money-making business."

"Does it involve killing innocent women and kidnapping?" Torres snarled.

Winter grinned and said, "Whatever gets the job done. It's not my way of doing things but it is what it is. It'll make all our lives a lot easier if you reconsider my offer."

Torres quickly pulled out his service pistol and shouted, "General you're under arrest for kidnapping and murder. Raise your hands and face the wall."

Winter walked to his desk and put the glass down. He sat back in his chair and looked at Torres then his eyes moved towards Ward. Torres turned quickly to see Ward had also drawn a handgun. Two shots rang out and Torres slumped to the floor.

∴ ∴ ∴ ∴

Finn heard the shots, stopped and spoke quietly, "Miller! Torres is in trouble. Winter is the only one who knows where the plane is going. I'll check on Torres and deal with Winter."

Finn quickly changed the magazine in his pistol to one with red paint, the lethal one, and replaced it in his holster. He swung the HK416 assault rifle from his back and held it at his hip. He knew the suppression would cut any noise while the armour piercing bullets would ensure elimination of the target, quickly. He started across the field making sure to check the positions of the security guards and looking for any additional surveillance equipment.

Hearing the shots, the security guards outside rushed to the front porch as Ward appeared at the door. He told them the General had shot his pistol at a rat, to forget it and get back to work.

Finn watched Ward return inside and the guards resume their rounds. He moved along a fence line, deciding to approach from the side. Studying the guards walking pattern around the building he timed their steps and calculated in his head where each pair would be. The precise formation they were using gave him the advantage of surprise. If he timed it correctly, he could take them out without warning the occupants inside the building.

Finn moved further around the fence and crouched near a bush. He noticed the guards wore bullet proof vests and decided accurate head shots would work best. If the guards became aware of his presence, he would have no cover and become an easy target.

Finn watched the first pair of guards come around the corner knowing the second pair would now be heading around the corner on the other side to the back, while the last pair walked along the front. From his position he would face the guards as each one approached.

Kneeling with his left elbow on his knee and his left hand supporting the barrel of the gun he waited. He heard them approaching, talking, closing in on his position. *Here they come, Now.*

Instantly he fired two shots in quick succession. The first tore into the first guards throat making him spin around spraying blood onto the other guard. Before he could react, a hole appeared in his forehead. The two guards slumped in a pile together at the side of the house.

Finn listened. *Nothing.*

Quickly he ran to the next corner knowing the second pair would now be about half way along the rear of the house, walking towards him. Jumping out Finn caught the guards by surprise. Before they could raise their guns, he cut them down with shots to the head. *Now the final two.*

The final pair of guards were now approaching the far corner. Finn had to move quickly or the guards would see the bodies and raise the alarm. He ran to within ten feet of the corner and took up a kneeling position again. Counting in his head. *5,4,3,2,1.*

As they turned the corner both he shot both men in the head, killing them instantly.

Finn replaced the HK416 on his back and took out the SIG Sauer P320 semi-automatic pistol. He moved around towards the front door of the house and climbed over the rail on to the porch. He crouched down, looked around for any remaining guards then moved towards the door. *There's at least two inside. How many more?*

Finn gripped and slowly turned the doorknob until the door opened, holding the handle so it remained ajar. He peeked inside seeing no one in the immediate vicinity. He opened the door fully and moved inside the entrance hall, shutting the door behind him. Looking around until he heard voices from a room on his right. Moving over to the door he stood and listened.

Winter shouted at Ward, "This is going to cause me a lot of trouble, and cost me a lot of money, if anyone finds him dead on the base. First, you make sure no records exist anywhere of him coming on the base. Clear all the security cameras and pay off the guys on the main gate, they don't work for us anymore. Also, get some of your guys in here to clean up this mess." Winter pointed to where Torres's body lay motionless, slumped on it's the side next to the drinks cabinet, "And get that sack of shit out of my office. Throw it into a lake, chop it up, feed it to pigs, anything. I don't care, just make sure there's nothing left that leads back to me."

"Yes. Sir." Ward declared before heading towards the door.

He pulled the door open and came face to face with Finn. Ward grabbed for his pistol. Finn reacted quicker and shot Ward in the stomach at point-blank range. The bullet lodged into Ward's Kevlar vest and the force knocked him backwards into the room. Finn advanced, Ward raised his head and Finn placed a bullet into his forehead killing him instantly.

Winter watched as Ward fell backwards onto the floor and looked up to see Finn advancing towards him. He fumbled in his desk drawer, trying to grab his gun. By the time he managed to put his hand on the grip Finn was already standing directly in front of him. Winter stopped moving and stared at the pistol aimed at his head.

Finn shouted, "I wouldn't do that General if you want to keep breathing. Put your hands where I can see them, and do it very slowly."

"Who hell are you? You're not an American, where are you from?" Winter demanded whilst placing his hands on the desktop.

"My name is Finn, British Army, SAS."

"SAS!" Winter hissed, "Son, we're part of NATO, on the same team. What is an SAS soldier doing on my base and killing my men?"

"Shut up Winter you piece of shit! I'm in charge here, not you."

Winter looked towards the floor, "You've killed Ward. The man was thick as shit but at least he was loyal."

"Shut it! I want to know what you've done with my sister," Finn demanded, waving the gun in Winter's face.

"How the hell would I know? We don't allow women on the base. It distracts the men and when they're distracted, they're not focused on their jobs. Now really son what's this all about, are you with him?" Winter pointed at Torres' lifeless body.

"You think you're an important person Winter, you're not. My sister is important and the only way you're getting out of here alive is by telling me where she is."

Winter cursed aloud, "I knew this shit would get out of hand. How did you manage to follow her here?"

"You're not answering me Winter. So far, I've killed nine of your men adding an extra one to the list won't make any difference to me. I followed your men from New Mexico to Texas. It looks like I missed you by a few seconds in El Paso but you got sloppy. Kathy left me a message which led me directly to you. Now stand up!"

"A message, what do you mean? And why do you want me to stand up? Look son can't we work things out?" Winter pleaded.

Finn ignored the questions and gestured with the gun for Winter to start moving, reluctantly he got up out of his seat.

"Come around here where I can see you," Finn said.

Winter pushed the chair away, came out from behind the desk and stood at the side in full view. Finn aimed his pistol and shot a single bullet. Winter's knee exploded into bone fragments and he dropped to the floor screaming in pain.

"That's going to hurt." Finn grinned, then demanded, "Tell me what you've done with my sister or I'll shoot the other one."

Rolling on the floor with a pool of blood growing around him, Winter struggled to speak eventually mumbling, "She's gone."

Finn shouted, "Speak up man!"

Winter gathered his strength and snarled, "She's gone asshole! She's on the cargo plane which has taken off."

Finn approached and pressed the hot barrel of the gun into Winter's cheekbone, he screamed in pain and Finn asked, "Where's she going? Why did you kidnap her?"

Winter rubbed his face and shouted, "She's going to Afghanistan...Amir Zafar wants her."

"Don't talk crap he's locked up in an Afghan jail. I put him there."

"True, but Zafar was an asset, key to the expansion of our business so Marshall arranged for his release. That said, I'm with you, I would've let the scumbag rot in jail. It was Zafar who asked for your records, it seems the man doesn't like you. Marshall used his contacts within the military to get hold of your records, interesting reading, I must say. I know all about you Finn...I know you're the person who captured Zafar."

"Zafar asked you to kidnap my sister and you've sent her to him in Afghanistan." Finn aimed his pistol and shot Winter in the other knee making him scream out in agony and calmly asked, "Where's the plane heading?"

Winter rolled in agony, blood now leaking from both knees, he composed himself and spoke through gritted teeth, "The cargo and contractors are scheduled to land at Morocco for refuelling then on to Kandahar."

"When does it arrive at Kandahar?" Finn snarled.

Winter held his shattered legs, trying to stop the blood oozing out onto the carpet, "The flight takes about twenty hours, it's scheduled to arrive at ten-thirty local time."

Finn had the final piece of information he needed. Winter had no value to him anymore, he raised the gun and aimed at Winter's temple. Winters eyes widened as he noticed the determination on Finn's face.

A voice from behind yelled out, "Don't do it Finn! Drop the weapon, he's not worth it buddy."

Finn fixed his eyes on Winter. Slowly he increased the pressure on the trigger.

The voice spoke again, "Come on buddy let it go."

Finn relaxed the trigger and turned to see Miller standing in the doorway with a team of men wearing plain clothes and bullet proof vests. He lowered the pistol and replaced it in the holster, "Where did you all come from?"

Things had moved quickly after Miller heard Winter shoot Torres. He contacted Colby who sent in the team of Paramilitary Operations Officers from the SOG he had secretly assembled locally. The officers secured the main gate by using tranquiliser darts on the security guards, moved quickly through the base, and headed for the ranch house.

Another voice shouted from the entrance hall, "Out of my way, let me through, come on move."

The officers moved to the side and a man in his late fifties with a bald head and glasses pushed his way in. Finn instantly recognised him, *Colby*.

The two men looked at each other. Finn turned away and moved over to the drink's cabinet and kneeled next to Torres's body.

Chapter 16
Akron Airport, Ohio

The white Exec-Air jet touched down at Akron Airport at 00:11. At the end of the runway the pilot followed air traffic control instructions and taxied to ramp seventeen. He reached a row of maintenance and storage hangers and continued along the front of them until he reached the final hanger. He looked through the cockpit window and read Foresight Air written in large letters above the hanger doors. Ground crew guided him to the parking area outside the aircraft hangar and he shut down the engines.

The pilot pressed a button in the cabin and the front door on the jet fuselage opened from the top edge, revealing a set of steps on the other side. The pilot looked through the cockpit window, watched until the stairs fully extended. He switched off the seatbelt sign and moved to the cockpit door, standing to watch his passengers disembark.

Two men wearing white slacks and sports jackets, one in light blue the other in green, descended the stairs to the tarmac. Nervously, they looked around the area ensuring they were alone and unobserved.

The one with the blue jacket said anxiously, "Where the hell is the car? You were supposed to arrange a car.

His green jacketed partner argued, "Of course I arranged a car!" He fumbled in his jacket pocket for his mobile phone, "It should be here."

The sudden appearance of a man and woman running towards them from behind the open hanger doors with guns drawn startled the men.

FBI special agent Gina Reed shouted, "Freeze! FBI, put your hands up."

The men noticed the yellow FBI logo on the blue windcheater jackets and turned to climb up the airplane stairs. The pilot, seeing the danger, ran into the cockpit and closed the plane door, leaving the men trapped outside.

Several police cars appeared and surrounded the plane. The area became flooded with flashing blue and red lights. Police officers got out of the cars with guns drawn and spread out, covering the plane and the two men.

Gina Reed's partner, Martin North shouted at the men, "Get your hands up."

The man with the blue jacket man raised his hands. The other followed then changed his mind and suddenly reached into his jacket, pulling out a handgun. Reed reacted faster and shot the man twice in the stomach. The man stumbled backwards and collapsed onto the ground. A large red stain appeared on the front of his pastel green jacket.

North shouted at the man with the blue jacket, "Don't even think about it."

The man raised his arms fully and asked, "What's this all about?"

"You're to be detained until we've had time to search the plane," North replied.

The police officer handcuffed the man and led him away to a police car. Reed and North directed their attention towards the jet.

Reed walked around to the front and pointed her gun towards the cockpit window. The pilot quickly raised his arms to confirm no weapon.

North banged on the door and yelled, "Come on guys you're surrounded. You're not going anywhere. Get this door open and come out with your hands up."

After a few moments the electric motor on the door reactivated and the stairs reappeared. The two FBI agents stood at the bottom of the staircase and pointed their guns at the opening.

Reed shouted, "Step out one by one, hands up."

A man with brown hair and a beard appeared at the top of the stairs and held his arms up. Seeing no weapons, she shouted, "Get down here and lie on the floor."

The man did as she ordered and a police officer moved over to guard him. A second man appeared, much older, followed by the pilot and the two men joined the first on the floor.

North ran up the stairs and quickly looked inside, turned to Reed and said, "It looks empty."

He then stood guard at the entrance while Reed gestured to the waiting police officers who came over, handcuffing, searching and then escorting the men to separate police cars.

Reed moved over to the dead man's body at the side of the stairs. The green jacket and white pants now covered in blood. She kicked his gun away and knelt beside him, checked for a pulse, and announced, "He's dead."

She searched his pockets and found a money clip with a large bundle of notes. She pulled out a wallet, flipped it open, revealing the man's ID card. In his trouser pocket she found a mobile phone. She took out an evidence bag and stashed the items.

The lead agent, Reed, spoke to the police sergeant in attendance with his men, "Process these guys at the station, don't let them speak to each other. We're going to search the plane for evidence. We need a full forensics unit out here straight away and the Coroner for the body."

She handed over the evidence bag, "Book this in for me." Reed continued, "Start the process of identifying them, I want backgrounds ready when I get to the station, and no one questions them until we get there."

"No problem, I'll ask for a detective to be assigned to support you." The sergeant confirmed and walked away to talk to his men.

Reed climbed the plane stairs to join North, smiling she stashed her gun and said, "Let's see what's on this plane. Dawson mentioned a possible kidnapped woman. She may still be hidden somewhere on board."

Slowly the two agents entered the cabin. The luxury interior contained sixteen seats set out in a staggered pattern, facing forward and back with tables in between. The seats lead all the way down to the rear of the plane with a galley on the left and a toilet door on the right.

North chose to search the cockpit while Reed moved along the inside of the plane heading towards the rear, checking between the seats.

North shouted down to Reed, "There's nothing in here, have you found anything?"

"Nothing in this main section I'll check the toilet and galley. Cover me."

Reed opened the toilet door finding it empty and quickly closed it again. She moved into the galley area and noted a countertop, the usual food preparation equipment, some drinks cabinets and under the counter three inflight meal trolleys. She slowly opened the door on the first trolley and shouted towards the front of the plane, "North, come here I think I've found something."

Reed continued to open all the other food trolley doors. They all contained the same blue bundles. She opened the food storage boxes above the counter revealing more.

North appeared in the doorway and said, "What have you found?"

"My best guess would be drugs of some kind." Reed announced before turning to face North and saying, "Let's photograph everything then we'll unload the bundles on to the table over there."

North nodded, "I'll check the overhead storage bins in the main cabin and go outside to check the cargo bay underneath."

"Good idea." Reed confirmed and added, "It looks like the woman is not here but this is definitely a big bust. The DEA will need to be involved."

North searched the front of the plane and opened the overhead lockers on the left and right, finding more blue bundles. He took photographs of them then placed them on the table. Once he confirmed to himself that he had discovered all the bundles he hurried to the front door of the plane and went outside to search the cargo bay.

Reed finished her photographs and moved the bundles from the galley on to the table with the others and waited for North to return.

North turned the handle on the cargo bay door and opened it wide enough to look in. He pointed his torch into the void only to find it empty, after locking the door he returned to the main cabin. He walked down Reed and announced, "Empty, nothing there. How many bundles are there?"

Reed raised her eyebrows, "I was waiting for you to return before starting. I wanted to be sure we had all of them." She counted the bundles and declared, "That's a total of one hundred and thirty-four bundles. I guess each one is about a kilo in weight. For the record, take pictures while I open this one."

Using a small penknife Reed made a small slit in the top of one of the bundles. She pushed the flat blade inside and pulled out a small amount of brown powder.

"It looks like brown heroin, not fully refined yet but this is still going to be a big haul. If my math's are right a hundred and thirty-four kilos will have a street value of anything up to twenty million dollars."

North grinned and said excitedly, "That's going to hit someone in the pocket. The traffickers are looking at spending a long time in prison."

Reed took a moment to think and said, "We'll stay here until the body has been collected by the Coroner and the forensics team have secured the plane. Then we'll head to the police station. We need to get a team started collecting data on the plane, where it's been, the flight logs and maintenance records, then we'll interrogate the prisoners. First, I need to call the DEA and report the drugs."

North nodded in agreement.

∴ ∴ ∴ ∴

Reed and North arrived at the Akron police station and checked in with the desk sergeant.

"So where are we with identifying the prisoners," Reed asked.

The sergeant replied, "I've taken down all of their details and we're currently searching for them up on the central police database. We suspect they've given us false ID's so we've taken fingerprints and DNA samples. We are hoping to get an answer soon on the fingerprints, the DNA results will take a lot longer."

"Thanks." Reed said, "So what's your opinion?"

The sergeant said sternly, "My opinion doesn't matter. All I know is that I've got a Cuban, two Americans and a Canadian…who claims to be a pilot, taking up space in my holding cells. What charges do you want me to put on the arrest forms?"

Reed replied, "There'll be a long list of charges for these guys. You can start with drug trafficking, resisting arrest and carrying concealed weapons. We may be adding kidnapping and murder. First, we'll interview them, can you get the pilot and the Cuban brought up to the interview rooms for us?"

The sergeant nodded, "Of course."

Reed turned to North and ordered, "You can interview the pilot and I'll speak to our Cuban friend?"

After spending thirty minutes interviewing the two suspects Reed and North met up in the main office to discuss the progress.

"What did you find out from the pilot?" Reed asked.

"He says he's only contracted to fly the plane. He did confirm however that he makes regular return flights from Lubbock to Akron, Miami, and Los Angeles. He said it's normally the same four passengers. Claims he knows nothing about what they do when they get to the destination. They never talk to him other than to give him instructions on the destination. They oversee any passengers and the loading of cargo. All he does is sit in the cockpit and wait till their ready." North shrugged his shoulders and added, "I think he's telling the truth. I'd be surprised if he's in on the drug trafficking."

"Agreed!" Reed confirmed. "Get his full statement typed up and signed off. I guess the DEA will want to speak to him about the flight history."

North nodded, "I'll get it done straight away. What did you learn from your guy?"

Reed shrugged her shoulders and said, "He's admitted he's a Cuban but apart from that he's not talking. My gut feeling is that he's just the hired muscle. Probably sent with the goods to make sure they arrive and to transfer the cash. Let's see what the fingerprint guys come back with before we speak to him again."

"That's if he's in the police database. A lot of the Cuban drug guys are ghosts, totally off the grid with no ID or traceable history." North said dismissively, "What about the two Americans are we going to talk to them now?"

"Let's look them up first, if their American surely we can find them on the database."

Reed walked over to desk and sat down at a PC. North followed and stood behind her. She logged on, typed in the details and waited for the information to display on the screen, she pointed at the data and read it out aloud, "The younger guy is called Douglas Brent, thirty to thirty-five years old but no significant information in the system. The older guy is Dave Ford, mid to late fifties, again no information in the system. Apart from the pilot, the Cubans and Americans look like they're career criminals. Must be false ID's. I'll be very surprised if none of them have police records. We'll have to hope the fingerprints are on the database and confirm who they really are. Let's make them wait until we get the results back."

"Good idea. We'll let them sweat in their cells." North said, rubbing his stomach, "I'm starving, I've not eaten since breakfast. Before we speak to them, I'm getting some food. What do you fancy eating, burgers?"

"Damn right!" Reed approved.

The two agents left the station, called in at their favourite burger joint and ate. They returned to the police station an hour later with a renewed energy, ready to interview the American suspects.

Arriving at the station they walked past the desk sergeant and stood at the access door.

"Buzz us through." Reed demanded, pushing her shoulder against the door.

The sergeant looked at her, "The fingerprint results have arrived."

He pressed the door lock button. The office door sprung open and the two agents rushed inside to where a local detective sat waiting.

Seeing the agents walk in, the detective waved a piece of paper at them and shouted, "We've found your guys."

Reed and North moved over to his desk and Reed said, "Tell us what you've discovered."

The detective read the details from the papers on his desk out aloud, "Cuban number one, the guy you killed, is called Rafael Gonzalez. Cuban number two, the guy downstairs, is Alberto Garcia. A nasty pair of dudes with lifetime criminal records. They're both wanted on murder and drugs trafficking charges in the US and in Columbia. The DEA have records on them but they've never been caught. It seems they've got nine lives, or a guardian angel. Every time they've been close to capture, they seem to escape."

The detective smiled, leaned back in his chair, and turned to face the two agents before continuing, "You'll both get a commendation for this one. I suppose their luck finally ran out when Dawson tipped you off about the plane and I guess Rafael didn't fancy a life in prison."

The detective stopped talking and thought for a minute. Reed and North looked at each other, then the detective.

An impatient Reed said, "So! Is there anymore?"

The detective turned his chair towards the desk and typed into his PC, pointing at the screen he started reading the text out aloud, "The report on the DEA system says they've got connections to a drug cartel, operating out of Florida, suspected of being responsible for distribution of drugs across the whole of the US. Until recently, responsible for bringing in large quantities of cocaine from Columbia. Latest reports say the government clamp down on drug harvesting put them out of business. Judging by what you've just discovered in the plane they've obviously found a supplier of opium-based products instead."

Reed took the papers from the detective and skim read the details, confirming what the detective had reported. She put them on the desk and asked, "What about the others?"

"The Canadian pilot has no criminal record. I guess he's just got mixed up with the wrong friends."

North spoke up, "He's still going to spend the next few years in prison."

"And the Americans?" Reed asked.

"The younger guy, Brent is ex Special Forces, looks like he did a few tours in Afghanistan, then he seems to have disappeared off the system. The other guy, Ford, he's ex-DEA. He left them under a cloud a few years ago. The personnel file says he was involved in a drug bust, the capture of a big cocaine shipment from Columbia. After booking the cocaine into evidence, the drugs somehow disappeared from the DEA lockup. Someone suspected that Ford was involved but what I can't understand is how quickly they closed the case, no arrests, or convictions. Fords was just pushed out of the door instead."

The detective handed the remaining papers to Reed who once again quickly read them and put them down. She turned to North saying, "Right I'm ready to talk to this Ford character. Get him brought up to the interrogation room."

North thought for a moment. Reed recognised the puzzled look on his face.

"Why Ford?" he asked.

"Brent was probably on the plane to protect Ford," Reed reasoned. "Ford is obviously the brains of the operation. He's most likely the one who'll tell us what we need to know."

North shook his head, grinned, and said, "That's why you're the lead agent. I'll go and get him."

The two agents entered the interview room and acknowledged Ford who had handcuffs looped around a steel bar fixed to the desk in front of him. Another set chained his ankles to a metal ring on the floor.

Sitting in front of him, North started the tape recorder while Reed read the arrest documents. Between sheets she glanced at the prisoner then continued to read. Ford moved uneasily in the chair while North stared at him intensely.

Reed placed the papers face down on the desk in front of her. She studied Ford and watched as beads of sweat ran down his face.

"Ford, I'm FBI special agent Reed, this is special agent North. The evidence we've found on the plane tells me you're currently facing a long time in prison. We've caught you trafficking over twenty million dollars' worth of heroin. That's a Federal offence, as an ex-DEA agent you already know that. I can't see you getting out of prison alive, I mean, based on your age, it's unlikely. You'll be a very old man in forty years." She paused and stared at him for a moment, studying his reaction to her words, "That's if you last that long, your drug dealing friends will be very upset at losing all that product."

She stopped and read some more before asking, "We know the plane took off from a private security base in Lubbock. Do you work for Iron Fist Security?"

"I don't know anything about drugs." Ford mumbled, "I'm just a businessman. I had a meeting with General Winter and he offered to give my driver and myself a free flight to Akron. I don't know the other passengers. I've never met them before."

Reed laughed aloud, "Really? A businessman? Do you take me for a fool? You're ex-DEA. We've just caught you on a plane with two Cuban hitmen wanted for multiple murders and drug trafficking. It also seems you lost your job at the DEA after a shipment of drugs went missing. And you sit there and say you know nothing about any drugs." She leaned forward and yelled, "Your career has been all about drugs! Now stop talking shit and tell me what I need to know! How did drugs end up on the plane? Where were you taking them?"

Ford ignored her rant and questions, choosing instead to stare at her with a blank expression on his sweaty face.

Reed banged the table with her palms and shouted in his face, "Answer me!"

"Like I said, I don't know anything," the blank expression on his face remained unchanged.

"That's not what Brent's told us, and the pilot said he flies your fat arse all over the US with your Cuban buddies. So cut the crap and start telling me what I need to know. I'll ask you again, how did drugs end up on that plane? What were you and the Cubans doing at the Iron Fist base?"

Ford continued to ignore her questions and mumbled, "Brent wouldn't talk to the law. He's trained to keep his mouth shut during interrogation."

Reed leaned back in her chair and grinned, "He's not in the forces anymore and when you're facing forty years locked up cutting a deal and talking is the only sensible choice. If he's ready to do a deal then you might want to consider doing the same. We can offer you some protection in return and possibly a shorter sentence. Are you interested?"

Ford shook his head from side to side, beads of sweat rolled off onto the table, "No! Never! No deals." Fear and desperation became evident in his voice, "If I talk, I'll be killed, it's that simple. You're fooling yourself if you think those Cuban thugs are pulling the strings."

Reed, seeing a crack starting to appear, leaned forward and urged, pushing for information, "Go on, tell me what you mean?"

Ford smirked and said mockingly, the pitch of his voice slightly raised, "You think you're in charge? You think you're the law? Who do you think arranged all of this? Who do you think has the power to put it all together? Some Cubans?" He laughed nervously, then stared at the FBI agents.

Reed ignored his questions and locked eyes with him for a few seconds, "Why did you steal the drugs out of the evidence lockup? It had a considerable street value. Why did the DEA decide not to charge you with the theft? I can't understand it, how did you get let off so easily?"

Ford smirked again then mumbled, "The drugs never went missing. The word missing suggests no one knew where they were. The drugs were moved, the whole thing was set up by Mars…" He stopped himself and a look of fear covered his face.

"Sorry! What did you say?" Reed asked.

Ford ignored her and looked down nervously at his hands mumbling words to himself under his breath.

Reed leaned back in her chair and looked at North who leaned forward and took over the interrogation, "Look buddy if you don't want to spend the rest of your miserable life in prison then you need to start talking. If we do a deal with Brent first, we won't need your help so you can go and rot in a cell. It's up to you."

"Brent knows nothing, he's just one of Winter's security contractors assigned to watch over me."

"We'll give you some time to think about our offer." Reed stood up, gestured to North and the two agents left the interview room, returning to the main office.

North grabbed two cups of coffee and they sat together at a desk.

"What do we do now?" North asked Reed.

"We've got to report to Dawson and let him know the woman was not on the plane. We also need to tell him about the drug shipment. There's a lot of unanswered questions and the waters are getting muddier the deeper we dig. Drugs on a military base...ex-DEA agents travelling with Cubans...we don't know where this is heading."

She drank some coffee and thought for a while before continuing, "Something is nagging me. The DEA has the Cubans on a wanted list but they've never caught them. Ford is ex-DEA and is involved in a drug bust where the evidence disappears. He's also not charged with anything. Instead, he leaves the agency, goes off the grid and reappears with the Cubans. It doesn't make any sense."

After another thoughtful minute she said, "Let's make Ford sweat while I make some calls. He's ready to crack. I'm confident he'll start singing soon. By the way did you catch the name he said earlier?"

North shook his head, "No! It tailed off, all I heard was Mars...Do you think that's the name of his boss...Mars?"

∴ ∴ ∴ ∴

"Hello Dawson, it's Reed, Ohio FBI. I'm calling with an update on securing the plane."

"How did it go?" Dawson asked.

"We discovered five people on board. A Canadian pilot, two Cubans and two Americans. One Cuban died at the scene resisting arrest, the others are under arrest at the local police station...."

Dawson interrupted her, "Did you search the plane?"

"I was just coming to that. When we searched the plane, we found no evidence of a woman. However, we did find..." Reed paused waiting for Dawson to interrupt again.

"Go on, what did you find?" Dawson said excitedly.

"A considerable amount of opium, refined into brown heroin. We estimate the street value to be over twenty million dollars."

"Wow, that's going to hurt someone."

Reed continued with her report, "We're in the middle of a drug epidemic up here so it makes sense that they'd ship the goods where they are needed most. One of the Americans is an Iron Fist security contractor, the other is an ex-DEA agent called Ford. Something doesn't add up. Why is a plane leaving a military base full of drugs? There seems to be some strange connection between Iron Fist, the DEA, and Cuban drug dealers wanted for murder and drug trafficking. We don't have a clue how this all fits together. We're in the process of interviewing the men to see what we can dig up."

"Have you called the DEA about the drugs?" Dawson asked.

"Yes, my partner called in the drugs haul to the DEA as soon as we seized it. They're sending some agents to check out the plane." Reed confirmed.

"Where is the plane and what have you done with the drugs?" Dawson enquired.

Reed responded, "The plane is impounded at the airport with a security detail. The forensics guys are examining it. A security team is shipping the drugs from the airport to the evidence store here. That's all I've got for now."

"Thanks Reed." Dawson replied with a concerned tone in his voice, "Things have moved on down here and the team in Texas are finding out things are not as legit as they should be at Iron Fist. Keep the information to yourself for now, and be careful. Keep me informed if there are any developments. Bye for now."

Chapter 17
DEA

The rain at Akron airport forced the forensics team to move the jet to the dry Foresight Air hanger. Once the security team collected the drugs, they began the task of searching the plane for evidence.

Two police cars parked outside the hanger doors to stop anyone getting close to the plane. A silver car drove up alongside one of the police cars so the two drivers' windows were opposite each other. The driver of the silver car wound his window down and gestured to the police officer to do the same.

The police officer wound down his window and spotted three men in the silver car, two in the front and one in the rear, "You're not allowed to be here, you need to leave the area immediately."

The driver of the silver car held up a badge, "Chavez, DEA," and demanded, "we need to see the plane."

The police officer read the badge and replied, "Not a chance the forensics team are still working on it."

Chavez responded angrily, "And the drugs? Are they still onboard?"

"Collected ten minutes ago by a security van. They are on the way to the Akron police evidence lockup."

"Damn it!" Chavez cursed. He turned and spoke to the passengers in the car before turning to the police officer, "Which security company?"

"VAULT. They have silver and black trucks. You must've passed the van on your way in."

The driver of the silver car wound up the window, the car quickly turned around and headed back the way it came.

∴ ∴ ∴ ∴

At the police station two men approached the reception desk, showed their badges, and announced, "Turner and Young, DEA. We need to see FBI agent Reed urgently."

The desk sergeant told the men to wait in the reception and called Reed. She came to the reception and the two DEA agents introduced themselves.

Turner said, "The men you arrested from the plane need to be handed over to us. We've got a van outside."

Reed laughed, "No chance, these guys are suspected of murder, kidnapping and drug trafficking. You're not taking them anywhere until I've interviewed them."

"You don't understand," Turner protested, "this has come from the top, we need to take them straight away."

"Sorry guys you'll have to speak to Dawson at FBI HQ. We're holding them as part of a joint task force investigation run by the NCS. If I'm sent some official paperwork confirming we've got to release them then you can have them. Until that happens, they stay here."

"You're making a mistake, and also a lot of trouble for yourself Reed." Turner threatened.

Reed grinned, walked to the door and said dismissively, "I'm used to trouble." Before disappearing into the office.

The desk sergeant laughed to himself and put his head down. The two DEA agents looking at each other bemused.

Turner cursed, "Shit! Come on let's get out of here."

They left the station and returned to their van. Young started the engine and drove out of the police station car park.

Turner spoke first, "A damn job's worth! That's all we need. What do we do now?"

"The shit's going to hit the fan if we return empty handed and those guys start talking to the Feds. Get on the phone to Marshall," Young demanded.

"Shouldn't we wait till we hear from Chavez? If he manages to get the drugs then they'll have no evidence to work with and they'll be forced to release the prisoners."

Young sighed and said, "Okay, let's park up and wait for half an hour to see what happens with Chavez."

∴ ∴ ∴ ∴

Taking a direct route to the police station the driver and guard sat in the front seats of the VAULT security van while sheets of rain hit the widescreen. The driver maintained a steady speed in the difficult driving conditions. The blue and red flashing lights in his rear-view mirror broke his concentration.

"Who do you think that is?" the driver asked.

The guard woke from his nap, "What?"

"Look behind," the driver demanded, "is that a police car? What do we do?"

"You know the rules. We're not allowed to stop for anyone unless we get instructions over the radio."

The car came up to the rear of the security truck and the siren began to sound. The security truck driver continued to ignore the car behind while concentrating on the road in front.

Chavez shouted aloud to his passengers, "I don't believe it! They're not stopping."

In desperation Chavez pulled the silver car into the middle of the road and pulled up alongside the security truck. The front seat passenger wound the window down. The security truck driver looked out to see the car and the passenger gesturing to pull over.

The driver ignored the hand signals and said to the guard, "Get on the radio. Find out if they know what it's about."

The guard picked up the radio handset and called the security company, "VS214. We've an unidentified car trying to stop us. Have you sent anyone?"

A voice came over the truck speakers, "VS214. No change to your existing orders. Do you need assistance?"

The guard didn't get a chance to respond. Looking out of the windscreen he watched the silver car overtake the truck, pull in front, and suddenly brake.

The truck driver noticed the brake lights but decided to continue regardless. He floored the accelerator and the truck ran into the rear of the silver car, the large steel bumper on the front of the truck shattered the car's plastic bumper.

The impact threw the guard forward, retained by his seatbelt but dropping the handset into the footwell.

The impact caused the silver car to weave on the road as Chavez lost control. The rear window shattered as someone on the back seat began shooting an assault rifle at the security truck. Bullets sprayed across the windscreen of the truck causing small white marks to appear on the glass.

The driver reacted instinctively by swerving the truck out into the middle of the road. He floored the accelerator and moved along the side of the car. Bullets hit the guard's door window which forced him duck below the dashboard. Headlights appeared on the road in front and the security van driver swerved the truck back into the correct lane, slamming into the rear wing of the car.

The force of the blow from the truck rotated the silver car across the front of the truck. The driver looked and saw Chavez's panicked face staring back at him. A grin appeared on the driver's face as he floored the accelerator again forcing the stricken car off the side of the road.

Both the truck driver and guard instinctively glanced into their rear-view mirrors only to see the car hit a tree and burst into a ball of flame.

"Who the hell were they?" the guard ragged.

"How the hell would I know?" the driver shouted back. "One thing is for certain if they were police officers, they wouldn't have shot at us. That bullet proof windscreen saved our lives. Get on the radio and call it in."

The guard picked up the broken handset from the floor and announced, "Radio's bust."

❖ ❖ ❖ ❖

Turner and Young sitting in their van observed the traffic on the road and ignored each other. The thirty minutes came and went before Young said, "Turner, it's time for you to call Chavez."

Turner, reluctantly, pulled out his mobile and called, after a few moments he hung up and called again. He turned to Young with a worried look on his face, "No answer. All I get is a damn answering machine!"

Young cursed, "Shit! There's no alternative, you need to call Marshall."

Turner nervously dialled the number.

"What the fuck are you calling me for?" Marshall raged. "Have you got the drugs and the men?"

"We can't get hold of Chavez. He should've been in contact by now. Somethings gone wrong."

"Shit!" Marshall snarled, "What about the men on the plane?"

"They're locked up at the local police station. The FBI agents won't let us see them without proper authorisation. Something about a joint task force taking over the investigation and we need to speak to someone called Dawson at J Edgar."

"Turner, you asshole!" Marshall shouted, "Unless we get the drugs back and stop those idiots talking, we'll all be sent down for a long time."

Young started the van and shouted, "Turner, look it's the security van."

"Sir, we can see the van they're minutes from the station, what do you want us to do?" Turner asked into the phone.

"Stop it anyway you can and get those men out of the station. I'll find out what I can about this task force and Dawson character. Don't contact me until you've got good news."

∴ ∴ ∴ ∴

Marshall called Winter at his office and got his secretary, "General Winter's office."

Marshall bellowed, "Get the General on the phone straightaway."

"Can I ask who is calling?"

"It's Marshall!"

"I'm sorry sir but he's currently unavailable. Would you like to leave a message?"

"Stop pissing me about and get Winter on the phone. Drag him out of his bed if you must. It's urgent!"

"I'm sorry sir but he's currently off the base."

"Off the base? Shit!" The line suddenly went dead.

∴ ∴ ∴ ∴

Young accelerated the van down the road behind the security truck, following it into the police station car park. The two men watched as the security truck stopped, turned and reversed down a ramp towards the roller door of an underground car park.

Turner proposed, "At this time of the night there'll only be skeleton staff in the station. If we hit them now, we might just pull it off."

Young parked the van in the main car park, "Too right, this is the only chance we'll get. They won't expect anything to happen here on their patch."

The two men watched as the guard climbed out of the truck and swiped a card along a reader next to the door. The roller shutter opened slowly. The guard waited impatiently then ducked under and disappeared inside.

"Let's Go!" Turner hissed.

The DEA agents climbed out of their van and ran down the ramp along the passenger side of the security truck. The driver, busy looking in the side mirror, couldn't see the two men on the other side. The guard banged on the rear panel to signal the roller door had cleared the roof of the truck and the driver reversed inside. The two men followed the truck's progress, walking, unseen, and alongside. Once inside, the roller door automatically closed and the driver pressed the override button, unlocking the rear doors. On hearing the deadbolts disengage the guard opened the doors.

Turner appeared from the side and grabbed the guard around the neck with one hand over his mouth. Young heard the driver get out, waited until he appeared and did the same.

Turner pulled the swipe card from the lanyard around the guard's neck and they bundled the two security guards into the back of the truck. Young slammed the doors, ran to the front, and locked the deadbolts. Turner looked around the garage area making sure they were alone.

Young reappeared and Turner pointed to the rear corner of the ceiling, "There's a camera up there but let's hope at this time of night no one's watching."

Young said under his breath, "Forget it, we'll know soon enough, there's the door, we need to get moving."

Turner swiped the security card and the door to the basement of the police station sprung open. Peeking inside he noticed a corridor with doors on both sides leading towards another corridor, "If we are lucky the detention cells will be down here somewhere, they normally are."

The two men entered the building with their silenced guns drawn, making sure to leave the entry door slightly open.

Turner whispered, "I'll check the door on the left, you do the right."

They edged along the corridor, discovering nothing in the rooms until they reached the intersection at the end.

Turner glanced to his left and spotted a set of stairs leading upwards. Looking right he noticed a row of ten metal doors. Pointing to his right he whispered, "There they are. You guard the staircase and I'll check the cells."

As instructed, Young took up a position guarding the bottom of the stairs. Turner walked along the cell doors. He opened the viewing hatch on the first cell. Finding it empty he moved to the next. Again nothing.

An alarm sounded in the police station office.

Reed turned to the local detective and asked, "What the hell is that sound?"

"I'm not sure, a warning of some kind, they're shown on the security panel over there. I'll check it." He ran over and shouted back to her, "It's indicating someone has left the access door into the garage open."

Reed stood up, sensing danger, "Is the garage access downstairs?"

A penny dropped with the detective and he yelled, "The cells!"

Reed, North and the detective drew their weapons and ran across the office to a staircase leading down to the cells.

The detective moved to go down, Reed pulled him back, "We'll go. Get on the phone and arrange some backup. Then get your arse outside to the outer door and stop them escaping."

She edged her way slowly down the stairs with her back pressed hard against the wall. North followed closely behind.

Turner opened the third hatch and discovered a person laid on a bench in front with a face he immediately recognised, unable to contain himself he smiled. *Garcia*.

Garcia, hearing a noise at the door, opened his eyes. Seeing the grinning face looking back at him he climbed from the bench as Turner pushed the barrel of the pistol through the hatch. Two shots hit the Cuban in the chest and stomach killing him instantly.

Young, heard the puff of the silencer and looked towards Turner who gave him a thumbs up sign.

Turner moved to the next hatch, *Brent*. Seeing the man asleep on the bench he shot three times into his body and waited. Seeing no movement, he continued to the next cell.

Reed stopped on the stairs and stooped down looking along the corridor and spotted a pair of shoes. She stooped lower seeing legs, then a man, guarding the stairs. Unseen in the darkness above she raised her hand and made a sign to North to indicate the danger. She continued to move out of the shadows for a clearer view seeing a second man shooting a pistol into a cell. Instinctively she rushed forward with her gun held up high, shouting, "FBI! Drop your weapons!"

Startled, Young turned and shot wildly in the direction of the shouting. Bullets hit the wall alongside Reed's head and she quickly moved back up the stairs to safety.

Young shouted to Turner, "We are blown! It's time to get the hell out of here."

Turner cursed as he pulled open the next cell hatch, "Not until we get Ford."

"Leave it! We'll take the truck with the shipment instead." He continued to shoot at the stairs until a loud click signalled an empty magazine in the pistol. With no more bullets he ran towards the garage door, leaving Turner behind.

Reed, also hearing the click, descended the stairs and found Turner with his gun at the hatch, "Freeze! Drop the gun!"

Turner ignored her. The excitement of the kill had overtaken his sense of self preservation.

She noticed his finger at the trigger and shot twice, hitting him on the side. As he fell, he squeezed the trigger and shot once into the cell. Seeing Turner fall to the floor she moved to the corridor leading to the garage. Behind her, North advanced, gun drawn and pointed at Turner's lifeless body.

She pulled open the inner garage door and discovered Young pulling at the handle on the driver's side door of the truck. "Freeze! Drop the gun!" Young froze, considering his options. "Forget it. You won't get out alive, there are more police outside."

Young dropped the pistol.

Reed moved forward, the gun pointed at Young's head, "Kneel down, put your hands on your head."

Young did as she instructed.

Reed handcuffed his hands behind his back before kicking him face forward to the garage floor. The detective, who had opened the shutter door from outside appeared and she shouted, "Guard him", before running to the cells.

She discovered North standing over Turner's body and asked, "Is he dead?"

North nodded.

"And what about inside the cells?"

"I don't have the keys for the cells but by the look of it both Garcia and Brent are dead. Ford is in there sobbing like a baby. I think he's ready to start talking," He smiled and added, "Strange how the threat of execution focuses the mind."

Chapter 18
Iron Fist Base

The taskforce operator turned to her partner, "That was a call for Winter, a man called Marshall...start a trace."

"I'm on it." The technician looked at his PC and ran the software, "An encrypted satellite phone, I'll trace the signal." After a few more moments he said excitedly, "Got it! Kandahar. Afghanistan"

Puzzled, the operator repeated the words, "Afghanistan? What the...We need to inform Miller."

∴ ∴ ∴ ∴

Finn looked at Miller and asked, "What are the plans now?"

"Well, we need to get this base locked down and find out what's really going on here. Colby is speaking to the National Security Advisor at Washington as he'll want to take over things down here."

"I don't mean this place, I meant what do we do now to find Kathy."

"Ah, yes! Don't worry. Colby has organised a plane to take us to Afghanistan. We are flying out from here as soon as it lands and has been refuelled." He looked at his watch, "They've got a four-hour head start on us. The C-5 Galaxy they're using will need to refuel, no doubt at a private airfield in the Moroccan desert. We're going to use a converted Gulfstream G650ER. It has a top speed and maximum range more than the C-5 Galaxy. We'll be able to get there without stopping. It'll be close but we should land in Kandahar at roughly the same time."

Miller looked intensely at Finn, tapped the desk and asked the question eating away at him, "What can you tell me about Amir Zafar? I asked Dawson to look him up on the inter-agency system and it seems the DEA have classified any files related to him. We need a person with the highest security clearance to let us in, and we don't have the time. I also heard you tell Winter that you captured Zafar, what's the history between you two?"

"Zafar is evil, an animal. A fanatic in every sense of the word but not in a religious way. He worships power and money. He's a tribal lord ruling his territory by fear and intimidation. The people who live there do as he says, the alternative is torture and murder." Finn stopped, stood up and walked over to the window, "He's the last person I want anywhere near my sister. What I can't understand is how he's managed to get out of prison. It took a lot of hard work to capture him, some of my best men were killed in the process."

He turned and faced Miller, with a look of determination in his eyes, "The Afghans wouldn't have released him unless an American agreed to it. The deal was he stayed there, in an Afghan prison, to avoid an uprising. I wanted him extradited. Who's got the authority over here to arrange for his release?"

Miller shook his head, "I don't have a clue buddy, but it'll be a senior person. Tell me how you managed to capture him."

Finn moved to the desk and sat down, "I'll tell you all about it once we're on the plane. Where's the damn plane? I just want to get moving, every minute we waste here she's getting further away,"

Miller sensed the urgency in Finn's voice, "Cool it buddy, it's on the way. Colby must get top-level clearance for what they're planning. He also needs to speak to people in both London and Kandahar. We need everyone on board."

"What about leaks?" Finn asked, "We don't know how far this web stretches. It only takes one person who's involved to find out we seized the small jet then get in touch with the cargo plane and warn them. They may ditch her rather than risk us finding her when they land. They're due to stop for fuel in Morocco, they may dump her there."

"Let's not worry about that just yet. There's been no information posted about Winter's arrest. As far as the workers here are concerned nothing has changed, most were off site when we arrested him. Apart from Winter it looks like only a few other men from his personal security team are involved in his drug dealing activities. The other suspects are locked up and Winter is in a secure medical facility. As far as we know there's only the four security guards left on the plane with Kathy to worry about."

Miller pulled out a cigarette, lit it and continued, "The plane passengers are also locked up and are not allowed to contact anyone. Only the people in the task force know what's really going on. That's Colby, the two of us, the agents at Akron, Dawson, the Paramilitary Operations Officers you met in Winter's office and some Specialized

Skills Officers. There shouldn't be any leaks to worry about. We're hoping to get an update from the FBI agents at Akron soon, but it sounds like we'll not get their full report until we're on the plane."

There was a knock, the door opened and the taskforce operator appeared at the door, "Sir, we've just had a call for Winter, someone called Marshall, he was agitated, and needed to speak to him urgently. We did a trace and the call originated in Afghanistan."

"Afghanistan!" Miller stood up and moved towards the doorway, "Did this Marshall person say why he wanted Winter? And where in Afghanistan?"

"The guy was too angry, he just hung up. We traced the call to the Kandahar area. The technician is currently trying to get a closer fix on the location. Dawson also has the details. We're hoping he can help us find who Marshall is."

Miller turned to Finn, noticed the worried look on his face and said, "It could be nothing, it may be one of Winter's drug contacts calling. Let's just focus on what we know and need to do."

He turned to the operator, "Any news on this damn plane landing?"

"That's the other reason I came to see you. It's just landed, we're starting to load our gear."

"Okay, thanks. See you onboard."

As Finn arrived at the hangar, he discovered a sleek, twin engine jet sitting on the tarmac with a refuelling tanker alongside and Colby's staff loading boxes into the cargo bay. He recognised the executive jet painted in the same colour as the helicopter Cooney had flown.

Miller noticed the curious look on Finn's face and announced, "Welcome to the National Clandestine Service. Colby sure has some nice equipment available to him. That's a ninety-million-dollar aircraft, crammed full of technology."

Finn watched as the pilot, dressed in a US Air Force uniform, appeared at the rear of the plane and began shouting at the men loading the cargo, "Guys! Dump the gear, only essential items remember. We need to save as much weight as possible if we're going to get to Kandahar in one hop. Who's in charge?"

The men looked over and pointed towards Miller and Finn. The pilot ran over, looked closely at the two men, and asked, "Where's the party guys?"

Miller, dressed in jeans and Hawaiian shirt over a t-shirt. Finn, also in jeans, t-shirt and torn leather jacket looked at each other, then to the pilot. Not getting a reaction to his question the pilot reached out a hand towards Finn, "Langford, I've got orders to get this plane to Kandahar. Are you in charge?"

Finn shook the pilot's hand and said, "I'm Finn. This is Miller, he's the one in charge."

The pilot finished shaking Finn's hand and reached out for Miller's, "Sorry! I'm still getting used to working with you undercover guys."

Miller took his hand and introduced himself before the pilot continued, "I've checked all the calculations and I'll have enough fuel to get us there in one go but it means I can only take seven passengers. One of your guys is already on board, so that's you two and four more. You'll also need to ditch most of the gear you're planning to bring. We're not going to Acapulco, it's essential items only on this trip, a toothbrush and change of underpants, anything else and we won't make it there without a fuel stop."

Finn interrupted, "We don't need gear Miller, your guys at Bagram and mine in Helmand have what we need to get Zafar."

Miller walked towards the guys loading the plane and after a short discussion they reluctantly began unloading the gear.

"When can we leave?" Finn asked the pilot.

"Now, if you're ready."

Miller selected two paramilitary officers and two special skills officers to join him on the plane then told the rest to stay at the base.

Finn walked over to him, "The pilot says we can leave once everyone's on board."

The pilot checked with air traffic, logged his flight plan, and moved the Gulfstream to the end of the runway. After a short wait a message came over his headset with clearance and he pushed the throttles forward. The Gulfstream accelerated to take-off speed, lifted off the tarmac and climbed to a cruise height of forty-nine thousand feet.

Chapter 19
Akron Police Station

Reed, sitting at a desk in the detective's office of the Akron police station, turned to North and asked, "So, what do we know?"

"By the sound of it the two security guards in the truck have had an interesting night. They said people in a silver car shot at them, then tried to run them off the road. Seems like they fitted out the car to look like an unmarked police car complete with siren and lights. We've just had a report of a crash earlier on the 241 involving a car which fits the description. It crashed and burst into flames. They found three bodies inside. The guards drove the truck here only to get mugged as they entered the garage. They were roughed up a bit, then locked in the back of the truck."

"A team of five men…they've gone to a lot of trouble to get the drugs back," Reed offered.

North noted the puzzled look on her face, adding, "And to stop the prisoners talking. No honour among thieves."

"It nearly worked, three are dead. What did we find out about the two DEA agents, Turner and Young?"

"The records show they both left the DEA a few years ago, since then it looks like they've gone off the radar. They've brought Young up to the interview room, he's ready to talk."

"Well Turner is not going to be talking, so let's go and see what Young has to say."

Reed and North, sitting at the desk in the interrogation room, stared intensely at Young opposite. Reed picked up a document, pretended to read it then passed it to North.

Reed spoke first, "You're looking at a long time in prison Young. If you don't help us, we'll not be able to protect you. Why did you come back here to kill the prisoners?"

Young arrogantly leaned back in his chair, "Don't try and make it sound like you're in charge. I asked to speak to you, don't forget. My only option is to do a deal otherwise I'll end up the same as them."

"Well start talking! Tell me something which will make me believe you know something of interest," Reed said impatiently.

"That's easy," Young announced arrogantly. "In a word...Marshall. He found out the plane was captured at the airport, called us in and told us we had to recover the drugs and release the prisoners...or at least stop them talking."

Reed offered Young a cigarette, he snatched it from her and placed it between his lips. North pulled out a lighter and lit it. Young took a long drag on the cigarette,

Watching the end of the glowing cigarette, Reed asked, "How did you get here so quickly? You arrived pretty damn quick after we arrested the men."

Young took the cigarette out and blew smoke to the side, "Security detail. We live in the area. When the drugs come in, we make sure they arrive safely and get shipped locally to where they're supposed to."

"Using two teams?" She asked, "We've reports of a silver car involved in a crash out near the airport. The same car was identified by the police guarding the aircraft."

"So that's what happened to Chavez."

"Chavez?" North asked.

"My boss, Chavez. Last time I saw him was at the wheel of a silver car. He went after the drugs with two other guys. Turner and myself were only supposed use our IDs to get the prisoners released. Once we noticed the security truck driving past, still on route to the police station, we knew something had gone wrong."

Reed studied his face, "You decided to do both jobs, the drugs and the men. Wasn't it a bit risky, I mean breaking into a police station?"

Young grinned and shook his head, "The easier option for us I suppose, the alternative was death. Marshall doesn't take failure lightly. If we returned empty handed, he'd kill us, and if caught trying, he'd send someone to kill us anyway."

"You need to tell me more about Marshall?"

Young dropped the cigarette on the floor and stood on it with his foot, "I've told you enough already. I want a deal and releasing, I didn't kill anyone, Turner did the shooting not me. Get me a lawyer, a deal and I'll tell you everything you want to know about Marshall."

Reed smiled, "Leave it with us, we may not need your help after all. Due to your failed assassination attempt, Ford is ready to talk."

The look of panic replaced the arrogance on Young's face.

North left the interview room for a few minutes and returned with a police officer who collected Young. The officer locked up Young then returned with Ford.

Reed leaned forward and looked at the twitching man in front of her, "Are you ready to talk now Ford? Your friends have already tried to shut you up. I'm losing my patience with you, if you don't start telling me what I want to hear you can go to the County lockup. I can't protect you there."

Ford moved uneasily in his chair, "You can't do that, I need you to guarantee my protection before I start talking."

"I'll see what I can do. Now stop pissing me about!" She snapped, "Who the fuck is Marshall?"

"Marshall?" He managed in a strangled voice, "He's got his fingers in many pies. He works for both sides. He's got access to all the agency information and money."

He paused and a tear appeared in his eye. The two FBI agents stared at Ford now a man on the edge, broken and desperate. Suddenly, he exploded in rage, "He's an evil bastard! If he wants to...he can destroy your life."

The FBI agents stared in disbelief, he calmed down, composed himself, then mumbled, "Can I have some water?"

North went outside and returned with a plastic cup of water and Ford drank it down in one.

Reed urged, "Go on…finish the story."

"I worked for the DEA for 12 years in both the finance and IT departments. My job involved following the drug money around the world and highlighting the banks which hid it. I learned all the tricks of how to clean dirty money.

I arranged for the seizure of millions of dollars. Marshall was my boss at the agency. He said I was the best in the business. One day he invited me to his home and that's when he asked me to join his 'organisation'. I refused his offer and a few weeks later he got me arrested for stealing evidence, ruining my career. While I was in prison Marshall came to see me and made another offer, join him, or spend the rest of my life in jail. I didn't have any other option than to accept his offer. He got the theft charges dropped and had me dismissed from my job. Ever since then I've continued to do the same work, but now I do it for him and his evil friends. And before you say it, I had no choice, it was made clear if I went back on the deal my wife and children would be killed."

North interrupted, "Your new job is to launder drug money for Marshall and the Cubans?"

"Only for Marshall and his organisation. The Cubans handle their own money. I look after the cleaning and distribution of the money raised from the drug trafficking ring Marshall has set up with Winter and the Afghan poppy grower. The Afghan doesn't have the means to launder money. It's a service Marshall offers him in return for a cheaper product price."

"And Marshall has ex-DEA agents working for him?" Reed asked.

"Not everyone is 'ex'. Some of his men are still working within the agency, and not just one agency either. He has men in most of the intelligence agencies. Marshall finds ways to make you work for him, blackmail or threats of violence. Chavez and Turner both told me their families would be in danger, not sure about the others."

"Why were you and the others on the plane today" North asked, "Talk us through the setup."

"The Cubans were there to make sure the drugs arrived with their people and to hand over the cash to me. Brent was there to protect me from the Cubans, Marshall didn't trust them."

Reed, sitting back in her chair, speculated, "Then you take the money to Lubbock for Winter…Correct?"

"No. It needs to be cleaned first through a number of legitimate businesses which have been set up around the country, a lawyer in Texas sets them up. Once clean, the funds are transferred into the personal offshore bank accounts I've set up for them."

Reed thought for a while, considering her options, "This is how I see things going for you Ford. I'm currently working as part of a task force which has been set up to investigate this drugs business. You've got the information we need to take down the whole organisation, access to the cash and you know who the main players are. If you agree to share your information with us, I'll speak to my boss and see what I can do to get your family protection."

The two looked at each other before Ford nodded.

Reed smiled, took out a notepad and pen, "Good man. Let's start at the beginning. I want to know everything…"

❖ ❖ ❖ ❖

Ford returned to his cell while the two FBI agents returned to the detectives office. Reed sat at a desk and North collected two coffees from the machine. He handed one to Reed and asked, "Do you believe what he just said? He said Marshall has contacts in all the major security agencies, men everywhere, with access to confidential information, no wonder he's got away with things for so long."

"Well put it this way, if only half of it's true, then Colby is right to say we shouldn't trust anyone. Damn!" Reed banged the desk and stood up, "North! It was us who brought the DEA in on this. Marshall found out about the detainment of the plane almost immediately, that's why those guys appeared here so quickly."

North complained, "How the hell could we have known they were involved in the trafficking?"

"That's not the problem. What we've accidentally done is probably blow Colby's mission in Afghanistan. The people over there will know we're onto them."

North threw his coffee cup in the bin, "You need to tell Dawson straight away. We need to warn them."

Reed grabbed the phone and called FBI HQ, "Dawson, we've had a busy night. Your hunch about the plane has opened a big can of worms. We've got some information which you need to get to Colby straight away."

"Let me have it," Dawson said blandly, sleepy from a day sitting at his desk looking at a PC.

Reed told the full story of the events that had taken place since the plane landed at Akron, including the incredible story Ford divulged.

Dawson suddenly woke up, his senses returning, and with panic in his voice warned, "You do realise what this means Reed? We know Marshall is based in Afghanistan. He most likely has already been in contact with the C-5 while it's on route to him. I need to warn Colby."

The line suddenly disconnected.

Reed leaned back in the chair and announced, "What a night. I'm beat. I think it's time for some sleep."

Chapter 20
Gulfstream Jet

Finn climbed the stairs and boarded the Gulfstream jet.

The pilot startled him when he suddenly appeared at the top of the stairs, "Welcome to Covert Air." he joked, "Grab a seat down the back with your buddies and I'll get this beauty in the air."

Finn smiled and the pilot disappeared into the cockpit. He expected to see a luxury interior, like the ones he'd seen in glossy magazines. He discovered a scene far from that idyllic view. A bank of computers, radar screens and other technical equipment filled the front of the cabin with two special skills officers working, including the woman who reported Marshall's call.

Finn pushed past the officers and continued towards the passenger area at the rear of the plane. A group of eight seats, four on each side with tables between. Beyond he identified storage racks, toilets, and a galley area. He noticed people already occupied some of the seats and chose an empty one facing forward. Getting into his seat he discovered Miller and a sleeping Colby in front of him.

Miller leaned forward and whispered, "We've lots to talk about on the flight but you'd best get some sleep first. It's been a long night."

Hearing the plane engines start Finn reclined his chair, closed his eyes, and let his mind drift away. *Kathy, I hope she's safe and can hang on until we get there. What's this all about? How did Zafar get out of prison?*

Another thought filled his mind and he opened his eyes again. *Torres!*

The catalogue of events which had taken place since he arrived in the US played out in his mind. He questioned himself. *I was the one who talked him into going after Winter? Why didn't I see the danger?*

He cast the thoughts from his mind and looked at both Colby and Miller asleep in front of him. He realised there was still a full team of people ready to put their lives on the line to help him find his sister.

Torres was helping me look for Kathy, he'd want me to carry on and finish the job.

He closed his eyes again and drifted off to sleep.

∴ ∴ ∴ ∴

A voice woke Finn, "Sir." One of the special skills officers talking to Colby, "Can you come to the front, we've got a call for you."

Colby rubbed the sleep out of his eyes, arose from his seat and walked to the front of the plane. Finn watched as he walked away, then fell asleep again.

∴ ∴ ∴ ∴

Finn opened his eyes again to see Colby and Miller talking together.

Miller noticed Finn waking and joked, "It's about time. You've been out for nearly six hours. I'll get you some breakfast."

Miller got up and moved to the rear of the plane and returned with a tray containing coffee cups and cakes. Finn took a coffee and a cake. He drank the coffee and quickly ate the cake.

"You must be hungry." Colby noted, "There's plenty more at the back, just help yourself."

Finn looked at the two men and asked, "Is there any new information?"

Miller left Colby to reply, "There's been a lot happening since we took off. I think it's time I brought you up to speed."

Colby sat up in his chair, drank some coffee and began, "Our guys have finished interviewing Winter and his men. It now appears Winter has been using his military contract as cover for importing opium from Afghanistan. You'll already know that eighty percent of the world's opium comes from Afghanistan poppy fields, grown mainly in the southern provinces like Kandahar, Helmand, Nimroz and Farah. Each one of the provinces has a tribal leader. In the olden days the leader was a wise man who looked after his people, today he's a drug lord who demands they grow poppies. Some of the drug lords are religious fanatics who grow poppies to buy guns, others, like Amir Zafar style themselves on the original Columbian drug lords of the Medellín and Cali Cartels which operated in the eighties.

"Cultivating and processing opium is big business, it adds about five billion dollars to the Afghan economy and employs about three million of its people. The problem is most of the money goes into the pockets of terrorists and corrupt officials. You won't see the average Afghan enjoying the good life. Most of the population live day to day not knowing where their next meal is coming from and wondering if someone is going to shoot or bomb them."

Colby stopped and drank some more coffee.

Finn asked, "You're saying Winter is part of a much bigger criminal network?"

"Zafar grows the poppies, harvests the opium and refines it into brown heroin. Marshall buys the heroin from Zafar and Winter ships it to the US, no questions asked. His military contract allows for regular air traffic and no customs people poking around the crates. They ship the drugs onwards to various locations around the US. It now seems he's using a Cuban cartel based in Miami to distribute the drugs down to street level. At the start of their chain of misery is a destitute Afghan farmer and at the other end is a broken-down American with a three hundred dollar a day addiction. Drugs are big business Finn, full of winners and losers."

"Where does the money go?" Finn asked.

"Into a series of offshore accounts controlled by Zafar, Winter and a man called Marshall."

"Who's this Marshall?" Finn enquired.

Colby replied, "He's a senior member of the DEA, based between the US and wherever the drugs business takes him. He's currently stationed in Afghanistan."

Finn listened to the words but found the story too incredible to be true and declared, "Sorry! You're saying a senior member of the DEA is behind all of this. I don't understand."

"It started months ago. The bad news about the increasing use of opiates back home finally landed on the President's desk. He spoke to my boss and I ended up with the task of investigating what was going on. It became obvious there was something wrong at the DEA. Drug busts dropped off and people within law enforcement complained the bad guys always seemed to know they were coming. We didn't know how far the corruption had spread. The only solution was a covert operation

"My team decided to feed false information and it confirmed my suspicion when it ended up in the field. We tracked several low-level agents, hoping they'd lead us to the principal players but we never got close. Finally, we got lucky, thanks to you and Torres. The FBI agents at Akron discovered a guy called Ford on board the small jet. It turns out he's the finance guy for a big drug organisation run by Marshall. By capturing Ford, we've discovered Marshall has used his position at the DEA to set up a drug trafficking ring. Ford is disclosing information on the whole organisation so things are starting to become a lot clearer. It was his job to launder the drug money through various shell companies and other legitimate business ventures. Coming out clean at the other end. We now know who the main players are."

"If that's correct then I assume it was Marshall who got Zafar out of prison?" Finn theorised.

"Definitely!" Colby confirmed, "Marshall needs Zafar to manage the farmers. A few bribes, forged documents and false ID's and a major terrorist and drug lord walks out of prison, courtesy of the DEA. It's a bit ironic. A man who works for an agency that was set up to eliminate drug trafficking ends up using his power to increase it."

"What does all this have to do with Kathy...and myself?" Finn requested.

"We intercepted some communications between low-level guys in the organisation indicating they were going to kidnap someone. When you called me, it was just a case of putting two and two together. I saw an opportunity to help you and maybe at the same time you could help me break the case. I know and trust your covert skills, and since you're not connected to any agency, I saw you as an asset I could use. It has worked, since you arrived in the US things have moved quickly, they've become sloppy and are making mistakes. That said, with what I know now, I suspect it's you they are after...not her."

"I've never met Marshall so why would he be interested in me?"

"You must've done something to get under his skin." Miller said, "He's most likely using her as leverage to get to you."

"But it doesn't make sense to send her all the way to Afghanistan."

"This is what I think." Colby suggested, "Do you remember a few years ago when the authorities set up a joint US and UK task force to destroy all the poppy fields? They called it the 'War on Drugs'. The goal was to stop the flow of cash from the drugs business going to the various terrorist factions which operate there. Recently someone reported the Taliban earns over four hundred million dollars a year from growing opium. They use the money to buy weapons and to make bombs, which they use to attack British and US soldiers. You were part of the British response, right Finn?"

"Yes! I lost good men. Some of the missions were a wild goose chase and we also walked into quite a few ambushes. I was convinced our intel was compromised."

"You can thank Marshall for that, and…" Colby paused and stared at his hands for a moment before adding, "unfortunately...it still is."

Finn noticed the pained look in the older man's eyes, "What do you mean?"

"Since capturing Ford we've tried our best to plug the leaks but we didn't count on Marshall being the big boss. Think about it, the drugs landed in Akron, the FBI agents informed the DEA about the drug haul and who do you think would be the next to find out?"

"Shit!" Finn yelled, "Marshall!"

"Exactly!" Colby confirmed, "We know he sent men to the police station to recover the drugs."

"And to kill his own men!" Miller added.

"Our problem now is not in Akron," Colby announced. "We have to assume he's already contacted the C-5 and told them we'll be waiting for them when they land. Additionally, we need to prepare for the possibility that Marshall's also decided it's time for him to run."

"How long is it now before we land?" Finn asked impatiently.

Miller looked at his watch, "About five hours."

"What's the status of the C-5?" Finn asked

Miller replied, "It's already landed in Morocco, it is now heading directly to Kandahar. We should arrive there at roughly the same time."

Finn looked at Colby and asked, "What's the plan?"

"In a nutshell, intercept the plane, find Kathy, make sure she's safe, destroy Marshall's network and take down Zafar. But we are going to have to react quickly. Things are fluid, changing by the minute." He stood up and announced, "First! I need to check up on something."

Colby ventured towards the front of the plane, leaving Miller and Finn alone at the table. Miller recognised the look in Finn's eyes and said, "Don't worry buddy we'll get your sister back."

"My priority is Kathy, but I'll you now, I'll settle the score with Marshall and Zafar." Finn said angrily, "I lost good soldiers capturing him and I'm not capturing him again just to find out later he's been released as part of some intelligence agency deal."

"While you're on the subject of Zafar, you didn't finish your story about him." Miller noted.

Finn sat back in his seat and stared out of the window, "There's something else that's on my mind."

"What's that?"

"Torres!" Finn muttered, "He told me a Cuban drug gang operating out of Florida killed his wife and daughter. I wonder if it was the same guys..."

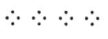

✧ ✧ ✧ ✧

Colby returned to his seat and announced, "I've got the latest flight information." Miller and Finn listened intently, "The C-5 is about thirty minutes ahead of us. Our pilot is checking to see if he can do anything to reduce that. I've spoken to the military staff at Kandahar Airport and they're getting prepared for the C-5 to land. They'll seize it and hold it until we arrive. If Kathy's in one of the crates, we'll be able to get her and arrest Winter's men."

"I want to be the first person on board." Finn demanded.

"No problem," Colby confirmed, "I'll speak to the Commander and have him hold off entering the plane."

Finn thanked Colby, turned to Miller and asked, "Do you know where your guys have stashed my gear? I want to freshen up and put my uniform on."

"Your pack is at the back in the storage lockers."

Finn got up and disappeared to the rear of the plane. Miller watched him go, turned to Colby, and asked, "How well do you know Finn?"

Colby thought for a moment then said quietly, "I know him well enough to know he's true to his word. That guy saved my life a few years back. And several of my men. I've owed him ever since."

"Can you be more specific?" Miller probed.

"When we decided to stop the flow of money to the terrorists, during the 'War on Drugs' fiasco, we received intel on a big haul of opium from Helmand going over the border to Pakistan. We called the British in to provide support on the ground and they sent a sixteen-man SAS squad. Their job was to recon the area, make sure it was safe for the US Special Forces team to land, seize the drugs and catch the traffickers. Finn led the SAS squad team."

Colby kept an eye on the rear of the plane making sure Finn was still busy in the toilet, "Our intel said the drugs would be shipped from Khanashin in two trucks, driven south and over the border to Pakistan. There's nothing down there in the south but desert, so it's easy to cross the border at night undetected. Finn's squad followed the drugs from the pick-up point in Khanashin and onwards to an abandoned farmhouse, about ten miles from the border. They set up a perimeter and staked out the place, relaying information back to my base. The intel said to expect two armed guards travelling with the truck drivers. I positioned an assault team in the desert nearby, a mixture of my guys and a US Special Forces team. Once we received the go ahead, we set off in two helicopters to capture the drugs. Before our choppers arrived four Toyota Land-cruisers containing twenty plus heavily armed guys drove into the area. They quickly took up positions around the farmyard with rocket propelled grenades, AK47's, the works, ready to shoot the choppers down."

Colby continued to look towards the rear of the plane as he talked. Miller listened intently, not wanting to interrupt, Colby continued to talk quietly, "Finn saw the helicopters approaching, recognised the danger and ordered his squad to take on the guys on the ground. We noticed the firefight taking place from the air, landed at a safe distance and went in by foot to support the British guys. By the time we arrived they'd already killed the hostiles. The intel was shit, we found no drugs in the trucks, they were empty. It was a set-up, there'd been a leak somewhere and it cost Finn five of his men."

Colby looked sternly at Miller and said forcefully, "Uncle Sam owes Finn, and that's why we're going to do everything we can to help him find his sister."

"Where did the bad intel come from?" Miller asked, "Did you manage to trace the leak?"

"The original intel was correct but they switched the trucks somewhere in the village, the drugs still managed to make it to Pakistan. At the time we were carrying out lots of missions, relentlessly bombing poppy fields, safe houses, warehouses and heroin processing factories. The ambush looked like a revenge attack and we never found out where the leak was..."

"Until now." Miller prompted.

"Exactly!" Colby nodded, "I'd keep that information to yourself for the moment. There's no way of knowing how Finn might react if he works it out for himself. He took it badly when he lost his men."

∴ ∴ ∴ ∴

Finn appeared from the toilet wearing his standard British Army desert camouflage uniform. He went into the galley and picked up three cans of coke, a loaf of bread, a hunk of cheese and some sausage before making his way back to his seat. He placed the items on the table in front of the other men and sat down. He tore a chunk off the bread and used his knife to cut some pieces off the cheese and sausage, and urged the others, "Dig in guys I doubt we'll have time to eat when we're on the ground."

∴ ∴ ∴ ∴

Miller returned from the Gulfstream cockpit and announced, "The pilot has confirmed we'll be on the ground within the hour. The C-5 is still thirty minutes ahead of us."

The communications officer approached and spoke to Colby, "Sir, on the radar the C-5 has just done something odd. We watched as it moved away from the standard flight path into Kandahar. It headed further north towards the Arghandab Valley, turned after a few minutes and joined the original flight path."

"Are there any clues as to what they were up to?" Colby asked, "Was there any radio contact from the plane to anyone on the ground?"

"Nothing," The officer stated. "It changed course, slowed down, then turned back and is now heading into Kandahar airport as planned. The only radio contact has been with the tower at the airport arranging for their landing. Something strange happened, we heard a sequence of beeping tones, a long tone, then silence."

"Okay, stay on it."

The officer returned later, "Sir, we've just been told the C-5 has now landed at Kandahar and the military police are escorting it to a secure area away from the main terminal."

"When do we land?"

Before the officer could reply an announcement came over the airplane speakers, "We've started our descent, please make sure your seat is in the upright position and your seat belt is securely fastened. All luggage must be stowed underneath the seat in front of you or in the overhead bins."

Finn heard the landing gear starting to come down, he put on his seat belt and looked at his watch. *Not long now.*

The pilot made a further announcement, "We've just been cleared to land at the Kandahar airport. Please make sure one last time your seat belt is securely fastened."

Finn looked at his watch confirming it had barely moved since he last looked. *Come on.*

The engines of the Gulfstream slowed, the wing flaps extended and the air speed decreased.

"Two minutes, take your seats for landing."

Chapter 21
Kandahar Airport

With a jolt, the landing gear of the Gulfstream jet touched down on to the tarmac at Kandahar airport. The pilot reversed the engines, slowed the jet, and stopped at the end of the runway. An airport security jeep guided the pilot away from the runway and to a parking area. The pilot applied the brakes, switched off the engines and switched off the seat belt sign.

Finn climbed from his seat and picked out his pack. Colby and Miller grabbed their gear and everyone walked to the front and disappeared, one by one, out of the door.

As Finn arrived in the doorway the pilot shouted from his seat in the cockpit, "Good luck Finn."

Finn waved to him, exited the cabin, and descended the stairs. A line of three US Army Humvees greeted the men. The last fitted with a fifty-calibre turret mounted gun.

Colby approached the soldier standing at the front jeep, "Are you Lieutenant Green?"

"Yes Sir!" Green saluted then shouted, "We're here to take you to the plane, everyone in the front two jeeps."

Green waited for Colby, Finn, Miller and one of the special skills officers to climb into his jeep. He followed, looked in the door mirror to ensure the remaining officers climbed into the second jeep then shouted, "Drive!"

The Humvee lurched into life, gaining speed quickly. Finn looked behind to see the other Humvees following in close formation. The driver weaved the big jeep between the various aircraft, refuelling tankers and cargo trolleys scattered around the airport. Once past the main passenger terminal the driver headed towards a line of maintenance hangers. In a space at the far end, beyond the hangers, Finn noticed the large C-5 Galaxy cargo plane. *There it is.*

More Humvees surrounded the plane, two with turret mounted guns and several soldiers had taken up covering positions, weapons drawn. The driver braked and the line of jeeps came to a sudden stop at the rear of the plane.

As the men climbed out of the jeep Miller handed Finn an MP5 assault rifle, 'You might need this buddy."

Colby turned to Green, "Lieutenant, is there some way to contact the pilot?"

Green reached into his jeep and spoke loudly into his radio handset, "C-5 Galaxy. You're surrounded by US Army personnel. As a precaution we're going to come onboard and search the plane. Everyone inside is to remain seated with their hands up. Place all weapons on the floor. Once you're ready you can begin to open the rear doors."

Suddenly two more US Army Humvee jeeps appeared from the direction of the terminal buildings, stopping at the rear of the plane near Green's jeep. Identical to the US Army vehicles, painted in standard desert camouflage apart from black doors. The dark blue crest painted on the door confirmed who owned the vehicles. A skull with crossed rifles where bones would normally be and underneath the phrase 'Iron Fist' painted in red. The US Army soldiers, including the gunners, turned and pointed their weapons towards the potential danger.

The doors of the jeeps opened and seven men jumped out wearing desert camouflage pants, black t-shirts and a harness which included the usual grenades, flash-bangs, and magazine clips. Finn recognised the uniform. *Like the guys at Lubbock.*

The men drew their weapons and took up covering positions. The passenger door opened on the rear jeep and a bald man in his forties with a Frank Zappa style moustache, stepped out. He held up his hand to protect his eyes from the glare of the morning sun, reached in his pocket and put on a pair of mirrored sunglasses. He looked around him, ignoring the US Army soldiers and walked out in front of his men.

He signalled to his men to lower their weapons then spoke with an arrogant tone, "Gentlemen, what seems to be the problem here? Who's in charge of this cluster fuck?"

"That will be me." Colby announced from the side of Green's jeep.

The man glanced, "A civilian!" A grin appeared on his face, "Tell me sir what the fuck are you doing spoiling my day?"

Colby motioned to reply when the man walked up to him and said forcefully, "This plane is under US military jurisdiction and is not allowed to be stopped, searched or delayed without the permission of the National Security Advisor himself." He lifted his glasses and sarcastically added, "You don't look like him."

The man stood and stared with a menacing look on this face.

Colby ignored him and calmly replied, "I might not be him but I've got this instead." He reached inside his jacket, took out a letter and handed it to the man. "This is a letter from that particular gentleman giving me permission to spoil yours and anyone else's day, whenever I want to."

The man read the letter and handed it back, "So you're Colby? I've heard of you before, back in my Navy Seal days."

Colby, not in the mood for chit-chat, dismissed the man's attempt to be friendly, "That's all good and well, we can swap stories later. First, you can tell your men to stand down, then extend the courtesy of telling me who the hell you are?"

The man turned to his men, made a gesture with his hand and they returned to their jeeps.

Colby shouted, "Lieutenant Green, can you ask your soldiers to point their weapons at the plane."

The man held his hand out to Colby and said, "Assistant Battalion Leader Kane, Iron Fist Security."

Colby accepted the hand and introduced his companions, "Mr Kane, this is Miller, he's a senior officer in the Special Operations Group, and this is Captain Finn, British Army, SAS."

Kane shook Miller's hand, turned to Finn and shook his hand, "A Captain in the SAS. What are you doing out here with this mob?"

Finn barked back, "I don't have time for your crap. I need to get on the plane straight away." The stern expression on his face unchanged.

Unfazed Kane said, "I see. How can I help you?"

"For a start, you can tell me how many of your men are inside the plane?" Colby growled, "Are they armed?"

"The plane is carrying replacement gear, supplies and a new batch of contractors. It's all legitimate, we've got all the permits."

Colby said angrily, "You didn't answer me. How many?"

Kane replied calmly, "There are two pilots, an engineer and navigator, plus a hundred and twenty men. A couple of the officers carry handguns as per regulations. The rest of the weapons are in crates."

Finn asked, "What about the guys who wear the all-black uniforms?"

Kane smiled, "Don't worry, there are none of those mongrels on board this flight, just my contractors, real soldiers."

"That's bullshit!" Finn shouted, "I watched the plane being loaded at Lubbock. The last men to board the plane were all dressed in black. Four of them, the one barking out orders was called Martinez."

"Martinez? Winter's lap dog? You must be mistaken."

Growing impatient with the lack of progress Finn moved closer, faced Kane, reached up and removed his sunglasses. He looked directly into the man's eyes, "Stop messing me about. I need to get on the plane," Finn handed back the sunglasses and shouted, "Now!"

"Look, we can sort this out quickly. I'll go on board with three of my guys. If Martinez and his security buddies are in there, we'll arrest them for you. I'm sure this is just some misunderstanding which we can resolve quickly."

Colby agreed, "That seems to be the best solution to avoid any bloodshed. But no one comes out of there carrying a weapon."

Kane summoned three of his men to come over and took the radio off his harness, "Pilot, open the rear hatch. I'm coming on board."

The rear doors opened, a ramp lowered to the ground and Kane and his men ran up into the plane. After a few moments, soldiers dressed in the same beige and black uniforms filed out of the plane. They gathered and stood in ten rows of twelve. Colby signalled to Green and a group of US Army soldiers and a Humvee with a turret gun moved around to guard them.

Kane appeared from the ramp and shouted, "It's all yours Finn. Martinez and his men are not in there."

Finn grabbed his MP5, with Miller covering him, ran into the plane finding a row of crates.

"Shit! It's not here." Finn shouted, "Where the hell is it?"

The two men searched along either side of the crates until they reached a ladder which gave access to the cockpit and flight crew. Finn climbed the ladder and found a navigator and engineer sitting at a desk in a room behind the main cockpit.

He pointed his gun and asked, "Where's Martinez?" Both shook their heads, as if mute and unable to speak. Impatiently Finn pushed past into the cockpit where the pilot and co-pilot sat at the controls.

"Where's Martinez?" Finn asked again, "And where's the crate they loaded at Lubbock?"

"We just followed our orders," the pilot replied nervously, "A guy called Marshall called on the satellite phone just after we took off from Morocco, he spoke to Martinez."

Finn raised the gun barrel and jammed it into the neck of the pilot, "Go on! I'm listening!"

"Hey man leave it out, he..." The co-pilot protested but before he could say anymore Finn elbowed him in the face, breaking his nose.

Finn pushed the barrel harder against the pilot's neck "Go on! You were saying."

"Alright!" The pilot howled, "Martinez spoke to the guy out there in the comms room. After he finished the call he came in and said we had new orders." The pilot tried to move in his seat to reduce the pressure of the gun barrel but Finn followed his move. "He ordered us to do a cargo drop over the Arghandab Valley. He gave me the coordinates and we redirected. He took the engineer and forced him fit a G-12 cargo parachute to one of the crates. When we arrived at the coordinates Martinez and his men pushed the crate out then jumped after it. The engineer said he watched the five parachutes open, then shut the doors. We just continued and landed as normal."

Finn removed the gun from the pilot's neck and stood back feeling the anguish of missing Kathy by minutes. He cursed under his breath and lowered his head. *What do we do now?*

The pilot leaned over and checked on the condition of the co-pilot who now had blood running down onto the front of his green uniform. Turning to Finn he growled, "You're an asshole, why is that damn crate so important?"

Finn muttered, "My sister was inside."

"What?" The engineer spoke from behind Finn, "Martinez, said it was supplies for the locals. I thought it was strange how the crate had holes drilled in it. If it's any consolation to you the parachute will take weights up to one thousand kilogrammes. If there was someone inside the crate, they should at least land safely."

Finn moved towards the ladder, "You guys need to get off the plane, and give all the information you've got to the officers outside. I want to know the exact coordinates of where you dropped the crate."

Grabbing the ladder Finn stopped and turned back, "Sorry about your nose, I'll get a medic to look at it for you."

Finn climbed down the ladder and found Miller checking some crates, "Did you find anything?"

"Nothing out of the ordinary," Miller replied. "What did you find up there?"

"They did a cargo drop, a crate, and the four guards parachuted out after it. Marshall had warned them, they knew we'd be here waiting for them."

The two men watched as the flight crew climbing down the access ladder and walked along the crates towards the exit ramp.

Miller noticed the co-pilot's face and turned to Finn. "What happened to him?"

"A moment of frustration," Finn replied in a guilty tone. "I'm not proud of it, anyway, we need to tell Colby what we've discovered."

Miller agreed and the two men moved towards the exit ramp following the flight crew. Finn stopped and took one final look at the inside of the plane, while Miller directed the flight crew towards his officers.

After several minutes of checking around the cargo bay of the plane, Finn walked down the ramp to the tarmac, only the three jeeps and Lieutenant Green remained.

"Where's everyone gone?" Finn asked Green.

"Colby's released the Iron Fist contractors and Kane arranged for trucks to take them to their base in Kandahar. The Army soldiers have returned to their base. Colby wants all the cargo checked before allowing it to be unloading. You should've seen the look on Kane's face...talk about unhappy."

"Where is Colby now?" Finn asked while looking around.

"He's in my jeep with Miller."

Finn opened the rear door of the jeep and climbed in.

Miller was just finishing his report "... nothing in the crates boss but Finn has some news." He looked at Finn. "Well go on tell him what the flight crew said."

Finn relayed the story to Colby who asked, "Do we know the coordinates of where the crate was dropped?"

"The flight crew are getting interviewed now. We're gathering as much intel as possible on the flight path and drop zone." Miller replied.

Colby shook his head and said, "Well gentlemen we didn't figure on that one, did we? I suppose it was inevitable that once they knew about the drugs, they'd contact the plane."

"All is not lost," Miller responded, "but now we need to focus our efforts on finding out what has happened to the crate, and clearing up the rest of this mess."

"This is not over by a long-shot." Colby added. "But if it helps you Finn, they wouldn't have captured your sister and brought her all this way just to kill her, they want her alive."

"What do you suggest we do now boss?" Miller asked.

"I've arranged for us to stay at an SOG safe house here in Kandahar. We'll use that as our base, they dropped the crate nearby. We'll get the special skills officers and the others set up to collect intel and they can liaise with Dawson in the US."

Colby turned to Miller, "Can you jump out and quickly tell the others that we're leaving. Once they've gathered all the intel, tell them to release the aircrew and meet us at the safe house."

Miller did as commanded, climbed out of the jeep for a few minutes before returning and announcing excitedly, "All set boss."

"Green!" Colby leaned forward and tapped the lieutenant on the shoulder, "We can go now, you've got the address."

Green nodded to the driver who started the Humvee's engine, beginning the journey into the city of Kandahar. At an agreed location on the outskirts the Humvee stopped.

Finn, Colby, and Miller transferred to a battered old car that replicated most of the other cars used in the city. Miller acknowledged the driver, a paramilitary officer from the SOG, and climbed into the passenger seat which left Colby and Finn sharing the back seat.

Chapter 22
C-5 Galaxy

Kathy woke with the sensation of falling. She could hear the air rushing around the outside of the crate. Sunlight shone through air holes on the sides and lit the inside of the crate. The crate spun round and round, creating strobes of nauseating light patterns.

She groggily pushed herself up from the padding and blankets. The noise, pulsating light and the effects of the sleeping pills made her feel sick. She managed to get up into a sitting position but the spinning force pressed her against the side of the crate. She moved her head and peered out of one of the holes.

Extreme fear replaced her thoughts of sickness at the frightening sight of the ground below approaching fast. The outside air turbulence drowned out the sound of her screaming.

With a jolt the crate hit the ground and tipped over onto the side. Kathy hit her head on the lid of the crate and cut herself above her eye. The blankets and padding fell on top of her. She pushed the materials away and got herself up again with her knees and palms on the wood of the crate. The parachute flapped in the wind until it filled with air and pulled the crate with it, slowly at first, then gathering more momentum. Dust and sand poured in through the air holes and filled the crate. The crate came to an abrupt stop throwing Kathy forward again, banging her head. She lost focus and slumped into unconsciousness.

Martinez landed near a grape drying hut and quickly disconnected the parachute harness, leaving it to float away, only to become trapped on the grape vines. He surveyed the area and searched for the rest of his men.

He ran towards the hut and climbed onto the roof to get a clearer view beyond the grape vines and vegetation. He spotted the large cargo parachute on the crate and the parachutes of his men scattered around within a radius of the crate.

Jumping down from the hut, he swung his assault rifle around to the front of him and ran towards the crate. He spotted two old men picking grapes and a younger man with some goats. He grinned at them and pushed on. After running past the grape vines, he entered a large poppy field which gave him an improved view of the location of the crate. After running another fifty yards he came to the spot where the crate had landed. He looked along the row of flattened poppies and discovered the crate wedged against a small group of palm trees.

Martinez ran towards the crate, discovering it wedged between two of the trees, and on its side. Two of his men appeared from the other side of the trees.

Martinez shouted, "Cut the parachute and get the crate upright,"

The men followed his instructions. After cutting the straps the parachute blew away in the wind. The men struggled to move the crate from the trees.

"Get on with it!" Martinez shouted.

The men finally managed to get the crate out of the trees and stood it upright.

"Get the lid off," Martinez ordered, "we need to check she's still alive."

The two men lifted the lid and threw it on the dusty ground.

"Get back!" Martinez pushed his men aside, "Let me see her."

He investigated the inside of the crate seeing a mass of padding and blankets, a blood stain on the side of the crate and Kathy's lifeless body.

"Shit! Get her out of there."

The two men lifted her out and set her down next to the crate. Martinez quickly brushed the hair away from her face with his fingers. He noticed the cut above her eye and a purple bruise on her forehead.

"Water!" One of the men passed a canteen.

Martinez ran water over Kathy's face and she slowly opened her eyes.

"There you are, good, stay still." he said. "You've banged your head. It'll ache for a while."

Martinez turned to his men, "Well don't just stand there, go and look for him."

The two men ran off in different directions while Martinez made Kathy comfortable by placing some padding under her head, "Sorry about that, using the parachute was the only option."

Kathy opened her eyes, "Why are you doing this to me?"

Martinez ignored her questions and continued looking for potential danger. He heard tree branches creaking to his left, stood up quickly and aimed his rifle. His men appeared, the first two carrying the third.

"He's got a busted ankle," one of the men announced.

"That's all we need!" Martinez cursed and pointed in turn at the two men either side of the injured one, "You help him and we'll put her on the crate lid and carry her out of here. We need to find a secure area to hole up until the transport arrives."

Martinez pointed, "There's a hut over there, come on move."

The group moved towards the grape drying hut and past the local people Martinez encountered earlier. The hut appeared between the grape vines and Martinez shouted, "There it is. Move!"

Martinez arrived at the doorway of the hut, approximately twelve by twelve feet with brick walls and a corrugated steel roof. He checked it was empty then barked, "Put her down in there!"

They laid Kathy down on the floor inside. Martinez checked her condition again and gave her more water.

Looking at one of the men Martinez said, "Go and speak to the farmers, we need some food for her and more water. And don't do anything stupid like threatening them. Ask nicely."

The man left the hut and returned with the goat herder who had brought some bread, meat, and a pouch with water.

Martinez took the items. He reached in his pocket and pulled out a dollar coin and passed it to the man, who smiled a toothless smile and quickly left.

"Eat something as it'll settle your stomach." He passed some chunks of bread and meat to Kathy. She snatched the food and quickly ate it.

"Slow down, you'll make yourself worse. Make sure you drink plenty of water."

He looked at the two able bodied guards and yelled, "Don't just stand there one of you strap his ankle up while the other gets the satellite phone out."

The men followed Martinez's orders.

He picked up the handset on the satellite phone and made a call which connected after several rings, "We're on the ground. I've got the package, we're sheltered, five in total, one injured, I need urgent transportation and medical assistance. I'm transmitting the homing signal now."

He listened to the response and hung up the phone, "Not long to wait. They're sending some trucks and a medic."

Martinez could finally relax. One of the men took up a position guarding the doorway and the others sat against a wall. Martinez heard the noise of vehicles and moved to the doorway asking, "What can you see?"

"Three pickup trucks," the guard replied. "How do you want to play this?"

"Take up a defensive position over there near the bushes," Martinez pointed to the line of grape vines. "Don't start shooting unless I do. These guys can be trigger happy and we need to make sure we know who they are and if they're on our side."

The guard moved in a crouched position across the open ground until he reached the grape vine rows. He picked a spot which provided cover and a wide-angle view of the hut and surrounding area.

Martinez shouted to the other guard and told him to find a similar position opposite the first. Once both guards were in position, they signalled Martinez, who came out of the hut, standing ten feet in front of the doorway, in full view of the approaching vehicles. The pickup trucks moved quickly, in a line, along the bumpy farm track and a cloud of dust following them. When they got within fifty feet of the hut the lead pickup braked hard and skidded to a stop. The driver, passenger and two men in the flatbed jumped out. The driver signalled to the vehicles behind to wait and the group of four started walking towards the hut.

The driver, who appeared to Martinez to be the one in charge, walked out in front. To Martinez he looked exactly like all the other Afghan fighters he'd encountered. Dressed in the traditional Afghan male dress of a dark green perahan shirt and beige tunban trousers. On his head he wore a patterned black and white kufi and a shemagh scarf wrapped around his neck. Along with a bullet proof vest, in his left hand he carried an AK47 assault rifle by the barrel. The driver stopped when he heard loud shouting behind him. He turned quickly and found his men pointing their guns at the two men they had discovered hiding in the grape vines.

He shouted, in English, "Come out of there! We are all friends here." Then in Pashto he told his men to lower their weapons. The two men stayed partially hidden, waiting for instructions from Martinez.

Ignoring the guards, the driver continued to walk forward until he reached within a few feet of Martinez. He paused, and like Martinez had done with him, studied the man in front of him, dressed all in black but now covered in dust and dirt.

He laughed aloud and said in English, "It's never a good idea over here to wear black." A wide grin appeared on his face, "Welcome to Afghanistan. I'm Abdul-Ali, Zafar sent me to collect you."

"Martinez!" He reached out and shook the Afghan's hand while he spoke, "Thanks for coming, I've got three armed men with me, one is injured, and the woman, who also has a head injury." He waved to the two guards to return to the hut, before continuing, "Did you bring a medic?"

Abdul-Ali turned and shouted in Pashto towards the men in the pickups. A small man in his forties climbed out of the passenger side of the second pick up, holding a small black rucksack. The man ran over and stood next to his leader, awaiting instructions.

"Martinez this is Hakeem, he was trained in the US, now he heals Afghan people shot with American bullets. Show him where your injured people are."

Martinez turned, walked towards the doorway and pointed inside, "They're both in there, the woman was unconscious before. She banged her head when we landed. The guard has a suspected broken ankle."

Hakeem pushed past Martinez into the darkened hut. On his left he found a sleeping woman lying on a blanket. On his right a man sitting against the wall with a rifle in his hands.

Hakeem knew his biggest priority was the woman. He moved to where Kathy lay motionless and kneeled in front of her. He brushed her hair away from her face and found the bruise on her forehead. He moved her head to the side and noticed the dried blood which had run down her cheek from a cut on her eyebrow.

He shook Kathy and she slowly opened her eyes, "Hello I'm Hakeem, don't worry I'm here to help you." Placing his hand on her shoulders he asked, "can you lay on your back for me please?"

Kathy rolled on to her back and raised her hand towards her head, Hakeem gently grabbed her arm and laid it down by her side, "Try not to move."

Hakeem looked in his bag and brought out a torch which he shone into Kathy's eyes, checking for a reaction to the light, then asked, "Can you talk?"

Kathy tried to move her lips, but no sound came out. Hakeem, picked up a water bottle and poured it slowly into her mouth. He looked as she gulped down the water, "Good yes?"

"Thank you," Kathy said in a soft voice.

"Can you tell me your name?"

"Katherine..." she mumbled searching her mind for the word, "Finn."

"Happy to meet you Katherine. Now can you sit up for me?"

Kathy slowly raised the upper half of her body, Hakeem helped her and she rested against the wall.

Hakeem looked carefully at the young woman's face, "How do you feel?"

While waiting for her response the medic checked her pulse.

Kathy mumbled "My head hurts and I feel dizzy." She paused for a few seconds, "and I think I'm going to be sick." She blinked her eyes a few times, "My eyes won't focus."

She grabbed Hakeem's hand and said in a whisper, "Where am I? Can you help me? These men have kidnapped me..." Her words tailed off as she passed out again.

Hakeem rested her head against the wall. He took out a cloth, covered it with water and cleaned the blood from her face. He took out a dressing, poured alcohol on it and cleaned the cut above her eye before adding a plaster. Taking some paracetamol from his bag he gently opened her mouth, placed the tablets inside and added water from the bottle.

Hakeem turned to the injured guard and said angrily, "You men did this to her? What happened?"

In too much pain to argue the Iron Fist guard put his gun down beside him and said, "Can you look at this for me." He pointed at his ankle, "I think it's broken."

Hakeem moved across the dusty floor towards the man. He felt around the top of his boot, inducing the guard to cry out in pain.

Hakeem looked at him with unsympathetic eyes, "It's not broken, you'll live. If you take the boot off it'll swell up so leave it on for now. Here are some painkillers."

He pressed a couple of tablets into the man's hand and, not caring to waste anymore of his time, stood up and returned to the men outside.

"Hakeem, report! How are they?" Abdul-Ali demanded. He looked to the sky for a moment, "We need to get moving. There are drones operating in this area."

Hakeem cleared the sweat from his face with his shemagh, his hands shaking, then mumbled, "The woman has concussion, she needs to be rested and monitored. I can't tell if she has internal bleeding. She should be ok but she will need a hospital if she doesn't show signs of recovery within the next forty-eight hours." Looking at Martinez he continued, "She has been drugged, an overdose."

"Can we move her?" Abdul-Ali asked.

"Yes, but we need to be very gentle, no sudden shocks, it could kill her."

"That may be difficult Hakeem," Abdul-Ali looked at the road surface, "But we'll do our best. We'll make a bed for her in the back of my pickup."

Abdul-Ali shouted orders to his men. One ran to the pickup, the other two proceeded inside the hut.

Hakeem pushed his way past and shouted at them in Pashto, "Be careful".

One of the men placed his hands under Kathy's armpits and raised her limp body off the ground. The other placed her arm around his neck and between them they carried her out of the hut and towards the pickup.

As he emerged from the hut Martinez grabbed Hakeem by the arm and enquired, "And what about my man?"

Hakeem brushed his hand away and hissed, "He'll live!" The two men stared at each other for a moment. Hakeem turned away and followed Kathy.

Abdul-Ali noted the angry response from Hakeem and commented, "Martinez, it seems you've upset my medical friend with your treatment of the woman. You know Zafar made it clear the woman mustn't be harmed in any way."

"We had no other option but to use the cargo drop," Martinez said with a worried tone in his voice. "The US side of the organisation has collapsed and the CIA were waiting for us at Kandahar. I discussed it with Marshall, it was my only option to make sure she arrived here..."

Abdul-Ali lost interest, walked away, and headed towards his pickup truck.

Shocked by his arrogance Martinez shouted after him, "And what about me and my men?"

Abdul-Ali stopped and slowly turned around, "I suggest you get into a pickup truck before we leave."

Abdul-Ali checked the flatbed of his pickup and found Kathy laid on some blankets. He climbed into the driver's seat and started the engine. He waited for a few moments as Martinez and his men climbed onto the pickup truck behind. He slowly pressed the accelerator and the automatic gearbox engaged. Carefully, he turned the pickup around on the dusty road surface, facing back the way it came. Once the other pickups had done the same, he drove carefully along the bumpy track, proceeding as slowly as possible, avoiding the potholes and ruts. As the truck moved the two Afghan men in the back held Kathy to steady her.

Chapter 23
SOG Safe House, Kandahar

After changing cars, the twenty-mile drive from Kandahar International Airport to Shafakhana Sarak had been uneventful. Finn had spent most of the time with his eyes closed, a car horn blasted and he quickly opened them. He gazed out of the window watching the local people busy going about their daily activities. Dust swirled around the street and the heat of the afternoon sun made Finn's throat dry. The road became much busier as they ventured deeper into the city.

The driver cursed under his breath as cars, motorbikes, carts, and pedestrians blocked his way along with random vehicles driving the same way in both lanes. He struggled with the clutch and gears on the old car before eventually turning off the busy road. The car travelled down a side street lined on both sides with walls over ten feet high. The properties built to the usual Afghan architecture style, with a high walled courtyard containing a house, invisible from the road.

The driver turned several times down similar streets until he stopped at a large metal gate. A man in traditional Afghan dress, sitting on the floor next to the gate, observed the vehicle pull up and banged on the metal panel. The gate opened slowly and another man peeked out. He acknowledged the driver and continued to push the gate fully open. The car quickly drove inside and the gate shut swiftly behind them. Finn looked out into the courtyard and found a two-story building in the middle.

"Here we are!" Colby announced. "Miller can you give Finn a quick tour and find a spare bed for him to dump his gear on? Then both come to the operations room."

Colby climbed out of the car. Finn watched as he ran towards the building and down some stairs on the side. He imagined the stairs led to the cellar of some kind.

"Come on buddy, let's get going" Miller urged, "I'll give you a quick tour of the safe house."

Finn collected his pack from the boot of the car and followed Miller into the building. "What's this place?" he asked.

"It's the Kandahar Hilton, let's find the cocktail bar." Miller joked and added, "It's an SOG safe house. Colby has a few of them set up across Afghanistan. They're used as bases for planning and implementation of covert operations. I'm sure you know the type of stuff that goes on here. If we're given a target to watch, or to take out, then this is where the planning starts. It needs a lick of paint but what you see on the outside is just for show. We want to blend in with the locals."

Finn followed Miller through the main doors of the property into a corridor with rooms off to either side. Miller carried on talking as he walked deeper into the property.

"As you know, the Special Operations Group or SOG, is a department within NCS responsible for clandestine, or if you like, secret operations with which the U.S. government doesn't want to be associated. The staff here are constantly changing, depending on the current operations which are taking place. You'll find both paramilitary and specialised skills officers here. They're the best in the business at implementing covert and undercover tasks, recruited from elite U.S. military groups like the Navy Seals, Special Forces, Army Rangers, and the Marine Corps. There are a more people here than normal. Colby has pulled in extra staff from other locations considering recent events. He's got about thirty staff here collecting intel on Marshall, his movements and network. They're also trying to track down Zafar. Buddy, these are the guys that are going to help us get your sister back."

Finn patted Miller on the back and nodded. The two men continued to walk deeper into the building. Finn investigated each of the rooms as he passed the doorway. He found men and women busy with their tasks, talking on phones, working on computers, analysing documents, and maps.

Miller pointed to a room on his left, "That's the kitchen. Take anything you want buddy, it's all free."

They walked to a double staircase, one section leading up to the next floor, the other leading down. Miller pointed downwards, "That's the Ops room. That's where Colby wants us to meet him. We'll be spending most of our time down there. But first! I'll show you the sleeping quarters and bathroom. Plus, I've got a little surprise for you as well."

The comment intrigued Finn and he followed Miller up the stairs. On the top landing he glimpsed a naked woman walking out of a room on his left. She smiled at him and carried on walking whilst towel drying her hair, before disappearing into another room.

Miller noticed the surprise on Finn's face and joked, "No one's shy here buddy."

"That's the first time I've seen a naked woman since I got deployed over here…six barren months."

Miller slapped him on the back, "Don't get any ideas buddy, that's Wilson, ex-Navy Seal, she'll kick your ass."

Finn took an extra look at the woman walking away from him. Miller pulled him away as the two men laughed together.

They entered a room with a row of bunk beds, "It's like my home in Helmand," Finn announced.

Miller banged on an empty top bunk, "This is yours buddy. Dump your pack on top so the others know it's taken."

Finn threw the pack onto the bed and a cloud of dust rose around it.

Miller said excitedly, "Now come and see this."

Finn followed him out onto the landing and climbed the staircase leading upwards. At the top, Miller kicked open the steel door and disappeared. As he stepped out onto the roof of the building Finn felt the blast of heat from the afternoon sun. He quickly looked around taking note of his new surroundings finding several satellite dishes on the roof, a three-foot high perimeter wall and poles in each corner contained security cameras pointing down into the compound. Avoiding the cables on the roof, Finn joined Miller at the far wall.

A smile appeared on Miller's face as he looked out over the city. He raised his arms up and shouted, "Isn't the view amazing, you can see for miles."

Finn took a moment to sample the atmosphere, hearing the noise of the city. The sun, almost at its highest, induced a hot dusty haze which hung over the city. He asked, "Can you point towards the direction where Kathy was dropped?"

Miller looked around, getting his bearings, walked over to another wall and pointed, "Out over there somewhere along the Arghandab river. It flows south down past Kandahar into Helmand and then onward to Pakistan. You know about the rivers running through here?"

"Not really, you travel on them in a boat or get wet swimming in them." Finn said blandly.

"The Arghandab river starts north-west of the city of Ghazni, in the northern mountains of Afghanistan. It flows south-west for two hundred and fifty miles. On its route to the south, it passes this place, Kandahar, then joins the Helmand river south of the city of Girishk. These rivers are the lifeblood of the people here. They provide irrigation for farms and drinking water for the population. That's why most of the vegetation and people are situated along the banks of the rivers. To extend the area the locals have devised a complex system of wadis which they use to irrigate the fields much further away. With the heat, and the water, this is poppy grower's heaven."

Already bored with the sightseeing tour Finn looked at his watch and asked, "Don't we need to meet with Colby?"

"Back to reality!" Miller dropped his smile, "Come on buddy, let's go!"

The two men ventured downstairs to the basement and operations room. Miller entered a code into a keypad and the door sprang open.

Finn walked inside and found a large desk with nine seats, one at the opposite end to a large screen and four on either side. The large screen currently showed eight different broadcasts in a grid pattern. He quickly scanned the images finding random computer data, overhead drone footage, TV broadcasts and security camera footage. He glanced around at the other people sitting at the table. At the other end to the screen Colby sat with two men on his left and a woman on his right.

Colby noticed them enter and stopped his meeting, "Come in, sit down. We're discussing the latest intel we've collected and drawing up ideas of how we put this business to bed."

Colby addressed the people sitting around the table and pointed, "I guess you all know Miller. This is Captain Finn, a British soldier in the SAS."

The people around the table all looked at Finn to acknowledge his presence.

Colby got straight to business, "I'll bring you both up to speed." He pointed to the screens at the other end, "We are monitoring data coming into the DEA field office here in Kandahar. The head of the DEA currently has a considerable amount of 'egg on his face' and has agreed to start sharing information. In the last twenty-four hours he's discovered one of his senior staff members is running a major drug trafficking ring, supplying hundreds of millions of dollars of opium-based products into the US." Colby smiled to himself, "I can't see him staying in his job much longer."

He looked to a woman on his left and ordered, "Cooper, can you tell everyone what we've found out about Marshall's current location."

"Gentlemen, on the screens you can see the various intel streams we're gathering from the intelligence officers upstairs and from other intelligence agency sources."

She looked on the table, moved the papers and found a handset, like a TV remote. She pressed the buttons and a box appeared on the screen. She continued to press the handset moving the box around the eight images until it arrived at an overhead camera image. She pressed a button and a single large image replaced the eight smaller boxes.

"This stream shows the footage from a drone that's currently circling above a house in Kandahar. The latest intel indicates that Marshall is holed up in there with some of his men."

She put the remote down, picked up a piece of paper, read for a few seconds then continued, "We've discovered that Marshall has been operating outside the law for a long time. He's established a supply line that's allowed high grade heroin to be shipped to the US using the Iron Fist transport links."

Colby interrupted her saying, "Explain a little about his relationship with Zafar."

"I'll be brief as I guess most people here already know. The Afghan opium trade is hundreds of years old, the locals grew a few poppies, produced small amounts of heroin, transported it to Pakistan and received cash for food to feed their families. That's until people realised it could generate vast amounts of money. Today, insurgents use the drug money to buy guns and explosives. The joint US and UK operations, which started around ten years ago, gradually reduced the supplies of opium by burning the poppy fields and bombing the drug processing factories. Covertly, there was also a drive to kill or capture the drug lords who forced the locals to grow the poppies. Zafar controlled the biggest poppy growing industry, gradually getting rid of the competition until he was the only one left. He ruled the locals by fear, intimidation and killing anyone who stood up to him."

Cooper looked down the table, "Captain Finn I believe you led the mission to capture Zafar four years ago."

"Correct." Finn said sternly.

"Can you tell us more about your operation?" Cooper looked at the head of the table, then back to Finn, "I know Colby was involved somewhere, but it may help the rest of the team understand how Zafar operates and how we recapture him."

Finn looked at Colby to check that he was comfortable with him sharing the classified information. Colby gave him a nod to confirm it was okay.

"It was a joint UK and US operation, the US Air Force provided air support with drones and intel, the UK provided troops on the ground. He went into hiding using a building in a village which he set up like a fortress. My squad had the place staked out for days, watching the routines and the various comings and goings. We watched them preparing some vehicles, getting ready to leave the compound. One of my men identified Zafar in the group so we set up an ambush. We took out the vehicles with the guards, captured Zafar, then battled our way out of the village."

Finn stopped, a stern look returned to his face, "I lost men capturing him. The mission brief said it'd help to reduce the drug shipments and stop the insurgent attacks on our patrols. They told me it'd save lives!" He looked at Colby and said angrily, "So why the fuck is he out of prison?"

Colby noted the pain in Finn's eyes, "It appears Marshall did a deal with the local officials to get him out of prison. Drugs provide money, and that money feeds corruption."

Finn banged the table and shouted, "I should've shot the bastard!

The people around the table looked at Finn but dared not speak. Colby paused, turned to Cooper and asked "Please continue your report. Tell us more about where Marshall is now."

"Once his organisation in the US began to crumble, he fled from the DEA field office here, taking a few of his men with him. The man arrested in Akron, Ford, has helped us freeze all his bank accounts, so he has limited access to resources. And he's fast running out of friends. The cameras at the DEA office showed him leaving in a car. We managed to follow the route of the vehicle by going back over drone and security camera footage of the area." She pointed to the screen, "The live footage you're watching is from a drone stationed over the house where we think he's holed up."

Colby spoke to the man on his left? "Dornell! Is that Reaper armed?"

"Yes sir, four hellfire missiles."

"You're not thinking of using them, are you?" Finn interrupted.

"Not yet," Colby replied, "But we might have to, it's an option we'll keep open for now, I don't want this guy getting away."

"It's not!" Finn shouted, "He's the only person who knows where my sister is. We need to capture him and find out where Zafar is located."

"What do you suggest?" Colby calmed the tone, reducing the tension in the air.

"Give me a couple of your men as support. I'll go in tonight, capture and bring him back here then your people can interrogate him. If you kill him, you'll never know how far his network reaches into all the different intelligence agencies in the US."

Colby looked at Miller, "What do you think?"

Miller thought for a few moments before he looked at Finn and replied, "I agree! But we'll do it together, Finn, Dornell and myself. We'll infiltrate the house tonight under cover of darkness, capture Marshall, his accomplices and secure any evidence. I'll also need you Curtis," pointing to the man sitting next to Dornell, "you can do the driving and keep the outside area secure while we're inside doing our stuff. We go in fast, get him and get out."

Colby stood up, "Sounds like a good plan. Miller you're in charge, use Cooper and her team here as your intel link. I'll follow progress on the drone footage and listen in on the live feed. In the meantime, if Marshall exits the property, I want to be the first person to know about it." He walked over to the door and shouted back, "And make sure you bring the bastard back in one piece, he's vital to bringing down the whole organisation, we need his knowledge."

Colby left and the others talked freely about the mission. Finn focussed his attention on the drone footage, taking mental notes of the road layout, building positions, and the entry and exit points.

Miller asked Cooper, "What do you know about the property?"

"It's not much different to this place really, just a little smaller, there are high walls, a main metal gate wide enough for a car at the front and a small metal door at the rear. There are security cameras installed on the roof." Cooper added, "So getting in undetected may be difficult."

"Is there a blueprint of the building we can use?" Finn asked.

Cooper shrugged, "No, sorry, blueprints are not really used over here, people buy a plot of land and build whatever they want on it."

A grin appeared on Miller's face and he announced to the team, "We'll just have to do it the old way, on the hoof. Everyone get some food, get some rest, clean your weapons, check your gear and be ready to go at one hundred hours."

Chapter 24
Marshall

Curtis turned the estate car around so it faced towards the compound gate. Finn and Dornell climbed in the back with Miller sitting in the front. The assault team had silenced handguns, MP5 assault rifles, flash-bangs, smoke grenades and wore standard Special Forces uniforms with Kevlar vests.

"Guys! I need a comms check," Cooper announced.

The four men in the car called out their numbers in turn until Cooper responded, "All received, loud and clear, and guys...good luck."

Miller nodded at Curtis who drove the car to the gate. The security guard slowly pushed the gate open, peeked outside to check the road, then pushed the gate fully open and the car sped out into the dark street.

"Dornell, shout out the directions." Miller ordered.

Dornell looked at the hand-held satellite navigation system, pre-programmed with the address of Marshall's hideout, "Go left here...Straight ahead...Watch out there's a sharp bend coming up..."

The car followed a route through the backstreets of Kandahar, avoiding the populated areas of the city and the areas known to be under insurgent control. They arrived at an area, on the fringes of the City, with a mixture of homes, industrial units, and farm properties.

"Curtis!" Dornell shouted. "That's the place, over there with the black gate, one hundred yards on the left."

"Park here," Miller ordered. "Stay close by and monitor the outside area, any people who appear, shout out."

"Yes sir," Curtis stopped the car.

Miller turned to the two men in the back, "We'll go around to the rear wall. I'll use the EMP to short the cameras. Once they're deactivated the two of you lift me up onto the wall. I'll check for any guards, drop down and open the back gate. Once inside we'll assess the situation and decide the best way to infiltrate the house. Ready?"

The two men nodded. Miller opened his door and crept towards the rear of the property with Finn and Dornell following closely. Things went to plan. Alongside the rear wall Miller took out the EMP device while the others covered him. The device scanned the area for radio frequencies. After a few seconds a list appeared on the screen showing identification codes for all the electronic devices in the property. Miller scrolled through the list and ticked the boxes next to the six CCTV cameras and pressed a button. The device transmitted a pulse of energy which instantly fried the electronic circuits in the cameras. He checked the device again and confirmed the six cameras had disappeared from the original list.

He whispered to the others, "Hopefully they're not watching. Ready?"

Dornell and Finn, formed a cradle with their arms and Miller climbed on. The pair raised their arms, lifting him high enough to allow him to grab the top of the wall. With a heave, Miller managed to get up onto the top of the wall. He checked the visible area inside the compound and signalled to the men below that all was clear. He moved onto his front and slid down from the wall onto the ground. He made a noise on landing, rolled over onto his side, froze, and waited. He spotted a lit room on the ground floor and waited for movement. Confident he had escaped undetected he stood up and edged his way along the inside of the wall until he reached the rear gate. Taking a crowbar from his harness he quickly broke the padlocks and swung the metal door open.

Finn and Dornell quickly entered, Miller shut the gate behind them. The three men moved across the compound to the rear wall of the house and took up a crouched position. Miller took point, Finn behind him and Dornell walked backwards to protect the rear. They advanced slowly. At the corner Miller held up his arm to stop them. He scanned the area ahead for danger then gestured to move on.

Finding the ground floor window, on the side of the building, illuminated by a light inside the men got down lower. Miller indicated to Finn and Dornell to stop on the left of the window while he crawled under the windowsill and took up a position on the right. Miller took out a mirror on a retractable stick and raised it up to the window. Through a small crack in the curtains, he noticed a man laid on a sofa, asleep, but with a pistol on his chest.

Twisting the mirror to gain a view of the rest of the room he discovered another man sitting in a chair, awake, and armed with an assault rifle. Miller gestured to Finn and Dornell, using his fingers to indicate what he had seen.

The three men froze when they heard shouting from inside the house, "This is a crock of shit! You told us that you could get us out of the country. While we're sitting around here on our arses, they're looking for us."

Miller moved the mirror for a clearer view but couldn't see the person speaking.

A second voice responded, "Be quiet! I'm still working on it. That bastard Winter has messed everything up with the security team. All he had to do was arrange for the capture and interrogation of a woman. He sent a group of meat heads. They couldn't get her to talk so decided to kidnap her! The whole mess they created in New Mexico has opened a hornet's nest. Winter and his men have led the FBI straight to me."

Finn whispered to Miller, "That must be Marshall talking."

The voice inside continued to rant, "Because of that idiot all of my accounts have been closed. All the money we've got left is in those bags."

The three soldiers continued to listen.

The first voice spoke out again, "What about Zafar? Can't he help us?"

"He's disconnected his phone. I guess he suspects we'll just sell him out to the US or UK military. Either way we can't rely on him to help us."

"I knew we should've left him to rot in prison. What are we going to do?"

Miller whispered, reporting progress to Colby and the intel team, "We've found Marshall plus at least three more inside the building."

The second voice inside continued to talk loudly, "We just need to get over the border to Pakistan. We need to load up the car and start driving. We'll steal an SUV on the way, the old thing outside won't be able to handle the border roads. Once we've got a new base established in Pakistan, we'll set up a new supply line. Don't you worry, once I'm back in the game...I'll deal with Zafar."

Miller twisted the mirror around seeking the source of the chatter and spotted two men standing near the bottom of a staircase. Miller returned to the other side of the window, joining Finn and Dornell and gestured for them to move to the rear of the building.

Miller whispered to the others, "Four men downstairs. We'll just have to assume there's no one upstairs. The first two targets are in the room with the light, to the left of the doorway. We have one laid on a sofa with a handgun, the other is sitting in a chair with an AK47. The other two are standing between the door and a staircase. The one nearest to the stairs is the main talker, looks like Marshall, but not sure. The last is standing between him and the door. Those two don't have any visible weapons. From what I could make out they're getting ready to bail, we need to take them now. We need Marshall alive, the others it depends on if they put up a fight. Dornell, you stay at the side window and when I give the signal, smash it and send in two flash-bangs. Finn, you're with me, once the second flashbang has gone off, we'll breach the front door and throw in two more. I'll take down the men on the sofa and chair. You need to get the two near the stairs. Remember, we need to take Marshall alive. Understood?"

Finn and Dornell both nodded. The group returned to the window and Dornell got into position. The other two proceeded to the front door. They stood either side of the door and listened to the men talking inside. Miller made a click with his mouth, Dornell stood up, smashed the window with his rifle butt and threw in the flash bangs. Quickly, he crouched down and covered his ears.

The grenades landed on the floor between the chair and sofa and immediately detonated, producing a blinding flash of light and an intense loud sound, 'bang', 'bang'. The noise of the smashing window woke the man on the sofa, and he grabbed his gun. The flash activated the photoreceptor cells in the men's eyes, blinding him for several seconds while the detonation induced temporary deafness.

The man with the AK47 tried to stand up, blinded, disoriented and unable to focus his eyes. Losing his sense of balance, he stumbled forward.

On hearing Dornell's flash-bangs, Miller kicked the front door in and Finn threw in more flash-bangs. The pair jumped back, against the outside wall with their hands over their ears and eyes closed. The grenades detonated. 'bang, bang'.

Miller and Finn quickly entered the property, guns drawn, their military training in full flow.

Miller found a man directly in front of him, stumbling forward but with his arms out, as if trying to feel for an invisible wall. Miller hit him in the face with the butt of his rifle forcing the man backwards onto the floor. Miller moved forward and added a second blow to make sure he was out cold.

Finn moved to the right of Miller and discovered a man making his way up the staircase. The fleeing figure bounced off the staircase walls with each footstep that he took.

As the smoke from the flash-bangs began to clear, Miller detected the two men near the chair and sofa and shouted, "Freeze! US Special Forces, stand down."

The man next to the chair raised his assault rifle and Miller fired two shots, hitting the man in the hand and arm. The injuries forced the man to drop the weapon and fall backwards into the chair.

Miller looked to his right and noticed the man from the sofa, now standing with his handgun pointed directly at him. In a split second the man's head exploded, spraying blood and bits of skull and brain over Miller. As he advanced on the injured man in the chair Miller caught sight of Dornell at the window with his assault rifle drawn. He grabbed the man in the chair, now minus two fingers, and threw him to the floor, kneed him in the back and handcuffed him with tie-wraps. He turned towards the unconscious man and did the same.

Miller looked up to see Finn disappear up the stairs.

Seeing the man now stumbling along the upper landing, Finn shouted "Freeze!"

The man immediately turned towards Finn and began wildly shooting his pistol. The effect of the light afterimage, still in the man's eyes from the flash-bang detonation, rendered him partially blind. His shots had no true direction, hitting the walls, ceiling, and floor.

Finn dived into a doorway for cover, hiding behind the frame. He peaked out and saw the man turning away from him, continuing to flee. Taking out his handgun Finn shot the man twice. The first bullet grazed the man's thigh, the second entered the back of the man's left calf. The man screamed in pain as the exiting bullet took a chunk of bone from his leg. The leg buckled, unable to support the fleeing man's weight and he collapsed, face down onto the stone floor, breaking his nose and cracking his front teeth.

Finn moved forward, kneed him in the back to wind him, then pulled his arms behind him and tie-wrapped his hands together. He dragged the protesting man along the floor and down the stairs. He dumped the body and looked around the room, finding Miller standing over two bodies, his face and vest covered in blood. He noticed Dornell next to the window and a headless body sprawled over the rear of the sofa. The flash-bang detonation ignited the sofa material and smoke slowly filled the room.

Miller shouted, "Curtis! We are coming out the front gate. Get the car there now!"

Dornell appeared at the front door. Miller grabbed the unconscious man and dragged the body outside, towards the courtyard, "Get the other two, we're leaving."

Finn and Dornell did as instructed and the three men each dragged a body towards the main gate.

Miller moved to the padlocked gate, quickly broke the lock, swung it open and found Curtis outside. He shouted "Open the boot!"

Curtis climbed out, ran to the rear of the estate car, and opened the hatch. Miller, Dornell and Finn dragged their prisoners out of the gate and bundled the bodies into the vehicle.

Miller took out his phone and took photos of the captured men's faces then slammed the hatch. He looked back to see the downstairs of the house completely engulfed in flames. The men climbed into the car and Curtis quickly gained speed. In the rear, two of the captured men groaned in pain from their injuries while the third remained silent, still out cold.

Miller, with dried blood covering his face and jacket, looked behind to face Finn and Dornell, "That went about as well as we could've expected!" Then laughed aloud.

"Miller, are you hit?" Finn enquired.

"It's not my blood. I hope for your sake Dornell the head shot wasn't Marshall."

"I didn't get the chance to ask him boss." Dornell protested.

"I owe you a beer, thanks for saving my life back there."

"You'd have done the same."

Miller grinned, "True, now let's get the hell out of Dodge."

Chapter 25
Zafar's Compound

Abdul-Ali drove his pickup from the rutted farm track onto an unpaved, gravel road. Whilst still uneven it allowed him to begin to increase speed with the other pickups close behind. He passed through a lush green landscape with many vegetation types but mainly poppy fields, grapes, and cannabis plants.

He continued driving south on the unpaved, gravel road joining a two-lane tarmac road heading towards Nalgham, and home. The improved surface allowed him to increase speed. He looked to his left and noticed the banks and flowing water of the Arghandab river.

He pulled the pickup off the highway, twelve miles north of Nalgham, and joined an unpaved road again. The dry gravel and the dust from the wheels engulfed the pickup trucks behind, making them slow down. A gap grew between the three pickup trucks and the ever-increasing dust cloud forced the fighters in the flatbeds to wrap their shemagh scarfs tighter around their heads and faces for protection.

The soldiers in the rear of Abdul-Ali's truck watched the dust generating chaos behind and laughed to themselves. One pulled a blanket up over Kathy to protect her from the dust swirling around the pickup.

The pickup drove between farmers' fields, stocked with crops of poppy, maize, alfalfa, and vegetables. Fruit trees with grape, peach pomegranate and figs lined the road and the banks of the irrigation channels. The road entered an area of heavier vegetation as they drove closer to the river. The fertile soil contained shrubs, bushes and fruit bearing trees which provided valuable shade for farmers and their animals. Abdul-Ali stopped to allow a herd of karakul sheep to cross the road. He waved to the shepherd and continued his journey.

From within the heavily vegetated area a large walled compound appeared at the end of the road. He swerved to avoid a goat and cursed a young boy who ran out into the road to collect it. He slowed to a crawl and approached the building. Two large steel gates stood in the middle of the fifteen-foot-high compound wall. Fruit trees on either side of the gate provided cover for the guards and pickups with mounted guns stationed outside. Out of sight of the regular drones operating in the skies above.

One of the guards noticed the approaching convoy and acknowledged Abdul-Ali returning. As if in a panic, he yelled aloud and banged on the steel gates. The gates opened inwards, the convoy drove in and the guards quickly closed them behind. After entering the dusty compound, Abdul-Ali parked up and climbed out at the same time as the other pickups pulled up alongside.

The men jumped out and Abdul-Ali shouted out orders, "Hakeem! take her inside. You men, move the vehicles to the stables, the satellite will be overhead soon."

He directed his attention to the four men dressed all in black.

"Stay with the men," he directed Martinez with his outstretched arm. "They live over there in the barracks. You're welcome to share their food and hospitality."

Before Martinez could respond, Abdul-Ali walked away and headed towards the main building. Martinez surveyed the high walled compound, a series of mud brick buildings in the shape of a 'U' facing on to the gated entrance. Along the full length of the rear wall stood a single-story property with curved window frames and a mix of open and closed shutters. In the centre several steps led up to a large wooden door. On the right side of the compound a stable building. Partly used to hide vehicles and the remaining used for housing the goats contained within a small wire fence at the front. An identical shaped building stood on the left side of the compound, converted into a kitchen, a canteen area, and several barrack rooms for the men.

Martinez turned to his men, "Let's get ourselves set up over there in the barracks, see what you can do for his ankle. Afterwards, I'll go and see Zafar. We need to arrange transport to Kandahar airport, hook up with the Iron Fist contractors and get home. I also don't like the look of these guys, so watch your backs."

Martinez headed towards the barracks. The others followed, two holding up the third with his damaged ankle. He looked in the first doorway and found a room with low level seating, carpets on the floor and several men talking and smoking. As Martinez appeared in the doorway the men stopped and turned towards him. Taking the greeting as moderately hostile, he decided to move to the next doorway, only for the same to happen again. After a similar experience at the next he came to the final door in the block. He looked inside, disappointed to find just a washroom and toilet. The smell from the drain made him baulk and he quickly returned to the compound outside. He decided to return to the previous doorway and walked inside. The fighters stopped talking and stared at him in silence. He chose a free space on a sofa, sat down and gestured to his men to join him. The Iron Fist men threw down their packs and settled down. Eventually the local fighters lost interest and continued talking among themselves.

∴ ∴ ∴ ∴

Two guards gently lifted Kathy from the pickup truck and carried her towards the garage area of the compound, Hakeem followed close behind. With her eyes half open, she drifted in and out of consciousness. The guards carried her through a small door into a corridor which led to a small room where they placed her on a mattress on the floor, Hakeem knelt beside her.

Kathy opened her eyes finding him leaning over her and behind a middle-aged woman wearing a traditional Afghan dress and a scarf covering her hair.

The woman came closer and looked down at Kathy's face, scrutinising her partially opened eyes and dazed look, the woman shouted at the guards as they left the room "What have you done to her?"

Hakeem mumbled, "She was injured by the men who captured her. They've drugged her and she may have a concussion. She will be ok if she gets rest."

"Take care of her," the woman barked. "And make sure you clean and feed her. He won't be happy if he sees her like this, you know the price of failure."

Hakeem nodded and the woman left the room.

Kathy opened her eyes and climbed from the mattress, "Where am I?"

"You're safe now," Hakeem confirmed. He pushed her down, "Rest! I'll return soon with food and water. I'll also get some pain killers."

Kathy opened her eyes fully and pushed the man away from her. She managed to sit up and shouted, "Who are you? Tell me where I'm?"

Hakeem moved away from the mattress, and nervously looked behind him at the doorway. He turned to her and raised his hands, showing his palms, "Please be quiet. Don't make a fuss. Making a noise will make him angry. I can't tell you anything but I'm sure things will be clearer soon. Take the opportunity to rest while you can."

Kathy watched as Hakeem left the room, shutting and locking the door behind him. Sitting up she looked around her. The ten-foot square, unfurnished, room contained only a bucket in the corner. Above her, sunlight poured in through a square hole in the ceiling, the bars too far away to reach. Light came in through a hatch in the old and battered wooden door. She looked at the pastel green coloured walls covered in writing and graffiti. Messages scratched into the plaster, words written in Arabic, English and French. Eventually the starkness of her situation dawned on her. *A prison.*

Kathy pushed herself up off the mattress and staggered, her legs struggling to hold the weight of her body. The concussion combined with the sleeping pills made her feel unsteady and queasy. Leaning with one hand on the wall, she gradually steadied herself and moved across the room towards the door. She peered through the hatch and noticed a corridor and a partially open door, leading to outside. The sun lit up the dry, dusty corridor as the dust blew in from outside. She racked her brain for answers, none came. She raised her hand to her face and felt the dressing covering the cut above her eye. She felt the bump on her forehead and winced in pain.

In some sort of ritual and to make herself presentable, she ran her fingers through her matted hair, finding it ingrained with dust and dried blood. She pulled it from her face and continued to use her fingers as a brush. Her attention moved to her t-shirt and cargo shorts. She banged her clothes repetitively to clear them of dust. Eventually, she gave up and moved to the rear of the cell, towards the bucket. The smell and contents told her why it was there.

She staggered to the mattress and laid down, staring up towards the small square opening. She listened to the noise of vehicles and men shouting outside and the sounds of bells ringing on the goat's necks. She smiled, finding some strange comfort in the sound, and drifted to sleep.

❖ ❖ ❖ ❖

Martinez grew impatient, sitting around doing nothing. He told his men to wait and ventured outside to look for Abdul-Ali. He wandered around the compound, unable to find him. He tried to ask various Afghan fighters but they all shrugged at him, unable to understand the language. His patience ran out and he headed to the house.

He banged on the large wooden door. The middle-aged woman opened the door then stood and stared at him.

"Hello!" Martinez barked, "Do you know where Abdul-Ali is?"

The woman remained silent, before Martinez could say more, Hakeem appeared in the doorway, grabbed his arm, pulling him away from the door which quickly closed.

"Don't do that again, no one is allowed in the house," Hakeem said anxiously.

"Get off!" Martinez protested. "Where the hell is Abdul-Ali? I must speak to him."

Hakeem looked around the compound nervously, noticing fighters gathering at the entrance of the barrack rooms, curious to see what the commotion was about, "Please sir, be quiet! Abdul-Ali is not here. He won't be here until morning."

Still protesting, Martinez shouted, "Cut the crap! Where's Zafar?"

Hakeem noticed the fighters approaching and pulled Martinez away from the house, leading him back to his men, "Stay here, eat, rest and sleep. Abdul-Ali will return in the morning. You can talk then."

Martinez gave up, one of his men asked, "So what happened?" He didn't reply.

Hakeem waved to the fighters and spoke in Pashto. Slowly, they returned to their barracks.

∴ ∴ ∴ ∴

Kathy woke to the noise of footsteps on the hard stone floor outside. The sounds of a key fumbling at the lock forced her to open her eyes. Looking up she found the man who helped her earlier, entering the room.

Kathy sat up on her elbows as he walked over and kneeled beside her, "Is your health improving?"

"Can you help me?" she asked in a hoarse whisper, all she could manage from her parched throat.

Hakeem opened a bottle of water and passed it to her. She gulped down the contents until it was empty.

"Please help me," she pleaded.

Hakeem looked behind nervously, and moved over to the door to check that no one was listening. He slowly closed the door and returned to Kathy.

He muttered, "Don't ask me questions, I can't tell you anything or I'll get into trouble, I don't know why you're here. I'm also a prisoner, my only crime is they need a medic. Please just do as they say, it's preferential to punishment, now sit up."

Kathy pushed herself up and sat on the mattress. He checked her injuries, put a new dressing on her cut and rubbed cream into the bruise on her head. He used a torch to check her eyes then reached into a pocket, pulled something out and pushed it into her hand. She glanced into her palm to see a small white plastic bubble pack, turned it over and in letters printed on the foil, she read 'paracetamol'.

Hakeem whispered, "You need to take two now and two in a few hours. There are a few spare ones, keep them out of sight in your pocket. You need to get the sleeping pills out of your system so don't take too many, save them until you need them."

He returned to the door, opened it wide, and said loudly, "I'm glad you're making progress, I'll bring some food."

The door shut and she heard the key in the lock. She pressed tablets out of the bubble pack and swallowed them, hiding the rest in her shorts.

Questions swirled around in her mind. She thought about her friends and recalled the events which had taken place at the campsite. Tears appeared in her eyes but she quickly stopped herself. Wiping away the tears she thought of her brother and how he would react if he caught her crying. Finn had always taught her to look after herself.

She remembered how he would always say 'No crying'. That was his mantra when she fell in the playground, when she failed to get her dream job or when her boyfriend cheated on her. She kept telling herself. *No Crying*.

She heard footsteps again outside. The door unlocked, opened wide and the middle-aged woman stood in the doorway. Seeing Kathy awake she walked over and placed a tray on the floor next to her, "Food. Eat!"

Kathy watched as the woman disappeared outside and heard the door lock. She glanced at the tray, a large bowl with a stew of meat and vegetables, bread, a bowl with figs and a large bottle of water. With a plastic spoon she quickly ate the stew, not caring about the ingredients. Between spoonful's she pulled chunks of bread, dipping it into the stew before eating. She liked the tasty stew even if the meat was a bit chewy. Once it was all gone, she used the final bit of bread to clean the bowl.

Replacing the stew bowl on the tray she picked up the bowl containing figs finding them soft and ripe. Splitting them with her fingers she sucked out the sweet meat inside. Afterwards she drank water from the bottle.

Finally, she pushed away the tray and sat up on the mattress with her back resting on the wall. With her bladder now bursting she could no longer hold the urge. After relieving herself in the bucket she laid back on the mattress. She stared above her and noticed the sky getting darker. Her eyes felt heavy and she drifted off to sleep.

Chapter 26
SOG Safe House

On the return journey, Miller sent the pictures to Cooper using his US made version of iBOW. She called back moments later to confirm the identity of the older man as Marshall.

When the news came over the radio Miller looked to Dornell and smiled, "You're off the hook."

At the safe house, the four soldiers climbed out of the estate car and moved to the rear hatch. Miller opened it and reached inside grabbing the unconscious man's ankles. He pulled him out far enough to be able to lift him and heaved him onto his shoulder. He turned to the others and barked, "Grab a body and follow me."

He set off towards a small building on the side of the compound. Finn, Dornell and Curtis looked at each other.

Finn reached inside and grabbed the man with a gunshot wound to the arm and pulled him out onto the ground. The man hit his head on the bumper and let out a groan. Finn punched him in the face, knocking him out and joked, "That makes life easier." He lifted the limp body onto his shoulder and followed Miller.

Dornell and Curtis looked at Marshall. Seeing the blood leaking from the gunshot wound on his leg Dornell said, "We're going to have to carry him."

With his arms tied behind his back, the two soldiers lifted him, using his armpits. They half carried and half dragged him towards the small building.

"Who the hell are you guys? I need a doctor. I'll bleed out if I don't get some medical treatment." Marshall protested, but they ignored him. "Are you Americans? I'm protected, you need to speak to someone at the NSA. Are you two listening!"

They continued to ignore him and followed Finn and Miller into the small building finding an empty room with equally spaced metal rings scattered around the walls, two-feet off the floor. Finn and Miller dumped the unconscious men on the dusty floor and handcuffed them to the metal rings. Once finished, they stood back and looked at the manacled prisoner's bodies slumped on the dry mud floor.

"What should we do with this one?" Curtis asked. "He's losing a lot of blood."

Miller walked towards the man, "Hope it hurts Marshall you piece of shit!"

Marshall struggled between the two soldiers and tried to attack Miller, who just smiled and said "In your dreams scumbag."

Finn looked at the injured leg, "We need to get that looked at, he can't tell us anything if he's dead."

"I'm not talking to anyone," Marshall yelled and Finn punched him in the stomach. Marshall doubled up, the two soldiers taking his weight.

Finn grabbed the injured man by the chin, looked into his eyes and said menacingly, "If you don't tell me what I need to know, I'll kill you."

Miller pulled Finn back and ordered the others to take Marshall to the medical room. Curtis and Dornell did as instructed.

Miller looked at Finn, "Cool it buddy. We only need to keep him alive long enough to find out where Zafar and your sister are…after that you can do as you like. We need to report to Colby while he gets fixed up."

∴ ∴ ∴ ∴

Finn and Miller joined Colby in the Ops room.

Colby asked, "What's the latest on Marshall?"

"Just waiting for the Doc to let us talk to him, hopefully soon." Miller replied.

"I need a full account of what Marshall has been up to and a list of all the people involved in his caper both here and back in the States. Leave no stone unturned."

"Don't worry boss," Miller said with conviction. "We'll get what we need out of him, then we can formulate a plan on what we do next."

∴ ∴ ∴ ∴

A man entered the room finding Marshall laid on a bed with blood leaking out of the wound on his leg.

Marshall cursed, "Who the fuck are you?"

The man calmly replied, "A doctor."

He picked up a pair of scissors and slowly cut away the remains of Marshall's trouser leg. He inspected the wound. The bullet had entered the back of the calf and shattered the bone as it exited. The injury was not as bad as first thought, despite the loss of blood. He picked up a syringe, inserted the needle into a small bottle, filled the tube and injected the liquid into Marshall's arm who gradually stopped moving.

"What's that you're giving him Doc?" Dornell asked.

"Just a sedative." The doctor looked at the two soldiers next to him, covered in dust, mud and armed with numerous weapons, "You two can wait outside, he's out now and won't be awake again until the morning. I'll fix his broken leg, stitch him up and give him some blood. He should be fit enough to talk to Miller in the morning."

Dornell replied, "He needs to be kept secure Doc, he's dangerous."

"I'll monitor him," The doctor ushering them towards the door, "Get out!"

∴ ∴ ∴ ∴

Marshall woke at 10:46.

The doctor immediately called Miller, "He's awake."

"Get Dornell and Curtis to take him to the ops room and tell them to be careful. He's not going anywhere fast with his leg in plaster but don't trust him for a second."

"Okay, I think I'll cope." The doctor confirmed.

Marshall raised his head and reached down to touch his leg, "How is it?"

"You'll have a limp," the doctor confirmed, "one leg is shorter than the other. Sorry, I did the best I could with what remained of the bone. You'll need to see a dentist when you get home and your nose is bent but apart from that you'll be fine."

Marshall flopped his head backwards onto the pillow, accepting his situation and asked, "Can you at least give me something for the pain?"

"I've already given you a shot of Morphine, you can't have any more yet. We don't want you getting addicted to the stuff." Marshall groaned before the doctor added, "It's a bit ironic isn't it that you're probably responsible for the death of hundreds of heroin addicts in the US and here I am trying to stop you joining them."

The two guards walked into the room and the doctor stood back as they lifted Marshall from the bed, "Be careful, keep the weight off his leg and let me know if anything happens."

Dornell replied, "Will do."

The two soldiers picked up Marshall from the bed and carried him between them down the stairs to the Ops room. Colby directed them to put Marshall in the chair at the head of the table. They stood behind him with their pistols drawn, waiting for the others. A few moments later Finn and Miller arrived. Miller sat next to Colby to the right side of Marshall while Finn sat opposite.

Colby lit a cigarette, "Do you want one?" gesturing with the packet to Marshall who shook his head in reply. He took a few drags on the cigarette and looked back to Marshall, "You've been a naughty boy Marshall but I can confirm your little game is up. We've arrested the people at the DEA field office here in Kandahar and we're shutting down your little organisation in the US. Bank accounts are frozen and we're in the process of seizing all the money." He paused, looked down, clearing some ash from the table with his hand. "Well, most of it. You people always seem to find a way to hide some of it away."

"What's all that got to do with me?" Marshall barked back.

"Shut up idiot!" Miller cursed, "We recorded your speech at your hideout."

"I'm a US citizen." Marshall mumbled, "I want to be taken to the USA. I need to speak to my lawyer."

"You seem to forget that no one actually knows you're here Marshall, this is a SOG operation." Colby grinned, "It's easy for me to just say you died at your hideout and in a few days…you'll be forgotten about."

"What! You wouldn't do that…would you?" Marshall looked around the table at the faces of the men in front of him. He made eye contact with Finn, noticed his eyes darken and a shiver ran through his body.

"Tell me everything I need to know and I'll promise you a long and happy life at Fort Leavenworth, Kansas." Colby urged, before dropping his cigarette on the floor and stepping on it, "I've given you the alternative."

Marshall could feel the pain in his leg slowly increasing, a regular throbbing, mixed with sharp stings of pains. Sweat covered his face and he became light headed. He rubbed his face to revive himself, looked at Colby and said hoarsely, "What about a deal?"

"No deals!" Colby shouted and banged the table with his fist, "You tell me what I want to know and you'll live. If not, I'll arrange for someone to dump your body in the street. It's your choice. Now start talking before I lose my patience."

"Okay!" Marshall shrieked, looking desperately at the men around him, "Get me a bottle of whiskey, some decent food, and get the doctor down here with his magic needle. Once you've sorted all that, I'll tell you everything." He shuffled nervously in his chair, "I also want it in writing that you'll be taking me back to the USA."

Colby nodded and instructed Curtis to get the items, ignoring the request for the doctor. After a few moments he returned with the whisky and a couple of ham sandwiches, placing them in front of Marshall.

Marshall grabbed the first sandwich and ate it in a couple of bites, his mouth full of food as he spun the top off the whisky bottle. The lid flew away onto the dusty floor as he took a series of large mouthfuls.

Miller leaned forward and grabbed the bottle from his hand, "That's enough! You need to start talking before you get anymore."

Marshall quickly ate the second sandwich, looked at Colby and asked, "What do you want to know?"

"Start from the beginning."

"The beginning? You mean at the DEA? In the beginning I thought I was doing something good until I found out how much money other people were making. I was moving around the world, following the drugs and money, surrounded by corrupt people. I soon realised on retirement I was going to leave the agency with no family, no home and just a basic agency pension. Once reality kicked in it was easy to switch sides." He reached for the bottle, Miller handed it back and he took a long drink.

"It started with the Columbians but that operation got shut down. The agency posted me over here to monitor the Afghan drug trade and that's when I met Zafar. We set up a network shipping opium product into Pakistan and Iran but there's no money in shipping small batches. To make the big bucks we had to get the drugs into the US. That opportunity came around when I encountered Winter overseeing the security at the airport. Once he was on board, it opened all the doors to expand the operation. Things were good, the money flowed in and I dreamed about getting out.

"The authorities in Washington decided to stop the flow of money to the insurgents and the US and UK military started bombing buildings, burning fields, and handing over the local tribe leaders to the Afghans to throw in prison. Zafar managed to keep himself hidden but once he was captured supplies dried up."

"That's why you got him out of prison?" Colby asked.

"Of course! The organisation had grown, there were bills to pay."

"Go on!" Colby demanded.

"When he went to jail, we collected product direct from the individual farmers across the Arghandab and Helmand valleys. It proved too much of a risk as it exposed Winter and his men."

"Why?" Colby asked.

"They were noticed moving in areas where the military were operating, questions began to be asked. Getting Zafar out of prison was the only way we could get things back on track. We used his local contacts and with a few bribes and blackmail it was easy to get him out. Once he was back in charge of the farmers the supplies soon increased back to the original levels."

"Surely it's not as easy as that, the locals would protest." Miller said.

Marshall continued, "It was easy for him. He took over all the poppy production here in the Arghandab valley, using his usual motivation methods, fear and brutality. He killed anyone who wouldn't work for him to warn everyone else against defying him. The locals grow the poppies, harvest the resin, refine it into heroin and Zafar takes all the profits. He gets the farmers to transport the goods to various addresses in Kandahar. That's when Winter's security guards collect it. They pack the drugs into crates at the airport and it's shipped to Lubbock, no questions asked. The money is cleaned then distributed by a series of accountants and shell companies, Zafar gets his share, Winter too."

Marshall drank more whisky from the bottle.

"Sounds like you had a good business going so why has it all come crashing down?" Miller asked.

"Zafar!" Marshall cursed, "He came out of prison a changed man, vengeful, bitter, full of hatred for people. He was nasty before but he'd become mentally unstable."

"That doesn't explain why the business has crashed. What did Zafar do?" Miller asked impatiently.

Marshall shouted back at Miller, "The woman! He became obsessed about that bloody woman! He wouldn't supply any more drugs until we captured her."

Finn looked at Miller and motioned to speak. Miller grabbed his arm.

"Who is this woman? Come on! Out with it." Miller demanded.

The mixture of the alcohol and the drugs affected Marshall's speech, "I don't know. Some British woman, Finn…Katherine Finn…I think…I'm not sure." He said in a slurred tone. "He asked about a Captain in the SAS…a soldier in the British Army Special Forces. I found some general intel, just some basic military papers, nothing classified and passed it on to him. He read them and asked about the Captain's sister, demanding that we capture and interrogate her. We had to discover if she knew the location of the British camp where the Captain's soldiers were based. I found out from her ESTA application that she planned to travel to the US for a holiday. Winter's job was simple, capture her, rough her up a bit and get the information. Instead, he sent some meatheads who decided to shoot her friends. From what I hear she wouldn't talk, Winter told Zafar and he ordered him to send her to him using one of his transport planes. It was just what Winter wanted to hear, he wanted to get rid of her off his base."

Finn stood up and grabbed Marshall by the shirt, pulling him out of the chair, "Where's this British woman now? Where have you sent her?"

"Get off me!" Marshall protested.

"Not until you tell me where the woman is."

Miller stood up to pull Finn back.

Colby grabbed his arm and whispered, "Leave it."

Finn hit Marshall in the face with a punch which would have knocked most men out cold, but the alcohol in his blood dampened the effects. Marshall cried in pain as his lip split and blood flowed down onto his shirt. He spat and two teeth spun away across the floor. He felt his misshapen nose and wiped blood from his lips.

Finn shook him, "That's just the start. I'll not ask you again, where she is!"

Marshall grabbed a tissue from the plate and held it to his nose to stop the blood.

Finn yelled, "Talk man or I'll kill you."

The look in Finn's eyes frightened Marshall and he held up his hands, "Okay," he mumbled. "As far as I know she's at Zafar's base. A converted farmhouse in the Arghandab valley. The last message I received said she was on the ground with four of Winter's security guards waiting to be collected by Zafar's men."

"That's enough for now," Colby threw a pen and paper on the table. "Give me the details of the location."

Marshall picked up the pen, scribbled some words, then threw the pen down.

Colby shouted down the table to Dornell, "Take him upstairs, get the doctor to look him over. And stay with him."

As the two guards helped Marshall up from the chair he turned to Finn, "How do you know this woman?"

Finn just stared at him, did not answer and picked up the paper. The guards dragged Marshall away. Finn read the words written on the paper and passed it to Miller, "Doesn't mean anything to me, do you recognise it?"

Miller read and replied, "Not sure, I think it's somewhere in the Zhari district, near Nalgham."

"That's on the Arghandab river south of here, right?" Finn asked.

Miller nodded.

"What do you know about the area?"

"It's a bit wild down there that's for sure," Miller replied. "Most of the people in Zhari are ethnic Pashtuns with strong links to Iran and Pakistan. There's a dozen or so tribes living in the area, plus some nomads which pass through the northern areas. Mixed in with the locals there are factions like the Taliban which specifically target our guys. They use IED's, suicide bombers and booby traps. A favourite trick is to injure one of our guys then wait until help arrives so they can send a suicide bomber in to get the rest. Most of the Pashtuns are decent, hardworking, people but they have had to learn to live with conflict day in and day out."

Finn turned to Colby, "We need to go to Zafar's compound and get her back."

Colby nodded, then turned to Miller, "So what's the plan?"

"We need to give Zafar's location to Cooper. I want a drone over the top of his base immediately gathering intel. We need to find out how many men Zafar has stationed there and what sort of firepower he has. To do that we will need access to the new drone design the Air Force are using. The one with combined Lidar and Thermal Imaging technology. What's it called?" He paused thinking to himself, "Echo! the Echo camera system. With that we will be able to create a map of the compound and buildings, plus see whoever is inside them." He looked at Colby and asked, "Can you speak to the Air Force and sort one out for us?"

"I'll see what I can do. What's it called exactly?"

"It's the new ECS Predator, a modification of the old MQ-1."

"Leave it with me."

Miller turned to Finn, "With the new camera system we may get lucky and even spot Kathy."

Finn smiled, "I hope so."

Miller stood up, "Come on Finn we've got some planning to do."

Colby looked at his watch, "It's just after midday, meet me here at fourteen hundred hours with a full action plan. We need to get moving on this today before Zafar finds out we're onto him and goes to ground."

Chapter 27
Amir Zafar

Kathy woke to see sunlight streaming in from the opening above her head. Slowly sitting up on the mattress she reached into her pocket for the tablets. She took two and washed them down with some water. After using the bucket, she returned to the mattress and waited.

She heard footsteps outside, the key in the lock and the door opened. The middle-aged woman stood in the doorway with a tray.

Kathy admired the traditional dress which was beautifully embroidered with many different coloured patterns woven into the fabric. She wore a silver silk head scarf covering her hair.

"Good morning!" The woman announced as she entered and placed the tray on the floor. As before, it contained some stew and figs.

Kathy noticed her accent and asked, "Are you English?"

"No, I'm Afghan, but I was educated in London. Eat while you can."

The woman turned to leave and Kathy shouted, "Please don't go, please stay, can you help me?"

The woman replied in a comforting tone, "Don't worry, I'm sure you'll be fine, but please do as you're told, don't make a fuss."

Kathy watched her leave and heard the lock in the door. She quickly ate the food then laid back on the mattress. Her head hurt and she felt sleepy. She felt herself slipping into a semi-conscious state and tried to keep awake by listening to movement in the house and outside in the compound. Her body told her to sleep and she slowly closed her eyes.

✧ ✧ ✧ ✧

The morning sun quickly warmed the air in the compound and barracks. Martinez woke seeing Afghan fighters moving around. He got up from the floor and walked outside. The fighters continued to ignore him. He walked to the canteen and joined a line of men collecting bowls of food and bread from a server. After receiving his ration, he sat on a bench outside the canteen and ate. One of his men appeared and he instructed him to get food for the others. He ate the food and returned the bowl to a sink in the kitchen area and walked casually around the compound, taking stock of the location both in boredom and curiosity.

Suddenly, he heard a commotion and watched as fighters ran towards the gates. A group of six removed a steel bar across the gate, threw it down and with three men on each side they opened the heavy gates. Three vehicles, two pickup trucks laden with men and supplies, at either end of a Land Rover, drove into the compound. Martinez noticed Abdul-Ali driving the front pickup. The pickups stopped, the gates quickly closed and the occupants climbed out. The fighters in the compound cheered, holding guns above their heads, and gathered around the Land Rover where a man climbed out, dressed the same as the fighters.

Martinez moved closer into the crowd to gain a clearer view of the man, considered his appearance, and decided he was in his early forties. It was hard to work out his age due to the long beard, heavily tanned face and shemagh wrapped around his neck and head. Regardless of his age and look, the reaction confirmed the fighters adored the man and held him in high regard.

The man raised his arms and waved the fighters away. Abdul-Ali shouted out orders, breaking up the crowd, men quickly unloaded the pickup trucks and hid the items away as the man walked casually towards the house.

Martinez followed the man and got within a few feet before fighters noticed his progress and began shouting, drawing their weapons. The man turned around to face Martinez, who gestured to speak but before he could, he felt a blow on the side of his head. He fell onto the dusty soil, rolled on to his back and looked up to see Abdul-Ali standing over him, pointing a gun at his head.

"Be careful my friend," Abdul-Ali warned. "This is no time to be brave."

Martinez held up his hands in submission. Abdul-Ali stood back to allow Martinez to get up. Once on his feet, he noticed a ring of fighters had gathered around him. He kept his arms aloft while Abdul-Ali spoke in Pashto to the fighters. Slowly they lowered their weapons and moved away.

Martinez watched as the man disappeared inside the house, "Was that Zafar?"

"You mean Amir Zafar?"

"Sorry, yes, I mean Amir Zafar."

Abdul-Ali lowered his AK47, "You don't talk to our leader. When he's ready, he will talk to you. If he wants to know something, he'll ask. Never do that again, I may not be able to protect you next time."

Martinez lowered his arms, "I just want to know how I get out of here with my men. We need to get to Kandahar airport so we can fly home."

"You can leave at any time, the gate is over there," Abdul-Ali pointed. "Just ask the guards and they'll let you out."

Martinez looked at the gate then turned back, not really knowing what to say. "But..." He mumbled. "How do we get to Kandahar?"

Abdul-Ali looked at him, laughed and walked away saying, "That's your problem my friend, you arrived, I'm sure you'll find a way to get back."

Martinez stood and watched Abdul-Ali walk away. He gathered up his men in a huddle, looked around then whispered, "We are in shits creek here without a paddle. They won't help us get to Kandahar airport, they said we can walk. I guess it's over 60km to the airport. We need to get clear of this place then we'll steal a vehicle." He looked at the guard with the injured ankle, "Can you walk?"

The guard nodded, "I'll give it a go boss if someone can make me a crutch, the sooner we get going the better."

"Good man." He pointed at the other men in turn, "You, go and find something he can use as a crutch. And you, collect up as much food and water as we can carry. We'll meet back here in fifteen minutes. Get going!"

The men split up, Martinez stayed with the injured man, checked the guns and magazines, counted the bullets, and checked his handgun.

One guard returned with a piece of wood, "Found this in the stables, smells of goat shit, but it'll do a job."

He handed it to the injured guard who pushed himself up onto his feet using the "Y" shaped yoke in his armpit. He nodded, "That's great thanks."

The final guard returned with bags of food and a couple of bladders with water, "I managed to get these, they'll do until we can get some more."

"Great work," Martinez said, "Now let's get going."

The four men set off towards the gate as the fighters watched. At the gate Martinez motioned to open the gate and the guards ignored him. He told his men to lift the steel bar and there was a sudden burst of gunfire. Turning, Martinez observed Abdul-Ali walking across the compound towards him with an AK47 raised above his head.

When he got close enough, he shouted to Martinez, "Where are you going my friend? Amir Zafar would like to talk with you."

In the distance Martinez noticed Zafar standing in the doorway of the house.

Abdul-Ali shouted, "You come with me, the rest stay there."

"Stay alert. I don't like the look of this," Martinez whispered to his men.

He approached Abdul-Ali and the two men walked together towards Zafar. When they got close enough to talk, Abdul-Ali stopped and held his arm out blocking Martinez's progress.

"You're the man in charge?" Zafar asked Martinez.

"Yes, I'm Martinez. I'm second in command of General Winter's security guards."

Zafar laughed loudly saying, "The great General Winter, he owes me a considerable amount of money for the opium he recently took from me. I hear from my sources both the DEA man and him have disappeared. My banker in Pakistan has told me that all my money has disappeared. Do you know where my money is?"

"No." Martinez mumbled nervously, "It was my job to deliver the woman, I don't know anything about money."

"I've been told you delivered the woman injured. I thought I told Winter she must arrive here in perfect condition."

"We received a message informing us the plane would be searched when it arrived at Kandahar. Marshall told us to do a parachute jump and bring her direct to you."

"You admit then you're responsible for her condition?" Zafar's tone grew ever more menacing.

Martinez noted the danger in his tone, "I did my best," holding up his hands as if to surrender. "It was a dangerous jump but she'll be ok in a few days. One of my men was also injured."

"This situation makes me very angry. You don't have my money and you have no way to get my money, instead, you want to leave, is that correct?"

"Yes, if you don't mind, we need to get to Kandahar Airport so we can get a plane back to the US."

Zafar's eyes darkened. He stared at Martinez for a few moments then gestured towards the gate, "Go! Get out of here, make your way back to the great USA."

Surprised, Martinez looked at Zafar and said nervously, "Thank you."

He turned, ran towards the gate and worked with his men to remove the steel bar. Lifting it clear, they threw it onto the floor and two used their weight to force open the heavy steel gate. Once wide enough, they grabbed their guns and pushed through the gap and out onto the dusty track outside. Behind them they heard the gate close and the steel bar refitted.

They started to walk down the dirt road. The man with the crutch turned to Martinez, "Narrow escape! What did the Afghan say to you? He seemed pissed off."

Martinez motioned to reply when he heard the fifty calibre guns on the pickup trucks engaging behind him. He turned quickly, pulling his assault rifle up in defence but the burst of armour piercing bullets cut him down. As if performing some dance his body twitched as the bullets tore into his body. When the shooting stopped the lifeless body collapsed onto the road. The gunner laughed in some mad battle cry.

Two guards scattered leaving the injured one stranded in the middle of the road. Bullets ripped into his body and he collapsed, dead, next to Martinez.

One guard made it to the left side of the road and dived into a ditch, the other went to the right. After shooting the first two, each pickup gunner chose a side and continued to rain bullets into the undergrowth on the sides of the road, cutting down bushes and ripping branches from the trees. Bullets tore into the back of the guard on the right side of the road killing him instantly.

The guard on the left crawled on hands and knees, staying in the undergrowth and creating distance between himself and the road. Bullets whistled over his head as he moved along the ground. He reached the banks of a fast-flowing river and crawled down to the water's edge. He lowered himself into the water, considering the swim to the other side then stopped and pushed himself under the branches of an overhanging tree.

He could hear the fighters, now on foot, shouting and getting closer, every few moments they shot bullets from their AK47's into the undergrowth. He pushed himself further into the mud as he heard footsteps on the bank directly above him and a man speaking in Pashto. He held his breath, slowly the voices moved away.

Zafar heard the shooting from behind the locked gate, turned and went back into the house.

✧ ✧ ✧ ✧

The sound of a key in the door woke Kathy. She looked to see a man standing in the doorway. He walked into the room and shouted, "Stand up!"

Kathy struggled to get to her feet, still hazy from the sleeping pills the cook had put in her stew.

The man shouted something in Pashto. Hakeem appeared, placed a chair in the middle of the small room and quickly disappeared.

"Sit!" The man ordered.

Kathy struggled across the room and sat down. The man looked her over and said, "I'm Amir Zafar. Welcome to my home."

"I don't care who you are," she said angrily.

"You're here to atone for the sins of others."

"What are you on about? I don't know anything about you."

"What would you like to know?" Zafar offered.

"Where am I?" She asked.

"You're at one of my homes in the Zhari district of Afghanistan. Do you know anything about this area?"

"No. Why would I?" The question surprised her.

"Let me inform you. Zhari is in the south of the country near the borders of Pakistan and Iran. Two rivers flowing through the country created the geology of this area. The rivers meet in the Helmand province. These rivers are the lifeblood of the land that surrounds them. The perfect conditions for crops to grow and provide a livelihood for the people. We Afghans are no different to you British, or Americans, we just want to live a life which allows us to survive and look after our families."

Zafar stopped talking and studied her face, undecided if she was taking any interest in his words. He decided to continue regardless, "From here I can control all of the farm production in the area. I'm a wealthy man in a country plagued by invaders who want to take all the riches for themselves. From the oil in the north to the poppies in the south."

"That all sounds great," Kathy interrupted, "but do you mind telling me why I'm here?"

"Don't interrupt me!" He shouted, then leaned forward so she could smell his sour breath, "I want you to tell me about your brother. Where is he stationed?"

"My brother?" Surprised by the question. "What's he got to do with this?"

"I want to know where he's stationed? I'll not ask you again."

"Fuck off," she hissed.

Zafar stood back and hit her across the face with the back of his hand. The blow knocked her off the chair and she stumbled across the floor. Zafar shouted in Pashto and Hakeem returned to the cell, lifted her onto the chair and disappeared again.

She rubbed her cheek feeling the warm flesh and a sting of pain.

Zafar leaned forward and raised his index finger towards her face. She watched the long dirty finger nail as he brushed it slowly along her red and swollen cheek, "You will learn to speak to me with respect I deserve woman." His finger continued to move down her cheek following the contour of her skin on to her neck and down towards her breasts. She moved uncomfortably in the chair as his finger slowly pulled the neck line of her t-shirt down. He glanced into the opening, observing her breasts, "Tell me where your brother is and I'll let you go."

Kathy noticed the lie written in his eyes, "I don't have a clue where he is. He doesn't tell me. He's not allowed to. You're wasting your time."

Zafar laughed and stepped back, "You'll understand that it's best to cooperate with me. I can keep you here for as long as I like. You will soon beg me to help you."

"I don't know anything," she screamed.

"Very well. I'll give you time to reconsider, but don't leave it too long. Once I lose patience with you, I'll kill you or if you're lucky, I may even let my men use you for their pleasure first."

Kathy hung her head, sobbed then composed herself. She imagined her brother telling her not to cry, gathered up all her strength and glared at Zafar. Under her breath she said, "Come here,"

"What did you say?" he leaned forward struggling to hear the words and quickly moved back as she spat in his face. He cursed, wiped his face, and hit her again across the face. The force of the blow knocked her unconscious and she fell to the floor. Zafar motioned towards her prone body and swore in Pashto, then stormed out of the small prison cell. Hakeem ran in, picked her up and laid her on the bed. He poured water on her face and she gradually opened her eyes.

"I've never heard anyone speak to him like that." Hakeem mumbled, "You need to be careful. He'll kill you without a second thought."

Kathy looked into his eyes, then passed out.

Chapter 28
Intel

Finn walked into the Ops room at the agreed time finding the others sitting around the table in the same positions as before.

Colby waited for him to take a seat then spoke, "Cooper can you bring us up to speed with what you've found at the location Marshall gave, is it Zafar's compound?"

Cooper stood up, moved towards the TV screens, pointing to one which was mostly dark, apart from green lines outlines and multicoloured objects moving around, "We think so. I'll explain what we're looking at. This screen shows a live feed from the Predator drone with the new Echo camera. It's positioned directly over the site. What you can see is live, happening now. Compare the Echo image to the standard camera image also being transmitted on this screen." She pointed to a second screen, in colour, "When we compare both screens together it's easier to understand the image from the Echo system. The standard camera works well in daylight hours but has limited capability on a night. The Echo camera lets us see at night, plus we can see what's happening inside the buildings. I'll talk you through what we've discovered so far from the data collected."

She took out a metal pen from her shirt breast pocket, extended it like an old car aerial, and pointed it at the green lines, "These are the solid walls of the buildings, and there are vehicles here and here. There are trees and other types of vegetation here outside the compound. On the buildings the depth of the green colour changes from light to dark, highlighting the thickness of the object. Dark items are walls, lighter lines are doorways or windows. It's hard to differentiate, but if you compare the live image you can make a judgement, for instance, this must be a doorway as someone has just walked through it."

She pointed at the multicoloured objects, "These are people, the colour represents the heat signature they're giving off. The hottest is white, moving through a range of colours to blue which is coldest. For example, yellow is hotter than red but colder than white. It will identify living objects, look here, these are small animals, goats, or sheep. And this room must be an outdoor cookhouse with hot ovens."

"This new equipment gives us a lot of usable information," Colby said excitedly. "Please continue."

"I'll summarise the overall layout of the base. The compound has a high twenty-foot wall all around with main gates here, at the end of the road, the only external entrance. The inside of the compound has a 'U' shape design. All along the left side it appears there's a kitchen, a canteen, barrack rooms and toilet. These are the main rooms where the fighters tend to hang out.

"Along the rear wall we have the main house with various rooms...we'll come back to them. On the right side we've got a garage with four vehicles, most likely pickups or jeeps judging by their shape. And finally, at the end there's a stable of some kind with small animals, probably food for the fighters.

"Going back to the main house. The local architecture is the same for most of the houses built around here so we've taken a guess on what the rooms are. A main bedroom, two smaller bedrooms with a hallway joining all of them to the entrance hall. A large living space, a lounge of some sort which connects to another small room and a kitchen."

See pointed at the screen, "We can see the heat again from the cooker here. From the kitchen there's a doorway into a small corridor that has two small rooms on the left and a door into the covered vehicle area on the right. To clarify, if you start in the main bedroom and want to take a vehicle you would walk down the corridor, into the entrance hall, lounge, into the small room, into the kitchen and down the corridor to the garage."

Cooper stopped and studied the faces of the men looking at her from the table, "Any questions so far?"

After a few moments of silence, she returned to her seat, and continued with her report, "In terms of personnel the most we've seen onsite is thirty-two people. It changes as regular vehicles come and go with men and supplies. We expect most activity will stop at night time and we should be able to say exactly what you're up against by the time you launch the attack. The personnel currently appear to be twenty-eight outside the house and four inside. The four people inside the house don't move about a lot. We suspect it's Zafar, some people he trusts...and the prisoner."

"Prisoner!" Finn roared.

The outburst took Cooper by surprise, "Er...No...Yes...I'll show you!"

She stood up, returned to the TV screen and she pressed a button on the remote. The eight smaller images changed into a full screen image of the live Echo camera stream. "If we zoom in on just the main house there's one person in the kitchen, probably the cook. In the main living area, there's normally just one person but occasionally, men come in from outside and sit in there with the person."

Pointing her stick at the multicoloured object on the screen she said loudly, "We're confident this person in the lounge is Zafar."

"It's a pity we can't just drop a Paveway on him and blow his ass to shit," Miller shouted.

"True but we've got a hostage to think of." Cooper pressed the remote and the screen split into two, with the echo image on the left and the standard image on the right. She zoomed the camera into a section on the right rear corner of the compound. "Look here, in the little room near the garage, there's a heat signature which looks like a person laid down. And, on the standard image you can see above the body, on the roof, there's a small opening with a grille of some kind."

She stopped and looked at Finn, "We think it's a prison cell. I can't say one hundred percent but it's highly likely the person we can see is your sister Captain."

Finn jumped up, knocking his chair over in the process, and rushed up to the Echo image. He leaned forward to get a clearer view, seeing a figure in the foetal position in the corner of the small room. He looked at the real image and the opening in the roof.

He looked at Cooper and asked, "Do we know if she's alive? Has she moved while you've been watching?"

"Whoever it is, Kathy, or someone else, they're giving off a heat signature so they must be alive. Periodically the person moves and we've seen people visit the cell."

Unseen by Finn, Miller had risen from his chair and now stood behind him. He placed his hand on Finn's shoulder and calmly said, "Come on buddy, sit down, we need to work out together how we're going to get her back."

Finn picked up his chair, sat down and turned to Cooper, "Sorry...please continue."

"No problem Captain," She pointed to the screen, "There's one other person, here in one of the small bedrooms, we think it's a servant of some kind, he moves around the house a lot and seems to be the one interacting with the person in the prison cell."

Cooper sat down and Colby commented, "Great work Cooper...as usual."

Colby turned to Miller, "What do we know about the defences and the potential forces we'll encounter?"

"They're heavily armed by the look of it." Miller stood up and moved to the screen, "Cooper can you put the live feed from the normal camera on the screen for me."

Cooper pressed a button on the remote and the screen changed to a colour image.

Miller continued, "They've got two pickups here, with mounted guns hidden under the trees outside, they were clearer on the previous Echo image, with two men on each pickup, they're guarding the road. Inside there's at least twenty plus fighters, probably armed with the usual stuff, AK's, RPG's, and grenades. Obviously, we don't know if these are hardened fighters who'll fight to the death or the types who'll run at the first signs of a fight. We should plan on the basis they're fanatics."

Miller pointed to the main house, "We suspect Zafar, Kathy, a cook and one other are living in the house. Out of them we expect only Zafar to put up a fight. Cooper, apart from the cell window in the roof are there any other windows, doors or openings on the outer walls of the compound?"

"No, the only windows face inwards to the compound. The place is a fortress."

"The only entrance being the main gates?"

"It looks that way."

"It's clear then. To get Kathy back safely, and capture Zafar, we need to incapacitate, or eliminate, his fighters first. Looking at the design and shape of his fortress I think we should hit them on all four sides and at the same time. They'll think a full assault force is attacking them, It'll totally confuse them. They'll expect any force to attack via the gates. We'll use the design to our advantage."

"What sort of force do you think we'll need to pull this off?" Colby asked.

"I've run through a few scenarios and it looks like I'll need about ten to twelve highly skilled fighters, there's only four of us here with that level of training," Looking at the men around the table, "Curtis, Dornell, Finn and myself."

"What about support?" Finn asked, "There are US military forces operating regularly in this area, can we get a Special Forces team to help us?"

Colby leaned forward with a worried look on his face, "That may be difficult, you already know the big boss in Washington is talking about pulling our troops out of here. I may be able to get someone to listen if I say there's a big drugs ring to break up, but they don't like hostage rescue missions, too many things can go wrong. They'd just send in a few A10's and wipe the place off the map along with all the people and the poppy fields." He sat in his chair and shook his head, "No, at this stage, let's forget that option. I don't want the US Army digging into our business, we're a covert organisation remember."

Miller shrugged his shoulders, "That's clear, but it doesn't leave us with many options, if the four of us go in, I doubt we'll come back." He looked around the table, "Anyone else have a solution?"

"What about using some of my men?" Finn offered.

The offer surprised Miller, "What?"

"My men!" Finn repeated, "They're in Helmand...probably going stir crazy."

"Go on." Miller said eagerly.

"If we use eight of them to join us, we'll have enough men to carry out your plan. We can also use Camp Griffin as the launch point."

Finn turned to Colby, "Can you speak to the people in charge of both the UK and US military forces over here and get authorisation for a joint assault team. All we need then is someone giving the order to my CO, Adams."

"A very interesting proposal," Colby said. "I'll speak to my opposite number in London. He was very supportive when I asked about you coming to the States, maybe he'll do it again. Let me make a call! Miller, in the meantime continue your planning with the others. We need a rock-solid assault plan putting together."

Colby left the room.

Miller sat down and looked at Finn, "What's your plan buddy?"

Finn took over at the TV screen, "Okay, this is what I think we should do..."

❖ ❖ ❖ ❖

Colby returned to the room and announced, "Finn you're on! Adams is waiting for your call to tell him what men and gear you need."

Colby sat down in his chair and looked around the table, "Do we have a plan?"

Finn got up, "Looks like it, we'll need more help from you. Miller will fill you in with the details..."

Finn proceeded upstairs to the communications office on the ground floor, currently occupied by Colby's staff, working on computers and other electronic equipment. He walked over to the woman who he'd seen naked, she smiled and he asked, "Hi, Wilson, right? Can you help me? I need to get in touch with Camp Griffin, it's a British Army base in Helmand. Is there a secure satellite phone I can use?"

Wilson returned the smile and declared, "No problem," she pointed to the desk next to her, "grab the handset and I'll hook you up. What name do I ask for?"

Finn sat down next to her, "The CO, Adams."

The woman looked up the details on her PC, picked up a phone handset and typed in a sequence of numbers and characters on the keyboard. After a few moments the line made a clicking sound mixed with a sequence of random tones. It fell silent and a voice announced, "Camp Griffin."

The woman spoke, "Camp Griffin, I've got..." The woman put her hand over the receiver, "What's your name honey?"

"Finn, Captain Finn."

She nodded and continued, "Sorry about that! I've got Captain Finn, he needs to speak to your CO, Adams."

"Finn?" Baker said excitedly, "Put him through."

The woman gestured to Finn and he spoke, "This is Finn."

"Finn, sir, how are you? People have been wondering what you've been up to since you made such a dramatic exit. Are you in the US?"

"It's a long story Baker for another time, I urgently need to speak to Adams. Can you get him for me?"

"No problem sir, I'll put you through to his office."

The phone clicked a few times and Finn heard Adams answer the phone. "Finn, I've been waiting for your call. I've just got off the phone with the top brass in London. It seems we're going to rescue your sister and get Zafar. Good news, what do you need?"

"Sir, I need eight of men ready to go later today."

"Okay, but I can't believe it's Zafar who's captured her, I thought the scumbag was in prison. You put him there, and not without losing some good men on the way. What is all this about Finn?"

"I don't have a clue why Zafar has taken her but I guess it's something to do with me, by taking Kathy I assume he's trying to get to me."

"Let's get things started, tell me the names of the men you need."

Finn took out a piece of paper from his breast pocket and started reading his notes, "I need seven men from B Squadron, Corporal Gray, O'Neill, Jones, Rowntree, Docherty, he's the best with a boat, plus Ryan and Stone. I also need a good communications guy to link up to the American intel team, Baxter will do,"

Adams wrote the names down, "And what gear do you need?"

"I need one of our boats, a RIB, plus the usual tactical weapons for the men including flash bangs, breaching charges, smoke and sleeping gas grenades. We are going in at night so add black uniforms and night vision gear."

Adams continued to write down the details, "You said later today, when exactly?"

"Get everything ready, we're going in tonight. We're hoping to use two US Air Force helicopters as transport. The US team is also controlling the intel and are using a surveillance system streaming live drone footage from the location. I'll be arriving with the American team later today then we'll arrange a briefing with the men. You'll be connected to the live stream so you can monitor the assault."

"Sounds good. When do you plan to arrive here?"

Finn looked at his watch, "Around nineteen hundred hours."

"Okay." Adams hung up, walked to his office door and shouted, "Baxter, get your arse in here."

❖ ❖ ❖ ❖

Finn returned to the Ops room finding the team members going over the final details of the assault plan. He grabbed a can of coke from the fridge in the corner, "Anyone else want one?"

Miller shouted, "Throw me one buddy."

Finn threw the can and asked, "Have you managed to arrange transport?"

"We've received clearance for the two helicopters. They're meeting us at Kandahar airport at sixteen-thirty hours."

"Good timing, I told them to be ready for us arriving at Griffin around nineteen hundred. Once we've pulled the squad together, done a full briefing, stowed the gear in the helicopters, we should be able to get airborne. We plan to hit them at zero two thirty hours. That'll give us enough time to complete the operation before the sun starts to come up."

Miller looked at his watch, "Shit! We've got just over an hour to get to the airport."

He turned to Cooper, "We need you to stay in constant contact with us. I want to know immediately if anything changes at Zafar's base. Watch out for reinforcements turning up or anything else that could affect the outcome of the mission."

Cooper nodded, "No problem, I'll hook into the comms system so I can hear what's happening and talk directly to you both."

"Perfect." Miller said with a smile, before turning to the others, "Right come on guys we need to get moving."

∴ ∴ ∴ ∴

The estate car arrived at Kandahar airport at 3:48 pm. They passed through security and drove out to a separate military zone of the airport. Once inside the secure perimeter they continued sitting in the car and waited. At 16:25 they heard the twin engines of a Chinook helicopter overhead. The men climbed out of the car and looked up to see the large green helicopter swoop over and gently touchdown on a large painted H on the tarmac.

"Looks like our ride is here," Miller shouted. "Grab the gear."

Finn looked up again, hearing a familiar noise and watched as a second helicopter circled around above him, *Cooney*.

The X-49 helicopter levelled off and moved to a second H next to the Chinook and landed. Finn picked up his pack and walked towards the helicopters. The rear doors of the

Chinook lowered as he approached. To his right he watched Cooney climbing out of the grey helicopter.

Cooney noticed Finn and ran over, "You're a sight for sore eyes. I hear you've been racking up the air miles."

Finn smiled, "Very true, it's great to see you."

"Colby said you needed some help, so here I am."

Cooney looked around, searching, "I've arranged for some guys to meet me here….there they are! We'll talk later bud, in the meantime get the gear on the helicopters. We leave here at sixteen-thirty hours."

Finn watched as Cooney ran over to a couple of US Air Force vehicles, a truck, and a jeep. He started talking to two men waiting for him, a lieutenant, and a sergeant.

"Hi guys, I'm Cooney, did you get the supplies I requested?"

"It's all here in the truck sir." The lieutenant replied.

"Okay, we need to get my chopper armed and both refuelled immediately."

He turned to the lieutenant, "You need to speak to the maintenance chief of Iron Fist Security. Their hangar is near the terminal, you can't miss it, it has 'Iron Fist' in big letters written on it. We need their fuel tanker over here now. Colby has already cleared it with Kane, the head honcho over there. If you get any lip let me know."

The lieutenant climbed into the jeep. The sergeant got into the truck. Cooney watched as the truck and jeep went off in opposite directions.

He ignored the jeep and followed the progress of the truck over to his helicopter.

The sergeant climbed out and banged on the metal side panels, "Let's go gentlemen, It's time to go to work."

The rear hatch of the truck dropped down and a team of Air Force engineers jumped out. Some unloaded crates while the others ran over to the helicopter with tool boxes.

Cooney broke off watching the engineers when he heard the jeep returning with the fuel tanker. He watched as the jeep parked up and the lieutenant got out and started walking towards the two helicopters. He guided the beige and black tanker into a space in between them to begin the refuelling process. Cooney laughed to himself when he noticed the large ensign on the side of the truck. *Iron Fist, who ever thought that one up.*

Men jumped down from the cab of the tanker and pulled hoses from the side. Cooney lost interest and decided to walk over to his own helicopter. Standing far enough away to observe without getting in the way of the engineers working. They split into two teams, one on either side of the fuselage. They first removed the extra fuel pods on the underside of the short wings. *We won't need those on this trip.*

The men carefully placed the pods into crates, opened crates nearby taking out 'X' shaped carriages and started fitting them where the fuel pods were. He instinctively retreated. *Now for the tricky part.*

Cooney heard the lieutenant shouting orders at the tanker crew behind him. Ignoring him, he continued watching the engineers, as they unpacked the Hellfire Air-to-Surface guided missiles. The engineers carefully fitted the missiles into the X shaped carriages. Once complete, the helicopter had eight missiles, four on each wing. The engineers then fitted mounted guns on the fuselage, either side of the cockpit.

The lieutenant walked in front of him and barked out at the engineers, "Come on guys, we've got to go faster," Clapping his hands, he spoke, "We need these birds in the air."

Cooney blasted back, "Leave it, they're going fast enough for me, I want it done properly so I know they'll work when my arse is on the line later."

The lieutenant looked at him, decided not to push his luck, and walked away, shouting at the refuelling guys instead. Cooney grinned.

From behind Finn asked, "What are you so happy about?"

"Ah, it's nothing, just having a bit of fun. Are you ready?"

"Yes, we're ready to go, just need to get airborne."

"These guys will be finished in about fifteen minutes. I'll be taking two of the engineers with me to do all the final checks on the weapons and guidance systems at Camp Griffin. They're travelling in the Chinook with you."

"Sounds good, I'll grab a quick coffee. Do you want one?" Finn asked.

"White, lots of sugar."

✧ ✧ ✧ ✧

The Chinook took off and quickly climbed to a height above two thousand metres, the maximum range of any possible RPG attack from any of the local insurgents.

Cooney watched the Chinook take off and move away to his right and begin to arc around, heading north west of the city of Kandahar. Once a safe distance had opened between the two helicopters he pulled back on the stick and lifted X-49 off the tarmac. With a much faster top speed he could easily catch, and pass the Chinook if he wanted. The Chinook pilot set a cruising speed of one hundred and seventy miles per hour. Cooney took up a covering position instead, behind the big twin bladed helicopter. With only seventy-four miles to travel, the helicopters arrived at the Camp Griffin on time at 19:03.

Cooney moved the X-49 to a position above the Chinook and circled the base, using his night vision radar to check on any possible RPG threats. Once convinced it was safe he radioed the Chinook pilot with an all-clear message. He watched as it quickly descended and touched down inside the base.

Cooney did one more circle of the base before landing the X-49 next to the Chinook. Once the helicopter blades finished rotating and the dust cloud dispersed, the Chinook pilot opened the rear door allowing the passengers out.

Finn took Miller, and the two SOG men, to meet Adams and his team. The two engineers collected their tools and walked over to meet Cooney at the X-49.

The first engineer met Cooney at the cockpit, "We'll run a system test and make sure everything is in working order."

"Thanks guys. I'm going to the briefing." Cooney began to follow the others, stopped, then shouted back, "Can you also check the oil, water, tyres and don't forget to clean the bugs off the screen."

The engineer laughed and waved him away.

Chapter 29
Briefing

The assault team assembled in the briefing room, sitting at desks like school children in a classroom waiting for the teacher to arrive. Some soldiers chatted casually amongst themselves while others sat patiently, choosing to sit in silence and wait. Adams, Colby, Miller, and Finn walked into the room and stood in the front of the men.

Adams spoke first, "Captain Finn will now brief you all on a joint UK and US task force mission. He selected each of you because you're the best soldiers available to ensure a successful outcome. Finn will now present the briefing."

Adams turned to Finn, "Captain, go ahead." Then retreated to the side of the room.

Finn looked around the room at the familiar faces in front of him, "Okay guys, this is Robert Colby, head of the NCS special activities division. With him are three of his paramilitary officers, Miller here, and the two guys at the rear, Dornell and Curtis. You can all get friendly with each other later."

Finn turned off the lights and pressed a button on a keypad and a projection screen rolled down the wall behind him. Once fully down, a picture flickered into life on the screen. "What you're looking at here is a live stream from a drone over the target site. Take note of the buildings and people moving about. Our target is a man called Zafar," Murmurs could be heard in the room, "Okay quiet. I know some of you have already had dealings with him.

Zafar is currently terrorising the local population, forcing them to grow poppies, and is responsible for large amounts of drugs shipped into Iran, Pakistan, and the US. These drugs go on to fund terrorists, insurgents and the various military factions which operate in this country. Overall, many British and US military personnel have died at the hands of people, funded by drugs. We need to capture Zafar, or kill him, I don't care. There is however one more problem. He has kidnapped a woman and taken her prisoner." He paused for a moment, "My sister!"

The room erupted into minor chaos with men talking to each other before Docherty shouted out, "How the hell did he manage to kidnap your sister Cap?"

Ryan added, "And why the hell has he done it?"

Finn raised his hands up to calm the men, "Why has he done it? The short answer is, I don't know. As you all know I've been out here several times over the last few years. I can only guess it has something to do with what I've been involved in or revenge for capturing him. My priority is to recover my sister safely."

From the rear of the room Gray shouted out, "Don't worry boss we'll get her back, and kill the bastard for you, no problem."

A cheer went up in the room and Finn raised his hands, "Okay guys settle down. Don't start thinking this is going to be a walk in the park."

Finn looked at the screen and pointed to the house, "We're fairly confident Zafar is in the main house, possibly in this room. There's a kitchen here and it appears there are two staff. This small room, a prison cell, is where we think my sister is held."

From the side someone shouted, "So the four inside should be easy to overpower, what about the fighters in the compound? Do we have numbers?"

Finn continued, "There'll be around thirty-two people on site. That means we can expect thirty plus armed fighters with the usual AK47s, and possibly RPGs. There are also two pickups and four men outside. The pickups have mounted guns, probably fifty calibre. The only entrance is the main gate at the end of the access road where the pickups are stationed."

"What's the plan boss?" O'Neill shouted.

"We've worked out a way which will allow us to get inside quickly, neutralise all the guards, secure the prisoner, and get Zafar out. We'll receive support from Mr Colby's surveillance team in Kandahar. They're streaming the drone feed you can see on the screen and are providing extra live onsite intel via a communications link. The US Air Force have provided the drone plus the two helicopters outside. With myself, the three paramilitary officers, and the rest of you we'll have twelve sets of boots on the ground."

"Where exactly is this place Finn?" Rowntree asked.

"It's near Halgram. Some of you guys already know the area and have operated around there before. The house is close to the west bank of the river, in an agricultural area, with lots of little farms and fields. We don't expect any trouble from the locals, they probably want to see the back of Zafar as much as we do. We'll travel in the Chinook, with the RIB. The other helicopter is there to protect the Chinook until we are on the ground. Afterwards it will be used to provide us with air support."

"You mean the fancy little chopper outside with all the guns and rockets?" Gray shouted out, "We should be able to kick some serious ass with that baby."

The men laughed, shouting, and cheering as the door opened, Finn turned to the visitor, "Right on cue…guys this is Cooney, he's flying the support helicopter."

Cooney nodded to the men, "Did I miss all the fun?"

Finn pointed to an empty chair at the front, "Sit yourself down, we are just getting started..."

∴ ∴ ∴ ∴

After the briefing ended Finn looked around the room and noted the silence, "Any more questions?" He waited a few seconds with no response, the men had mentally moved to the serious phase of the operation. "I'll take the silence as confirmation everyone knows what's expected of them. We'll leave here at zero-one-forty to arrive at the LZ at zero-two-hundred. Once we're in position the assault starts at zero-two-thirty. Dismissed!"

The men climbed from their seats and began chatting among themselves as they left the room.

Colby turned to Finn and Miller, "Good luck!" Shaking each of their hands in turn, "I'll stay here with Adams in the command centre to monitor the drone feed and to listen in on the comms link."

Finn looked to see Adams at the side of the room. He knew what he had to do. He waited for the others to leave the room and walked over, "Sir, I owe you an apology."

"Why?" Adams said, the stern expression on his face unchanged.

"It seems I've been blaming the wrong guy. I found out from Colby there was a leak on the US side and that's why they overpowered us at Khanashin. I thought it was at our end. I'm sorry...I was wrong."

Adams offered his hand which Finn accepted, Adams grinned back at him and said, "Now get the hell out of here Captain you've got a mission to complete."

∴ ∴ ∴ ∴

The Iron Fist security guard hid under the bushes on the bank of the river until it was dark. After waiting a while, he noticed the noise of the vehicles and men begin to dissipate and checked his gear. *They've given up. Pistol, a flash-bang, a couple of spare magazines, no radio, no water, no food, damn it.*

He crawled along the river bank away from the compound. Stopping every few feet to listen, each time he was sure it was safe, he moved on. He repeated the cycle until clear of the compound. He moved up from the river bank and on to the flat dry soil. With the river on his left, he assumed the access road was now far enough away on his right and stood up. He moved forward and walked straight into a bush. He felt around and discovered he was in a field of fruit bushes. He picked one of the round fruits and took a bite. *A Peach.*

The sugar and warm juice in the flesh gave him some small comfort. He pulled off more of the fruits and stuffed them in his pockets. Continuing along the irrigation track between two rows of the bushes, he noticed the shape of a large hut appear on the skyline in front of him. Edging up next to the hut he walked around the perimeter to find the doorway. He peeked inside and found it empty. He walked in and sat in the corner facing the doorway with his gun in his hand. *This will do until morning and the heat dies down. Maybe I can find a boat to get over the river, or steal a motorbike, or a car. Damn, I'm a long way from home with no friends, not how I thought I'd end my days.*

Slowly he fell asleep.

Chapter 30
Assault

Night descended on Camp Griffin and the security increased, guard towers staffed with soldiers wearing night vision goggles ensuring any movement outside would be immediately detected. The twelve-man team boarded the Chinook at 01:30. They sat in the cargo bay, six on either side of the RIB sitting in the centre. They performed a final comms check and received the all clear to take off at 01:40, as planned.

Cooney lifted the X-49 off the ground and made a security sweep of the area. Once happy it was safe, he contacted the Chinook pilot. The big helicopter lifted off the ground and immediately flew towards the agreed coordinates with the X-49 following in close formation.

After a journey of approximately twenty minutes, the Chinook descended to ground level. Landing on the east side of the river one mile north and on the opposite bank to Zafar's compound. The rear hatch opened and the men ran out, carrying the RIB, using the rope handles on the side of the boat.

Once clear of the cargo bay door, the soldiers crouched down alongside the RIB. The Chinook pilot closed the hatch, took off quickly and returned to the safety of Camp Griffin. Keeping their heads down while the dust cloud dispersed. Finn heard the Chinook pilot on the comms system saying, "Good luck."

Finn stood up and gestured to his men to do the same. Finn at the front, on the left, with Miller opposite, "Let's go."

All the soldiers stood up and lifted the RIB off the ground. They ran directly towards the river. At the river bank, they split into two teams, one team with the boat, the other taking up defensive positions around it. The boat team pushed the boat down into the water. The fast current pulled the boat away and the six men struggled with the handles.

"Hold on to it," Finn ordered. "Docherty, get the engines started."

Docherty jumped up inside the RIB, pressed the starter and the twin engines burst into life. He accelerated the propellers to counter the speed of the water and the men loosened their grip on the handles. With Ryan and Stone holding the main anchor rope off the front, Docherty forced the front of the boat onto the bank.

"Everyone in," Finn ordered.

In a precision movement each man climbed in and took up their position in the boat, kneeling on either side. The last two jumped in with the anchor ropes and knelt at the bow.

Docherty put the engines into reverse and pulled the RIB off the bank and out into the river. Following an agreed route, he kept the boat moving with the river current while gradually moving towards the western bank. He continuously monitored the depth gauge and the GPS. The light turned green on the GPS, signalling their arrival at the agreed drop off point. He slowed the engines and let the boat cruise up to the bank, running slightly aground and killed the engines.

Ryan and Stone jumped out and secured the anchor ropes to trees on the river bank while the other soldiers climbed out. Docherty, last off the boat, grabbed an extra anchor rope from the back of the boat and secured it to another tree. The men all gathered, crouched down, looking around for signs of danger.

Finn observed the area through his night vision goggles, following the outline of trees to the high rear wall of the compound, in the distance. He gave a hand signal and the men split into three agreed troops. Each troop had a unique call sign so the base communication teams could monitor progress. Troop A contained Finn, as leader, Corporal O'Neill, Dornell and Baxter, with the radio equipment. Troop B consisted of Miller, as leader, Corporal Gray, Rowntree and Stone. The final group, Troop C included Corporal Jones as leader, Docherty, Curtis, and Ryan.

Finn looked at his watch, 02:09, and used his fingers to signal to the other troop leaders to move to their agreed assault positions. Troop B would take up a position on the eastern wall, nearest the river. Troop C, who had the longest distance to travel, and the biggest risk of detection, headed to the western wall. Finn, with troop A, headed to the rear wall.

Finn watched as Troops B and C moved away from him, all the men crouching and holding silenced MP5 assault rifles.

※ ※ ※ ※

Cooney watched from above as the Chinook landed. He hovered the X-49, while constantly looking at his monitors for danger signs. Once the Chinook took off, he climbed to a higher position, remaining on the eastern side of the river. He watched as Finn and his men launched the RIB into the water and travelled towards the other side. Slowly moving the helicopter around, he scanned as much of the area as possible, ready to warn the men of any danger. Once the men arrived at the opposite bank, he moved the helicopter to a position five miles south of the compound, at a high altitude waiting for the signal from Finn.

∴ ∴ ∴ ∴

In the briefing room of Camp Griffin, Colby and Adams stood, watching the projector screen. The Echo camera on the drone picked up the twelve separate heat signatures of the men. They watched as the soldiers arrived at the other side of the river and split into their agreed troops. Through the speakers they could hear the movement and breathing of the men as they ran.

"So far so good," Colby said.

"Now for the hard part," Adams added.

∴ ∴ ∴ ∴

At the Kandahar safe house Cooper gathered the latest intel and reported it to the team, "Squad intel. I've got an update on numbers. We count a total of thirty-one persons on site.

In the main house we've got someone in the main bedroom, possibly Zafar, the other two members of his staff are in the smaller bedrooms. The prisoner is in the cell. Over."

Finn heard the report and did some basic math in his head while he moved along with his troop to the assault position. *Take off Kathy and the servants and that leaves us with a twenty-eight strong force. There are four outside and twenty-four inside. That's two men each to take down.*

∴ ∴ ∴ ∴

Tawfiq, at the front gates, walked past the front of the pickup truck and found the driver asleep, he laughed to himself and began to climb into the back, then stopped. To his right, along the outside of the compound wall he noticed something move. Picking up his AK47 from the flatbed he walked along the outer wall trying to find the distraction.

Ikram leaned with his back against the bonnet of the other pickup. He lit a cigarette and looked to the other side of the road. He found the other pickup driver asleep in the driver's seat and the guard, Tawfiq, walking around the far side. He turned to look at his own pickup and acknowledged Jamil stood smoking a cigarette in the flatbed next to the mounted gun.

∴ ∴ ∴ ∴

The men of troop B moved along the perimeter of the compound. Gray looked out from the bushes to see a fighter with an AK47 walking along the wall towards them and suddenly crouched down. They all stopped. He gestured to the others to warn them of the danger and gave a signal to Stone, who retreated into the bushes and disappeared.

Tawfiq, already bored with looking, stopped and gave up. *Nothing, damn water rats again.* He turned away and returned to the pickup.

Watching the man stop and turn away from him, Stone took his opportunity. In an instance, he came out of the darkness, grabbed the man from behind, placed his hand over his mouth and slit his throat in one quick movement. He pulled the body into the undergrowth and returned to the other squad members.

∴ ∴ ∴ ∴

Finn arrived at the rear wall and looked at his watch, 02:23. He signalled to O'Neill to set the breaching charge near the main bedroom area. He watched as O'Neill took out the C4 sticky bomb and pressed it against the wall, the thick jelly coating sticking the bomb onto the dusty brick. The soldier moved the power switch on the bomb into the live position and a red light began flashing. He returned to where Finn and the other squad members were hiding with the hand-held remote trigger. He looked at Finn, with his thumb positioned over the switch.

Finn looked at his watch, 02:31.

Finn called in over the comms, "A, ready." He waited for a response which quickly came back.

"B, ready."

"C, ready."

Finn looked at his men and gave the final agreed call signal. "All teams ready, Flycatcher engage! We go on your signal."

∴ ∴ ∴ ∴

Cooney heard the call sign and headed towards the compound in the distance. He flew the helicopter to the western bank of the river and dropped to a height of thirty feet. Sweeping over the storage hut, the field of small bushes and finally over the dirt road.

Using night vision goggles, he fixed his stare on the compound gates in the distance. He activated the HUD system, which displayed the missile radar system on the windscreen of the helicopter. He pressed the target seeking switch on his control stick and a box rotated around in front of his eyes as the targeting system searched the landscape. In an instant it locked on to the first pickup. He pressed the button again and another red box rotated around until it locked on the second pickup. With a smile on his face he announced, "Goodnight gentlemen," and pressed the trigger.

Ikram looked along the dirt road and heard a strange throbbing noise in the distance which gradually grew louder. He strained his eyes to see in the darkness and spotted a shape hovering above the road. He began to speak as he watched two bright lights appear in the distance.

Two Hellfire missiles launched simultaneously, one from each wing, speeding towards the two pickup trucks

❖ ❖ ❖ ❖

A loud noise over the top of the farm hut woke the Iron Fist security guard. Startled, he grabbed his gun and stumbled towards the doorway. Outside, he looked up and spotted a grey painted helicopter moving along the peach trees, towards the road. He walked slowly alongside the row of bushes and watched the helicopter until he reached the road. He noticed the US Air Force marking on the grey fuselage then stumbled backwards as the rocket engines on the missiles ignited and two bright flames raced along the dirt road towards the compound.

❖ ❖ ❖ ❖

The two missiles struck the pickup trucks at the same time, wiping them out. One lifted off the ground in a ball of flame, turned over and landed on its roof. The other burst into flame and became a burnt-out shapeless shell, within minutes. Cooney quickly locked another missile on to the gate and fired. The missile struck the gate and ripped the two metal doors off their hinges which fell noisily onto the ground, inside the compound. Cooney climbed the X-49 up to a height of two thousand feet. With the fighters alerted, the danger of RPG attack on the helicopter became a deadly reality. From his new elevated position, he watched as the breaching charges exploded on the compound walls and the soldiers stormed inside.

※ ※ ※ ※

Corporal Jones and the men of troop C stood in position at the far wall of the compound. Curtis placed the C4 on the wall behind the middle barrack room. Hearing the rockets making quick work of the pickups and gate, Curtis pressed the remote trigger. The wall exploded and a large opening appeared. Docherty and Ryan threw in flash-bangs and crouched down. The grenades exploded with a deafening sound and a bright flash of light. Instantly, the troop moved towards the opening, with their MP5 assault rifles ready.

Jones entered first and discovered the mangled bodies of four fighters who had been sleeping next to the wall. Other fighters stumbled around injured, disorientated, grabbing for their guns, bumping into each other as they tried to reach the doorway. Jones squeezed the trigger and in short three bullet bursts began cutting the men down. The other members of C troop joined him in the room and finished off the rest of the fighters.

Troop B, at the opposite wall, heard the rockets explode and Rowntree set off the breaching charge. The explosion blew a hole in the wall and threw the pickup on the other side into the middle of the compound. The troop advanced through the hole, first taking up defensive positions and then surveying the current situation.

B troop's objective was to eliminate all the enemy fighters in the compound. Corporal Gray motioned to Rowntree and they moved to a position alongside the pickup and watched the fighters running from the barracks on either side of the one where C troop had entered. The soldiers picked off the Afghan fighters, some reacted and returned fire. Others, seeing their comrades dying outside, decided to stay in the barrack rooms and returned fire with AK47s from the windows.

Stone and Miller moved to the wall adjoining the stables. Miller gestured to Stone to confirm he was ready to move to the stables and required covering fire. Miller ran into the compound, bullets ripped along the dirt floor, following his footsteps. He dived into the stables, landed in a pile of goat shit, rolled onto his back, and climbed up onto his feet. He moved to the doorway and threw a smoke grenade into the compound, the signal for Stone to get moving.

Stone ran, following the path of Miller, who had now moved to the stable window shooting at the barracks room opposite. Stone dived in, meeting the same fate as Miller. He looked up and found the petrified goats crowded in the rear corner of the stable. He pushed himself up off the floor, with goat shit all over his hands and jacket. He joined Miller at the window and began shooting towards the barracks.

Troop A, with Finn, heard the rockets explode and O'Neill pressed the trigger, the wall of the master bedroom disintegrated leaving a large opening. Finn entered first, aiming his MP5 at the bed. He noticed a figure in white sitting against the far wall, blood pouring from his ears and a cut on his head. Finn ran directly to him, raised his gun, and squeezed the trigger, ready to shoot. Hakeem looked up at the man in front of him dressed all in black.

Finn released the trigger. "Shit! It's not him." he whispered into the comms system. "He must be in another room."

He hit Hakeem on the head with the butt of his rifle, knocking him out, then turned to see O'Neill opening the bedroom door. In the distance he watched a figure all in white running away from him.

Dornell advanced down the corridor and the others followed. Baxter, at the rear, turned Hakeem's body over and tie-wrapped his hands before joining them.

Dornell found the closed door of the first small bedroom and moved to the far side of the door frame, guarding the men from any attack which may come from the darkened space at the end of the corridor.

O'Neill kicked in the bedroom door and advanced rapidly with his MP5 at shoulder height. He discovered an armed woman cowering in the corner of the room and ran over. Taking no chances, he turned her over and tie-wrapped her hands behind her back and left her on the floor. He gave an okay signal to the other troop members in the corridor. Finn tapped Dornell on the shoulder and the troop advanced to the second bedroom door, finding it open. After looking inside, Dornell signalled it was empty and they advanced to the entrance hall. O'Neill engaged the lock on the front door into the compound and the squad moved onwards to the lounge.

They spread out, taking up agreed positions. Finn took up the point and with his MP5 ready moved slowly to the next room. *We've managed to take down two, only Kathy and Zafar left.*

That's when Finn realised who the white dressed figure was. *Shit he's going for her.*

Corporal Jones and the men of C troop looked outside seeing the men of B troop opposite, shooting at the fighters in the rooms on either side of them. Splitting into two groups they set breaching charges on the internal walls on both sides of the room then exited through their original entry point. They hugged the outside wall and Jones pressed the remote trigger.

The blast generated a cloud of dust which blew back out of the opening. Once the dust cleared, they returned to the barrack room with guns drawn and noticed the walls on either side of the room had disintegrated. They stayed in groups of two and attacked the rooms on either side.

Jones and Curtis took the room to their left, throwing in flash-bangs before advancing into the room, picking off the last of the fighters then took up a position at the doorway.

Docherty and Ryan headed to the room on the right. Inside they found several injured fighters crawling on the floor, a couple grabbed for guns and the SAS men shot them. Like the other two, they took up a defensive position at the doorway.

Miller, on the other side, gestured to Docherty to move on and check the kitchen and canteen area. He left the doorway with Ryan in close formation behind. He quickly peeked into the canteen and a burst of bullets ripped into the walls around the door frame. Docherty dived to cover outside and pulled out a flash-bang. He chucked it inside and pressed himself against the outside wall. There was a loud bang and flash of brilliant light. He looked in again and discovered some fighters crouched behind a table, shielding themselves from the light burst. Once the dust settled in the room, they stood up again and peppered the doorway with bullets.

Miller and Stone, seeing the men opposite meeting strong resistance, ran across the compound towards the kitchen door in support.

Docherty pulled out a sleep grenade, pulled the pin and chucked it in. A blue mist gradually filled the room. Unseen by Docherty, the two fighters had guessed he might throw a grenade and had already ran through an adjoining door into the kitchen, joining the last two fighters in there.

This is where the Zafar's remaining fighters would make their last stand. Four, armed with AK47s until one spotted an RPG on the floor, dropped his rifle, and snatched it. In quick action he disabled the safety switch, slung the launcher onto his shoulder, aimed through the doorway into the canteen and fired. The rocket powered grenade exited the launcher, through the doorway, detonating as it hit the far wall of the canteen. There was an explosion and an explosion of flame which brought the canteen roof down.

The blast knocked Docherty off his feet and he landed on his back outside the doorway. Ryan, who had anticipated the danger the RPG presented, pressed himself against the outside wall. The blast buried him under a pile of rubble from both the wall and roof collapse.

Miller looked in from the kitchen doorway, noticed the four fighters and watched the RPG launch. He raised his MP5 and cut down two of the men in a single burst of fire. One of the remaining men went on a suicide run, firing his AK47 continuously as he ran directly at Miller. One bullet hit Miller on the leg and he dropped to the floor outside the kitchen door.

Stone moved to take his place and took the full force of the AK47 bullets in his chest. The 7.62 high velocity bullets lifted the SAS soldier off his feet and threw him backwards onto the ground outside. The shooter continued running until he arrived outside, at which point his gun ran out of ammunition. Miller, from the side, blasted rounds into his body and head, killing him instantly.

Docherty crawled up onto all fours, then climbed to his feet still dazed from the blast. Seeing Miller and Stone in trouble he pushed through the rubble and headed towards the kitchen with his assault rifle ready. Miller managed to get up on one knee and blindly fired rounds into the kitchen from the outside doorway. The remaining fighter returned fire at Miller, not seeing Docherty approaching from the internal doorway to his left who cut him down in a final burst of bullets.

Finn quickened his pace, moving from the dining room to the kitchen and out into the small passageway. He arrived at the prison cell door, finding it open and the room empty. He looked to his right and noticed an open access door into the garage. He ran to the doorway and looked outside, only to see Zafar getting into the driver's side door of a Land Rover.

Once the shooting in the compound had stopped, Corporal Gray and Rowntree advanced into the compound. Zafar, with great one-handed skill, fired an AK47 over the roof of the jeep making Finn retreat inside. Gray and Rowntree turned as they heard the shots behind them, followed by an engine starting up. Suddenly a Land Rover appeared in the compound. Gray reacted quickest and spun around with his weapon ready to shoot but froze when he heard Finn shouting over the comms system, "Don't shoot! It's Zafar, he's taken Kathy."

※ ※ ※ ※

Cooney, from above, watched as the vehicle sped from the covered garage. The jeep accelerated, drove around the blasted pickup truck, across the compound, over the metal gates and out onto the dirt track outside. Cooney spotted a second larger jeep driving out from the garage in pursuit. Over the radio he heard Finn shouting, "I'm going after him, Gray, call the chopper and get everyone to the LZ. Don't wait for me."

※ ※ ※ ※

Docherty checked around to make sure the last of the fighters were dead, then turned to see the two cars speeding out of the compound. He moved towards the doorway and found Miller crouched over Stone's dead body. He returned to the canteen and dug with his hands into the rubble searching for Ryan.

Jones and Curtis cleared through all the rooms in the compound, ensuring all the fighters were either dead, or dying then noticed Docherty digging. They joined him in the task. They all moved away from the scene when they discovered the crushed body of their comrade.

Jones checked for a pulse and confirmed, "He's gone."

The men from all the troops regrouped in the compound. They placed the bodies of Ryan and Stone in black body bags. Miller had his leg strapped by a soldier and another gave him a makeshift crutch. The others swept through the area setting charges.

Corporal Gray spoke over the radio, "We need extraction, twelve in total, two dead, one with a gunshot wound."

Cooper sighed upon hearing two of the soldiers had died. After a moment of silence she composed herself, "Meet at the LZ, thirty minutes, confirm."

Grey replied, "Confirm, over and out." He looked at the men around him, "Docherty you're in charge of the boat, Dornell and Curtis take Ryan, Rowntree and Baxter get Stone, O'Neill you help Miller, once we're clear I'm going to blow this place."

"What about these prisoners?" Corporal Jones asked, bringing Hakeem and the cooking woman out from the house.

"Let the woman go, we'll take him with us to see if he has any valuable information. You're responsible for him."

"Great, babysitting a scumbag, just what I want." Jones complained, while cutting the tie-wraps behind the woman and pointing her towards the gate.

"Can someone let the goats out, they're trapped in the stable." Miller shouted.

Dornell waved to him, ran to the stable and pulled down the wire mesh fence. He entered the stable and the goats stayed huddled together in the corner, he cursed and ran towards them to make them scatter, once one found the opening the rest followed.

Dornell laughed as they trotted out of the gate behind the woman, creating a surreal scene.

Gray watched the goats, smiled, then announced, "Right! If everyone is happy, can we get going?"

The men ran out through the gate, turned left, and doubled back along the compound wall. Once they arrived at the corner of the wall they arched right and down towards the river bank, where they found the tied-up boat. Gray pulled out the remote trigger and several explosions ripped through the compound.

Once all the men, the two bodies and the prisoner were in the RIB, Docherty started the engines. They cut the anchor ropes and the boat swirled around, caught by the current in the river. Docherty pushed the throttles and the big engines rapidly gained speed. The RIB took hold against the current and moved upstream towards the LZ.

O'Neill turned to Miller, "Jesus man, what the hell is that smell?"

Miller didn't reply, he continued to stare at the two body bags laid at his feet on the RIB floor. Once they arrived at their original launch point on the eastern river bank, Docherty swung the boat around, accelerated, and ran the boat up onto the river bank.

"Go! Go! Go! Move it!" Gray shouted.

Docherty kept the engines running while everyone dismounted the boat, taking the bodies and the prisoner with them. He ran the full length of the RIB and jumped onto the river bank turning for a moment to see the RIB floating downstream and disappearing into the darkness.

The men regrouped and proceeded in formation, towards the LZ. When they arrived, they arranged themselves in an armed defensive circle, each on one knee with the prisoner and body bags in the middle of the circle. After a few minutes, the Chinook reappeared from the dark sky above, this time without the protection of the X-49. It landed with the rear door already open. The soldiers ran inside and the helicopter took off immediately, with the rear door still closing, and returned to Camp Griffin.

Chapter 31
Kathy

The Land Rover weaved out of the compound gate, swerving to miss the burnt-out upside-down pickup and ran over Ikram's burnt body. Once on the straight dirt road Zafar pressed the accelerator to the floor. The jeep lost traction on the loose dirt and the rear end swung out onto the verge. There was a loud thud and he looked in the door mirror to see something spin away into the field alongside the road. To avoid losing control of the vehicle Zafar pulled the steering wheel in the opposite direction to the skid and the rear end of the vehicle snapped straight.

∴ ∴ ∴ ∴

The Iron Fist security guard walked along the verge of the dirt road, watching the firefight taking place in the compound ahead of him. He heard a hard driven engine and the screeching of tyres. In the blink of an eye a vehicle appeared in front of him. The force of the impact threw his body away from the road and he hit the ground under a tree. He looked up to see something hanging above his head, pain gripped his body, his breathing stopped and his lifeless eyes continued to stare at the peach.

∴ ∴ ∴ ∴

Zafar headed down the road, struggling with the wheel as Kathy lay on the back seat. She shouted out at him and he lashed out at her, "Shut up woman."

He looked in the rear-view mirror and spotted another vehicle on the road behind him. He continued to follow the dirt road, checking his mirror, and watched the vehicle behind gaining ground on him. Kathy managed to sit up on the back seat, leaned forward, and hit Zafar with her fists. With his left hand gripping the steering wheel, he used his right to pick up the pistol from the passenger seat and he hit her across the face. The metal barrel crashed against her temple and she fell backwards on to the rear seat.

※ ※ ※ ※

Cooney brought the X-49 to a height of one hundred feet above the road following along the route of the dirt road. His instinct told him to blow the Land Rover off the road but he decided to wait and see how things developed.

※ ※ ※ ※

Finn floored the accelerator on the Toyota Land Cruiser and the big turbo diesel engine sprung into life. The Japanese vehicle was well suited to the dirt road and soon gained ground on the Land Rover. Finn got to within a few feet of the rear bumper. The single-track dirt road presented no safe overtaking opportunities. Finn noticed T-junction approaching which led onto a main road. He backed off the accelerator unsure which direction Zafar would choose.

Zafar braked hard and swung his vehicle left out from the dirt road on to a twin lane tarmac road. Finn followed close behind. With no other traffic on the road Finn took the opportunity to overtake. On each attempt Zafar would weave the Land Rover from side to side blocking his path.

Within a few moments the two vehicles were travelling at more than eighty miles per hour on the dusty tarmac. Cooney followed from above, in the X-49.

Zafar slowed for a sharp bend and Finn managed to get along the right side of the Land Rover, cutting the corner. Zafar moved over into the centre of the road and slammed the jeep into the Land Cruiser. Finn momentarily lost control, took his foot off the accelerator and fought hard to keep the heavy vehicle on the road.

The Land Cruiser fell away and Zafar managed to pull out a lead of over two hundred feet. Finn struggled to get the Land Cruiser up to speed. Once back on the rear bumper of Land Rover, he waited again for an overtaking opportunity to appear.

They weaved through several small villages and raced between farmers' fields. Zafar suddenly slammed on the brakes and swerved left to go over an old wooden bridge.

Finn almost collided with the rear end of the Land Rover but managed to react fast enough by swerving and braking at the same time. The Land Cruiser missed the bridge entrance as Zafar continued over. The old wooden planks groaned under the weight of the Land Rover. At the end of the bridge Zafar swung the Land Rover right onto a single-track tarmac road.

Finn angrily reversed the Land Cruiser past the bridge entrance then engaged drive and followed Zafar over the bridge. Several planks broke as he sped over them, the forward motion keeping the vehicle safe from crashing through.

Zafar looked in his mirror and watched the Land Cruiser losing ground and smiled to himself. He continued to accelerate along the tarmac road, knowing the vehicle behind wouldn't be able to overtake. In the distance he noticed the desert road approaching which provided a direct path towards the Pakistan border...and safety. He braked and swerved off the tarmac road onto the new dirt road, Finn followed. They drove through a desert landscape of hills and sand dunes, mixed with small amounts of vegetation flanking the road. Clouds of dust swirled around behind the Rover, making visibility for the chasing Finn difficult.

The poor road conditions forced Zafar to slow down, handing the speed advantage back to Finn. Despite having the advantage in performance, Finn could not risk overtaking without running off the road or getting bogged down in sand. He knew one mistake now and Zafar would escape...taking Kathy with him.

Zafar kept going, leading Finn further out into the desert. Ten miles or more passed before Finn noticed a right-hand bend approaching, with a ditch, a small group of trees and several large rocks on the inside of the curve. He floored the accelerator and pulled the Land Cruiser off the side of the dirt road and up along the left side of the Land Rover. Zafar checked his mirror finding clouds of dust behind him, not realising Finn's vehicle had moved into a blind spot, at his side.

Finn waited for the perfect moment and when it arrived, he did not miss. He pulled the steering wheel sharply to the right. The front wing of the Land Cruiser slammed into the rear door of the Land Rover, forcing it to turn towards the left. Zafar pulled his steering wheel hard to the right to correct the spin of the vehicle, however he over compensated for his current speed and the front right wheel slipped off the road and down into the ditch. The front wishbone scraped along the desert floor and the wheel lost contact with the dirt road.

Zafar panicked, he noticed the trees rapidly approaching and pulled the steering wheel hard to the left, trying to get the wheel, and Land Rover, back on the road surface. He failed and the front right wheel hit a large stone in the ditch, tearing the wheel from the front suspension mounting and forcing it under the vehicle body. The sudden braking force of the wheel under the vehicle pulled it further right and into the ditch. The front bumper dug into the dirt and the momentum lifted the rear of the Land Rover off the ground. The vehicle continued to rotate until the driver's side door crashed into the small group of trees, where it came to a stop.

Zafar banged his head on the window glass and a cut appeared above his eye. The crash threw Kathy against the rear passenger door and onto the back seat, unconscious.

Finn hit the brakes as hard as possible and the Land Cruiser snaked from side to side until it stopped fifty yards further down the dirt road. Grabbing his pistol from the holster, he jumped out of the vehicle and ran towards the wrecked Land Rover.

The small group of trees blocked Zafar's door from opening. Sliding over to the passenger side, he grasped the passenger door handle and kicked the door open. He looked down, searching for his pistol. He scrambled around on the floor unable to find it. In a panic he threw himself out of the passenger door and landed on the dry ground. He scrambled on all fours then up onto his bare feet. He turned and noticed a man in a military uniform approaching.

Dazed, he stumbled from side to side searching for a hiding place, the desert landscape offered no protection and left him with only one option, run!

Finn arrived at the Land Rover and noticed the man, dressed in white robes, running away from him. He looked through the back-passenger window and found a motionless body on the back seat. *Kathy.*

He reached inside the back door, checked her neck and found a pulse. *Alive.*

Dust swirled around as the X-49 circled above. He shut the Land Rover door and ran after the fleeing man.

Zafar looked back again, noticed the soldier gaining ground, panicked, and continued to run into the desert.

Seeing the fleeing man heading into nowhere Finn grew tired of the chase. Within ten feet he raised his pistol and shot at the man's leg. The man shouted out in pain and collapsed face forward onto the sand.

Finn shouted, "Freeze Zafar, or the next one will be through your head."

Zafar turned over on his back, sat up and looked at the face of the man with the gun, "You!"

"You made a bad decision the day you took my sister. You must've known I'd come to rescue her."

"I did and welcomed it. But this is not how I expected things to turn out."

Finn raised the pistol, "Give me a reason not to kill you. No one will miss a scumbag like you anyway."

"That's very true," Zafar hissed. "Thanks to you!"

"What are you on about? I've only ever done what my superiors told me to do. That's how it works in the military, you follow orders. I was told to capture you and that's what I did."

Zafar held his hand over the wound on his leg and looked at Finn with hatred in his eyes. "Don't make the mistake to think this is about you capturing me…I'm not important. I don't care about imprisonment, that's the downside of the business I'm in. But it saddens me to hear you pretend not to know the full price of capturing me."

"The price?" Finn said angrily, "What the hell are you going on about man, tell me why you captured my sister?"

"When in prison, I had a lot of free time to think about the day I was captured and I swore one day I'd kill the man responsible."

"You have always known it was me who captured you. If you had a problem with me, why not just come after me?" Finn asked. "Why did you involve my sister?"

"No, that's incorrect. I knew your face but not your name. The task of identifying you became much easier once I began to work with Marshall and Winter. They had access to all the confidential information I needed to help track you down. They informed me it was a British Army unit run by a Captain Finn which carried out the mission to capture me. I demanded all the personal information they could find on you. I read about your parents' death when you were just a young boy. That was hard for you, maybe you feel some hatred for that situation like the hatred that I now feel for you."

"If you had the information then why not just come after me?"

Zafar noted the annoyance in Finn's voice and it pleased him, "Believe me I tried. It would have given me great pleasure to capture and torture you, like you've tortured me. Do you remember the drug shipment from Khanashin to Pakistan which you intercepted near the border?"

"Yes?" Finn replied, unsure of the question. "But no drugs, it was an ambush."

"That's correct. I leaked the information about the drug shipment and Marshall monitored the response. Once I knew your unit would be involved, I set up the ambush. I sent my brother to capture you but..." A feeling of grief swept over him and he paused for a few moments, "He was foolish not to anticipate the strength of resistance he'd receive from your men…he was killed."

"You're saying that you set up the whole thing just to capture me? My men died taking part in your sick plan. I was just following my orders. My mission was to observe a drug shipment for the US forces to capture, that's all. A group of men turned up in pickup trucks, shouting and waving guns about. They had RPGs which threatened the US helicopters so it left me with no other option than to attack. How'd I know it was your brother attacking?"

"After you killed my brother, I became more determined to torture and kill you."

"You really are mad aren't you Zafar. But it still doesn't answer the question of why you took my sister." Finn raised the gun up to Zafar's head, "Speak!"

"No one could tell me where you and this mysterious British base were located. They said the location was known only at the highest levels, outside of the information stream that Marshall had access to. I suggested they capture and interrogate your sister to see if she knew anything about it. When they messed that up, I decided it was best to bring her here so I could do it."

"You're talking in riddles man! Why bring her all the way here?"

"I have just told you! To interrogate her, to find out the location of the base where you and your men were located. I planned to launch an attack, capture you and kill everyone else. The bungled kidnapping gave me another opportunity to punish you, I could imprison her and make you feel the same pain and anguish you've brought down on myself. Once under my control, I could keep her hidden, making you search for her. You'd spend every day wondering, not knowing if she was alive or dead. The uncertainty a torture you'd endure every day. And you'd also know what it's like to lose all of your family."

The comment puzzled Finn, "You mean because I killed your brother while he was attacking my men?"

Zafar noted Finn's blank stare and calmly said, "You really don't know, do you?"

"No! I don't." Finn barked.

∴ ∴ ∴ ∴

Cooney in the X-49 looked towards the ground and watched Finn standing over the man. He checked the area to make sure no other forces were nearby. He identified a place to land, flew over the top of the two men and disappeared over the crest of a sand dune.

∴ ∴ ∴ ∴

Finn's patience ran thin, desperate to return to the vehicle and check Kathy but he had to hear the full story.

Zafar said quietly, "Do you remember when you captured me?"

"Yes, we ambushed your armed convoy when you left your safe house."

"No, that wasn't a convey. It was me moving away from the repeated bombings we've endured for many years. Constant attacks on fields and buildings by invading forces. Imagine your life never knowing if your home will be the next to be wiped out from the unseen threat above."

"The intel I had said you planned to relocate to a new base where you'd be able to continue your attacks on military personnel."

"And the vehicles? Do you remember the vehicles?"

Finn thought for a moment, "Yes, there was a pickup with a mounted gun in front, your vehicle, a Land Cruiser behind that and another pickup with a mounted gun at the rear. An armed convoy."

"In order to get to me your men eliminated the other vehicles by firing hand held rockets from the rooftops of the houses."

"Yes, that's correct," Finn confirmed. "It was quick and easy, nicely executed. Wipe out the threat and take the target. You!"

"You've forgotten to mention my wife, daughter and two sons who were also travelling in the Land Cruiser. Your decision to blow up the vehicles killed all of them. My whole family wiped out, taken from me in one moment from a decision made by you."

"Incorrect!" Finn protested. "The intel said your family was safe and living in Pakistan."

"No. You killed them and your decision left me dead inside, filling my life with hatred and loathing. I want you to know the same feeling, to wake up every day knowing someone has taken the person you love away from you. That's why I captured her. Revenge! I took her as an act of vengeance. It's that simple."

Finn stared at Zafar, "So you're telling me you captured my sister as revenge for what happened to your family, and your brother."

"When a man loses everything he loves, the only thing left to fill the void in his heart is hate. Taking your sister was my way to make you feel the same hatred and suffering which you gave to me."

"Does it look to you like I've suffered?" Finn enquired. "I do my job, I'm given a task, or an order, and I follow it through to the end. I don't hate you or anyone else. You're using me to excuse yourself from guilt. The reason your family is dead is because of the evil life you immersed them in...you killed them."

Zafar exploded in anger as Finn dismissed his story. He raised his arms and yelled, "You will know the hatred I feel. I'll go to prison but I promise you I'll use all my power to hunt both you and your sister down and when I do, I'll..."

Bang.

Zafar did not get the chance to finish his threat. A gunshot rang out from behind Finn and a red hole appeared in the Afghans forehead. Finn spun around to see Kathy standing behind pointing a pistol at Zafar's dead body.

Finn moved towards her and said quietly, "Kathy, put the gun down."

She dropped the gun on the sand and stood with a blank look on her face, "Is he dead?"

"Yes, he's dead." Finn put his arm around his sister and walked her slowly back to the Land Cruiser.

"Finn, wait." A voice called from behind and he turned to see Cooney running down a sand dune towards him. The pilot stopped near the dead body laid on the sand and pointed, "Is that Zafar? What happened to him?"

Finn looked at him, "He died in a car crash in the desert."

Cooney looked at Finn then turned towards the body, noticing the bullet wound in the forehead. He shrugged his shoulders, "That's just what I thought. They say it's dangerous driving out here in the desert, anything can happen."

Finn stood with Kathy, and watched as Cooney dragged Zafar's body back to the Land Rover. The pilot lifted the corpse and placed it into the driver's seat, then ran back towards Finn and Kathy. He sprinted past them and shouted, "Let's get the hell out of here."

They watched as he continued running ahead of them and disappeared over the crest of the sand dune.

Finn followed with Kathy, holding her arm, rushing her forward. At the crest of the sand dune, he spotted the X-49 parked with Cooney climbing into the cockpit.

Finn carried on pushing Kathy forward until they arrived at the helicopter. He opened the rear door and guided Kathy inside. Sitting her down, he fitted her seatbelt then climbed in next to her. Cooney started the engine and increased the revs until the helicopter lifted off the sand.

He turned to Finn, "How is she?"

"In shock I think," Finn said, while pushing the hair away from her dirty face, noticing a cut over her eye and a bruise on her forehead, "Looks like she's banged her head, concussion probably. We need to get her to the medical centre at Camp Griffin."

Cooney raised the helicopter away from the desert floor, sweeping around to the small group of trees. Using the mounted guns, he fired at the Land Rover until the vehicle burst into flames.

Cooney pulled on the stick and climbed up to a safe height and said, "That's the last we'll see of that madman."

Finn tapped him on the shoulder, "Thanks buddy."

❖ ❖ ❖ ❖

The X-49 landed at Camp Griffin and a medical team took Kathy away on a stretcher. Finn held her hand as the medics carried her across the dusty ground towards the medical centre.

Kathy woke, slowly opened her eyes, and looked at Finn, "Who was that man?"

Finn looked down at her bruised and bloodied face, "No one."

She closed her eyes.

Epilogue

"Come on let's get you sitting up, in the bed," The nurse helped Nico Torres up and bent him forward. She leant over him and puffed up the pillows behind his back. Torres couldn't help but notice her large breasts straining at the buttons on her uniform.

"There you go." She said with a smile, "It's time for your physio but before you go you've got a visitor."

"Who is it this time?" Torres moaned, "Not Dawson again, any chance of you telling him I've escaped."

"You're going to have to leave one day Nico. You know, return to the real world, dealing with all the bad guys out there. Your friend Dawson has been on the phone every day, badgering the doctor, trying to get him to discharge you."

The nurse straightened her dress and slipped a piece of paper into his hand. "And when you do make sure you give me a call."

A voice spoke out, "I see you've not lost any of your charm FBI special agent."

Torres looked past the nurse and found a beautiful blonde woman, standing in the doorway. The nurse blushed and quickly departed the room.

"If I remember, lover boy, the last time we spoke you promised me a meal," Rivera followed the nurse out the door with her eyes and added, "That's if you can fit me in."

Torres smiled and quickly slipped the paper under the sheet, "It's great to see you, thanks for coming, I'm going stir crazy here."

She raised her eyebrows and said, "You look like you're coping. What have they said about your injuries?"

"On the mend, I should be out of here next week."

Rivera walked up to the side of the bed and held his hand, "That'll be great, I look forward to it." She leant forward and kissed him.

A familiar voice shouted from the doorway, "Am I interrupting, I can come back later if you like."

Rivera broke off the kiss and they looked up to see a man in the doorway, in one hand a burger, in the other, a six pack of IPA's.

Torres recognised him instantly, "Finn!"

THE END

Abbreviations

SAS - Special Air Service (British Army, founded 1941)

CIA - Central Intelligence Agency

NCS - National Clandestine Service (part of CIA)

SAC - Special Activities Centre (part of NCS)

SOG - Special Operations Group (part of NCS)

DEA - Drug Enforcement Administration

NSA - National Security Agency

RPG - Rocket Propelled Grenade

RIB - Rigid Inflatable Boat

APB - All Points Bulletin

SMG - Sub-Machine Gun

LZ - Landing Zone

HUD - Head Up Display

NPR - Number Plate Recognition

MP – Military Police

Equipment Used

SIG Sauer P320 - Semi-automatic Pistol.

Heckler & Koch HK416 - Assault Rifle

Heckler & Koch MP5 - Machine Pistol

Glock 17M – FBI issue 9mm Handgun (used by Torres)

X-49 SpeedHawk - Experimental four-bladed, twin-engine, high-speed helicopter developed by Piasecki. Versions for military use exist.

RIB - High speed inflatable boat commonly used by special forces troops including the SAS.

Lockheed C-5 Galaxy - A heavy-lift aeroplane with four jet engines and access doors at both ends of the fuselage. Developed to transport military equipment, including tanks. Top speed is 532 mph (856 km/h), maximum range is 5,500 miles (8,900 km) with a 54,431 kg (120,000 lb) payload.

Boeing CH-47 Chinook - An American twin-engine, tandem rotor, heavy-lift helicopter, manufactured by Boeing Vertol.

Gulfstream G650ER - An executive passenger jet capable of taking up to nineteen passengers and two flight crew. The ER version of the standard G650 has an extended range and can fly up to 8,600 miles (13,900 km), top speed 530 mp/h (900 km/h).

AGM-114 Hellfire - The Hellfire Air-to-Ground Missile (AGM) has multi-mission, multi-target precision-strike ability, and can be launched from multiple air, sea, and ground platforms, including Predator and Reaper drone aircraft and has Laser Guided and Radar Seeking capability with a 45kg (100-pound) weight class and 180mm (7 inch) diameter. Used by US armed forces and many other nations. The Longbow version can seek a target after it is fired.

MQ-1 Predator Drone - The MQ-1 Predator is an American unmanned aerial vehicle (UAV) capable of remotely controlled or autonomous flight operation. It's used primarily by the United States Air Force (USAF) and Central Intelligence Agency (CIA). Conceived in the early 1990s for aerial reconnaissance and forward observation roles, the Predator carries cameras and other sensors.

MQ-9 Reaper Drone - The MQ-9 Reaper is larger, heavier, and more capable than the earlier MQ-1 Predator. The MQ-9 is the first hunter-killer UAV designed for long-endurance, high-altitude surveillance and targeting. Most often fitted with Hellfire missiles.

Paveway – Laser guided bomb.

Fictitious Equipment (Possibly?)

Rubber Suit (used by Finn)

ECHO camera system

ECS Predator

EMP device (used by Miller)

iBOW comms device – (used by Finn/Miller)

(iBOW name created by the author.)

Opium

The farmers collect the milky sap from the ripe seed pod of the poppy flower. The sap is converted to resin which is further refined to create drugs like Morphine and Heroin. Heroin, the most lethal form of opium, is manufactured in the highest volumes to meet demand. Opium based drugs are highly addictive. Estimates are that, Worldwide, over 15 million people regularly use opium-based products recreationally. Reports suggest 85% originates from Afghanistan.

Printed in Great Britain
by Amazon